ROUGHED IN

EVA MOORE

Copyright © 2019 by Eva Moore

All rights reserved.

No part of this book may be reproduced in any form or by any electronic or mechanical means, including information storage and retrieval systems, without written permission from the author, except for the use of brief quotations in a book review.

Cover Design by Render Compose

Edits by Jennifer Graybeal, JenGraybeal.com and Julia Ganis, JuliaEdits.com

This is a work of fiction. Names, characters, places, and incidents either are products of the author's imagination or are used fictitiously, and any resemblance to actual persons, living or dead, business establishments, events, or locations is entirely coincidental.

Roughed In/Reclaimed Dreams Print ISBN: 978-1-950345-05-2

CONTENTS

Chapter 1	1
Chapter 2	9
Chapter 3	16
Chapter 4	27
Chapter 5	37
Chapter 6	47
Chapter 7	53
Chapter 8	60
Chapter 9	72
Chapter 10	84
Chapter 11	93
Chapter 12	101
Chapter 13	108
Chapter 14	120
Chapter 15	124
Chapter 16	130
Chapter 17	139
Chapter 18	149
Chapter 19	159
Chapter 20	172
Chapter 21	179
Chapter 22	188
Chapter 23	194
Chapter 24	203
Chapter 25	211
Chapter 26	218
Chapter 27	229
Chapter 28	235
Chapter 29	241
Chapter 30	248
Chapter 31	257
Chapter 32	266

Chapter 33	274
Epilogue	281
34. Reclaimed Dreams	290
Content Warnings	291
35. Chapter 1	292
36. Chapter 2	298
37. Chapter 3	306
38. Chapter 4	314
39. Chapter 5	323
40. Chapter 6	337
41. Chapter 7	349
42. Chapter 8	361
43. Chapter 9	367
44. Chapter 10	379
45. Chapter 11	393
46. Chapter 12	400
47. Chapter 13	406
48. Chapter 14	415
49. Chapter 15	425
50. Chapter 16	441
51. Chapter 17	448
52. Chapter 18	457
53. Chapter 19	468
54. Chapter 20	476
55. Chapter 21	487
56. Chapter 22	496
57. Chapter 23	505
58. Chapter 24	515
59. Chapter 25	521
60. Chapter 26	529
Opened Up Chapter 1	539
61. Valenti Family Timeline	548
Christmas Spirits Excerpt	551
Someone Special Excerpt	557
Acknowledgments	563
About the Author	567
Also by Eva Moore	569

For S-
May you always approach life with a laugh and a smile, and never be afraid to work for what you want.

CHAPTER 1

FRANKIE VALENTI WAS JUST ABOUT DONE with this shit. She grinned at the camera and prayed it wouldn't pick up her clenched jaw. If she needed caps on her molars, Jake Ryland was going to pay for them. She raised the can of ridiculous hot pink spray paint with her name on it and began marking walls.

"All right guys! It's demo day. We've got three walls that need to go down quick. You two, grab a wall and a sledgehammer. First one to take down their section wins. Aaaannnd GO!"

She let out a berserker yell and tore into the wall nearest her. Coming up with silly shit on a construction site was easy. Keeping it fresh, but the same, for the camera was harder. She had one shot to get the first hit right if she didn't want Trina to make her reshoot it by tearing into a wall she'd planned to keep.

Since she refused to let the guys beat her, she channeled all of her frustration into the sledgehammer she wielded against the drywall. The Kaufmans' living room was toast.

Every stupid retake. *Bam!*

Every stupid delay. *Wham!*

Every stupid change Mr. High-and-Mighty Dick-rector Jake wanted to make at the last fucking minute. *Slam!*

Jake Ryland was getting on her last nerve with his controlling attitude and his know-it-all smirk and those damn forearms. She refused to examine why forearms pissed her off, and refocused her ire on the demolition.

A two-by-four stud splintered behind the force of her anger-driven sledge.

When her family had signed on for Million-Dollar Starter Home, she had been one hundred percent on board. She agreed with her father that it would help grow their business and solidify their reputation as quality builders in Silicon Valley. Leaning in to making the show a success made sense. She just hadn't anticipated that she'd be cast as the class clown and forced to submit to the whims of an arrogant asshole. It had chafed for years that she'd had to bide her time and follow orders from first her dad, and then Adrian and Sofia. Jake added insult to injury. The thought of knocking him out with her hammer made her grin like a fool. A sweaty, manic fool.

Someday, Frankie thought as plaster dust rained down on her, *I'll be running Valenti Brothers...*

Thunk!

...and then this...

Whack!

...will all be worth it.

Crack!

Until then though, she'd keep hustling and trying to prove that while she might look like her petite mother, she could absolutely fill her father's shoes.

Frankie tightened her grip on the sledge so it didn't fly into the next room, and hit as high as she could reach.

Yes, she was the baby of the family, and yes, she was a woman in a man's field, and yes, she was only five foot four, an injustice she intended to have words with God about.

But she'd be damned if she'd let any of that stand in the way of fulfilling her promise to Gabe.

Her entire childhood, she'd looked up to her big brother. They'd planned to run Valenti Brothers together, but then Gabe had gone off to war while she was still growing up, and hadn't come back home. Chasing their dream kept him alive in her heart, and Frankie was more determined than ever. She just had to convince her father, and now Jake Ryland, to give her a shot.

The upcoming spin-off was the perfect opportunity.

"Hey!"

Frankie whirled, sledgehammer raised, and whipped off her much-protested pink safety glasses.

"What?"

Rico stepped back, hands raised. "You won."

Frankie looked at the destruction she'd created and grinned. She'd gotten her whole section done while she'd been lost in thought. Mugging for Trina, the camera operator and only other woman in the room, Frankie shook her hips and pumped her fists in a victory dance.

"And cut."

Speak of the devil, and he shall appear.

Jake Ryland strolled into the rubble-filled room, looking crisp and clean and utterly infuriating. How the hell did his starched button-down shirt and pressed jeans never get dirty? His Italian leather shoes, which she imagined cost more than her monthly salary, gleamed as he stepped over the demo debris to look at the screen on Trina's video camera. While they discussed something in whispers, Frankie brushed at her own shirt. She self-consciously knocked off chips of plaster and wood and tried not to react to the fact that he hadn't even acknowledged her presence. And failed. She cleared her throat.

"Are you not entertained?" she asked as she held out her arms and half bowed.

Frankie couldn't keep the snark from her voice. She did feel a bit like a gladiator, performing feats of strength for the masses. Jake gave her a side-eye glance and shrugged a shoulder. He wouldn't give her the respect of turning to face her. If the show ever did run to blood sport, she'd be gunning for Caesar.

"It was a good bit. But I need to talk to you. Outside."

A bit? Why did she feel like he was looking down at her for giving him exactly what he asked for? *Fucking emperors.*

She tucked her glasses into the V-neck of her T-shirt and leaned the sledge against the wall, so she wouldn't be tempted to brain him with it, before following him out the front door. By the time she caught up with him, he was already at the craft services table set up in the side yard, because the garage at this house was currently packed with the owners' belongings. She took off her hard hat and propped it against her hip as she resisted the urge to reach for a cookie with her filthy hands. She drummed her fingers against the hard plastic, eager to get back to work.

Because of those stupid delays, they'd gotten a late start on this house. The Kaufmans had needed to move out of their old house before the crew had even gotten started on their new one. It grated on her conscience that Valenti Brothers was behind schedule because of the show. *Good work, on time, and under budget* was their motto for a reason. If the show killed their reputation, what was the point? Brick upon brick, the wall of her annoyance rose taller, blocking her in.

"So, what do you need?" Irritation sharpened her tone. Jake held up a finger as he slugged down what had to be his eighth cup of coffee, judging by the height of the sun in the sky. Frankie fumed.

Just another fucking delay. Was this some stupid power play? She crossed her arms and tapped her foot as he drank the hot coffee like water, her eyes involuntarily resting on his bobbing

Adam's apple. He looked like a fucking coffee model. Was that a thing?

His short dark hair framed his face, fading into the perfect balance of facial hair. Not short enough for a five o'clock shadow, which would hurt during a lip-lock, but not a burly lumberjack beard that would catch food either. Just a soft, sexy beard that highlighted his ridiculous cheekbones and a dimple. A fucking dimple! On a grown man! *Unfair advantage*, she groused. Even his bared forearm was perfectly muscled and lightly hairy.

She half expected a wind machine to crank up and theme music to start playing. She looked around to see if Trina was filming this. The man was a walking advertisement for drinking your weight in coffee every day. She couldn't explain why, but his unrelenting perfection made her want to muss him up. She clenched her fingers against the desire to crinkle his shirt in her fists. And when he licked his lips after the last swallow, her own felt dry. Why was she paying attention to his lips?

The man treated her like a child, giving orders, talking over her with Dom, assuming she would jump to do his bidding. How could she hate the things that came out of that mouth, but still be obsessed with its shape and texture? She deliberately stretched her fingers out and shoved them in her back pockets out of harm's way. Uncomfortable with the direction of her thoughts, she did what she always did: she fell back on sarcasm and bluffed her way past it.

"If you're done caffeinating, I have a house that needs work. What did you need?"

"I need you to change clothes and run over to the Rancho project," he said while he refilled his coffee mug.

"But I'm in the middle of demo here."

"I'm aware." He raked his eyes from her head to her toes. "That's why I asked you to change."

She growled, and he continued.

"The crew here can handle this without you. Adrian is here to do his walk-throughs. There was a glitch with the cameras, and we need to reshoot the final walk-through with the inspector. He's giving me half an hour. Get over there, and do something about your hair."

Frankie felt her cheeks flush hot as she raised a hand to her habitual ponytail and dusty particles of plaster fell to her shoulders.

He'd managed to waste her time, dismiss her importance on the jobsite, and insult her appearance in under two minutes. The man was a management marvel. "What did that half hour cost you?"

"A bottle of eighteen-year-old scotch."

"Why can't Adrian cover it?"

"Because I need you to make this funny."

Of course he did. Not because he needed her building skill or her project lead ability. He needed her to be the class clown, because that was all he valued her for. And didn't that just burn her up inside. But she'd use that fire to push forward. She would prove her worth if it was the last thing she did, just so she could rub his nose in it.

"Damn. Okay, let me go over the plan with Rico, and I'll head over."

"I'd go now." Jake turned his wrist to check a watch worth more than her monthly salary. "He'll be there in twenty."

It was a fifteen-minute drive.

"Nothing like cutting it close," she muttered as she fished her keys out of her pocket.

"I'm not stupid. If I'd told you earlier, I'd have had to listen to you complain about it longer. Besides, you don't need time to primp. Just change your shirt and brush the dust out of your hair."

His detached assessment slapped at her feminine pride. Her

temper flashed to the tip of her tongue, but he was already walking away.

"Oh, and the Glenfiddich is in your front seat. Don't forget to give it to him."

She spluttered at his retreating back, her molten ire bubbling over and its target out of range. Someday she was going to have the perfect set-down on the tip of her tongue. But clearly not today.

She stormed off to her truck, muttering about asshole emperors and their fucking dimples, while pulling her sweaty T-shirt off over her head. She had a strappy cami on underneath. It would have to do. She tugged at the uncooperative damp cotton that decided to stick to her shoulder blades and cursed Jake anew.

"Hey, hey, hey, this is a family show."

Adrian was standing in front of her with a grin on his face when she emerged from her cocoon.

"Ha ha, very funny. Hey, can you keep an eye on Rico and the boys? I've got to run over to the Rancho project."

"Sure, no worries. Everything okay?"

"Some mix-up with the inspector's film. How's my sister today?"

Adrian hooking up with Sofia had surprised the hell out of her, but now it seemed so obvious that they fit. Her big sister was pregnant with their first baby, and the first trimester had been brutal.

"Feeling much better now that the smell of garlic doesn't send her running to puke."

"That's good. You guys coming to Friday dinner?"

"Wouldn't miss it, *manita*."

She held her fist up for their special handshake, and grinned when Adrian returned it with a bump and finger wiggles. Right now, she was cool with him running the construction side of the firm alongside Fi's design work. It helped with the waiting for her break to know the company was in good hands. But soon she'd take her place as his business partner and her dad could retire without worry. Soon.

Temper defused, she pulled her ponytail out and shook her hair out as she walked to her truck. For now she'd play the clown and make nice with the inspector for the cameras.

Eye on the prize, Valenti.

CHAPTER 2

Jake grimaced as he tried to sip from a now empty mug. He contemplated getting up for another cup of coffee, but no. That would mean leaving the trailer and running the risk of bumping into Frankie on his way to craft services.

Not worth it.

He wasn't hiding exactly. He was busy. Lots to do. Lots to keep track of. Lots of…complete bullshit.

Frankie was back from the Rancho project, and he'd gotten a thank-you call from the inspector, so he knew it had gone well. Which meant he didn't need to seek her out for confirmation. No matter how much he wanted to. And damn it all, he really wanted to.

He'd seen her hop out of her truck as he ducked into the production trailer, and the sight of her in a strappy cami with her hair flowing over her shoulders was now seared into his mind, tempting him to go back for a longer glance. When he'd told her to change her shirt, he hadn't thought she would just whip off her T-shirt and go on cable television in her undershirt. He tried not to think about the lovely, trim body and small, firm breasts that her tank top revealed. He failed. Miserably. Again.

Damn it.

Ever since Christmas Eve, he'd been distracted by her presence on the set. He couldn't afford to be. There was too much riding on the success of Million-Dollar Starter Home and his new project, Valenti Vineyards.

These shows were his springboard. He refused to be known as a child actor burnout. Once he made his name as a showrunner, he planned to move on to bigger and better things. Jake could leverage his new name and his track record to get bigger projects green-lighted. One step at a time, he was building his own empire now.

His cell phone rang, pulling his thoughts back to business. He glanced down at it and sighed deeply. His agent, Melody Payne. He liked the woman who had helped him transition from J.R. Hudson, child actor, to Jake Ryland, showrunner. She was a damn good agent and kept track of his residual rights from his early career, but she had a soft heart and often reached out to him about projects he'd been asked to participate in, even though he'd told her a thousand times he was done with acting.

"Melody, how are you?"

"Living the dream, Jake, living the dream. I'm glad I caught you. I've got a proposal for you."

"I thought you were married," he quipped. "How is Eddie doing?"

The image of her stocky bulldog of a husband flashed through his mind and made him smile. Eddie Payne, retired stuntman, was one of the few guys in Hollywood he could stand to have a conversation with.

"As cranky as ever. I'll tell him you said hi. But I'm not falling for that distraction trick. The proposal is from Brittani."

Brittani Belleview. The actress who had played his sister on the long-running family sitcom, *Hudson House*, had grown up on set with him. She'd been his first off-screen kiss. She had gone on to star in a slew of teen dramas and horror movies before she disappeared from the screen. Jake tried to remember the last time he'd seen her. He could at least hear out her request. "What does she want?"

"She wants to put together a reunion show."

Well, that was an easy answer.

"No."

He knew it was rude, but he'd been over this a thousand times. He wasn't that kid anymore, and he couldn't afford to look back. Plus, he wasn't going to give his parents one more dime off his childhood.

"Jake, you might want to consider this one." Her softer tone did little to soften his opinion.

"Melody, what's the one thing I've always been crystal clear on?"

"No looking back, I know, but—"

"No buts. Was that all? I've got to run."

Melody sighed heavily on the other end of the phone. He could practically hear the expletives she wanted to hurl at him racing through her head. From long acquaintance, he knew she'd let them fly as soon as he hung up.

"Yes, that was all."

"Okay, talk soon. Bye, Mel."

"Take care, Jake."

He returned his attention to the dailies running on the screens in front of him. His job was to craft the best damn forty-three minute show possible from days' worth of footage. This would be his legacy. He didn't want to be remembered as the boy with the dimple, or the awkward teen from the few high school rom-coms he'd done. That's why he drew a hard line at projects that reminded everyone he'd been a cute kid. Jake Ryland refused to believe that the peak of his career was behind him.

He had zero intention of stepping in front of the camera

again. No, he preferred being the man behind the curtain, pulling levers and keeping everything moving forward.

Speaking of pulling levers, he needed to nail down the first laughter beat for the Kaufman project. He checked the log and scrolled through the time-stamped takes from the demolition race.

He watched as Frankie took down drywall like a machine. He hit pause. *That right there. That smirk was gold.* No wonder the camera and their audience loved her. He would love to know what put that smile on her face. He would love to know too many things about her.

Trina, as usual, had found magical angles. The light filtered through the dust and rubble, making Frankie seem to glow as she went to town on the wall. Jake cursed when he realized he'd been watching the playback at regular speed for five minutes. He needed to keep his brain working in fast-forward. He couldn't afford to get distracted by the repetitive flex and release of Frankie's lithe form in motion.

She wasn't the kind of girl he could pursue.

Not only was she nearly a decade younger, and the daughter of a man he was doing business with, but he was her director. And he wasn't at a point in his life where he could indulge in anything more than a fling. He was crazy busy and living out of a hotel room in a city far from home. If he had a Magic 8-Ball, all signs would point to no.

And yet when her T-shirt rode up on an upswing and revealed the trim flesh at her waist, his fingers twitched at the memory of how surprisingly soft she was. Jake couldn't help but recall the way she'd pressed that lithe body against his, his hands sliding over her hips as she'd pinned him against her door on Christmas Eve. Haunted by that smirk, he remembered that she'd done that right before she'd kissed him senseless. He licked his lips as if that would bring back her taste. Her taste... He reached for his coffee again, needing to erase the memory of sweetness and wine, and cursed to find it still empty.

It had been a memorable moment for him.

Even if she didn't remember it at all.

He'd just have to do his best to forget.

Tired of being alone with his uncooperative thoughts, he reached for his walkie and called his head camera operator. "Hey Trina, can you come in here?"

"On my way, boss."

When she arrived moments later with a fresh cup of coffee, he nearly kissed *her*. Trina always seemed to anticipate him. That's what made her an invaluable part of his team. Jake inhaled deeply, letting the rich, dark scent swirl through his head, before savoring the first sip. It didn't matter that it was made in a five-gallon drum. Coffee was his sin and his salvation all rolled into one deliciously bitter mouthful. Maybe now he'd be able to focus beyond Frankie.

"Let's talk strategy for tomorrow. We are two houses from the end of season two on MDash and I want to end on a high note, really amp up the tension for the last two shows. What's our conflict?"

Trina didn't answer and stared down at her rapidly tapping Chuck Taylor's.

"What? No ideas?"

"No, I just... How can you keep putting them through the wringer? I'm starting to feel bad about how hard they're all working to pull off these renos."

"Going soft on me, Trina?" Jake teased. "So close to the end?"

"I like them. They are good people."

"They are."

"Then how can you torture them?"

"Why do people watch reality TV, Trina?"

"Entertainment?"

"Sure, but more specifically, they want to believe. They want the good guys to triumph. They want to feel better than the bad guys. They want to go along for the emotional ride. Our show? The Valentis? Definitely good guys, and our viewers want to see them triumph against all odds to give a regular couple their perfect home. If there's no struggle, there's no drama. You know this. You're the queen of catching those small moments that feed the whole narrative."

"I just think that renovating a home is stressful enough without adding extra obstacles."

"Right. And that was fine for the first few episodes. We're now nearing the end of season two with an extended break before we start filming three because of all the baby leaves. And a new spin-off I'm trying to get approved to fill in the gaps. And I need high drama to keep our viewers. Now, help me figure out what that looks like."

Trina shook her head and shrugged her shoulders. A change in tactics was in order.

"How's everything going with Winston's demo?"

"Good. He's gotten a few nibbles, but it's slow."

Her boyfriend worked on the crew here but had recently gone down to LA to pursue a singing career. He knew the temporary long-distance aspect was putting a strain on their relationship, but he had also promised to recommend Trina for a movie gig once they wrapped the special. She'd agreed to stay until after the babies came to help smooth the transition to a new crew once everyone was back, and he was grateful. But she was still going to have to prove herself to any new director she worked for.

"I know you are dying to get down there and help him. But I've got you until at least the fall. Help me make these shows shine, so when it comes time to pitch you to movie folks, you'll be putting your best work forward."

She couldn't argue against her own self-interest. With a defeated sigh, she muttered something.

"What?"

"Power outage," Trina repeated. "It's supposed to rain tomorrow. They'd have to work in the dark and without power tools. It'll create interesting lighting challenges too."

"Brilliant! There's our finale. I knew I could count on you." Jake grinned but Trina didn't return it.

"Then why do I feel like I just snitched on my best friend?"

"It's just the job, Trina. And you do it damn well."

Jake turned back to his master binder as the gears began to whirr in his head around the new idea.

Blackout for the Bakshis. Fucking genius.

And just like that he was back in the game, his preoccupation with Frankie finally pushed from his mind as it filled with technical details and shot lists for the coming weeks. This was his sweet spot, everything under his control, even his own thoughts. He grinned and rubbed his hands together in anticipation. This was gonna be good.

CHAPTER 3

WHEN JAKE WALKED into Dom Valenti's office Friday morning, he was ready to negotiate. He'd combed through his proposals to both Dom and the network, looking for tangles. Launching the spin-off series for Valenti Vineyards would be a feather in his cap.

He'd gone out on a limb for the pilot of Million-Dollar Starter Home. When Dom had frozen on camera, Jake had thought he was screwed. But the sexual tension between Sofia and Adrian, coupled with a broody but competent Enzo and the comedic stylings of Frankie, had saved the show, endearing the Valenti family to millions of viewers, and green-lighting the second season.

With the original show now on hiatus due to imminent family leaves, he'd leaned into the winery renovation idea that Dom had pitched. He could keep his crew working during the break, get everyone their hours for insurance, keep his little tribe together for as long as possible. Letting a crew lapse could mean months of trying to find replacements when things got rolling again, with no guarantee that people would be available to come back.

After so many years in the business he knew the value of a

great crew, and he'd handpicked this one. They were like family, and he wasn't going to let them go just because his stars kept pairing off and making babies.

The spin-off special location miniseries would not only solidify their market share. It would translate into dollars in the bank for the Valentis and more respect and freedom for him at the network.

The last step was getting everything under contract.

Dom sat behind his massive desk, his large frame stooped, his salt and pepper hair disheveled. Jake tried to raise the energy in the room with his voice. "Good morning, Dom! Ready to sign some papers?"

The older man wasn't buying into Jake's hype. "Is this going to work?"

"Of course it is. The network is very excited."

"I don't give a shit about the network. Is this going to fix things with Jo?"

Jake grimaced, but kept his question calm and even. "How do you see this fixing things with Jo?"

Josephine Valenti had made her feelings about the original show crystal clear. Although her name was on the contracts, she wasn't active in the business and was rarely seen on site. She wanted Dom to retire, and she saw the show as another hurdle on that path. Jake hoped that this vineyard renovation would set them down a new path together. Hell, he prayed he could get her on-screen to help Dom carry the show.

Dom cradled his head in his hands, elbows propped on his desk, and Jake could feel the older man's frustration. "I want my wife back. I want her to talk to me, like we used to. I want her to want me again. I wish I fucking knew what to do."

Jake dug deep for his patience, but this was way beyond his pay grade. "What does this have to do with the vineyard, Dom?"

"Jo kept talking about wanting to go to Italy and eating the food and drinking the wine. Well, what do we need to fly to Italy for? We've got all that right here. Giving her a little slice of Italy here at home seemed like a good compromise." Dom ran his fingers through his hair and then pointed at Jake, as if he needed convincing. "And the property was a steal. It's a solid investment. Jo is going to be great at running a winery. Hell, look how she kept this business going for years." Dom couldn't keep his hands still, gesturing wildly while he spoke.

From everything Jake had seen and pieced together, Jo had very firmly stepped back from her work life. Was she seriously considering taking on the start-up work for a winery and event space? Something wasn't sitting right here. "What has Jo said about the project?"

"She doesn't know."

Oh shit. All of his work pitching this to the network would swirl down the drain, and his reputation along with it, if Jo wasn't on board with all this. Who the hell bought fifty acres of land, three outbuildings, and a farmhouse to renovate into a working winery and event space without consulting his business partner? He admired Dom's decisiveness, but this was too much.

"Don't you think you should tell her about it before you invest all this time and money?" Jake refrained from changing *this* to *my*, but that was what he was thinking. This would be a colossal waste of money if Jo didn't want it in the end. Prospects for future marketing and filming options withered on the vine of Jake's imagination.

"It's a surprise, to celebrate our retirement."

Jake sighed and looked back at the worthless contracts in his hand. So much for an easy negotiation.

"Hey, what's going on in here? You okay, Dad?" Frankie popped her head in the doorway. Concern for her father pulled her eyebrows together and narrowed her eyes. At Jake, of course.

"I'm fine, baby girl." Dom beckoned his youngest in for a hug. "Just talking through some business with Jake here."

Frankie pulled back slightly from her father's hug to skewer Jake with a glare. "What kind of business?" She perched on the arm of her father's desk chair and crossed her arms, settling in for a fight.

"We're signing contracts for the Valenti Vineyards project," Dom said.

"Dad, we talked about this—"

Dom slapped a flat hand against his desk, cutting her off. "You and Sofia are treating me like a child. I am still head of this company, and I don't need anyone holding my hand through a simple contract signing!" Dom's outburst seemed to tire him and he slumped back into his chair.

"So you've read through the contracts? Sent them off to our lawyer Cousin Giulia for a read-through?"

Dom just stared blankly at his desk.

"Dad, do you know what you're signing?" Frankie's sharp tone snapped Dom's head back into the game.

"I'm sure it's the same as the contracts for Million-Dollar Starter Home," Dom argued.

Frankie muttered under her breath, "Yeah, and those contracts weren't a problem at all." Jake watched this all play out stone-faced, but behind his facade he was scrambling for a new negotiation strategy. Never let it be said he'd completely abandoned acting. By the time Frankie turned to him and said, "I'm staying," Jake had the beginning of a plan.

There was something about the jut of her chin, the challenge in her tone, that made Jake want to win.

"Okay. Do you want to walk through the agreements?" Jake asked.

"No."

"Yes."

Dom and Frankie's opposite reactions were rare. Usually they were peas in a pod.

Frankie laid a hand on Dom's shoulder. "Humor me. I haven't heard it yet."

At Dom's reluctant nod, Jake took out the contract and set it in front of them.

"Basically, you all agree to participate in this six-part miniseries featuring the renovation of Valenti Vineyards. The network will assume twenty percent of the raw material cost and will pay the local production crew. You will cover the remaining eighty percent of the budget and all of the labor costs for your subcontractors. Anyone considered part of the family will not be compensated biweekly, but rather granted one lump sum for rights to use the family name and business logo, the idea being that you will benefit from the exposure for your brand."

"So far I follow. The network won't retain any rights to the property though, right?"

Frankie skimmed the contracts as he spoke, and he couldn't help but admire her mind at work. She might be the youngest Valenti, but she was no baby. Frankie gave as good as she got. Jake would bet money on her being the person to take Valenti Brothers into the future. He refused to let her wrest control of the conversation from him though, deliberately keeping his answers dismissive. "No, they won't. Moving on."

Negotiation strategy number one: if you can make your opponent's concerns sound inconsequential, they might just believe it too.

"We will stick pretty closely in terms of format to the current show, but we will focus on a different part of the property for each episode."

"No, we won't."

Frankie's flat reply had him leaning back in his chair. *What the hell?* His own negotiation strategy turned back on him? Where had she picked that up? "Elaborate."

"Similar format, fine, but we will not stick to the current roles."

Since Jake's plan of featuring Dom and Jo together had just gotten skewered, he nodded for her to continue, but she had already turned to her dad.

"I've got ideas about how the property should be developed. I know what Ma would want, and I'm not giving up control to some suits." Whirling back to Jake to drive home her point, Frankie drilled her index finger into the desk. "Saving my parents' marriage is more important than a silly show."

Jake bit back his flare of temper over having his work called silly. This was why he'd wanted to deal with Dom. This negotiation was going to take forever if she fought him on every point. "No one said you wouldn't be involved. You'll still do your thing."

"My thing?"

He could practically see her hackles rising. If he got her mad enough, maybe she'd stomp off and let him get these damn contracts signed. He had better things to do with his morning than argue with her. Plus, he got a perverse joy out of pissing her off.

"What exactly is my thing? The comic relief?"

Jake shrugged. That was a close enough descriptor. Yes, she was a talented builder, but he already had one of those—one beloved by audiences after that proposal stunt—in Adrian. Shifting from established roles wouldn't go down well with his bosses.

Frankie moved to sit on Dom's desk, turning her back on Jake. "Dad, listen. I want this project. Sofia can help me with the details around what I've already laid out. But with all the babies coming, no one else is going to have time for this. Plus, what better way to prove that I can handle taking my place in the business than by running this project by myself?"

Jake could see the idea of grandchildren race through Dom's head, pulling a smile from him—a rare sight these days. The man he admired had changed so much from the bold, fearless man who'd pitched him the show two years ago. His cheerful confidence at the beginning of the project had slowly diminished as his marriage had deteriorated. The tragic loss of their eldest son Gabe had strained Jo and Dom's connection, and the show had only made things worse. But Sofia and Adrian were expecting their first, and Natalie and Enzo were going to give little Daisy twins for siblings. Maybe three grandbabies in two months would help them figure things out. Didn't people always think babies would solve all of their problems?

"Imagine, me getting to be a grandpa to three babies all at once. The only thing that would make it better would be a trifecta." Dom lowered his chin and sent a heavy glance Frankie's way.

"Dad, please. I'm not even dating anyone."

Interesting. Jake filed that information away.

"Besides, right now I want this company with Adrian. Let me prove I can do it. Go play with babies and fix things with Ma. Let me be the head contractor on this job. Please, Dad?"

Frankie wrapped Dom around her little finger with an ease born of long practice. What would it have been like to wield that much power as a child? No doubt she'd been doing it since before she could walk. He could only imagine it led to a confidence that the world would bend to her liking. Instead of feeling trapped and helpless.

God, if he'd been able to convince his parents just once... But that had been a lifetime ago, and he'd done okay doing things his way.

He pulled his mind back into the present. The past was past. He clicked his director filter back into place and assessed the family dynamics at play with a dispassionate eye. Dom was softening, his face relaxing at the thought of his wife and his grandchildren.

"This is a big job," Jake interjected, trying to get them back on track. "I'm not sure this is the time—"

"I know exactly how big it is. I've got schematics and timelines already figured out," Frankie tossed back. She turned back to her father and stared him down. "If not now, when? I'm twenty-six, I got the degree you said I should have, and I've been working with you on jobsites since I could walk. Don't you trust me, Dad?"

Dark brown eyes flashing in her bronzed pixie face, she leaned across the desk. Her long dark ponytail was pulled back tight, highlighting her earnest ambition as she leaned forward. Her eyes flashing, she braced her arms on the desk. She was compelling.

It would have been damn entertaining if he didn't already know how the networks would react to this change in plans. Putting the comic relief with no leadership on her résumé in charge of this massive project was a nonstarter. No way could he sell that to the network.

Her small frame, tightly packed with lean muscle, vibrated as she waited for Dom to answer. Jake couldn't fault her ambition. It was one of the few things they had in common. He had it himself in spades, which was part of the reason he'd left acting. He'd wanted more serious roles, but he'd never managed to climb out of the "cute kid/hot teen" box he'd been shoved into, and he refused to stay boxed in.

He began to formulate what he would ask for in return, since he could see Dom wavering. He wished like hell that he could just step in and unilaterally say no. But until he had Dom's signature stating that the network had final creative control, he had to play ball. He was happy enough to ride the wave of popularity from

MDash, but if he lost this special after all the hyping up he'd done for his execs, all of that momentum would be lost. He was only as valuable as his current property.

Clearly not pleased that Dom hadn't already crumbled, Frankie pulled out the big guns. "Dad, listen. I'm going to run this company because I promised Gabe I'd look after it while he was gone." She paused to swallow hard. "No one expected him to be gone forever, but a Valenti keeps her promises. You taught me that. I'm not going to let him down. Consider this a dry run. If I can handle running our largest renovation to date, not only will you have proof you can trust me, but you and Ma can have that dream retirement she's been planning."

Jake broke into her monologue, unable to let her completely run over his plans. "What if you fail?"

Frankie looked at him blankly, as if the possibility hadn't even occurred to her. "Excuse me?"

Dom still hadn't spoken, but his attention bounced between them as quickly as their words. He was known for his snap decisions. This indecision was new, and Jake did not like surprises during a negotiation.

Jake pushed back, his voice deliberately hard with sarcasm. "Hey, let's invest half a million dollars in a project run by a twenty-six-year-old woman with no track record. It'll be fine. Is that what you want me to sell my executives?"

"I don't give a flying fuck what your executives—"

Jake stood and cut her off, slapping a hand on Dom's desk, getting in her face. "Yes, you do. If you didn't care about the show being a success, you wouldn't be in here fighting to lead it."

"Of course I want it to succeed. Why would I want anything with the Valenti name on it to flop? I just don't care that your network doesn't think I can handle it. Or is it really that *you* don't think I can handle it?"

Jake dodged the jab and leaned in even farther. "Where is the money coming from? Their approval is the only way this show gets green-lit and funded. If you want the money and exposure from this, you need to get them on board, baby. Cold selling the class clown as the project leader is going to be damn near impossible. Give me something to work with."

Frankie was twisted like a pretzel over the desk now, and it was a real struggle not to close his eyes and remember. He couldn't afford to lose focus.

"And whose idea was it to make me the clown in the first place?"

"You wanted a bigger role—"

Dom cleared his throat, breaking through their bickering. "Frankie, you will be head contractor on the show. All designs will go through Sofia and will be done before the baby comes. Adrian will help with the local builds off camera so he can be flexible for Fi. Our architects will approve any structural changes. You will run the build crews. Enzo's crews will handle the outdoor design as we've already agreed on a timeline that works around the twins. Jake, you will tell the network that she has my full support and oversight. And if we fail to hit production deadlines, we will pay back twenty percent of their seed money." Decisive Dom picked a hell of a time to show up.

"Dad! That's a hundred grand!"

"I know, and you'll be the one covering it. You want to run the business for real, you've got to have skin in the game."

"I can sell that," Jake quickly agreed, recognizing the value of that statement as a bargaining chip. Doubt and desire warred on Frankie's face, but her ambition was stronger than her fear. Jake had yet to see her back down from a challenge.

"I'll do it." Her hand was shaking but she held it out to Jake to seal the deal.

He was the one who had to suppress his reaction to her handshake. Electricity zinged up his forearm, and his grip contracted unconsciously around her fingers. He couldn't let go, even though he knew he should.

She was too young. And the daughter of a friend and colleague. And now a business partner in her own right. He forced all the reasons he couldn't indulge in this attraction to parade through his mind so he could let go of her hand and finish this damn negotiation. It was going to be a long six months on this project.

But when it was done, he'd be that much closer to his goal of being a respected and sought-after showrunner.

"It's a deal." He released her hand finally, extending his fingers before clenching them tight around the lingering buzz. *A very long six months.*

CHAPTER 4

"Dad, I promise you won't regret this."

No promises I won't, though. Frankie took a deep breath to steady herself and hopped off the desk. What had she done? Had she really gotten what she wanted? At what cost? Jake had left to update the altered contracts and get approval, leaving her alone with her father as her adrenaline dropped.

"I hope *you* won't regret it. This is a big step, baby."

Frankie ignored the nickname that always drove her nuts as her father seemed to read her mind. Today was a day for picking battles.

"Dad, how could I regret chasing the dream I've had for so long? I would regret *not* stepping up more than trying and failing." Frankie edged toward the door, eager to share the good news with Fi and Enzo.

"I want you to remember that if you end up working for free for a few years to pay down the debt."

That stopped her in her tracks. Turning back to Dom with her hands on her hips, she stared. "Wow. Thanks for the vote of confidence, Dad. You really think I'm going to fail?"

Dom pushed back in his chair and met her annoyed glare steadily, calm now that he'd settled everything to his liking. "I didn't say that. But I've been in this business long enough to know that sometimes things don't go according to plan. You've never held all of the cards before. I think it's going to be more challenging than you expect."

"And I know I am up to the challenge. In fact, I'm going to clear a few things with Sofia so we can hit the ground running." Frankie turned once more to leave, but Dom stopped her again, this time with a gentle hand on her wrist, his voice low and gruff.

"Francesca, you know I love you. It's hard not to want to protect you from the ugliness of the world, especially now."

Especially now that Gabe is dead was what he meant. So much had changed with that terrible news four years ago. Didn't he understand that was exactly why she had to try? "Playing it safe doesn't get you anywhere good. Did you and Zio Tony play it safe when you built this place? Or did you make sacrifices along the way to grow and thrive?"

"I did those things so you wouldn't have to." He turned his hand into hers and squeezed.

"But what if I want to, Dad? After all, I learned from the best."

She kissed his forehead and crossed the hall to her big sister's office. Despite having the utmost confidence in her ability to pull off this project, Frankie knew that Sofia's talent with interior design and deep knowledge of their mother's taste would play a big role in that success.

She dropped into the upholstered chair in front of Sofia's desk and waited for her sister to finish a call. Sofia pulled fabric swatches out of the mismatched cabinets that served as both storage and samples with her cell phone tucked against her ear. Buster rose from the blanket he had carried from Frankie's office into Fi's corner and nudged his head under her hand, demanding his welcome.

"Hi, big boy. Got lonely, huh?" Frankie ruffled his ears and laughed when he took that as an invitation to put his paws on her thighs and cover her face with big doggy kisses. "Were you a good pup for Zia Sofia?"

Her dog was almost four now, but he was still a big puppy at heart. He was her best boy, and she hoped he never lost his playful joy. It had been the reason she picked him out of the pound. She'd desperately needed a reason to keep moving after losing Gabe. Buster had forcibly pulled her back from the edge of her grief with every tug on his leash. He'd needed her to save him, and so she had. And he'd saved her right back.

Sofia ended her call and sat back in her chair, rubbing her slightly swollen belly. "He was an angel. I don't know why you complain about him so much," Sofia said, setting her phone on her desk and picking up her coffee mug. She grimaced after one sip. "God, I will never get used to that not being coffee."

Frankie didn't know how Sofia was functioning, having switched to herbal tea for the little peanut. Buster turned his head and gave her a snuffly woof. He had learned early on that Sofia was not one to mess with. She was a clear alpha in their little pack. He had no such respect for Frankie, even though she was the one who fed and housed him. Ungrateful little wretch. But then he plopped his head on her thigh and gazed up at her with eyes full of love, and all was forgiven.

"I wanted to see if you'd had any more thoughts on the vineyard project. We are finalizing the contracts today so it seems like it's a go." Frankie tried to play it cool, but she felt her face stretching with the grin she simply couldn't contain.

"What are you so giddy about?" Sofia teased.

"It's my show. I'm going to run the build. I'm finally getting my chance, Sofia."

Sofia sat upright in her chair and bumped into her desk. "Really? Dad went for it?"

"What is it with all the surprise today? Your faith in me is overwhelming." Frankie's smile faded. Did anyone think she could do this?

"Shut up. You know I'm happy for you." Fi reached into her chocolate drawer and pulled out a 100 Grand bar and tossed it at Frankie. "Congrats, Pip. I'm just surprised Dad went for it. But I'm not going to look this gift horse in the mouth. I'll be honest—I was worried about how Adrian would juggle filming with the baby coming. You're sure you're ready?" Sofia longingly stroked a Snickers bar before setting it firmly back in the drawer and closing it.

"I'll never know if I don't try. And I am so ready to try."

"Well, you know I'll help out however I can. Sooner would be better," she said as she patted her belly and reached for the ever-present bottle of Tums on her desk, "but I'm here for you."

"I'm going to take you up on that. Dad's got a lot riding on Ma loving this. I really want to nail it, and no one knows her taste better than you."

Frankie gestured to Fi's office. Despite the mismatched cabinets, Sofia Valenti's style shone in this room she'd made her office. Sofia was classy, colorful, and scrupulously organized—Frankie often wondered how they'd grown up in the same household and come out so differently. Fi had taken after their mother, with that inherent understanding of how to make things beautiful. From fashion to decorating to wrapping a Christmas present, Sofia and Ma were peas in a pod.

Frankie, on the other hand, was Daddy's little tomboy and could deconstruct a toaster to fix a short, but still managed to burn the toast. Her decorating style could best be described as "Adolescent Boy Dream Designs." Functionally cool, but not super tidy. She would install every bell and whistle on this winery, but Sofia would make sure they all shined.

"I've got Dad's take covered, but you are the pro at making things functional and beautiful. I can do the legwork if you can point me in the right direction."

"I've started a file…" Sofia reached for her laptop and pulled up an idea board within seconds.

Once again, Frankie marveled over the ease with which her big sister operated in her sphere. Since making a push for her design business, Sofia had really come into her own. Frankie hoped she could do the same. Although Frankie's desk would never look this clean.

It didn't matter. She needed to see things in order to find them, but she could always find them. And she could juggle details for multiple jobsites in her head. She tried to remind herself of her strengths.

They had been so different growing up, and with Sofia often having to help Ma with the younger kids, she had felt more like a little parent to Frankie. Frankie had hated that and had rebelled by becoming her oldest brother Gabe's little shadow. He'd never said she couldn't tag along on his adventures, and she'd never made him regret that, always pushing to keep up with the guys, always quick with a joke. He'd given her all the skills to succeed as a woman in construction. She'd just never anticipated she'd be doing it without him.

Frankie tried not to make comparisons between her life and her sister's, but it was hard. She was struggling, while Sofia had her dream job, a gorgeous fiancé, and a baby on the way. Frankie's job was literally a joke, Buster was the leading man in her life, and she could potentially be bankrupt a year from now. It was hard to keep her chin up when the calculus slapped at her.

But at least one of those things was about to change. She just had to make this show a success.

"So these are the finishes for the main house, and these are for the event space." Sofia turned her monitor so Frankie could see the details. "We should go with rustic stonework or stucco for the main building, with at least one big arched doorway, since Dad wants it to remind Ma of Italy. And I think that should carry over to the barns as well."

She clicked open a picture of a stucco-plastered building that vaguely resembled the shape of a barn with a travertine-tiled pavilion out front.

Barn, my ass. Frankie's jaw dropped. "Jesus, Fi, that's the barn? What the hell are you going to do to the house?" Frankie eyed the 100 Grand bar melting in her hand, wishing it was actually worth that much, and wondered how on earth she was going to keep to her contract.

"We'll get to that. This is a sound investment, Frankie. It will be a gorgeous backdrop for pictures, and it will be a completely multipurpose space. We can get married in the courtyard, move everyone inside for the meal, and then clear the patio for the dance floor. It'll be perfect."

Frankie caught the *we* slip and the stars in her sister's eyes. She wasn't building an event space. She was building her sister's wedding venue. To spec.

"When do you need it ready?" Frankie asked.

"Well, the baby comes in April. We were thinking October?"

Frankie let out a deep breath. That was going to be tight, but she would move mountains to give her sister the wedding of her dreams. "I may have to make a few tweaks, but I'll have it ready. I promise. Lay out the details for me."

While Sofia pitched the relative merits of marble vs. quartz countertops and complementary flooring options, Frankie mentally tallied price per square foot and installation man-hours. Between the barn and the house, Sofia was on track to spend over a million on the decor alone. When she clicked over to the picture of the walk-down wine cellar concealed beneath the kitchen cabinets, Frankie raised a hand.

"Fi, how are we going to afford all of this?"

"Frankie, this place has to knock Ma's socks off. We need to go all out."

"Yes, but Dad isn't made of money. I can't go over budget on this."

"You'll figure something out. Maybe you can work some of your Frankie magic on Jake and get him to up the budget."

As the baby of the family, she had developed a magic formula to get people to do what she wanted with a cute smile and circular logic. "I doubt Jake is susceptible to my magic." Which made the fact that she couldn't stop noticing his forearms inconvenient.

"I'd pay good money to see Jake Ryland wrapped around your little finger." It was no secret that Sofia barely tolerated the man's meddling. If he'd gotten between her and Adrian, Frankie doubted he'd have all of his limbs intact. Luckily, all of Jake's maneuvering had only thrown them closer together, but clearly Fi wouldn't mind seeing him get a taste of his own medicine. "It's a shame he can be such a jerk, or I'd tell you to flirt like hell."

Frankie stared at Sofia. Had she sprouted a second head or started speaking Latin? Both would have made more sense than the words she'd just said. "Hello? Have you forgotten who you're talking to?" Frankie gestured to her nonexistent curves. "He'd laugh in my face."

"Hey, that's my sister you're talking about. I'm just saying you are the only person I know who could beat him at his own game. And it wouldn't exactly be a hardship."

"What are you talking about?"

"Don't tell me you haven't noticed that our showrunner is smoking hot." Sofia opened the chocolate drawer again, dropping her gaze from Frankie's while she rifled through her stash.

"Sure, he's handsome, but..." Frankie was at a loss for words. For the last year, she'd heard nothing but shade from her sister about their tricky dick-rector.

Snapping the drawer closed without choosing one, Fi looked back up and laughed at Frankie's slack-jawed astonishment. "Hey, I'm pregnant, not dead."

"I think those hormones have warped your brain, sis. What are you looking for?"

"Twizzlers. Either the baby or my heartburn doesn't like chocolate."

"First coffee, now chocolate? Inconceivable! Does this baby not know who it's messing with?"

"I know!"

Frankie was glad her sister could laugh about this, since the pregnancy had been unexpected. She was going to be a great mother, but Frankie knew Fi was struggling with all of the changes coming so fast.

When Fi leaned forward in her chair and whispered, "Want to know a secret?" Frankie was pretty sure she was about to hear about another horror of pregnancy.

After the last diatribe on cankles, she was cautious. "Oh God, I don't know. Do I?"

Sofia nodded with a grin. "I had a copy of the *Tiger Beat* that had J.R. Hudson on the cover. Kept it for years."

"What are you talking about?" Frankie's mental whiplash had her brain scrambling to catch up.

"Hello? Hudson House? He played the son? And that role in *Full On 3*? Don't tell me you don't remember him."

"When on earth have you ever seen me watch a teen rom-com? I'm sure I was watching the baseball game with Dad and the boys."

It was Sofia's turn to goggle. "Are you telling me you had no idea he was a child star? My God, the man had a full career before you were out of kindergarten!"

"Who the hell cares that you had a crush on this J.R. Hudson dude?"

Sofia turned back to her computer and pulled up the images of this actor, and it finally clicked. She was looking at a younger, impossibly cuter version of her showrunner.

Sofia spoke slowly so Frankie could catch up. "Jake. Ryland. Hudson. I didn't just moon over the pictures. I read the articles too. He dropped his last name when the show went off the air, trying to distance himself from the role. I had such a thing for him. That's why I was so angry when he showed up and turned out to be an asshole."

"I had no idea."

Frankie sat back in her chair, shell-shocked by the explosion of information. She couldn't quite picture Jake Ryland taking direction from anyone else, but he certainly had the kind of male beauty that belonged on camera. Why had he walked away from the limelight? The cut of his jaw, his high cheekbones, the dark hair and eyes that contrasted with his naturally bronzed skin, and his perpetually perfect beard made him star material. He'd been an adorable child, but as a grown man he was dangerous. He carried his power and his sensuality with a casual confidence that flipped all of Frankie's lady switches.

Working around big and burly meatheads her entire life had inured her to their charms. The guys on her crew were like brothers to her, and when they were on-site she was just one of the guys. She'd worked damn hard to earn that privilege. Jake Ryland was a different kind of man, sexy and refined and confusing. Frankie didn't like things she couldn't take apart and figure out. It might be fun to figure out what made him tick…

But that was all hypothetical. She wouldn't be messing with

him, not with her career on the line. He was a distraction she couldn't afford, no matter how pretty.

Sofia snapped her fingers in front of Frankie's face. "Didn't mean to blow your mind, Pip. So, do you think you can get him to approve more money for these changes?"

"I'll do my best, Fi. You can count on me."

CHAPTER 5

Jake pinched the bridge of his nose and closed his eyes, dropping his head heavily onto the headrest of the driver's seat of his car. A sigh would have transmitted his frustration through the phone, so he bit it back. His development executive and current executive producers were going back and forth, hashing out the implications of what he'd promised Dom and Frankie, while he sat parked outside the Valenti Brothers offices.

Jake didn't doubt he'd bring them around eventually, but the two suits seemed determined to talk through every single point of the contract in depth, as if they hadn't just done this two weeks ago. He didn't have time to listen to them verbally process what he already knew to be a good deal. The extra hour of dickering was cutting into his already packed schedule. He had a million details to see to for the show he was currently producing. This was a waste of time.

But no matter how much he wanted to tell them to call him back when they'd pulled their heads out of their asses, he couldn't do that.

"Jake, my biggest concern is Frankie Valenti."

"Brian, I told you. I'm confident she can handle it."

"I respect your opinion." *Bullshit.* "But the world knows her as the crazy little sister who chucks crowbars through windows. That is the character they tune in to see."

"That's not the only reason they tune in." He made a well-balanced show that appealed to a broad audience. Even if they shifted Frankie's role, he was sure he could maintain the comedic beats that broke up the tension of the dramatic segments.

"Fair, but changing established roles midstream is risky." Alexander Prikov, the other exec, chimed in.

"Keeping everything exactly the same is boring."

Alex kept talking as if he hadn't been interrupted. "If her leadership role falls short, we need to be able to recut her scenes back to her humor role and backfill with supplemental footage of Adrian or even Dom."

"I can manage that. It shouldn't be too hard to get some insurance rolls, especially since we won't release any shows before the entire project is complete."

"And I want to meet her at the wrap party next week."

His producers had griped about having to travel up for the day, but Jake held firm. The party would be up here so the pregnant women wouldn't have to travel. These guys could tough it out for one day. "I'd be happy to introduce you."

"Any woman who can hold her own in a negotiation with you is a woman I want to meet." Jake bristled at Brian's tone, but bit his tongue. "Okay, between the backup and the buy-back clause you negotiated, I can fund this. That was some smooth wrangling. Of course, I expect you to do your best to trigger that clause."

Brian joked, but Jake couldn't tell if he was really joking or fake joking for deniability but actually expecting him to sabotage the project. He forced a laugh, hoping it was the right response.

"I'll get this over to legal to clean up, but good work, Jake. Keep this up and you'll have your choice of projects."

Counting on it, he thought as visions of future productions danced through his head. He wanted that Emmy in the next five years, and he wanted it for his created content, not his acting. He wasn't going to get it for Million-Dollar Starter Home or Valenti Vineyards, but if they built his name within the network so he'd have freedom to develop his own projects, well, he'd take that trade-off. He'd do just about anything to have control and the career he'd chosen.

For now, he'd jump through whatever hoops they put in front of him.

∽

JAKE SIPPED his Sonoma Imperial Stout and smiled. The smooth, creamy beer helped soothe the rough edges caused by the hectic production schedule. Starting a show at the same time one was ending might be great for crew retention, but it was hell on the nerves. But it was done.

The second season of Million-Dollar Starter Home, affectionately known as MDash, was filmed, mostly edited, and scheduled to air. Now it was up to other people to wrap things up.

He could sit back, enjoy his beer, and let all of his worries about Valenti Vineyards drop for the night. The wrap party was a time-honored tradition, and this one was just getting started. Jake loved and hated these parties. Celebrating a job well done was important, but it also signaled a goodbye.

He scanned the San Francisco Brewing Company, full of the cast and crew from the show enjoying the night and each other, and his throat clenched up. It would never again be exactly the same. People would move on to other gigs, half of his stars would be parents soon, and the new show would have its own energy. If there was a third season of MDash, it would be different. Change happened, whether he liked it or not, but one last party together helped ease him through the transition, even as he held himself apart and watched.

Against the burnished wood and exposed brick decor of the brewery, Lorena, his assistant director, and Rico faced off at the shuffleboard, while Enzo and Dom debated the offerings available on tap at the self-serve beer wall. Brian and Alex, his executive producers, had flown up from LA and were chatting with Trina and Winston, his carpenter with a voice of gold who had just gotten back into town himself. They were likely trying to convince him to do a spin-off show of his own instead of pursuing a solo music career.

Winston was the reason he'd be losing Trina after the vineyard project. They had fallen in love on set and were ready to settle down. Trina was eager to move into movie camerawork, and Winston's recent stay in LA had already snagged him agent interest and a few offers to get him in the studio. They had delayed a permanent move for him, and Jake was grateful. He'd help them out, of course, with his connections, but he felt like he was losing his right hand.

But not tonight. He had a commitment of six more months and another show before he had to cross that bridge. He took a sip of beer to push the lump back down his throat.

"You know, it's okay to join in the fun."

Jo Valenti's voice in his ear surprised the beer from his mouth up into his nose. He coughed and wiped his face, tears in his eyes.

"Sorry! I didn't mean to startle you." She tried, and failed, to hide her laughter.

He waved away her apology and laughed along with her. "Enjoying the party?" he asked once he could speak.

"We never get into the city. It's nice to have an excuse." Her eyes sought out and fixed on her husband. Jake was a pretty good judge of emotions, but he couldn't read the complex jumble glittering in Jo Valenti's expression. "It's good to have something to celebrate."

"I'm glad you came." Jake sipped his beer with exaggerated care, giving Jo the moment and the laugh she needed to collect her thoughts.

"Jake, I want to apologize." Jo fiddled with the rings on her left hand while she stared at his shoes.

"Jo, there's no need…"

"No, let me get this out. I'm sorry I haven't made more of an effort with the shows. You might have noticed my husband can be impulsive. When he signed on for these, I was ready for us to retire. These shows seemed like a hell of a lot more work."

"They are," Jake said, but Jo held up a finger.

"I hated you and this show for taking Dom further away from me."

"Ouch." Jake rubbed his free hand over his chest. "Tell me how you really feel."

"I'm trying to." Jo chuckled. "Over these two seasons, I've seen the changes that have come to our business and to Dom's state of mind. Your project has strengthened them both. He needed something to work on to get him through the worst of his grief, and the business is booming. My kids have found love and are starting families. Your work on this show played a big part in that."

Jake didn't know what to say, so he held his tongue and let Jo keep carrying the conversation.

"I won't say I understand why Dom needs to renovate a vineyard for someone, but Frankie is very excited for her chance to run the build. You've done so much for my family." She pinned him with what could only be described as a Mom Look. " I don't hate you anymore. I still want Dom to retire, but for the rest of it, thank you, and I'm sorry. If you need more from me on the vineyard project, I'll try."

Of course, on the one project he needed to keep a secret from her, she volunteered. Jake chuckled. "I will keep that in mind, though Frankie has things pretty well in hand. I might ask you for some design help once Sofia is out with the baby."

"Whatever you need."

"Thank you, Jo."

"Tell me more about this vineyard. I know Dom bought it to flip for a client, but I don't have any of the details."

Danger alarms began to sound in his head. He let his eyes scan the room, searching for a distraction. The one most guaranteed to distract him was nowhere to be seen. "We are still nailing them down. That's probably why he hasn't told you anything. Actually, you just reminded me. I need to talk to Frankie about something. Have you seen her?"

"She stepped outside for some air."

"Great, thanks. And thanks for what you said too. It means a lot."

"I'm trying to own my mistakes better, and I think I was wrong about you, Jake Ryland."

Jake turned and headed for the door, rubbing a hand over the back of his neck where it prickled.

Why did her reluctant approval send warmth down his spine? Straight-up compliments from his mother generally had the opposite effect, turning his blood ice-cold. It was good preparation so he could freeze out whatever request was coming next. But this, this apology, came with nothing attached, no emotional blackmail, no expectations. Jake was glad he'd already turned away, or he might've given in to the urge to hug Jo and let loose the tears clutching in the back of his throat. He had a feeling she'd understand.

Instead, he coughed the tightness free and set his empty beer on the bar before heading outside into the crisp San Francisco evening.

Coming from LA, he was always amazed at how different the weather could be in the Bay Area. It was a cold and clear March night in Ghirardelli Square overlooking the bay, but that afternoon had been warm and sunny farther down the peninsula. The other day the vineyards had hit eighty. He shivered and rued forgoing a jacket.

Scanning the bustling courtyard, he frowned. Even though he'd only used Frankie as an excuse to avoid giving away the surprise of the vineyard to Jo, he didn't want to be a liar. He did have things he could talk to her about.

But he'd have to find her first.

He crossed to the raised fountain and climbed the short stairs for a better view. How hard could it be to find one person? Jake turned slowly in a circle until his eyes snagged on a pair of truly excellent legs in high heels. Trim ankles, muscular calves, scarred knees, toned thighs that disappeared under a tight black sweater dress. His eyes kept traveling higher, admiring the fit of the dress and the long swing of dark hair that reached nearly to her waist.

It wasn't until his gaze landed on her face that he realized he was staring at Frankie.

Thank God she was staring longingly at the steaming cup in her hands.

"Hey, there you are." He sloughed back down the stairs and crossed the courtyard to her. "You're missing your party."

"It couldn't be helped. I needed to get my hot cocoa hit. How can you stand there, smelling the Ghirardelli chocolate, and not need a fix?"

"You're right."

For a hot second, Jake considered the best way to get a taste of that chocolate. He could kiss her again, but even though she looked like a different person with the hair and the legs and the shoes, she was still Frankie Valenti and still out of bounds.

Instead he snagged the cup from her hand and took a deep

swallow that singed his tongue. Her brows furrowed and she yelped in protest, snatching her treat back.

"Damn, that's hot," Jake cursed.

"Serves you right for stealing my cocoa, asshole. What is this, third grade where you make moony eyes at a girl and then steal her pencil and pull her braid?"

Shit, she'd seen him stare. And it was a bad idea to think about how he wanted to pull her hair right now. Awkward. *Divert! Divert!*

"I don't know. I never went."

Now she was staring at him like she'd never seen him before. "What do you mean, you never went?"

"I never went to third grade. There were on-set tutors for me and the other kids on the show, so I don't know what third grade was like."

Her face blanked, like he'd truly stunned her, before she rallied her snark. "Well, then let me inform you that it is not polite to snatch a girl's hot chocolate from her hands and drink half of it. If we were still in third grade, I'd kick you in the nuts for that."

Jake knew he was pushing it, but he deliberately took a step closer and leaned into her space. "And what are you going to do about it now?"

Frankie's face turned red and her mouth opened and closed like a fish. "God, I really want to dump the rest of this over your head, but also what a waste of good chocolate. Why is adulting so hard sometimes?" she whined with a grin, before turning and walking away from him.

Those heels added a swinging saunter to her step that her steel-toed work boots did not. He followed two steps behind her as she made her way back to the brewery, and manfully tried not to stare at her ass.

When her heel betrayed her on the bricked pavement of the

patio, he was close enough to catch her. With a hand on her hip, his arm wrapped around her waist, he looked down into eyes the same molten brown as the chocolate in her hand and lost his breath. Under the hanging strands of bulbs, she leaned into his side and the chill in the air disappeared. Heat flared where she touched him. The quick contrast of hot and cold sent a chill down the back of his neck, and he ran a hand over it to make it disappear.

"Thanks," she whispered before righting herself and clearing her throat. "I hate these things." She pointed her toe out in front of her, calling his attention back to her sexy ankles. "Fi talked me into these for the party."

"I'll be sure to let wardrobe know. No stilettos for Frankie," he teased, trying to bring things back to their normal vibe. God, what if she did start wearing heels around the work site? He'd be toast. She righted herself and he offered his elbow.

Frankie looked at it like he'd tried to jab her in the chest with it, before tentatively accepting it, placing her small but capable hand in the crook. "Why did you come looking for me anyway?"

"I was talking to your mom, and she asked me point-blank about the vineyard project. I didn't know how you'd spun it to her, so I said I needed to talk to you and ran."

Frankie laughed at that, breaking the tension between them. "Jo Valenti is a force to be reckoned with." Frankie confirmed that his intuition was correct. Like mother, like daughter. "We've basically kept her in the dark. She knows we bought the property and are renovating for a potential client, but we didn't really get into details. I will probably try to play it as straight as possible, without naming the client obviously, because my mom can smell a lie a mile away."

They walked back into the bar side by side, laughing over outrageous excuses to tell her mother. Jo hovered near the door and her eyebrow went up when she saw them together. Frankie crossed to where Alex and Brian were still chatting with Winston, and Jo stepped up to him again.

"You found her."

"I did. Hot cocoa run." He watched as she charmed his executive producers and had them laughing at whatever smart-ass comment she'd made. The smirk on her face and the glance in his direction told him it had likely been about him.

"Did you get your question answered?"

Jake turned his attention back to Jo. He thought about all of the uncomfortable revelations he'd run up against in the last fifteen minutes and grimaced. "I think so."

"You should come to Friday dinner soon."

The non sequitur pulled Jake into the present, and left him stuttering. "Um, yeah, sure. I'd like that. Can I bring anything?"

"Just your patience and a sense of humor," Jo replied. She hugged him briefly before rejoining the party.

The warmth in his cheeks he felt from her invitation was nothing compared to the searing heat in his chest he'd experienced with Frankie pressed up against him, but it stayed with him long into the evening.

Christmas had been a pity invite, but Friday dinners were for family. This simple invitation shifted his entire relationship with the Valentis. He couldn't help but wonder why Jo had invited him now? His director brain wanted to pick apart her motivations, but the little boy always on the outside looking in just wanted to wallow in that hug.

CHAPTER 6

"This isn't a hallway, guys. Maybe a secret passageway, but that's not in the blueprints. Oh dear God! No one tell Sofia I said that, or she'll have me add one just for fun."

Jake suppressed a smile at Frankie's banter as he walked into the main house of the vineyard property. The rest of her crew laughed freely, and she chuckled right along with them.

He had to give her credit. She was walking the line between crew boss and court jester well, keeping her men in good humor while holding them accountable. Jake checked that Trina was catching this little dramatic moment on camera. *Good.* The misplaced wall would be the tension trigger for the living room episode. With any luck, they'd get their shots on the first take.

"But boss, the schematic says the stud walls should be at twenty and twenty-two feet from the eastern wall." Rico pointed to the build plan they were working from.

"Son of a... That should be twenty-four. Who builds a two-foot hallway? That's not even to code! Whatever. This wall needs to come down and move two feet that way. I've got a lotto card for whoever volunteers to do it first." She pulled the scratch-off card from her pocket and wiggled it between her fingers.

"I got it!" Rico enthusiastically snatched the card from her and tucked it into his back pocket before reaching for his sledgehammer.

"Easy there," Frankie said and slapped a hand on Rico's chest. "This isn't demo day. Get an electric saw and cut through the nails, top and bottom. Then slide the wall in one piece. Work smarter, not stronger."

Jake took a deep breath when she dropped her hand. He hadn't realized he'd been holding it. Was there something between them? Were they looking at another Sofia-Adrian situation? Why did that piss him off?

He stepped up behind Frankie as she pored over the drawings. "Problem?" he asked directly in her ear, chuckling when she jumped.

"Only the heart attack you just gave me." She turned back to double-checking the blueprints, head bowed, her lip caught between her teeth.

Rico covered by a fixed cam, Trina stepped up behind Jake and filmed Frankie's arresting face from over his shoulder. She was so good he didn't have to tell her to catch any sound bites he might pull from Frankie. Trina was a gem and would frame the perfect shot. He was going to miss her like hell when she transitioned into movies.

The tape of Frankie torturing her poor lower lip was going to torture him later, but it was worth it to get the shot.

"What about the wall you just told Rico to rebuild?"

"Minor snag. Rico will have it done in twenty. He'll just slide it over and reattach it."

Damn, he'd hoped it would take her a little longer to recover. A quick fix did not create the drama he needed. "Resorting to bribery this early in the build, Valenti? Can you afford that?"

"You let me worry about the budget and keeping my crew motivated. Did you need something?"

He'd come in from the trailer because he wanted to see how the delay caused by his changes to the schematic drawing filmed. He couldn't tell Frankie that, or he'd ruin her reactions to it. He'd take the humor, but he'd hoped for more of a meltdown. Her equanimity was not what he'd promised his executives. He needed more from her.

"Just keeping an eye on my inexperienced crew boss." As he'd hoped, his comment riled her up.

"I don't need a babysitter." Her dark brown eyes flashed with anger, and he couldn't look away.

"That's not what the network thinks—"

"Screw the network!"

"—and since they are paying my salary, here I am. Do you think you could grab a sledge and help Rico? Or is that beneath you now as crew boss?" His taunts had the desired effect.

"I've never walked away from hard work in my life." She whirled away from him with Trina in her wake, her long ponytail nearly slapping him in the face—as he imagined she'd like to do with her palm right now.

For a split second, he contemplated how her hair would feel wrapped around his fist as he exposed her neck for a kiss. Visions of her challenging him for control flashed hot, searing his brain with new fantasies.

When she'd kissed him on Christmas Eve, she'd unlocked this side of his brain. He couldn't stop thinking about how it would feel to kiss her again, in a variety of new and interesting places. But that night she'd been drunk and happy. Pliant. Not a word he would use to describe the woman currently taking out her frustrations on a stud wall. And yet…

He'd given her a ride home from her parents' house after a particularly eventful Christmas Eve, intending to see her inside her apartment and then crash down in Enzo's empty pad so they could ride back to Jo and Dom's house for Christmas morning.

Even though he knew they'd only invited him because Jo had found out he didn't have anywhere to go, he'd loved being included in their traditions, something his own family hadn't attempted in years. He'd spent the one-time-only evening absorbing all of the details and dramas for future reference. If he ever had to film a Christmas special, he'd be all set.

The unexpected arrival of his makeup artist and Enzo's fiancée Natalie Carras's mother and ex-boyfriend had set everyone on edge. Frankie'd had a few more drinks than she'd intended. It was only polite to offer to drive her home. It had been good manners to walk her up to her door and see her safely inside. When she'd pinned him to said door and kissed him senseless, all of his civilized reactions disappeared. They had devoured each other. He rubbed his thumb over his lower lip, remembering how she'd felt in his arms, lips pressed against his. They had finally made it inside, and he'd let her go to strip his shirt off.

But when her knees had buckled and she'd leaned unsteadily against him, sanity returned. He'd carried her into her bedroom, laid her down on her bed, and walked back out.

Talk about a blue Christmas.

He'd crashed on the world's most uncomfortable couch with a very unhappy erection and a dog who insisted he should sleep curled up behind Jake's knees. But instead of waking to Christmas morning with the kisses and sexy times under the tree he'd been dreaming about, he was yanked from slumber by a shriek and a slamming door. She'd forgotten he was there. And, he discovered shortly thereafter, she'd forgotten that incredible kiss. The one he couldn't help but remember every time he looked at her lush lips.

He'd like to nibble on that bottom lip—

A large hand clapped down on his shoulder, jolting him from his thoughts.

"Hey, Jake. Catch you dreaming?"

Heat flooded his face, and he thanked God for his beard. Dom didn't seem to notice the blush or the direction he'd been looking. Getting caught mooning over a girl by her father was embarrassing, no matter how old a guy was. At least at the ripe old age of thirty-five, he hadn't outgrown it. "Dom! Good to see you. I was just thinking about you."

"Oh really?" Dom sounded skeptical.

Come on. Head in the game. You're the one in charge, so charge.

"Yeah, we have to take down and rebuild this wall. The crew made an error with the schematic."

"That's not like them." Dom frowned, and Jake waved Trina over to join them.

"I was hoping I could get a quick explanation from you of how this affects the build."

"I don't know…"

The last time Dom had tried to talk on camera, it had been a disaster. Thank God Sofia and Adrian had stepped in. But Jake had promised his execs backup rolls. No time like the present. "Let's just give it a try. You're more comfortable with all of this now. Trina will stand right next to me. All you have to do is look at me and answer the questions, okay?"

Dom nodded nervously but drew his shoulders back and down.

"So, Dom, can you tell us why reading a schematic drawing is important?"

"Wasted time is wasted money. Every time a mistake is made, it takes man-hours and supplies to fix, and it costs us homeowner goodwill. How hard is it to build a wall in the right spot in the first place? This is a rookie mistake."

"What do you think of how Frankie handled it?"

"She's always been smart about fixing things. Much easier to move the damn thing over than to rebuild it. Less wasted time and minimal supply loss. Smart."

"Got it," Trina whispered in his ear.

Boy, did they ever. That one clip gave him three different sound bites he could weave in as needed. "That was great, Dom. Why don't we go see what goodies they have at craft services today? I need some coffee."

No sense in pushing Dom too far, too fast. Besides, he'd gotten what he needed out of this little snag. A few audio clips he could play with, some great shots of Frankie and Rico working together to move the wall, and they weren't too far off schedule. In fact, he might just have time to throw another hurdle in their way. His mind was already spinning to the next day's filming schedule, plotting possibilities and mapping out the episode in his head.

This was what he loved—the energy and excitement of running a show, the camaraderie with his crew, the challenge of getting enough raw material so that he could create something entertaining...he thrived on it. This was his passion. But this was also a business, and he had a million other details to see to now.

He glanced at Frankie again, now dripping with sweat. The unseasonably warm inland California spring and her unexpected exertion made her shirt cling to her in interesting ways. He'd love to stick around and watch her work, but he had a job to do. Guilt perched on his shoulder, chastising him for making her job harder. But Frankie was tough. She could handle it.

He shook off his discomfort and nodded to Trina that she should go get shots of sweaty Frankie before he turned away, texting his assistant director to cover. Lorena could supervise the rest of the scene. He had to stay focused. Eyes on the prize.

Despite his pep talk, Jake stole one more glance at Frankie on his way out the door, and she stuck her tongue out at him. He laughed and followed Dom toward coffee and sanity.

CHAPTER 7

Frankie rolled her shoulders and winced. She walked gingerly toward her truck, so tired that she registered the rosy sunset happening over the hills, but couldn't stop to appreciate nature's light show or she wouldn't get moving again.

Gravel crunched beneath her work boots and compounded her headache. The day had been a minefield. She could hardly take a step without a new problem exploding in her face. And Trina had been there to catch each one on film. *Damn it.*

She still couldn't understand how the schematic had changed from what showed on the blueprint. She sure as hell hadn't expected to be the one fixing it, but she'd let Jake get the better of her temper and now she was paying for it. One small blessing was that the crew had already gone, so no one was around to see her pain.

Stretching her arms toward the sky, Frankie folded one arm behind her head and leaned into the stretch. She was regretting her upper body day at the gym yesterday. Switching arms, she groaned as her shoulders protested as she rounded the back of the house.

This was all Jake's fault, she groused. He'd gotten her into this mess by pushing her buttons. He should follow up with a massage to make up for it. The image of him putting his hands on her made her cheeks flush, and she stopped beside her truck and folded forward to hide her reaction and stretch her upper back. She took a deep breath and grimaced as a pair of shiny leather shoes stepped up into her inverted field of view.

She straightened and turned to face Jake Ryland head-on, and if she wasn't hallucinating, he pulled his gaze from her ass to her face a second too late.

No one looked at her that way. Certainly no one scoped out her ass. She'd accepted long ago that her body was built like a boy's. No ass, no hips, no boobs. Sofia had gotten the full family quota for those desirable parts. So Frankie had tried to look at the bright side: her body made it easier for her to fit in with the guys. But it was not so great for attracting men.

What was he playing at? At the party the other night she'd caught him looking too, but she'd written that off as the surprise of seeing her dressed up. Ripped jeans and a dusty T-shirt did not justify a second glance, let alone a hard look at her rear.

Frustrated, she pushed him away with her words. "I'm off the clock, Ryland, and the wall is fixed. What do you need?"

To his credit, Jake kept his expression neutral in the face of her anger, but that pissed her off even more. Why did her emotions always go haywire around this man?

"A word. We are due to start working in the event space next week. The timing is going to be tight because we have to be filming in three different areas simultaneously, and today put us behind in the living room. Is there anyone you can call to beef up the crews? I don't want them looking too sparse."

Frankie sighed and turned her mind to work. She ran through her mental list of backups, but calling these guys would all add expense. She refused to bug Adrian since he was carrying Valenti Brothers' regular building contracts, and she'd already stolen

Rico. Enzo's crew was hopping right now between their regular yard maintenance gigs and working on the landscaping here. Maybe she could ask Seth and his business partner Nick to help out. They were custom woodworkers, and she was already counting on their help for the tasting room bar. They were also former servicemen, so they might have some veteran buddies who wouldn't mind being extras. She hated burning all of her matches this early in the show, but she couldn't afford to look weak either.

"Sure, I'll have it covered." She could juggle with the best of them.

"Make sure that you do." He turned to walk away.

"Are you always such a hard-ass?"

"Thinking about my ass, Valenti?"

Her gaze involuntarily dropped before she yanked it back up to meet his. "No more than you were thinking about mine a second ago."

He chuckled at that, and Frankie buzzed with pleasure over making him loosen up and laugh.

"So you *were* checking me out, then," he teased back.

It took her a second to catch on to what he was saying, but when she did she flushed hot and ruddy.

"For the record, I'm not a hard-ass. I'm in control. There's a difference."

"Sure there is," Frankie teased, checking out his ass blatantly and frowning. She had no idea what pushed her to trade barbs with him but she couldn't resist. He could hold his own against her sarcasm, and damn if she didn't find a man with a smart mouth and a smart mind attractive.

"So you like a man with a hard-ass who takes control..."

"I never said I liked you."

"That doesn't mean you don't."

Darkness had fallen while they spoke. They stood toe to toe, sparks arcing between them like a poorly wired light switch. She needed to flip that switch off before those sparks turned to flames.

She opened her mouth, but before she could say anything to defuse the situation, his phone rang.

Saved by the bell.

"Hold that thought." He looked at the display and cursed. "I have to take this."

He deliberately stepped away and turned his back on Frankie before answering. The better to stare at his ass. She suppressed a chuckle and crossed her arms. How had they gotten from barely tolerating each other to flirting? Was this flirting? Or was he just messing with her?

That had to be it. He had no problem manipulating her temper to get a reaction for the show. Why wouldn't he try her other emotions as well?

All of the lovely heat coursing through her body began to fade. Of course he wasn't attracted to her. Why would he be? He could be with any Hollywood starlet he chose. A woman with no curves who could out-curse a sailor and wield a hammer better than Thor didn't stand a chance.

"What is it now?" Frankie wasn't deliberately eavesdropping but she couldn't help hearing his voice go icy and sharp. He could turn that heat on and off so quickly. He was still a talented actor despite leaving the limelight.

Frankie couldn't hear the other voice well enough to make out the words, but Jake's shoulders tensed and he pinched the bridge of his nose.

"No." The finality in his voice was clear, but the other person kept talking.

Jake half turned and Frankie admired the shift of his shoulders beneath the crisp cotton of his shirt. She shook the thought from her head, and reminded herself of what Sofia had said. He was an actor, so far out of her league as to be laughable, who had one hundred thousand dollars to gain by her failure.

He was clearly setting her up for something. Letting his looks or his charm distract her would only make it easier for him to win. If he slowed her down or shot her budget to hell, he'd be a hero, but she'd be broken.

Standing up a little taller, she brushed her dusty hands against her well-worn boyfriend jeans, reminding herself of just where she belonged. She'd never hesitated to go head to head with the boys before. She wasn't going to start now. Sometimes being *one of the guys* came in handy, even if it was one more reason she didn't have a chance in hell of attracting him. Even if she wanted to. Which she totally didn't. Like not at all.

His terse voice cut through her musings. Who was he talking to like that? An employee? An enemy? An ex-lover?

"Think I'm bluffing? Try me."

He tapped the phone to hang up, and his fingers flexed into a fist around it. Frankie could tell he was resisting the urge to chuck it against the rocks. He shoved it in his pocket with a growl instead.

"Trouble in paradise?" Frankie asked.

"Something like that." He hissed out a breath and pinched his nose again, as if that could relieve the pressure headache behind it.

Frankie had the bizarre impulse to smooth his hair from his brow. She tucked her hand in her back pocket and reached for humor instead. "What was that you were saying about not being a hard-ass?" she teased. "Remind me not to piss you off."

"Hey, Frankie, don't piss me off."

She couldn't help the chuckle at his bad joke. In the quiet wake of their shared laughter, she asked the question she should have asked long ago. "Why this project? Why are you so invested in us?"

"I'm not looking to spend the rest of my career shooting reality shows. If I have a breakout hit, I can parlay that into bigger projects, ones that I produce. I believe your family will get me there."

Frankie let that soak in. His ambitions were riding on this project just as much as hers were.

"Where were we?" Jake asked, trying to find his train of thought.

Frankie wasn't about to let him off the hook. He thought he could manipulate her? "You were throwing kinks in my build schedule." She emphasized the word kink, and got the desired reaction. He was focused on her again, eyes hot. His gaze strayed and lingered on her ponytail. *Interesting.* "And I was calling you out for being an ass about it."

"As I recall, I was explaining how we are going to run the shooting schedule next week and you were distracted by my butt."

She was not going to let him win by distracting her with attraction again. "Agree to disagree. Look, we both want this show to succeed, right?"

"Sure…"

"I need to prove myself to Dad and not lose a hundred grand, and you need to prove yourself to the network?"

"Also true."

"I propose a truce. We are both going to need to do what we need to do to make this show a success. All this"—she waved her hand back and forth between them—"is a waste of time. I just want you to deal honestly with me."

"Where's the fun in that?" he teased, but she could tell he was thinking about it.

"I wasn't aware we were having fun," Frankie tossed back pointedly. "I thought this was about business. You don't have to pretend to flirt with me to get me to play along. I'm not some

Hollywood actress who needs smoke blown up her ass. I'd rather you treat me just like everyone else."

He cocked his head to the side and assessed her through hooded eyes. "And how is that?"

"You know, just like one of the guys. Play it straight, Jake, and we can both succeed with a minimum of fuss."

"I don't know. Fussing with you is damn entertaining."

"I'm not here to entertain you. I'm here to win. Let's win together." She held out her hand and waited for a heavy moment until he took it in his and sealed the deal with a handshake.

"Deal. Here's to getting what we both want."

Frankie pulled her hand back from his and shivered. She chose to believe he hadn't meant that as a double entendre, but damn if it didn't make her think about all the things she wanted from him and couldn't have.

CHAPTER 8

JAKE STOOD in front of a beautiful Craftsman-style home with an immaculate lawn, and shifted the flowers and wine onto one arm so he could ring the doorbell. The house was a showcase for their businesses, and the care and attention to detail was obvious in every trimmed rose bush and freshly painted shutter. The house glowed in the California sunset. It was Friday night, and he'd been invited to the Valentis' home for dinner.

He had been here for Christmas Eve, and Christmas morning as it turned out, but this was the first time he'd been invited to their weekly family meal. His stomach flip-flopped at that thought. Jake laughed under his breath and shook his head. He was being ridiculous, but being invited to this smaller dinner felt like more of a triumph than joining a huge crew of people around the Christmas tree.

He hoped this boded well for the family trusting him, and that he wasn't walking into an ambush. Things had been quiet since he and Frankie had reached détente, but he wasn't sure how Jo was handling the demands of the new show on her family.

Still, he jolted when Frankie opened the wide wooden door instead of Jo.

"Hey, what are you doing here?" She leaned against the doorjamb with her arms crossed, a beer dangling from her fingers, dark eyes suspicious. Her feet were bare and crossed at the ankle. He caught himself staring at her toes, so small but so strong. Like everything else about her.

Jake cleared his throat and lifted the gifts in his arms. "I'm here for dinner?"

"Oh. Ma didn't mention it."

"Do you think I'm lying?"

"No, I only thought it was odd for the doorbell to be ringing. Friday night is family night."

"For God's sake, let the man in!" Jo called from somewhere behind Frankie.

Frankie stepped back from the door as Jo bustled up the hallway.

"I swear I raised them all with manners. Some took better than others." Jo leaned up and bussed his cheeks before relieving him of the wine and flowers he'd brought. "Come on in, Jake. It's good to see you again."

"Thank you for having me. I hope it's not too much trouble."

"The more the merrier on a Friday night." Jo smiled and nodded her head toward the kitchen. "Come with me while I put these in water."

Jake followed Jo, and Frankie trailed behind him. He was sure the burning sensation he felt at the back of his neck was just his imagination and not Frankie watching him. Maybe she was checking out his ass again... He suppressed a chuckle at the memory.

He marveled as they walked through the beautifully restored bungalow that magically seemed the perfect size for however many occupants it had on a given night. At Christmas, they'd had nearly twenty people comfortably around the table. Today there were half that, and it still felt full of love and warmth. How did they manage to do that?

Frankie peeled off and flopped on the couch in the family room between Adrian and Dom, lost to the lure of the Giants' home opener. He peeked out the back picture window. Sofia and Natalie sat on the deck, rubbing identical swollen bellies. Seven-year-old Daisy was supervising her soon-to-be stepdad Enzo as they expanded a fairy empire in the garden.

Jo alone ruled the kitchen. Jake perched on a barstool at her island and watched her fill a crystal vase and fuss with the hydrangeas and tea roses he'd brought. He had nothing but admiration for a woman who could make this house a home, keep these people a family, and manage to make it look effortless, even as she dealt with the emotional strain of the past four years. It was a skill and a talent that was often overlooked.

But Jake was a director. He'd been raised on a set swarming with people instead of in a home with a family. He was a pro at recognizing power dynamics and unseen labor. Josephine Valenti was the key to this family. Everyone was happily bending over backward to give her this dream vineyard as a surprise. Her children adored her. Her husband was concerned enough about the state of their marriage to go to extreme lengths to make her happy. Jake wanted to know what made her tick.

He couldn't imagine his own mother inspiring that kind of devotion from anyone.

"Thank you again for inviting me to dinner." Jake reached for the bottle of wine. "Can I open this for you?"

Jo buried her nose in the flowers and inhaled deeply. "Someone's been spilling my secrets."

"Pardon?"

"People only bring my favorite wine when they're trying to butter me up. Who told you and what do you want?"

"No one had to tell me. You served it at Christmas, and I

figured it would be one you liked. And I might be angling to get invited back for whatever is making this kitchen smell amazing." He winked and made Jo laugh and hand over the wine key. *Gotcha.*

"Well, aren't you clever? Are you a useful sort in the kitchen or should I dismiss you and your wine to go join the crew on the couch?"

"I can boil water, and I grill a mean cheese sandwich, but please don't make me go watch baseball."

Basketball was the only sport he could abide, because it moved fast enough to hold his attention. Hockey was a close second. But dear God, baseball and football drove him nuts. All the starting and stopping and time between plays left him too much time to think about the thousand and one things on his to-do list.

"Okay, you can stay and get your first lesson in Italian cooking."

She set him to slicing eggplant and zucchini for sautéing, and he soaked up her instructions and her charm, his director's brain tucking away details. This was how he'd imagined family dinners when he was a kid. His own mother hadn't been capable of this. His parents were both only children, as was he, so there hadn't been any extended family to pick up their slack.

His father had spent most of his time trying to revive his own failing acting career or drinking himself stupid. His mother had given up on him and instead devoted herself to Jake's career in the limelight from his infancy. First baby food commercials, then bit roles on sitcoms. Neither parent had cared when he said he'd rather go to school. Neither had listened when he said he felt sick. They had never put him first. He never knew how his mother got the Hudson House show to be written around him, but once filming began, it had been full-on. His mother had abandoned most of his care to on-set tutors and nannies who ferried him back and forth. She was much happier living the LA life she'd been promised.

"Can I ask you a question, Jo?"

"Sure." Her hands didn't miss a beat, sautéing the veggies.

"After Gabe died, why didn't you leave Dom? What kept you together?"

She tapped the wooden spoon against the pan and braced herself against the stovetop. She took a deep breath and turned to face him. "That is complicated…and simple to answer. I love him. I wanted more time with him, not less. When Gabe died, I realized that none of this time is promised, and it shook me out of the rut I'd been in. I want to shake Dom out of his, so we can do the things we always said we'd do together. Before it's too late." She shrugged and turned back to the stove, cutting him off from the hard emotions that had flickered across her face.

His parents hadn't wanted anything to do with each other by the time he was twelve. His mother always felt that his father had wasted his potential, and by proxy, hers. Boy, had she been pissed that his father had finally started getting more roles after their divorce. It had been another blow when Jake had quit acting at eighteen and fired her as his manager. To this day, she believed she'd been robbed by everyone in her life. He wondered if she'd ever learn that no one owed her a damn thing. Not likely.

"Try this and tell me what you think." Jo handed him a forkful of linguine in a light, creamy sauce speared to the utensil with a clove of roasted garlic and a sun-dried tomato. One perfect bite.

He moaned as the flavors burst and melted on his tongue. "I think you are a treasure, Jo Valenti." He captured her hand that reached for his fork and pressed a kiss to her knuckles.

"What's all this?" Dom blustered as he entered the kitchen and traded his empty beer for a full one from the fridge.

"I'm trying to convince your wife to run away with me and

cook linguine every day," Jake teased, but Dom didn't laugh. His face fell, and Jake let go of Jo's hand.

"Don't be ridiculous. He's helping me put dinner together, which is more than I can say for any of the rest of you."

"Come on, Jojo. That's not fair. You always shoo us out of the kitchen!" Dom protested and he snagged a stuffed pepperoncini from the tray of appetizers in the fridge.

"Because your idea of helping is snacking on the antipasti!"

"I fixed the leaking faucet last week," Dom grumbled.

"And after only two weeks of me nagging. I am truly grateful." She patted Dom's cheek. "Now go round up our children. Dinner's ready."

The hustle of people washing up and trading barbs raised the decibel level significantly, but Jake didn't mind. Jo didn't seem to either. She was in her element, helping Daisy dry her hands and directing Frankie to start moving food to the table. Once everyone was seated, grace was shared and the platters were passed.

Most of the time, Jake lived off craft services. It was convenient and fit his schedule. And he hadn't been joking when he'd said he could basically boil water and make grilled cheese. But craft services had nothing on this spread of sautéed vegetables, creamy pasta, crisp salad, and rich chicken cutlets. Jake loaded his plate and tucked in with gusto.

Frankie sat across from him, and he watched, amused, as she quarantined all the zucchini to one corner of her dish.

"I didn't poison it. Scout's honor."

She looked up, and he swore he caught embarrassment in her eyes as she bit her lip.

"Oh, Frankie can't eat zucchini," Sofia said before bursting into laughter.

Frankie turned beet red and glared at her sister.

"It sounds like there's a story here." Jake deliberately popped some zucchini in his mouth and chuckled at the way Frankie's face scrunched up in disgust.

"When we were kids," Sofia began, but Frankie cut her off.

"It's my story. I'll tell it." Frankie looked him square in the eye. He had to respect that. "When we were kids, Gabe convinced me that the budding zucchini out in the garden were trolls' toes that would soon sprout into full-grown ogres."

"How much older was he?" Jake wanted to know more about who the man had been before his death had torn a hole in the tightly woven fabric of this family. It was rare for anyone to talk about who he was before he left for the army.

"I was five. He was nine and old enough to get a kick out of grossing out his little sister. I was always tagging along behind him, and he tried to run me off by teasing me. Eventually, I learned how to take a joke and give as good as I got. But I hadn't gotten there yet. When Enzo came along and took a bite of a baby zucchini fresh from the garden, I ran screaming into the house. Traumatized for life." Frankie shuddered dramatically while the rest of the family cackled at the memory.

"I should have realized something was up when he offered me a dollar to go eat a vegetable," Enzo said through his laughter.

"It would have saved you from getting grounded alongside him," Jo said.

"I always got punished by association." Enzo stabbed a zucchini with his fork and ate it fiercely. Frankie gagged dramatically.

"So you still can't eat zucchini?" Jake asked.

"I've tried, but every time the texture makes me think of nasty toes, and I just can't."

At this point the whole table was in hysterics over the faces Frankie was making, her embarrassment shifting to bravado as she hammed it up. Jake couldn't help but join in. She played her role as the family jester well.

In a clear attempt to wrangle her unruly brood back to civility, Jo cleared her throat. "So, Jake, tell me how things are going at the vineyard. Dom has been remarkably vague about it."

Frankie and Dom froze. They had terrible poker faces. Jake knew Dom still intended the vineyard reveal to be a surprise for Jo, despite his own objections to that plan. He needed to tread lightly. "Well, we are through demo and starting in on the kitchen and tasting rooms."

"Oh, it's moving quickly, then. How on earth did Dom get involved in this project?"

"Dom saw the property and thought it would make a great renovation special, and the client wants it for a retirement investment," Jake hedged. Technically it was all true, but he couldn't help feeling a little bad about being evasive with the woman who was feeding him.

"It just seems a little odd that we purchased the property instead of the client." Jo wasn't going to let this go.

Dom jumped into the gap. "The client needed a bit more time to get his finances in order."

"But what compelled you to tackle a winery? You've never done commercial spaces."

"Remember that wine tasting tour you dragged me to with your group? I figured I could make it look better than that place," Dom bragged.

Jo's mouth tightened and she set down her fork.

Sometimes Jake wished he could shake the older man for the way he talked to his wife, but it wasn't his place.

"Don't go poking at my group. You know they are the only way I get out of this house anymore. I was just curious about the new show, since it is clearly interesting enough to make you break your word." Jo jabbed her finger at him.

"Now Jo, don't start—"

Jo slapped a hand on the table and cut him off. "Did you or

did you not promise me that you would retire once MDash was doing well?"

Even Jake knew better than to argue with that tone of voice when logic was on her side.

Dom clearly hadn't learned that lesson, despite their lengthy marriage. "I did, but..."

"Ma, I'm the one who pushed for the show." Frankie jumped into the fray. "Dad was going to pass, but I wanted a chance to prove to him that I can run the business. If I can pull this off, he's agreed to step back and let me run things day to day with Adrian. Isn't that right, Dad?"

Jake had not heard any of this from Dom. He had to assume Frankie was taking advantage of the situation to get Dom on record with her plan. She had him over a barrel, and he knew it.

"Um, uh, that's right. I'm not really involved in the new show."

"Then what's the holdup? When are you retiring?" Jo pressed.

"After the kids' weddings. I want to be able to cover for them for their baby leaves and honeymoons, but then I'll be done. I'll walk away."

"I'll believe it when I see it," Jo huffed. "You all heard him. When you get back from your honeymoons, he is done." She turned a steely glare first on Sofia and Adrian, then Natalie and Enzo, and finally Jake and Frankie. Everyone nodded dutifully. "I'm holding you to it this time." She jabbed her finger at Dom again, who hunched his shoulders as if she'd actually made contact.

The rest of dinner passed innocuously enough. The tense moment was quickly subsumed beneath the updates from Daisy's school and the tale of the skinny hallway from the vineyard. Family stories, inside jokes, and shop talk flowed around the table as people cleared their plates without missing a beat.

Jake just marveled, completely entertained. He couldn't turn off his analytical eye, and an intricate web of connecting relationships and conflicts mapped in his brain. This was why families were compelling. Million-Dollar Starter Home wasn't a hit because of Sofia's designs, or Adrian's biceps, or Enzo's lawns, or Frankie's pratfalls, or any of the behind-the-scenes work Natalie did. It was the genuine love and humor they held for each other that made them sparkle on-screen.

By the end of Hudson House, Jake had developed that kind of vibe with his TV family. The other actors had genuinely cared for each other, and after eight years on the set together, they'd known each other inside and out. When the show had been canceled, he'd lost much more than an income. He lost the only family who had ever given a damn about him. Just in time for puberty to put him through the wringer.

At the wrap party, they'd all promised to keep in touch. Martin Milton, who had played his on-screen father and often off-screen as well, had spun him a story about barbeques and pool parties. As a twelve-year-old, Jake had believed him. He hadn't understood that it was what everyone said at the end of a project, but that it very rarely came to pass. Another reason he refused the reunion events was that he didn't have anything worth saying to them anymore. They'd abandoned him when he'd needed them most and made him question whether the connection they'd shared had simply been good acting.

He'd gone back home to his mother who had immediately booked him into the first role he was offered, a particularly bad tween remake of *Much Ado About Nothing*, without even asking him. A series of teen movies with truly awful plot lines and even worse directors followed as he grew out of the awkward phase and into his cheekbones.

But the day he turned eighteen, he'd fired her as his manager, paid off the house she was living in, moved out, and quit acting. He couldn't do anything about the residuals, but he wasn't going to earn her one dime more than he was legally obligated to pay.

Jo pulled him from his deep thoughts with a hand on his arm.

"It's a nice night," she said. "Come sit on the porch with me while everyone else cleans up. Bring your wine."

Following her out the back door, he sat down next to her on the stairs leading down to the garden and sipped his Montepulciano. Jo had great taste in wine.

The backyard stoked Jake's admiration of the Valenti childhood even higher. The tree house in the corner must have been the envy of every child in the neighborhood. Even now he was barely resisting the urge to check it out. Combined with the sandbox, the raised garden beds, and the fairy empire, and he could picture the Valenti kids, past and present, having the time of their lives.

"You must think I'm crazy."

Her non sequitur pulled him from his jealous thoughts. Jo stared down at her hands and fiddled with her wedding ring, her wine forgotten on the stairs.

"Why do you say that?" Jake turned to lean against the newel post so he could look her in the eye.

"Here you've gone and made my family famous. You've made us a household name and business is booming, and all I want is for Dom to walk away from it."

"That's not crazy."

"It's just… Look, I devoted my adult life to making sure the kids were raised right, and Dom had what he needed, and the business stayed afloat. And I did it out of love. We built a good life, and we always planned to slow down and enjoy it all later." She gestured to the yard and the house, but clearly meant the memories and the people contained within. "We aren't guaranteed a tomorrow, and I want to enjoy whatever days I may have left with the man I love, instead of watching him work himself into an early grave."

"I get it. When I left acting, it was against the advice of every adult in my life. But just like you said, life is short, and I'd already missed out on most of my childhood. I couldn't lose the rest of my life as well. I truly think Dom is nearly there."

Jo took a long sip of her wine. "This vineyard project…how involved is he, really?"

"He's very hands-off on the build. Honestly, it's practically an honorary role. He's done some short explanations of what's going on, but Frankie is running the build."

"Then where the hell does he go everyday?" Jo's frustration leaked into her voice. Jake shrugged and she waved him off. "Not your job to be his babysitter. But this has to be the end of it for him. No more shows."

Jake felt her words land heavily on his shoulders, but what could he say?

CHAPTER 9

Jake stared at the floor and blinked. Two days! He'd been down in LA for two days. Leaving the jobsite hadn't been ideal, but it had been unavoidable. Pitching to advertisers during the network upfronts was a big part of his job. He'd had some good interest from the food and bev markets for the vineyard project. Revved and ready to dive back in, he'd come straight to the build from the airport. He hadn't even made it to the production trailer yet, and now he was staring at a hole in the middle of what should be the kitchen floor.

"What the hell is this?" Jake yelled. The crew building out what looked like plank walls on the floor all kept their eyes on their work.

"Good morning to you too, sunshine." Frankie rounded the corner with a smirk.

It was perverse the way his heart leapt and his shoulders clenched at the same time in reaction to that smirk. "Why is there a ten-foot hole in the middle of the fucking floor?"

"Actually it's twelve feet deep to accommodate a poured concrete foundation." She flippantly tossed her ponytail back over her shoulder, and he clenched his hands against the urge to strangle her.

"Why are we pouring a new foundation? What is this going to cost?"

"Sofia wants a hidden wine cellar beneath the cabinets. I altered the plans and got everything approved by the architects."

"You just neglected to tell me."

"I'm telling you now," Frankie pointed out, as if this solved everything.

"Yes, but now there's a twelve-foot hole in the floor that I can't exactly argue with."

"So my timing is perfect."

Frankie grinned at him and it took all of his acting training not to smile back. He'd bet she got away with murder with that look. He could count on one hand the number of people who were willing to oppose him. She was the only one who'd actually figured out how to get ahead of him, and had taken advantage of his recent absence to handle show meetings. And she was so damned pleased with herself, he almost hated to be the voice of reason. Almost.

"Where is the money for this coming from?" He knew her remaining budget to the penny. She didn't have the funds for this big of a project.

"I did some juggling. Went for cheaper materials in some nonpublic areas. And my cousin Seth is going to custom-build the cabinet surround, so all we had to order was the mechanism."

"I need to see the quote—"

Frankie held up a hand to cut him off short. "Already on your desk."

He pushed on, needing to retain control of the conversation. "—and adjust the filming schedule."

"You've got time for that. Today we're pouring concrete. I figure we won't need cameras until we start trimming it out."

Jake shook his head and sighed. "This is why I make the filming schedules. Of course we need to film the concrete. Who is supervising the install?"

"I am."

"Interesting, since I have you scheduled at the barn today."

Frankie rolled her eyes and bit back a huff. "Oh, come on. Don't be upset that we shifted some things. That's the nature of the construction business. Can't I quick-film the intro over there and get the guys going and then come back up here? I've got a three-hour window before the concrete sets up and the truck is already on the way."

Jake couldn't give her the inch she wanted, because she already assumed she had the mile. His anger seeped into his voice as he chewed her out. Everyone else in the room had frozen, waiting to see who would emerge victorious.

"This is why you get things approved." Frustration drove his voice louder over the buzz of saws and nail guns from outside.

"You weren't here. I had to make a call." Frankie matched him decibel for decibel.

"It was the wrong call."

"I jumped through all your damn hoops. Lighten up." She poked him in the chest with her finger and he growled and snapped.

"When you are carrying the responsibility for the project, then you can tell me to lighten up."

She got right up in his face at that jab, refusing to back down. Damn it. Why did he admire that? She pissed him off to no end and was digging herself into a hole, literally and figuratively. He needed drama for the show, and she was determined to do things her own way, so why did he keep trying to be the voice of reason?

"I *am* carrying the responsibility for this build. I'm telling you this is the best path to get it all done on the timeline you need for your precious fucking show!"

"Children, children." Dom strolled in, hands tucked into his pockets. "What seems to be the trouble?"

"Just a hiccup, Dad. Right, Jake?"

"Like you said. You're the one on the hook for overruns. If you say it's just a little hole in the ground, who am I to argue?"

Jake raised his hands in surrender and backed out of the room, his mind rapidly juggling shooting schedules and personnel. He might as well quit trying to protect her. If she caused them a delay or took them over budget, he would be a hero at the network. A show that made money on production? Unheard of. But that's just what they'd do if she had to pay back the hundred grand.

He strode into the production trailer, and sure enough there were the changes, printed and engineer approved, sitting on his keyboard. *Damn her.* True, he'd been gone for two days, but she could have reached him if she wanted to. No, this was a power grab. He could play that game too.

He dialed the number listed on the supply list.

"Hello? Yes, this is Jake Ryland. I'm the man in charge on the Valenti Vineyard show site. I need you to delay your delivery time by about an hour. Yes, sorry it's last minute. Unavoidable… Yes, I understand that the concrete has been mixed and is en route. I'll take responsibility if we exceed the window. Thank you."

As he disconnected, the door behind him slammed open, bouncing off the wall behind it.

Frankie caught the recoil as she strode into his office, face red and fuming. "You want to argue with me? Fine. I can take it. But I will not tolerate you being disrespectful to my dad."

She stood in the doorway, chest heaving and breathing fire. It was a good look on her. Why did he find her more attractive when she wanted to gouge his eyes out? She was fully alive in this moment, and he knew not one of her emotions was feigned. He'd been around enough actors to tell the difference between real emotions and ones worn like a mask. She was angry to her core.

"You thought that was disrespectful?"

"You walked away, dismissing him in the middle of the conversation." She stepped farther into the room and shut the door behind her.

Jake stepped closer, careful to keep a safe distance, but needing to meet her challenge for challenge. "Did you really want me to lay out the details of your scheming in front of your father?"

"I didn't do a damn thing wrong! I cleared all the changes with the engineers and architects. I kept my budget balanced. I updated the plans and sent you the details. And I kept my promise to you and to Sofia." Ticking her points off on her fingers, she advanced on him until she was close enough to touch.

Her eyes glittered with angry tears, and he momentarily got lost in them, trying to figure her out. He hated tears. They'd been used as tools against him for too many years for him to take them at face value, but he would swear these were real.

"Why can't you be more flexible?" She shoved at him, blinking back her tears and breaking the spell. He was impressed that she didn't let them fall to manipulate him. She was clearly angling for a reaction though. Well, he'd give her one.

He moved in even closer, his height towering over her. When she retreated, he advanced until her back was against the door. Bracing his hands on either side of her head, he leaned in close enough to smell the peppermint gum on her breath. "You want to see how flexible I can be, Frankie?"

The frustration in her eyes flickered and, for a second, surprised curiosity took its place. It was the wariness that quickly replaced the surprise that had him stepping back from temptation. He liked her angry bravado, but he couldn't enjoy her fear.

"I'm sorry. That was out of line." He stepped back even farther, running his hands through his hair.

Frankie reached out a hand to his hip, and he froze. "Maybe," she whispered.

"Excuse me?" He couldn't have heard that right.

"You asked if I wanted to see how flexible you can be. My answer is maybe. I just got the strangest sense of déjà vu. You want to kiss me." She said this with a certainty that she'd read him right. And she had. *Shit.*

"No. That's crazy. We can't."

"Why not?" This time she was the one advancing, cutting off his retreat, her hand never leaving his waist.

"You're Dom's daughter. I respect him."

"Good, then you won't treat me like shit. Next?"

He took another step back until his thighs bumped against his desk. "We work together. I'm your boss."

"You are not my boss. You run the show. I run the build. We are colleagues."

"Maybe." She glared as he grasped at straws. "You said maybe. Why maybe?"

"Maybe yes, we kiss, get all this awkward tension out of the way," she said, "and we can work together without all the sniping."

That was a terrible idea. No way he could forget another kiss. He hadn't even managed to move past the first. Her tone was pragmatic, but the way she was staring at his lips was far from it. When she pulled her own lip between her teeth, it was all he could do not to groan. "That's maybe yes. Why maybe no?"

Pulling her eyes up to meet his, she smirked again. "Maybe you might waste my time."

She might as well have waved a red flag in front of a bull. His male pride rose in his defense. The smug smile on her face said she thought she'd won, right before he covered those lips with his own. Little did she know they were both lost now.

Jake poured months of pent-up longing into that kiss, savoring every familiar taste and sound. When she sighed against his lips, he pressed his advantage and angled for more.

Frankie met him with equal enthusiasm, all of the energy between them crackling as they shifted from a negative to a positive charge. She slid her hands up into his hair and pulled his head down to better match hers. God, he loved a woman who could hold her own. She met him challenge for challenge, giving as good as she got. How could he not want more?

He held her face in his hands, steadying her as he bent to meet her mouth. Sliding one hand back, he wove his fingers through the ponytail that tempted him daily and tugged, just enough to tip her head back and expose her neck for his exploration.

He flashed back to Christmas Eve. This was quite a different kiss from the sleepy, tipsy lip smash they'd shared at the door to her apartment. Hotter, more explosive, infinitely more satisfying. Their first kiss had lingered in his mind. This one threatened to blow his head right off his shoulders.

As much as he wanted this kiss to continue, the hairs on the back of his neck rose and he tried to ease back. They were at work. Work they both needed to be doing. And this trailer wouldn't stay private for long once people knew he was back on set. Sooner or later someone would come for approvals or solutions. And though he wouldn't want it any other way, he also didn't want to expose her to gossip around the set. Getting caught kissing the talent wouldn't be a good look for him either.

But he couldn't make his hands release her head or his tongue stop tangling with hers. He wanted this kiss to go on and on, and preferably much further. He slid a hand down her back to the exposed stretch of skin between her T-shirt and her battered jeans.

She jolted in his arms and pulled back as though he'd shocked her. It was lowering to admit that she'd been able to step back and he hadn't. Her bemused and glassy-eyed expression made it a little easier to swallow. She wouldn't forget this kiss so easily.

"Hmmm, well, yeah. Now that we've gotten that out of our system, we should be able to work together just fine. No more tension. Okay, good. Right..." She rambled and retreated, bumping into the doorframe again, before she fumbled with the handle.

He let her retreat. This was far from over, even though it should be. A fling with Frankie would be his best worst mistake. "Yep, all good. No more tension," he parroted, willing to give her the space to walk away now. He definitely wanted more, but he could wait for her to be ready. They needed to figure out how they would keep this quiet. Better to have that conversation when they weren't so...heated.

"I'll just go work on the barn until the concrete truck shows up."

"I'll let the crew know. See? I *can* be flexible."

"Ha. Right. Good one." She shut the door behind her with an audible click.

Jake reached for his coffee cup and his equilibrium, and came up empty for both.

Damn it.

He let out a deep sigh and pinched the back of his neck. Nothing was going to plan today.

Mug in hand, he waited a beat to make sure Frankie had walked away. He didn't want his need for caffeine to be interpreted as giving chase. If he was lucky, he could get his fix at craft services and get back to his trailer without running into anyone.

He really needed to get caught up on the daily notes Trina and Lorena had left him while he was away. He had to get his head back in the game. Caffeine and distance from Frankie would help.

Jake snuck out of the trailer and headed to craft services, his source of that blessed nectar of the gods. As he turned the corner, his mind already ten steps ahead, he stumbled to a halt. Between him and his salvation stood Domenico Valenti, arms crossed, face carved in granite.

No way around him. Jake would have to bluff his way through whatever hiccup had pissed Dom off without his liquid crutch.

"This is not what I would have chosen." Dom spoke first, his voice full of gravel.

"I know the wine cellar looks like a big expense, but Sofia seems to think Jo needs it. Frankie and I just had a misunderstanding since the change hadn't made it to my desk yet."

"Screw the wine cellar. Fi can have whatever she wants. And I know Frankie is handling the job just fine. I'm not blind."

Shit, he'd guessed wrong. Before he put his foot in it again, he decided to let Dom lead. "No sir, you're not. What do you see that I don't?"

"Francesca. I wouldn't have chosen you for her."

That was not what he had expected. Dom kept his gaze steady and level, and Jake had to fight the urge to avert his eyes. Unsure what emotion would win the battle for expression, surprise or offense, Jake kept his face deliberately blank. Dom saved him from having to decide.

"Don't get me wrong. I like you, Jake. You've got a solid head on your shoulders, and you've delivered on your promises."

"I'm not sure what we're talking about."

Dom chuckled darkly. "You've never parented teens, and it shows. I know what my daughter looks like after she's been kissed. I caught her sneaking in from a date more times than I care to admit. She had the same face leaving your trailer."

Busted. By Dad-dar.

"Dom, I can explain."

"No, I don't want to know. That's between you and her. Just be careful with her."

Lorena approached the table, but she must have sensed the tension in the conversation because she did the ridiculous look-at-the-watch-and-walk-the-other-way maneuver.

"But there isn't anything between us." Jake lowered his voice. The entire crew didn't need to hear that he'd been kissing Frankie.

"Why the hell not?" Dom blustered, clearly not caring who heard him.

"Wait, what? You just said—"

"I said I wouldn't have chosen you, not that she shouldn't have. Don't be an ass."

Jake covered his face with his hands. "I am so confused."

"Then take some time to figure out what you want, so you don't mess around with her feelings. Next?"

God, it was scary how much father and daughter were alike. "I can't believe we are having this conversation. We work together."

"I worked with her mother. You will both work harder to make the show a success."

Jake's mind was spinning. "Why did you say you wouldn't have picked me?"

He was close enough to smell the freshly ground beans he insisted on. He desperately needed something to do with his hands, preferably that involved caffeine. Maybe that would help this all start to make sense, because he was at a loss. Jake had drifted toward the carafe when a meaty hand clapped down on his shoulder, and pulled him around the front of the building.

For all of his experience, he'd never actually met the father of a woman he was dating, let alone worked with him. This was all uncharted territory, and that made him nervous as hell. And

Dom wasn't helping with that smirk and his random-ass conflicting statements.

"Not so fast. I want us clear on this. I wouldn't have picked you because you're ruthless."

Now there was no question. Offense won. "I resent that, Dom."

"I'm not saying that's a bad thing. I've seen how invested you are in this show. You'll use any advantage you've got to get what you want. Frankie is the same way. She's never heard a no she couldn't change. You two will drive each other nuts, each wanting your own way."

"So then why are you encouraging me?"

"Because Frankie tends to get what she wants in the end, and apparently she wants you. You might as well get on board."

"I am only going to be here through the end of the vineyard show. Then I'll be back in LA working on other projects. My life is crazy when I'm home. It would never work."

"Uh-huh. I'm hearing excuses. If Frankie has decided she wants you, you don't stand a chance." Dom fairly cackled, as if he was going to extract the maximum pleasure possible out of watching his daughter bring Jake to his knees.

He'd be damned if that was going to happen. How had his plan for a few kisses, a simple fling, gotten so complicated? "Well, she's not going to get me."

"Son, she already has."

Dom strolled off with his last words hanging heavily in the air between them, as if he hadn't just swung a sledgehammer through Jake's peace of mind.

Where the hell was the coffee?

Stalking back to the beverage cart, he filled his mug to the brim and burned his mouth on his first furious sip. Natalie was the poor unfortunate soul who happened to cross his path just then.

"Hey, Jake. Can I ask you—"

"No. You can't."

He stalked back to his office before he could snap at anyone else and locked the door behind him. If only it was that easy to lock away the messy feelings ricocheting around his chest.

Head down.

Do the job.

Make it shine.

Soon enough he'd be gone and leave the wrangling of this crazy family to someone else. Once everyone was back from maternity leaves and ready to tackle another season, a new showrunner would step in, leaving him to pursue other projects that he'd earned the right to pitch with these successes. Absolutely nothing in his future looked like staying in the Bay Area long-term for a girlfriend. Hell, he hadn't even thought that far ahead.

Most women who were attracted to him wanted to hook up with someone famous or wanted to tap his connections. No one lasted long enough to be considered a girlfriend. Hell, even his early "relationships" had all taken place on set and had crumbled once the movie wrapped. How had he gone from that to dealing with an irrational father and a skittish love interest?

He didn't know, but he'd figure it out. Puzzles were his specialty. Frankie Valenti was a ten-thousand-piece jigsaw of a brick wall, and Jake couldn't resist running at it full tilt.

CHAPTER 10

Frankie practically crawled into her apartment. After another emotional day of not kissing Jake, a full week after the kiss that was supposed to fix things, she was ready to fall into her bed and sleep through her disappointment. She fed Buster and hooked him up to his yard tether instead of taking him for a proper walk.

She'd pay for that bit of laziness later when Buster was bouncing off the walls, but she simply couldn't muster the energy to do anything more than grab a beer and get herself into the shower.

She scrubbed herself clean, trying to wash away the tension of the day along with the drywall dust. Her traitorous hands lingered places they shouldn't have and left her right back where she started. Exhausted but aroused.

Reaching for her untouched beer, she paused and poked her head around the curtain. Her phone was buzzing on the counter. Ignoring whatever new critique Jake had for her, she took her first cold sip and turned to rinse the conditioner from her hair. If only it was that easy to ignore him in real life. Working with him after her stupid plan to get him out of her system had become a disaster.

They bickered all day long over stupid shit, and it was exhausting. But she had to stay strong and resist her urges. He was Jake-freaking-Ryland, dick-rector extraordinaire and Hollywood star. And she was Frankie Valenti, tomboy and temporary distraction.

Her phone rang again and clattered into the sink, buzzing madly.

Damn it. Couldn't a girl shower in peace?

She snapped down a towel, wrapped it around her body, and snatched up her phone, ready to chew him out once again.

Huh. It was her mom, not Jake. And she'd called three times. The phone began to ring again in her hand as she stared at the caller ID.

"Hi, Ma. What's up?"

"It's time." Her normally unflappable mother sounded breathless and a little manic.

"Time for what? Did you put something on the calendar?"

"No, babies don't tend to follow calendars. Get your butt to the hospital. Sofia just checked in."

Jo relayed the details to her, but beyond which hospital she was driving to, Frankie had stopped listening. Grabbing underwear, she dropped the phone on the bed to put them on.

The baby was coming.

She pulled a sweatshirt on and a pair of jeans.

The baby was coming.

She left her wet hair down and stuffed her damp feet into socks and gym shoes.

Racing down the stairs, she brought Buster in. "Now you be a good boy. Zia Sofia is having her baby." She ruffled his ears, and kissed his head, and closed him in her bedroom before sprinting back downstairs and into her truck. It had been five minutes. Adrenaline was an amazing thing. Her fatigue had completely vanished. Her hands shook as she gripped the wheel.

The baby was coming!

~

BY THE TIME she got to the hospital, and circled, and parked, and found the right waiting room, that adrenaline buzz was wearing thin.

Dom rose from a hard plastic chair and hugged her. "Hey, baby girl."

"Hey there, Nonno."

Dom teared up and pulled her closer. He was such a sentimental softy.

"Where's Ma?" Frankie pulled back from the hug, scanning the waiting room.

"She's staying in with Fi until Adrian gets here."

"He's not here?"

"No, he was out on a job and Jo and Fi were working at the new house on the nursery when things started happening." Dom waved a hand over his belly as if using actual words to describe labor was too difficult. "He's on his way though."

"And Enzo and Natalie?"

"They'll come once the baby arrives. It's no good having Nat sit up all night on these chairs eight months pregnant with twins." Dom lost his battle and a tear chased its way down his cheek. "All these babies. My heart is so full."

Frankie was grateful he didn't push the conversation toward her baby-making plans. Just because she could didn't mean she should. Having kids wasn't something she could see herself doing, at least not where her life was right now. But she was also too tired and emotional to defend her choice eloquently.

Luckily, Adrian derailed that train of thought by bursting through the doors.

"Sofia? Sofia? *Mi vida?*" His eyes searched the room frantically, landing on Dom once he'd determined Sofia wasn't actually there. "Dom! Where is she?"

Dom clapped a hand on his shoulder and pulled him in for a hug. "She's fine. Everything's fine. Room 326." Frankie couldn't tell if Dom was reassuring Adrian or himself.

"Dad, let him go."

"Oh, right, of course."

Dom dropped his hug, and Frankie slapped Adrian on the shoulder. "Batter up, *papi*. Go catch that baby."

Adrian grinned and took off down the hallway with such speed that Frankie was nervous for the nurses in his path. She didn't think he even saw them.

A minute later, Jo joined them out at the chairs.

"Everything is good. She is in active labor, but it's early yet. It will likely be hours before anything really picks up. But she's as comfortable as can be expected. Now that Adrian is here, she has calmed down. The good news is we put all of her nesting energy to good use. The nursery is completely finished, and it's gorgeous. Wait until you see it, Frankie." Her mother rattled out her update, nervous energy pushing her words quickly out of her mouth.

"I'd expect nothing less from Fi. How's the rest of the house looking?"

Her mother had been around enough build sites to give her an accurate assessment. "It's coming along. They really only have to finish the tiling and paint the walls. Then it's just punch out."

Adrian and Sofia had been sharing the efficiency apartment over Adrian's mother's house so they could be close for Graciela in case she needed them. Her therapy for agoraphobia had been going well, but some days were better than others. They were planning to move back into the main house for the first month with the baby, so Graciela could help out. But Sofia had wanted their own place, so they'd bought a fixer-upper on the same block and Adrian had spent every minute he wasn't at work renovating it. He'd hoped to be done before the baby came, but the wee one apparently hadn't checked the work schedule before deciding to arrive.

"That close, huh?" Frankie pulled her phone from her pocket and dialed Jake. "I'll be right back," she told her parents and slipped out into the elevator lobby. If Jake was game, she might be able to pull off the best baby shower gift ever.

"Frankie. What's up?" Jake answered, his tone brusque and distracted. He probably hadn't even looked away from whatever clip he was editing.

"I'm at the hospital."

That got his attention.

"What? Are you okay? Who's hurt? Tell me where you are. Did you contact the network's insurance?" The questions flew rapid-fire from his mouth, and she could hear a door close behind him, his keys jangling and his feet crunching on the gravel drive. Two beeps announced his car door unlocking.

"Jake, wait. I'm fine. Everyone's fine. Sofia is in labor. We're having a baby!" Frankie crowed.

"Oh! Oh. Wonderful." He exhaled heavily and his voice dropped a whole octave.

"It *is* wonderful. I'm feeling so happy and giddy right now that I'm even going to ask you a favor."

"Oh really?" he teased. "You're finally going to ask instead of wheedling or manipulating to get your way? I should get you in a good mood more often."

"First of all, I don't manipulate, I convince. Second, pot, kettle. And third, I'm too happy to let you pull me down." She didn't even respond with suggestions for how he could get her in a good mood. She mentally added points for her restraint to her win column.

"What's this favor?"

"I want you to pull a crew together and send them to Fi and Adrian's new place. If they haul ass, we can get that house done before they head home from the hospital."

"That's going to impact your schedule and budget here at the vineyard."

"Yeah, yeah, I'll make it up."

"You're a real softie, Frankie Valenti."

Just another thing she and her father had in common, she mused. "Can we swing it?"

"Sure. I'm going to film it, maybe use it as digital-first extra content... But yeah, consider it done."

"I owe you one."

"Believe me, that's a big factor in my yes."

"Smart-ass."

"Takes one to know one."

Frankie hung up and rubbed her hands together with glee. They were going to be so surprised. And if anyone could pull this off, it was Jake Ryland.

She walked back into the waiting room and saw her parents sitting side by side, her mom leaning her head on her dad's shoulder. She couldn't remember the last time she'd witnessed physical affection between them, and smiled. If it took a baby to bring them back together, she was damn glad they had three arriving in quick succession.

"Our baby is having a baby," Jo murmured, joy and concern fighting for top billing in her voice.

Dom put his hand on Jo's thigh, and Jo put hers on top of his. He turned it over and gripped hers tightly. Frankie didn't want to interrupt this tender moment, but she'd been spotted.

"And what are you grinning about, young lady?" Jo smiled and sat up, breaking contact with Dom's shoulder, but he didn't let go of his grip on her hand.

"Just got off the phone with Jake. Plotting a little surprise for the new parents."

"That sounds interesting." Jo paused and stared at Frankie, before she turned back to Dom. "Do me a favor, honey. Can you go see if the hospital has a coffee shop? I'd love a skinny latte. It's going to be a long night."

"Sure thing, Jojo." Dom strode from the waiting room, and Jo patted the open seat next to her.

"Come sit with me, Francesca." Frankie cringed but obeyed. "Your father does better with waiting when he has a job to do."

"Then why do you want him to retire so badly? He'll be bored out of his mind without something to do."

"Oh, I have plans for what we'll do." Jo wiggled her eyebrows and laughed at Frankie's reaction.

"Ew! Ma, seriously. I don't want to hear about any sexy plans you might have for Dad. Just… Gah! My mind's eye is burning."

Jo chuckled. "There are other things I like to do with your father, like traveling."

"Sure, that's what you meant." Frankie enjoyed this teasing with her mom. For too long, Jo had been buried by the grief of losing Gabe.

"Speaking of plans, what's this you're cooking up with Jake?"

"I asked him to send the crew over to knock out the last of the list at the new house, so it'll be done by the time they're ready to go home."

"That's very sweet of him to help." Jo's toned shifted subtly, and suddenly Frankie realized that her mother likely didn't need the coffee she'd sent Dom to find, and that this wasn't an innocent conversation. If there was one thing that hadn't changed her entire life, it was her mom's we-need-to-have-a-talk voice.

"Ma…"

"I just want to know what's going on in your life."

"There is nothing going on except me busting my ass to make this show a success."

"So much like your father." Jo sighed and ran her hand down Frankie's still-wet hair.

She *was* a lot like her dad. Only when her mom said it, it didn't sound like a good thing. Frankie couldn't help herself. "And that's bad?"

"I know you idolize your father, and that you are trying so hard to keep your promise to Gabe. But I am your mother and I have a few things to say. Brace yourself."

Frankie took a deep, deliberate breath before turning in her chair to fully face her mother. "Hit me."

Jo smiled softly at her antics before she crossed her hands in her lap and all of the expression leached out of her face. "I married a man who is very headstrong, driven, ambitious. He poured his energy into his family business, and we've had a good life. Losing Gabe…it woke me up. I'd been going along, making everything work, to follow his plans, for years. I didn't realize how little voice I had in our marriage until I spoke up and tried to use it, only to be ignored. Over the last two years, I've seriously considered leaving."

Frankie picked her jaw up off the floor long enough to ask, "Why did you stay?"

"Because even when he's driving me insane, he's my person. I love him. And I haven't given up hope that we can find a new normal. It's also terrifying to think of starting over alone after a lifetime together."

"Why are you telling me this?"

"Because I see the way Jake watches you when you're not looking. And I see the way a phone call makes you beam. Be careful, baby. Working with the person you love is complicated and hard. I don't want you to compromise your dreams like I did."

"Ma, you are way ahead of me. No one said anything about

love or marriage. Hell, we've only shared one kiss. There's no chance of anything there."

"Just be careful. You are too much like your father to react well to someone trying to run your life."

"Like I'd ever let that happen. You don't have to worry, Ma." Frankie leaned over and pressed a kiss to her mother's cheek.

"Whatever you say, baby."

CHAPTER 11

Frankie and Jo were alone again, Dom off on a dinner run, when Jake walked through the waiting room doors later that night and hovered, a gold and white gift bag dangling awkwardly from his fingertips. She replayed her mother's words, checking them for truth. They had only shared a kiss, and most of the time she wanted to throttle him. But looking at him all shy and unsure of his welcome made her want to pull him closer and indulge in a few more.

But a few kisses, no matter how hot, did not a relationship make. They were too alike, both too used to being in charge. They would burn hot and fast, going down in a blaze of mutually assured destruction. But damn, what a way to go.

Still, he looked so alone, standing there looking ready to bolt. She couldn't leave him hanging. She rose to meet him.

"Whatcha got there?" she asked.

"A little gift for mama & baby."

"And the house?"

"I left Rico and Winston with the punch list. Trina is hanging out to do a little filming."

"Fi is going to be so surprised. I can't believe I didn't think of this sooner."

Jake's excited grin drew her in. She liked sharing this secret with him. For a moment she just stood there a little too close, and watched him smile a little too long, and matched it with her own. The shared joy was palpable.

Jo cleared her throat and broke the spell. Stepping back, Frankie sat down and Jake took the seat next to her, replacing the sterile, cold, antiseptic smell with his own warm, manly scent. His thigh pressed into hers, firm and unyielding, cloaked in denim. Frankie tried to pay attention to the conversation, but her focus was consumed by the fire burning through her leg where it touched his.

"I'm just going to duck in and see how we're doing." Jo rose from her chair. "If Dom comes back with food, send him in."

"Sure, Ma."

Jo abandoned the field and left Frankie trying to jump-start her brain from a lust-induced dead battery back into conversation gear. It wasn't working. She scrambled for some conversation starter just to fill the awkward silence, but her brain kept pinging her dash with warning lights.

If he would just quit shifting in his seat, maybe she'd have a chance.

"Are you upset that I'm here? Jake stared at his hands and toyed with the braided strings of the gift bag, pointedly not looking at her. His fingers flexed and pulled as he worried the soft rope into frays. He had his sleeves rolled up, and the easy flex of muscle in his forearms captured her gaze.

She grabbed an arm to stop him so she could focus. "What? No. Of course not. Why?"

"Because you got real quiet once we sat down."

It is taking all of my considerable control to not kiss you again in the middle of a hospital waiting room, in front of God and my mother, and you want to know why I can't speak?

She shifted her grip and tugged down his shirtsleeves instead. "There, that's better. I was just a little distracted," she teased. A bit like Icarus, she skimmed too close to the sun of her truth, but secretly she hoped to get a little burned.

Ever since their kiss, she felt herself distracted by the most ridiculous things. His forearms were just the tip of the iceberg. His thigh. The way his hair curled at the back of his neck. His Adam's apple bobbing as he drank his coffee. The tendons in the back of his hand as he curled his hand into a fist in front of his mouth while he watched film. She was a hot fucking mess. Emphasis on hot but a decided lack of fucking.

"I get that. After all, you're about to be an auntie."

Sure. Let's go with that.

"I'm definitely going to be the 'cool aunt' for these little rugrats."

"You're lucky. I'm an only child of two only children. I'll never get to be the cool uncle."

"Never say never. The great thing about aunts and uncles is that they don't have to be blood relatives. What would you do if you were the cool uncle?"

"I'd fly the kids to wherever I was filming for a vacation and take them to premieres and stuff."

"Wow. I was just going to show up with candy and the obnoxious loud toys their parents won't buy them. You're setting that bar way high."

"You think it's too much?" He was trying to joke, but she heard the underlying anxiety and wanted to hug him.

"I think you need to ease up to that. Don't jump in the deep end."

"Noted. You know, for those hypothetical nieces and nephews." He bumped his shoulder into hers and she grinned and bit back a yawn. She liked this playful side of him.

"So, what did you bring them?" Frankie tapped the bag.

"A mini hard hat and a plush cube with different fabrics and colors on each side and...taggies? Not sure what those are but the article said babies love them, and this lady on Etsy said she could add them."

"Wait, wait, wait. Let me get this straight. You did research?"

"How else do you figure out what to bring for a baby?"

"And then you went on Etsy and had something custom-made?" Frankie's heart melted a little more in her chest. This man, so exacting and rigid, had turned into a marshmallow over her sister's baby. Damn, he was hard to resist. Why hadn't that kiss worked like it was supposed to?

"I support local artists when I can..."

"And everyone thinks I'm the softie," Frankie teased.

"I can promise you, no one thinks that."

Part of her wanted to take offense at that, but the way he said it wasn't a dig. More a statement of fact. His face was full of truth, and her gaze snagged on his full lips. She was so tired, she couldn't resist replaying their kiss in her mind.

"Something about you makes me feel soft," she said, before she could think better of it.

"You must be exhausted." Jake checked his wristwatch.

God damn it—why the hell was that little move sexy too? It wasn't fair. She hoped she could get this infatuation under control soon. She needed her wits about her again.

"It's nearly midnight."

"Mmhmm." She wished she could stretch out in her bed for the next twelve hours straight, but that was not in the cards. She blinked slowly when he wrapped an arm around her shoulder.

"Why don't you head home? Come back when the baby gets here?"

"But…we're family. She's my sister. No, I'll stay in case anyone needs anything." She stifled another yawn and snuggled her hip against his. "Maybe I'll just close my eyes though."

"Here." He placed a hand on her head and gently drew it down to his shoulder. "Rest. I'll wake you when there's news."

"You sure?"

She desperately tried to keep her eyes open, but they had been given permission to close and were acting of their own accord.

His deep voice rumbled beneath her ear. "I've got you" was the last thing she heard as she drifted off.

∼

FRANKIE WOKE to someone shaking her shoulder. She sniffed in sharply and sat up, taking a healthy noseful of Jake's cologne with her. How did he still smell good after a full day on site and an evening sitting up in a hospital? She blinked rapidly and checked her watch. Scratch that, it had been a full night. She couldn't believe she'd slept through.

"Frankie!"

"Wha? Huh?" Still disoriented, Frankie swiveled her head until her eyes focused on her mom, who was still shaking her shoulder.

"He's here."

"Who's here?" Frankie turned to look at Jake, who still had an arm draped over her shoulder and a small wet spot on his shoulder where her head had been. Oh Lord, she'd drooled on the man.

"The baby!"

Her mother's excitement broke through her muddled thoughts and pulled her back to the reason she'd slept in a chair all night. The baby. The baby! "It's a boy?"

Jo nodded with tears in her eyes.

"Enzo and Natalie are on their way. Mrs. Félice is going to take Daisy to school. You'll all get to go in together to meet him."

Dom joined them and wrapped Jo up in a big hug. *Please let this be a new beginning for them*, Frankie prayed.

"He's so beautiful. So perfect. And he cried so strongly." At this point the tears were flowing down Jo's cheeks with abandon.

Graciela, Adrian's mother, tentatively walked through the doors, leaning on her daughter Mahalia.

"Oh, Abuela Cici! He's here! Come and meet him!" Jo wrapped her daughter's mother-in-law in a big hug and hustled her back. Frankie rose to follow them, but her mother stopped her. "No, let us go alone. The rest of you wait for Enzo and Nat."

By the time her brother and his wife arrived, Frankie was dying. Sure, it had only been ten minutes but there was a baby to meet! "Finally! What took you so long?"

Enzo glanced at Natalie's prominent belly but wisely kept his mouth shut.

"We made it. That's all that matters. Can we go see them?" Natalie said.

"Yes, let's go!" Frankie shooed Enzo and Natalie ahead of her. Jake stayed seated in his chair, gift bag settled between his feet. "Are you coming?"

"I figured I should wait, let the family go first."

"That's ridiculous. Come on. We're all going together, room limits be damned."

A pleased smile crossed his face, and he took the hand she offered and followed her down the hallway to the room where her sister had just become a mother.

Frankie peeked her head in the room, to make sure everyone was decent, before leading in her band of merry rabble. Sofia sat up in bed, holding a little blue and pink swaddled bundle, while Graciela smoothed the sweaty hair back from her forehead. Both held identical expressions of awestruck love on their face. Adrian stood behind Jo, his arms wrapped around her shoulders in a hug as they both grinned like idiots at the tableau. Dom rested a hand on his son-in-law's shoulder.

"Knock, knock, can we come in?"

"Yes. Quietly though. He's had a rough morning, being born and all, and he's dozing." Sofia smiled at Frankie, and something shifted in her chest. A new love for this baby, a deeper love for her amazing sister, a fuller love for all of the people in this room who had gathered to welcome their newest member... Her heart filled up her chest as it found new ways to expand.

Frankie looked at the tiny swollen face, red and shiny, and thought he was the most beautiful baby she'd ever seen. "So much hair!" She gently touched the dark black shock of hair peeking out from under the knit cap that refused to stay on his big head. "Hello there, little man. I'm your Aunt Frankie. I'm going to teach you all the best jokes and be your favorite partner in crime. So when you want to get messy, or go a little nuts, or play chase with Buster, come on over. My door will always be open for you." Frankie stopped talking and looked up at her sister, surprised to see tears streaming down Sofia's cheeks. "What? What's wrong?"

"Nothing. Everything is perfectly right."

"Does little man here have a name?"

"He does." Sofia cleared the tears from her throat and addressed the whole room. "His name is Gabriel Luis Valenti Villanueva."

Both grandmothers burst into tears at hearing their beloved's names honored with new life. He would carry the legacy of his maternal uncle and his paternal grandfather into the next generation. This little boy had big shoes to fill. Frankie would make sure he knew he only had to fill them in the way that felt right to him.

"You named him for your papá?" Graciela reached a hand to her son.

Adrian squeezed it and nodded. "And Sofia's brother. They were both men we'd be proud for our son to take after," he said.

Jo gasped out a sob and proceeded to drench Dom's shirt with happy tears. Her tears sparked everyone else's, and by the time the nurse showed up to shoo them all out there wasn't a dry eye in the house.

It was a good day. For the first time in years, Frankie felt like their family circle was complete. She looked at all the beaming faces on the way out, leaving Fi and Adrian to settle into this new adventure of parenthood, and noticed one missing. Jake had left without her noticing. Where had he gone?

CHAPTER 12

It had been three weeks, two days, and maybe an hour since *The Kiss*. Italicized because it still made her cheeks flush hot. Capitalized because she couldn't stop thinking about it. Singular. Because it hadn't happened again. Frankie sighed.

What had gone wrong? After how sweet Jake had been at the hospital, she'd gone in to work the next day expecting that same camaraderie. Instead, she'd gotten perfunctory requests and terse replies. They weren't even bickering anymore. This deep freeze didn't make sense. Icicles dripped from his lips as he relayed the bare facts of the day's schedule. She hated it.

She wanted to rage at him, melt his icy control, and release the heat she knew he had inside. Just the memory of that kiss turned her bloodstream molten gold. She wanted that sparkling rich burn again.

But she couldn't. She was being "professional" about it and coolly ignoring her pants feelings at work. At home, she wasn't sleeping well, tormented by dreams of kissing him (and more) under the mistletoe. It was completely out of place in late April, but so vivid that she woke up hot and bothered. In another obnoxious twist, her ability to self-pleasure had hit a dry spell.

All of that pent-up energy was making her itchy. Adulting sucked.

Not like she didn't have enough to worry about with the build going off the rails. It seemed like every time she made a little progress, something new and disastrous would happen. There must have been something in the air at the hospital, because less than a week after Sofia, Natalie had delivered her twins three weeks early. This meant that all of the new parents were out of commission at once. So Frankie was now running point for Enzo's projects on the build, while Zio Tony pitched in to manage the outside crews. She and Dom were also juggling crews for Adrian's active builds, which were thankfully few just then. Then came all the issues with her own work.

When they'd assessed the barn for structural stability and readiness for Sofia's stucco dreams, they'd gotten their first bad news. The rustic interior they'd wanted to keep couldn't support the added weight of the stucco on the existing foundation. But they didn't have the time or money to pour a new foundation, so the country barn exterior had stayed. She knew Sofia had her heart set on it, and she hated disappointing her sister. But the change meant less work for Frankie, although the days they'd lost in the process still pissed her off.

Sofia would still get her indoor/outdoor entertainment space. It would just be whitewashed pine instead of Tuscan stucco.

Then there'd been the trouble with the landscaping. Enzo's team was excavating and building the gardens and the terraced patio for outdoor ceremonies. Despite having gone through all of the city documents and getting the all clear from PG&E to dig, they still ran into a nasty surprise. No old septic field showed on the plans. But it sure showed up when they'd started digging into it with a backhoe. That had left them with a stinky, muddy swamp for a week while they cleaned up and relocated the septic field. Thankfully, the main house had sewer access so only the outbuildings had been impacted.

Even the simple concrete foundation for the wine cellar a few weeks prior had nearly been a disaster. The truck had gotten delayed which left them with only an hour to unload and pour the entire batch. If the concrete had stayed in much longer it would have set up in the truck, costing her thousands of dollars in removal fines.

Luckily, they'd managed to pull it off by dumping the sidewall concrete into a series of wheelbarrows so if it set too soon, they'd only be out a few barrows.

Mismeasured floor joists, misordered tiles, unreliable subcontractors... Everything that could go wrong had. And all of it was caught on camera.

Frankie was still within her expected time frames and budget overages, but each day was a battle to stay there. She hustled to keep up with everything and pick up any slack, but she was exhausted. Something had to give.

In a fitting turn of events, installing the bar was the project that nearly drove her to drink. She sat down on the floor of what would one day be the public tasting room and leaned against the bottom cabinetry for the back bar. The tiny hammers were pounding in her head. She had pulled all of her strings to get the bar done today but had still come up short.

She'd been counting on Seth and Nick to get the custom bar top here before the union rules capped out the film crew. But a poorly timed flat tire had delayed them. The weight of the bar made putting the truck up on a jack precarious, not to mention the likelihood of blowing the donut. So the crew had left for the day, and her bar remained incomplete, her time slowly slipping away.

Fuck. My. Life.

She was so tired of going full speed on all fronts just to stand still. It would be years before this room would even be put to use. Why did it fucking matter if the bar got installed today or tomorrow?

Because Jake Fucking Ryland, of the lush lips he was keeping to himself, said it mattered. Selfish bastard.

She closed her eyes and dropped her head against the cabinet with a heavy thunk, hoping it would jar the repeating memories of his lips against hers from her mind. His hot and cold routine was getting real old. She wished the bar was already finished so she could pour herself a full glass of wine.

"Hello? Is someone in here?"

Damn, is he psychic too? She heard the scuff of shoes over the sawdust and grit on the floor as Jake stepped closer. Daring a peek, she found him peering at her over the unfinished bar.

"So the bar's not done?"

"Hi, Jake. It's nice to see you too. My day's been shit. Thanks for asking."

"Where. Is. The. Bar?"

"The bar is on the side of Highway 101 with a flat tire, so everyone went home."

"What?" Those lips pulled down in a frown as his eyes darted quick glances around the empty room, as if she was lying and a crewmember was miraculously hiding behind her cooler.

"The guys were on their way over with it..."

Jake already had his phone out, dialing. Resentment bubbled up in her chest. Seth wasn't going to tell Jake anything different than he'd told her fifteen minutes ago. She counted to ten as she listened to a one-sided replay of her earlier conversation.

"I'll be there in twenty minutes." As he disconnected the call, he strode for the door without even a glance in her direction.

"Hey! What's the plan?" She rose from her seat on the floor and chased after him. As she brushed the dust off her butt, she noticed his eyes follow her hands and felt a tiny ping of satisfaction. But his gaze returned to hers, all business.

"Just stay here. I'll be back in an hour. I'm fixing it."

"Sit. Stay. Good dog."

He didn't comment since he was already out the door. Frankie was so tempted to leave. After all, it was—she glanced at her phone—five thirty on a Friday. It had been a hellish week, and all she wanted was a shower, a beer, and a bed, in that order. She didn't even care that she'd be solo for all those activities. She was done.

But if he pulled it off and got the bar here, there was a chance she could still salvage her schedule for Monday. So Frankie stayed. She began to pick up the workspace. He'd better pull this off or she would seriously hold the delay against him. Hell, she was so horny, she'd hold any part against him.

No. Stop it.

He'd made it clear he wasn't interested in any further holding or kissing or anything. She had to put it out of her mind. If only it hadn't felt so right. If only he hadn't made her want more.

She'd dated plenty of boys and kissed her fair share, but she'd never felt this compulsion for more.

She spent the hour he was gone convincing herself that it couldn't possibly have been as good as she remembered. She was just coming off a long solo stretch. That's why it had hit her so hard.

And yet when she heard the crunch of tires, her stomach still flipped upside down.

Judging by the smug smile on his face, he'd succeeded in his quest.

"So where's the bar?" she asked, tucking her hands in her back pockets so she wouldn't be tempted to use them on him.

"In a van in the driveway."

"Are Seth and Nick bringing it down?"

"No, Seth stayed with the truck to wait for the tow, and Nick was late for an appointment with his wife, so I drove him back to his car."

Frankie was calculating weight and angles. There was no way she could manage this alone. The space was awkward at the moment, being set into the hillside on a lower level than the rest of the house. Everything had to be carried down a set of construction stairs. Eventually there would be easier exterior access, but they hadn't gotten that far yet with the landscaping and parking lots. "How are we going to get this downstairs?"

"I can help carry it."

Frankie snorted and bit back a chuckle as his eyebrows drew together above the bridge of his nose.

"I work out. I can carry it."

She weighed the cost of humoring his ego against the cost of repairing a dented bar top. The bar itself was meant to look rustic. She shrugged. It couldn't hurt to let him try, even if it turned into a controlled slide down the stairs. "We can carry it. Okay, let's get it down here."

She followed him up the stairs, and succeeded, barely, in not checking out his ass. But when he stepped out into the glow of a spectacular sunset and began rolling up his shirtsleeves, her mouth watered and she swallowed hard. She couldn't look away.

The man had spectacular forearms, taut and ropy, rippling as his fingers flexed and folded. He hadn't lied about working out, clearly. He couldn't get those arms from texting and typing or pointing a finger and ordering minions.

Spending her days around the guys, she was immune to a lot, but talented hands and strong forearms were a particular weakness.

"I'll go down backward," Jake offered.

Images of just how that would work flashed through her very

active imagination. She blinked hard and shook her head. "Do you think I can't handle it going down?" Frankie asked.

Why did everything suddenly seem to have an added layer of weight, deep in her belly?

"I think you could go down just fine," he teased.

Her eyes locked on his, and they were heavy with lust, reflecting her own needs back at her. The intensity excited her in all the best ways. "Let's just finish this thing." She picked up one end of the bar while he climbed into the van to handle the other end.

"Are you okay?" he asked.

"Would you quit? I said I've got it. Just because I'm a woman doesn't mean I can't manage a heavy piece of wood." She was deliberately poking him now.

"You are determined to make me crack, aren't you?"

"How'm I doing?"

He kept his face carefully blank, but his lip quirked at the corner. *Gotcha.*

"Get a good grip, Valenti. Let's go."

"That's what he said."

He grunted out a laugh as he hopped down from the back of the van and she started to walk backward, still teasing as she went.

CHAPTER 13

"What's that saying? 'Fred Astaire was great, but don't forget Ginger Rogers did everything he did...backward and in heels?'"

"She also survived five marriages, three to guys named Jack. But you're no Ginger."

"Oh really?" she huffed. The bar was fucking solid.

"No, you're more Katharine Hepburn."

"Excuse me?"

"Katharine Hepburn made a career of being the woman who could do anything a man could, but better and with heavy sarcasm."

"I think I'd rather be the pretty one in heels," she muttered and sucked in a labored breath.

"All I'm trying to say is you're strong, and everyone sees that. You don't have to keep proving it."

"That's..." She grunted and shifted her grip as her fingers slipped with sweat. "...where you're wrong. The minute I show weakness is the minute there is ammunition for Dad's argument that I'm not ready to handle the company."

When they reached the stairs, they carried the bar in silence. She refused to give him the satisfaction of hearing her moan and groan as they muscled the long oak plank downstairs. But words were also impossible to get out through her clenched jaw. She adjusted her grip on the rough natural edge. It would be beautiful once it was installed, but the bar was hard to get a handle on. Step by step, she proved herself capable, and when she reached the last stair, she grinned. *Take that!*

"Lean it here against the stairs for a minute." Jake lowered his end to the tread where he stood.

"Why? You need a breather?"

"No. I need to attach the dash cam. The crew is gone for the day."

"Anything for the shot. Let's just get this thing installed so I can go home. I still have to walk Buster."

Working together, in charged silence, they heaved the bar up onto the newly stained wooden base cabinets. Once it was up, he filmed her with his phone as she leveled and shimmed the top before screwing it down. Finally, something had gone right with this darn install.

With a satisfied grin, she stepped behind the bar and opened her cooler. "First official drink at the bar. What'll it be?"

"What do you have?"

Frankie laughed as she displayed the cooler's contents. "I can offer you the finest in diet soda beverages or bottled spring water."

"No coffee?" he teased. "I'll take a water. I don't need the caffeine bad enough to pour that crap into my body."

Frankie handed him the water and boosted herself up to sit on top of the bar with her feet on the lower counter. She cracked open a can of the diet and drank deeply. "Be careful. This 'crap' is the only thing that keeps me civil."

"This is civil?" he joked.

"I haven't finished it yet."

When Jake hopped up next to her, his legs dangling over the

front of the bar, she leaned over to tap his bottle with her can. The silence stretched, comfortable appreciation of a job well done.

"Do you really think you can't make a mistake?" His quiet question had her brain clicking to catch up.

"I don't think it. I know it. Do you know how many years I've spent trying to convince him to even give me a chance? All he needs is one error to throw heavily on the scale to prove he was right. You know how he hates to be wrong."

Years of arguments and well-meant insults replayed in her mind. She'd fought tooth and nail since before Gabe had left for the army to be included in the plan for the future. She was not about to lose all of that progress when she was so close to the finish line. He was staring at her as if he could see what was going through her brain. Why did he care so much? His hot and cold reactions were confusing the hell out of her.

"Well, I haven't seen anything so far that makes me concerned for the show."

Frankie bit back a laugh. Forever damned with faint praise. She bumped his shoulder with hers. "Aww gee, thanks."

"I mean it. That's my bottom line, and you're doing great. You play the game and get shit done. If Dom can't see that, he's blind."

The intensity of his voice made her turn. She studied his profile as he drank deeply from his water bottle. He sat facing opposite her, so she had an excellent view of that Adam's apple she wanted to lick.

Was there anything about him that wasn't ridiculously attractive, other than his attitude? It wasn't fair. She tried not to stare, and failed.

Stop looking. You can't sit here and moon over the man.

Her internal self-preservation mechanism was poking her. *He kissed you and then gave you the cold shoulder. He snuck out of the hospital without even saying goodbye. He can have any Holly-*

wood starlet he wants. But what had been a comfortable silence was quickly becoming awkward because she could not stop staring.

Gah, I need to get laid. This is ridiculous.

Working hard on all these projects made Frankie a dull girl. Her dating life had definitely taken a hit, both because she was exhausted by the end of each day, and every new guy who popped up on her dating app led with seeing her on the show. She was even getting recognized at the grocery store now. She hadn't considered how fame would impact her dating life, and it sucked.

Frankie cast around her tired mind for a conversational gambit that would give her an excuse to keep looking at him, since she clearly couldn't get her eyes under control. "So what was it like being a child star?"

She watched as the shutters fell down and his eyes lost their sparkle. *Shit. Wrong topic.*

"It was pretty much just like being a regular kid only with more people telling you what to do." He peeled the label off his water bottle and set the bottle down between them.

"Yeah, right. I'm not buying it. Sofia told me how popular your show was. That must've been crazy."

She watched as he folded the paper into a carefully creased accordion and then into tiny triangles. "That's a good word for it. My mom coerced the writer to base it on me, and it got picked up. I was just the cute kid saying lines. I didn't have any real skills, just dimples and a good memory."

"You must've developed some skills over an eight-year run," Frankie pressed.

He stared off into the mid-distance, reflecting. "I learned a lot from my director, watching how he ran things, the choices he made. Hell, I was around him more than my own father."

"So that's where you learned to be a control freak," Frankie teased again, trying to drive away the sadness that had gotten through his shields and settled in his eyes.

"Ha ha," he deadpanned. "Yes, that's where I figured out what I wanted to do. But it was years before I could get anyone to give me a chance to be more than a pretty face. That's why these shows mean more to me than Hudson House ever will. These are my work, my talent, my foot in the door."

That was a whole lot of self-worth tied up in a couple of reality shows. She knew exactly how he felt. "So is that why you're such a hard-ass? You've got something to prove?"

"When I'm done, people are going to know me as the award-winning director, not some stupid kid with million-dollar dimples."

Frankie poked him with a finger below his rib cage, and he jumped and laughed at the surprise tickle attack.

"They are cute dimples though."

He poked her back. "Brat. They were cuter when I was six and on the cover of magazines."

"I wouldn't know." Frankie flinched and held up her hands to block any more tickle attempts.

"What do you mean?"

"I've never seen the show. I know the memes, but I don't think I've ever watched an episode start to finish."

She blushed when he dropped his jaw in mock horror. "But it's syndicated! You could stream it now."

"But it's baseball season, and then football season."

Her snark prompted more retaliatory tickles until she was breathing heavy and hunched over nearly in his lap with his arms surrounding her. Heat flushed her cheeks and she sat up abruptly, trying to get herself under control. He allowed her to scoot back into her own space, and she was grateful. If he'd put up any kind of resistance, she wasn't sure she'd have been able to fight it.

"So why are *you* so invested in this business?" he asked once she'd settled.

"Because Gabe and I always talked about running it."

"So you're working this hard just because you promised your big brother?"

"No, I'm doing it because it's what I've wanted to do since I was a kid, and I'm good at it."

"Then why did you bring up Gabe?"

The question set her back. Why had she prefaced her dream with Gabe's death?

"When we were kids, Gabe and I were inseparable. Sofia was always more interested in fashion and coloring. Enzo liked to be alone in the back garden. Gabe and I were the same, full of energy and impulsive, much to Ma's chagrin. He and I built birdhouses together and worked on the tree house with Dad. I was never happier than when we were tinkering with something." Frankie grinned at the memory. "Even when he got older and hanging out with his baby sister wasn't cool, he didn't push me away. I made him and his friends laugh, so they kept me around."

"So that's where it comes from," Jake murmured.

Frankie pushed on, searching for words to explain this thing she'd taken as a given for most of her life. "This plan to run Valenti Brothers, it was never his plan or my plan. It was ours. When he died…"

Her throat closed up, tightening around words she still wished she didn't have to say. She coughed and took a sip from her soda can before realizing it was empty.

"That's when the plan became mine alone. Fi started working for the company when Ma quit, but that wasn't her dream. Enzo got roped in on landscaping, but he'd always planned to establish that on his own. Seth was very clear about not wanting to step into Gabe's shoes. Now Adrian is part of the mix, which in some ways is like working with a brother, but it's not the same. I'm the only Valenti who really loves the building. Before, Dad had Gabe, and Gabe had me, and we had a plan. Now I need to prove to Dad that he can count on me even without Gabe."

Jake absorbed all of what she said without looking at her, and nodded. "I see. You're very lucky."

Frankie's jaw clenched. *What the fuck?* "Lucky that my brother was killed?"

Jake's eyes snapped up to hers, shocked. "No. No!" He held up his hands as if he could stop her thoughts. "Lucky that you have the family you do. Shit, this is coming out wrong. You're lucky that you've got people to back you up." He let one of his hands fall to her shoulder, and she didn't shrug it off.

"They sure are backing me up, right into a fucking corner..." Where deadlines met the budget with a really low ceiling of parental doubt.

Her siblings' wish list changed almost daily, making it impossible to stay on track. She knew everyone wanted the project to be perfect, but it seemed like everyone had a different idea of what perfect was. They all believed Frankie could magically make it all happen though. She refused to let them down. But lesson learned. This was the last project for family that she'd stake her reputation on. They were the worst clients ever.

She couldn't admit any of that to Jake however. She couldn't let him see her struggle, or he'd milk the hell out of it for the show.

Thankfully, he picked up the conversational gauntlet and changed the subject. "So tell me something I don't know about you, Frankie Valenti."

"I hate snakes."

"Really?"

"Yeah, it's a good thing Enzo handles all the landscaping because the minute I see one I go all Indiana Jones."

Jake bit his lip and shook his head.

"What?"

"Just picturing you draped with snakes and wielding a whip. Director's curse."

"So you like things a little kinky?" Pleased that she'd made his dimple reappear, she turned the question back on him. "Tell me something about you, Jake Ryland."

"I hate carrots?"

"Uh-uh, something good. I'll remember the carrot thing though."

"Why? You gonna cook me dinner?" He leaned closer into her space, bringing his expensive-smelling cologne that much closer. She couldn't help her deep inhale, filling her senses with his scent.

"In your dreams, or maybe your nightmares. I hit my culinary peak the day I mastered Easy Mac. It's three minutes forty-two seconds on my microwave, FYI. Come on, what's your deepest fear? I told you mine."

"Stage fright." His voice softened, letting her hear the vulnerable little kid pushed into the spotlight too early.

"No. That's… That's awful. How long were you an actor?"

"Fourteen years."

"Did it ever get any easier?"

"The closed-set shoots were manageable, but live audiences or public events only got worse. And my parents didn't seem to care. No one else on set knew except my tutor because she saw me throw up once."

Frankie scooted closer so that her hip pressed against his thigh, even as their legs dangled over opposite sides of the bar. Her family liked to razz her about stupid stuff like troll toes and snakes, but they would never actually make her do anything she was truly afraid of. Imagine having parents who cared more about fame and a paycheck than about their son's well-being…

No wonder he didn't talk much about his past. What else was lurking under his polished surface?

Going on instinct, she wrapped her arms around his chest and hugged, tucking her head into his shoulder. "I'm so sorry that happened to you. It sounds awful."

"Well, you did ask my deepest fear. It wasn't going to be a walk in the park."

"Yeah, but I expected 'I hate spiders,' or 'Fucking glitter.'"

He laughed and she leaned back. He halted her retreat this time, a firm, warm hand gripping her forearm. "Thank you. I think that's the first time I've ever laughed about it."

They were so close. She focused on his lips instead of his whole face as he spoke. This time the scent of coffee and starch joined his woodsy cologne as it teased her nose.

"You're welcome," she whispered, mesmerized.

"Are you thinking about kissing me again?" he teased.

"Yes." She nodded, unable to look away. His perfectly trimmed beard framed his plump lips, making them stand out like a target.

"Fuck, Frankie." He exhaled hard. "You can't just say shit like that."

"I didn't just say it. You asked. Are *you* thinking about kissing *me* again?"

"Yes. I am now," he whispered, his hot breath tracing her cheek as he leaned over to place a kiss on the sensitive patch of skin right below her ear. She ran a hand down the front of his shirt, the buttons bumping under her palm, his chest solid and unyielding.

"I think I need a second kiss. The first one didn't work right."

"Technically, this would be a third, but if at first you don't succeed…" He leaned in with a confident smirk, but she straightened her arm between them, pushing him back into his space.

"What do you mean that's our third kiss? I'm pretty sure I would have remembered a second one."

"Actually, it's the first one you forgot," he teased, and she felt like an idiot.

"Explain."

"Christmas Eve, I drove you home after the debacle with Natalie's mom and the asshole. You pinned me to your door and kissed me stupid, and then your knees gave out and I carried you to bed. I crashed on your couch? Is any of this ringing a bell?"

Frankie was reeling. She'd kissed him Christmas Eve? That explained so much about her unrelenting fascination with his mouth. "Why didn't you tell me sooner?"

"When you didn't remember and were mortified that I'd slept over, I figured it would only add insult to injury. I didn't want you to regret our first kiss, and I was hoping to make a better impression with our second."

"Well, this just confirms it." Jake's face went carefully blank, and Frankie let a small smirk through her shock. "Even drunk, I have excellent taste."

It was comical how quickly his face lit back up. She liked him better this way, open and laughing. His mask frustrated the hell out of her.

Her new knowledge cast their whole relationship in a different light. Had he really been into her since Christmas? She shuddered and gripped his shirt, keeping him close. "Why did we stop doing the kissing thing?" she asked.

Frankie gasped as his beard tickled her ear and he gently bit her earlobe.

"Don't remember."

"Me either." Frankie managed to push the words out between breaths that were getting caught in her chest as he continued to work his way across her cheekbone.

Jake's hands rose to grip her face, and he finally gave her what she wanted. He took her mouth with abandon. He held her firmly, as if he expected her to pull away or disappear. She wished she could tell him she wouldn't. That she'd been waiting weeks for this pleasure again. That he'd ruined her mouth for all other kisses. But her own lips were too busy kissing him back to form the words.

Each press of his lips against hers, each slide of his tongue, drove the ache at her core higher.

After weeks of imagined foreplay, Frankie was too wound up to just settle for kisses. She gripped his wrists hard and he pulled back, dropping his hands to her waist. She got her knees beneath her, braced herself on his shoulders, and practically climbed the man. Awkwardly settling herself in a straddle across his lap, she was just grateful she hadn't kneed him in the process. Being short was the worst.

Lining up the ache between her legs with his front zipper, she rocked her hips forward. Jake groaned and dropped his forehead to hers. The length of her legs meant that she was resting all of her weight on that sensitive spot, her legs just barely reaching the bar top. Being short was the best.

When he began to kiss her again, she struggled to stay still and enjoy it, but she wanted to rock her hips again so badly. With just a little effort and the pressure of her jeans, she could find the full release she craved.

She'd never had a problem taking care of herself between boyfriends, but ever since Christmas, selfies had been hard to come by. Literally. Something had been missing. She had a feeling Jake was the answer to her problem, but she didn't want to scare him off by moving too fast.

Unfortunately, her hips didn't get the message, twitching impatiently beneath his hands as he kneaded her ass. When he shifted a hand to palm her breast through her T-shirt and bra, Frankie yelped and jerked her hips forward. Feeling the full length of him pressed urgently against her, even through two layers of denim, was the last straw. She wanted to feel that pleasure again and again. She clasped her hands behind his neck and rocked herself on his lap until the pressure peaked. Everything contracted and she pulled his face into her chest as she clenched and shook. Spent, she collapsed, shivering and panting against his shoulder.

She didn't know if it was a good thing or a bad thing to confirm that he was indeed the thing that had been missing from her orgasms these last few months. She did know that she'd just changed the game between them.

Frankie scooted backward, relieving the pressure on her too-sensitive clit, and Jake winced.

"Um, I, uh..." Words had deserted her. Her brain was complete mush. She pressed her lips together. *Please don't say anything stupid*, she prayed.

Jake gripped her hips and gently set her off his lap, before hopping down from the bar and adjusting what had to be a painful erection.

"Do you need any help with that?" she asked, her voice shakier than she liked.

"No, I'm okay." He backed away, heading for the door. He wouldn't look her in the eye.

"But I could..." Frankie gestured toward his rapidly retreating crotch.

"You've done enough."

Frankie's jaw dropped as he literally ran away from her, up the stairs.

What the hell?

CHAPTER 14

JAKE HUSTLED up the drive and into the production trailer as fast as his stiff cock would let him. Thank God everyone was gone. He was about to lose it, and he didn't need an audience for that.

Locking the door behind him, he leaned against it and pressed a hand hard against the front of his jeans, trying to make his erection go away. He refused to come in his jeans like some horny teenager, but if he'd stayed any longer on that bar with her sweet heat seated firmly in his lap, he'd have done exactly that. Or he'd have stripped them both bare and taken her up again, satisfying them both this time.

But bare was a problem. He'd had responsibility drilled into his head by a mother who wanted to protect him from fortune hunters who would try and sleep their way into child support. True, she'd only wanted to ensure her cut of said fortune didn't get garnished, but the lesson had stuck.

No condom. No sex.

He hadn't carried one in his pocket specifically to avoid temptation. How could he have known that when temptation sat and came on his lap it would be so damn hard to walk away?

Jake sighed. The throbbing was going down a little bit. He

ROUGHED IN

tried to remember why he'd been avoiding her, why they'd stopped "the kissing thing" as she'd called it. The kiss in his trailer hadn't gotten anything out of his system, but it had clearly spooked her. He'd let her retreat, fully planning to keep pursuing her. And then the night at the hospital had happened.

Talking with her, watching her sleep, being invited in to meet the baby with the whole family...it had been too much. Standing in the back of that hospital room, the emotions in his chest had grown so quickly he hadn't been able to breathe. Panic had hit him hard and fast, leaving him reeling and needing to escape. He'd dropped the present by the door and snuck out like a coward, but he'd told himself it was for the best.

He didn't do "family." He didn't build relationships. He hooked up with people for short periods of time until they'd both gotten what they needed and moved on. Something deep in his soul told him Frankie was dangerous. He wanted her too much. And though it terrified him, being included had felt...nice. He could get used to that too easily, and it would hurt like hell when he left.

She wasn't the kind of woman who thrived on flings. She was the kind who supported her family by sitting up all night, just in case. She was the kind of woman who chased down a dream because she'd promised her dead brother.

He wouldn't even know what to do with feelings like that. She was better off without his selfish ass. And that was why he'd spent the last three weeks trying to rebuild the walls between them, despite the fact that she was the better builder.

All he'd managed to keep erect was pressing insistently against his jeans, urging him to go back to her.

This would go down in his personal history as a fail. A mental image of Frankie going down popped into his head, and his other head popped up again with a vengeance. *Shit.*

He glanced over at the monitor on his desk and saw the live

feed from the portable mounted camera still attached to the bar playing in real time. Frankie was adjusting her clothing and packing up her tools. He imagined that her skin felt too tight and tingly all over, like his. The cotton of her shirt brushing over her sensitive nipples would send a shiver down her spine. As if on cue, she shuddered and straightened her shoulders, hefting the heavy toolbox and heading for the stairs. Damn his director's eye for seeing every nuance in her movements.

He crossed to his chair and dropped into it. He rewound the footage to the beginning. If he couldn't fuck away this hard on, he'd work it away. He trimmed and clipped footage of the first fifteen minutes. He'd gotten some decent shots of her carrying the bar and leveling it during installation. Perfect. When he got to the part where they sat hip to hip on the bar, he was tempted to fast-forward, but his analytical side took over again.

He watched her face as she flirted with him. The camera had thankfully captured the back of his head. He could only imagine the sappy grin on his face as she teased him. When she laughed, his lips quirked along with her. When she pulled him into the hug, he leaned closer to the monitor as if he could still draw in her comfort even though she was miles away by now. When she looked at his lips and chewed on her own, Jake pulled his own lips between his teeth, remembering every touch and taste. By the time she straddled his lap, he was a goner again.

He watched as she leaned into the pleasure of his hands, his mouth, his teeth. His hips rose in response to her repeated rocking on the screen, his hand providing the pressure where the seam of her jeans had been. Watching it should have felt wrong, but since he'd been there to witness it firsthand, it felt more like a visual memory than voyeurism. The look on her face as she came was visceral, and he committed it to memory. He'd been trying to hold back the tide so intently that he'd closed his eyes against the stimulation and missed it the first time around.

This time it blazed across his brain, searing itself in his mind's eye. His hand shifted from providing a calming pressure to rubbing frantically, wanting to join her as he hadn't allowed himself before. Messy jeans, be damned. His self-control was in tatters after months of denial.

His orgasm tore through him, too quickly. He shook in his office chair, eyes closed, until it rattled into the wall.

Next time he'd be prepared, and he'd take all the time he wanted. Next time he'd have a damn condom. He cringed at the way his underwear slid and stuck to him. And next time there would be a spare pair of clothes in his car.

He stopped the tape. Next time? Who was he kidding? There couldn't be a next time. What could he offer her? How could he sell a short-term fling? No matter what, he was heading back to LA after this show wrapped. But there was no denying he wanted more of Frankie any way he could get her.

His mind already plotting, he reached to rewind and delete the footage before anyone else saw it, but the look on her face stopped him cold. He had been so focused on his own need to escape that he hadn't thought much about his exit. Judging by the sadness in her eyes and her dejected expression, his quick retreat had left a mark. *Damn it.* He'd have to figure out how to fix that. After a shower. Tomorrow for sure. Right about the same time he figured out how to be with her, but keep things casual. But one thing was certain: he'd figure it all out because he really wanted a next time.

He deftly maneuvered his program and kept only the scenes he needed for the show before deleting the rest. He shut down his monitors and retreated to the long-term stay hotel room that served as his home base in the Bay. A warm shower beckoned, and for the first time in a year and a half, he looked forward to heading home.

CHAPTER 15

"Damn it, Frankie, get in here!" Dom's voice reverberated in the tight space of Frankie's office.

Jake leaned against the wall, waiting for Dom to find whatever it was he was looking for so they could have their status update before he headed over to the jobsite for the morning scenes. He'd followed Dom in here, thinking they could have a quick walk and talk, but that clearly wasn't going to happen with Dom so distracted.

Dom rifled through the piles of paperwork and flooring samples on Frankie's desk, cursing.

How anyone could function in this office was beyond Jake's comprehension. His fingers twitched with the urge to straighten the piles Dom was destroying in his frustration.

"That girl. Never could keep her room clean. How does she find anything in this mess?" Dom muttered under his breath.

"I can find things just fine if no one touches my stuff," Frankie said as she hustled into the room.

She hadn't noticed Jake against the wall, and he didn't alert her. She'd been avoiding him since their encounter on the bar, and Jake missed the sight of her in person. Seeing her in edits wasn't cutting it.

He needed the real Frankie, but any time he entered a room she found a reason to leave it. He hadn't even gotten a chance to apologize and explain why he'd left the way he did. Now a week had passed, and he felt awkward even bringing it up.

My God, I've gone back to high school.

He'd managed to get two full years of actual high school in between movies, and he'd spent most of that time wondering normal things like, "Did that sound totally lame?" or "Why do I lose the ability to speak around girls?"

He'd also pondered abnormal things like, "Does this girl like me or the character I played? Is she looking for a walk-on or an intro to my agent?"

Either way, he'd thought he'd left this level of internal angst behind him. Apparently all it had taken was one confusing brunette to bring it all back.

"Stop, Dad. What do you need?" Frankie bent over her desk to protect her piles from Dom's destruction, and Jake almost groaned.

Don't look at her ass. Do NOT check out her ass in front of her father. Don't... Too late.

Now that he'd gotten his hands on it, had felt the pleasure of it grinding in his lap, he was helpless to resist a glance that turned into a stare. His fingers twitched again as he repressed the urge to move her hips into place as well. The way she wore denim was criminal.

She was his siren. Despite his firm belief that he was not cut out for relationships and that she deserved better, he couldn't resist her call. All he could see was her. He'd toss himself against the rocks if it meant a chance to be with her one more time, and this time he'd be prepared. The condom in his pocket and the box in his car testified to his readiness.

If he could just get her alone long enough to convince her that he wasn't the asshole he seemed. Well, he *was* an asshole, but not a *fucking* asshole, and that had to count for something.

Dom cleared his throat, breaking the spell Jake had fallen under, before answering Frankie. "I need the paperwork on the supply agreement we negotiated with the Lumber Jills last month. Sofia didn't know anything about it, so Meena didn't see it and was sending orders with the wrong pricing. I can't find my copy."

"So you lost your copy and now you're tearing apart my desk to find mine?" Frankie rounded her desk and pulled a manila envelope from two-thirds of the way down a precarious stack. "Here. Next time wait for me. Or better yet, ask."

"I don't know how you manage to work like this. Okay Jake, let me make a quick copy of this for Meena and we can have our chat."

At the mention of his name Frankie finally noticed his presence, her eyes flashing to his. If he was a list-keeping kind of guy, and he was, he'd add betrayal and embarrassment to her ever-growing list of grievances with him. But at least there was a spark of emotion in her eyes that had been painfully blank the last few days. He wasn't about to blow this opportunity.

"Why don't you go handle that, Dom, and we'll talk after? I need to clear something with Frankie."

"Okay, give me five minutes."

Dom left, and Frankie crossed her arms over her chest and sighed. "What's wrong now? Are you going to add your critique of my organizational skills?" she asked.

"No, you find what you need when you need it. That's not what this is about. I think… I know… Look, we had a misunderstanding the other day in the tasting room."

Her face flamed red, and she looked away. "I'd rather not talk about that."

"Yeah, I got that impression from the not-so-subtle way you pretend you can't see me."

"I wasn't going for subtle. I don't like you very much right now, and I don't see the need to hide it behind overrated acting skills like some people."

She still refused to look at him, and he wasn't making any progress. This wasn't the time or place to get into it deeply. But he needed to at least put a crack in her defenses so he could scale that wall later.

"Listen, I *do* like *you*, but it's complicated… I was an ass, and you deserve a better explanation and apology than I can give you here. Let's talk about it. Later today?" She glanced up and he seized the advantage. "Please?"

She kept him in silent suspense as his heart pounded in his chest in anticipation. He could tell the minute she gave in because her shoulders dropped to reasonable levels and she unclenched her jaw enough to speak.

"You've got ten minutes, later. Now get out of here. I have work to do down at the vineyard."

He'd take it. She left, and Jake found Dom coming out of Sofia's office.

"Now that's a functional office," Dom blustered as he crossed the open showroom. "Even on maternity leave Sofia's got her office neat as a pin. That girl's got a knack. Those two are like night and day."

"Easy there. It takes all types to run the world." Although Jake would choose Sofia's style of organization for himself, Frankie's worked for her. He hated to hear Dom put her down.

"I don't know how Frankie thinks she's going to run this place with a desk like that." Dom shook his head and tossed the manila file back on top of the mess on Frankie's desk.

"Seriously? She found that file for you in under thirty seconds."

Dom crossed his arms and pinned Jake with an intent stare. "If you were a client, would you trust your money and your home to someone with that office?" He waved a hand toward Frankie's pit.

"Meena does a great job keeping the common areas clean and tidy. Frankie could meet them out here."

Dom brushed away that suggestion as if it was a gnat annoying him. Jake knew there was more to it than that.

"What's your real worry about Frankie?" Jake pushed.

Dom ran his free hand through his hair and sighed. "She's so young."

"She's older than you were when you started this place," Jake pointed out.

"Exactly! I know just how much of my life this place has eaten up. I've given it so much, and I still can't walk away from it. She's not even married yet. What about kids? I don't want that life for her." Dom ran a hand over a face that seemed to have aged years over the course of their conversation.

"It's not about what you want for her. What does she want? Is this the life she'd choose for herself? Has she said anything about marriage and children?"

Dom latched onto the last question in that string. "Why? Does that make you nervous?"

Jake ignored Dom's significant glance and not-so-subtle prying. "Even if she does want that with *someone*, should she put all of her ambitions on hold until she has them? How did that work out for Jo?" Jake watched as Dom's brain stuttered over that thought.

"It's not... Jo didn't... That's not what I'm saying," Dom growled.

"That's what I'm hearing though. And she's hearing that you don't trust her or respect her abilities."

"I respect her ability. Girl can swing a hammer. Taught her myself, didn't I?"

"Your ability to defend her and doubt her in the same breath is mind-boggling."

"You'll understand when you're a parent, young man."

Jake chuckled. He'd decided long ago that parenting wasn't in the cards for him. His father had been so driven by his own ego and ambitions that he'd seldom been around during Jake's childhood. The fact that Jake had earned more by the age of ten than his father had in a full career had only widened the distance between them, which had allowed his mother essentially free rein over his career choices. She had taken full advantage of his father's long absences, playing the role of stage mom to the hilt.

Jake's parental role models weren't exactly stellar. He didn't know what good parenting looked like. He'd only had scripted bits on TV for reference, and those had never lined up with real life. No, he would never bring a child into the life he led. No way was he going to subject a child to the unique hell of him trying to figure out what he was doing. With the demands of his job, even well-adjusted couples struggled to make parenting work.

"Not happening, old man. Not. Happening."

CHAPTER 16

"So the hidden cellar is finished?"

After the debacle in her office that morning, Frankie would take any good news she could get. Seth nodded and grinned as he flicked the latch open. With one hand, he pushed the edge of the quartz countertop back, and it slid easily on the hidden tracks built into the island cabinetry. With the top open, he lifted another catch and pulled open the end of the island to reveal a hidden staircase descending to the secret wine cellar Sofia had insisted on. The whole operation glided effortlessly and Frankie clapped her hands.

"It's perfect! Oh Seth, Ma is going to love this."

"It's definitely one of the coolest installs I've ever done. All that's left to do is putting together the wine racks down there and wiring the lighting. Two racks are already down there, but the other four are on back order. They should be here today or tomorrow."

"I really can't thank you enough for making this project happen for free."

"Not quite free. Don't forget, we're having Brandy's nursing school graduation party here next year free of charge."

"Absolutely. A deal is a deal." She shook her cousin's hand with a cheeky grin. She'd have agreed to get him the moon if he'd asked.

She was elated to have this done on time and under budget. Something on this damn project should follow the family motto. She was also glad she wouldn't have to eat crow in front of Sofia. Frankie had promised she'd get it done, and she had, and that was all that mattered.

The humiliation of overhearing her dad and Jake doubting her abilities and criticizing how she organized herself had cut her confidence to the quick. She'd needed something to go right to prove that she was as competent as she thought.

Jake had stripped down her defenses on top of that bar without removing a single item of clothing. Now she felt open to every attack, intentional and accidental.

Between all the low-key flirting on site and the connection she'd felt at the hospital, she'd thought this was heading somewhere. But after he'd left her high and decidedly not dry on the bar, she was questioning everything. Had she read him wrong? Was he laughing at her? This probably happened to him all the time.

Despite hashing things out between Ben & Jerry and Buster on her couch, Frankie was no closer to understanding where things had gone wrong.

She had always hated feeling awkward or unsure of herself, so she was falling back on old habits. She was avoiding him. If she didn't see him, he couldn't hurt her further. If she did have to spend time with him, she snapped at him with snarky sarcasm to keep him at a safe distance. She was terrified of what he would say in the ten minutes she'd granted him.

Once she figured out these feelings and got them wrangled back into submission, things would be better. Maybe some time alone in a quiet space would help her sort things out. Frankie heard Trina come in the back door, talking to Jake on her walkie-talkie, and she winced. The last thing she wanted right now was a camera in her face. Especially not while she was still processing how Jake's silent judgment had made her feel.

Was that what she was afraid of? Opening up and being found not good enough? Taking the risk and not succeeding? This fear on all fronts paralyzed her, but she wasn't going to let it slow her down today. She was going to take her win into her cave and protect it.

"Could you let someone on the production crew know to keep an eye out for those other racks? I'm going to go down and start drilling in anchors and assembling the two we have," she asked Seth.

"Sure, but then I've got to run."

"It's okay. I've got it from here. Thanks again, cuz." Frankie wrapped her arms around his waist for a tight hug. "You really are the best."

"Aw, come here, kiddo." He wrapped his arms around her shoulders in return. "This place is going to be great."

"I know."

He chucked a knuckle under her chin. "You're already great."

"Tell that to Dad and Jake."

"You'll show them yourself when this project is complete. Just maybe stop adding things to the plan…"

Frankie faux-punched him in the stomach. "Tell that to Enzo and Fi."

"You can always say no," Seth prodded.

"Sure I can. It's so easy to tell your brother and sister that you're going to spoil their perfect weddings. Why didn't I think of that?"

"Okay, smart-ass. Just don't lose sight of the bigger goal. You're making this place for your mom, not them, and you need to succeed."

"I know. I do," she protested at his raised eyebrows, and grabbed the impact drill then tucked the concrete drill bits into her tool belt. "I'm working on it. I'll catch you later, cuz."

"Bye, Frankie."

She walked down the stairs and pulled the countertop back into place above her. She didn't want to telegraph her location to anyone with a camera.

She flicked on the utility light hanging from the ceiling. The mini chandelier was still in its box in the corner, but they wouldn't install it until they were done assembling the bulky racks. The yellow bulb glowed through the orange metal cage, swaying back and forth from the J-hook in the ceiling, illuminating the small ten-by-eight-foot space. Caged in and off-balance. Boy, could she relate. Something was going to have to give soon. She couldn't keep swinging from extreme to extreme trying to make everyone happy.

Pulling a pencil and tape measure from her tool belt, Frankie efficiently measured and marked up the walls, noting the length of the wine racks and where the anchoring holes would need to be drilled into the reinforced concrete.

This whole wine cellar felt like a microcosm of this project—it was crazy, a pretty, shiny idea that had taken longer and more money to complete than she'd expected. When it came down to the nuts and bolts, Frankie was confident and capable, but with so many delays, she was beginning to wonder if Dom was right. Maybe she wasn't ready to take the lead. Maybe her project management skills were too rough around the edges. She had a really hard time saying no.

She hated when doubts crept past her confident veneer because they were hard to chase back out, especially when she was struggling. They ran on a loop through her head, beating down her conviction that she could handle things. When a build went bad, a few late nights with a hammer could usually make things right. But when her thoughts spiraled, she struggled to pull out of the tailspin. Maybe it was the combination of the stress, the show, the added workload... Whatever it was, she needed to find a way out of this hole she'd dug herself into.

Pulling out her phone to call Sofia to share the good news and hopefully get a boost, Frankie realized the downside to putting a wine cellar in a concrete box. Great for earthquakes, terrible for cell service or Wi-Fi. She heard steps up above in the kitchen, and decided her alone time was more important than risking discovery to make a call upstairs. She could muddle through this crisis of faith on her own.

The sound of the counter sliding back pulled her attention up the stairs, box-cutter in hand, only to see a most unwelcome pair of polished Italian leather shoes descending. Those shoes could only mean one man. Damn him and his ten minutes. If he thought anything he could say would erase walking out on her in the tasting room and witnessing her humiliation this morning, he was crazier than she'd thought.

Jake clicked the cabinet shut and slid the counter flush, closing them both in the small space, while giving her an excellent view of his ass.

If only he wasn't an actual ass ninety percent of the time...

She deliberately turned her attention back to the wall.

"Frankie..."

She cut him off with a blast from the impact drill as she drilled the hole for the first anchor. If he continued to speak over the loud, percussive blasts, she couldn't hear it. When she'd drilled far enough, she reluctantly let go of the trigger and pulled the bit out of the wall. She didn't want to have this conversation while she was fragile.

He tried again. "I just wanted to..."

Frankie moved over to the next marked spot and drilled again. *Nope. Not today.* She would make this wine cellar look like a bunker made of Swiss cheese before she'd give him the satisfaction.

She stepped over to the next drill marking, which took her into the corner created by the staircase cutting into the room. They'd designed the staircase to hold bottles in custom cutouts beneath the treads to maximize space, and the rest of the racks curved around the corner. It was a tight fit, but she'd have just enough room to assemble everything. Well, she would if a certain irritating director would get out of her space. But no, he'd come the rest of the way down the stairs and stood directly behind her.

"Would you just..."

She drilled again, practically feeling the waves of frustration emanating from the large man at her back. This time, as she pulled the bit out of the wall, Jake reached over her shoulder and snatched the drill from her hands.

"Give that back."

"Not until you hear me out." He held the drill behind his back and crowded her into the corner.

"I already heard my dad question my abilities and you not say a damn thing. I also heard your footsteps on the stairs when you left me in the tasting room. I'm not sure there is anything else I need to hear from you." Frankie crossed her arms over her chest and looked at her scuffed work boots. Even their footwear showed what a mismatch they were, despite what she'd felt in the hospital. She pushed that insecurity away and tried for bravado. She hadn't done anything wrong. He'd been the asshole. Why did she feel so defensive?

"Not even 'I'm sorry'?"

She paused at that, and looked up. The sincerity and remorse in his eyes was new. Something about that caught in her brain, and she was hooked. Maybe if she let him have his say, they could move past this. "Fine. I'm listening."

"About the other day, on the bar. It was the end of a long and stressful day, and I hadn't planned on…"

"This is your apology?" She shook her head in disgust and tried to step around him. He was just going to give her bullshit excuses? She'd been tired and stressed too. She hadn't planned to get off in his lap either. But she also had somehow managed not to shove him away and storm out of the room.

Jake dropped the drill and stepped forward, arms spread wide to stop her. "Getting to it. You were incredible and so damn hot. I wanted you—badly—from the minute I walked in the room." He hooked a finger in her tool belt and pulled her closer until her hips bumped his. "There's something about watching you work. Your body drives me insane, all of that power in this tight little package. It makes me want to set you off."

He dragged a finger down her bicep and gripped her wrist, turning her palm to the light.

"And your hands." He kissed her palm. "The way they take on the world makes me want you to take on me. Your mind pulling problems apart and putting them back together is compelling. Your competence is sexy."

That last word was whispered against the sensitive skin of her ear as he leaned closer. Frankie jerked her head and stepped away, unwilling to let him off the hook so easily. He was turning her inside out with his words, but he hadn't said the ones that mattered yet.

Feeling backed into a corner, she went on the offensive, pushing him for a better apology. "Still waiting for that 'I'm sorry.' It was a shit thing to do, walking away like that."

"I know. I'm sorry. I was trying to protect you, me…us, and I panicked. Like I said, I hadn't intended for any of that to happen, and then it did, and I wasn't prepared. I didn't have any protection, and I was about to explode. The slightest touch from you would've done it. And I didn't trust that I would have walked away from the temptation of being inside you. If you'd said so much as 'Stay,' I would have, and we'd both have more regrets. I wish I'd been able to find the words to explain in that moment, but I couldn't think straight."

Well, that was certainly a different interpretation of events.

"So you were so turned on that you had to leave?" She knew she sounded incredulous, but this was hard to believe. She didn't have the kind of body that drove men mad. And yet here he was, Hollywood heartthrob, nodding in agreement.

"I had to get myself back under control."

Control. That finally made sense. Jake Ryland thrived on control. She wrenched her wrist from his grip. "No, you didn't. You were afraid of losing control. That's different."

"That's not—"

Frankie cut him off, unwilling to let him hide behind his words. She pinned him down with a finger to his chest. "You were just as turned on as I was. But instead of letting me return the favor of a manual orgasm, you didn't trust me to take control."

Jake was silent. Frankie pushed on with her theory.

"I think you were scared."

He didn't deny it. The silence stretched between them, until Frankie broke it with a question that had been bugging her.

"You know, I realized later that there was probably video from that stupid camera. Should I be worried that any of it is going to get leaked for publicity?"

"No. You don't have to worry."

"Are you sure? Can I trust *you*?"

His eyes flashed angrily to hers when she questioned his honor. *Too. Damn. Bad.* Trust had to be earned, and he'd badly damaged her faith in him.

"Yes. I'm sure. I deleted it before anyone else saw it."

So, there had been video… "Did you watch it?"

"Yes." Jake's voice deepened around the single syllable.

Frankie lowered her voice to match it, curiosity spurring her onward. "Was it any good?"

Jake let out an unsteady exhale and nodded.

"Did you touch yourself while you watched it? Did you come?"

Jake paused and dropped his gaze.

"You did!" Frankie advanced, poking him hard in the chest. "You stole that from me. And you made me feel like shit while you did."

Jake pressed his hand over hers, flattening her accusing fingers against his chest, trapping her close. "How can I make it up to you?"

Knowing now that his disappearing act had been driven by his own battle for control and not by anything she'd done made her decision easier. Despite her best efforts, she hadn't been able to get him out of her head. Staying out of his way had felt like the best choice to move on from his callous dismissal, but it hadn't worked. Clearly it hadn't worked for him either, because here he was, chasing her into a hole in the ground so she would listen to his apology. Maybe taking back a little of that control would help her find the balance that had gone missing after that one-sided panty party.

"Give it back."

Jake looked confused, but he still hadn't released her hand from his chest. She bunched his shirt into her fist, deliberately wrinkling the pristinely ironed cotton, and pulled him right into her space.

"The orgasm you stole from me? I want it back."

His eyes went dark and dilated. He stepped forward, reaching his hands for her face.

"No," she interrupted. "I don't want you to give it to me. I want to take it myself."

CHAPTER 17

JAKE WAS helpless to resist as Frankie used her grip to push him off-balance into the concrete wall at the base of the stairs. He'd had more words to say. A plan. It was hazy now. He raised his hands to her hips to steady himself, and she slapped them away.

"My. Turn."

If this was how he broke through her walls, who was he to argue?

Her nimble fingers were easily unfastening the row of buttons down his shirt, tugging it from his jeans as she went. She pulled his shirt off his shoulders and down his arms, the sleeve snagging on his wrists because of the buttoned cuffs.

He reached behind to help her undo the now hidden buttons, but she stopped him again.

"Leave it. Maybe it'll help keep you from interrupting."

His need for control flared, unaccustomed to being denied.

Frankie ran her hand under his undershirt, raising it up to expose his chest, and tweaked one of his nipples before lowering her lips to soothe it. His hands rose of their own accord and were jerked to a halt by his makeshift cotton handcuffs. He hadn't even made it thirty seconds.

She laughed against his chest, and his chagrin dissolved. "This is gonna be fun." She chuckled again as she licked from his clavicle to his ear, tugging the lobe between her teeth, pulling a groan from deep in his chest unbidden.

Fun. When was the last time he'd relaxed and just had fun? The closest he'd gotten had been on the bar with her, talking and flirting. Even then he hadn't been able to fully let go, which had gotten him in this current situation. When Frankie stepped back from him to whip her own T-shirt over her head, he deliberately made no move to free himself or reach for her. He'd play her game and give her everything she'd asked for and more.

She slid up his torso, her breasts still hidden by her scrap of a bra. She was all lithe energy and strength as she literally climbed him and captured his mouth in a searing kiss, pinning him against the wall. He met her kiss for kiss, but kept his hands between him and the wall. He wanted to help support her, grab her ass, hold her close. But he was playing by her rules and he didn't want to lose.

She locked one arm behind his neck and used the other to cup his face while she explored his collarbone with her mouth. Between little kisses she asked, "Why...do you...wear...so many...layers?"

"Excellent question. I'm happy to shed a few for you. You can even tie my hands back again."

Frankie lifted her head at this and eyed him suspiciously. "You'd let me do that?"

This was a test. He had to prove himself worthy of her trust. "I'd let you do that. Promise."

She slid down his front and he wished those layers had burned off from the friction. God, he wanted to touch her again. He closed his eyes and groaned.

She laughed again, that joyous sound bursting from her like a surprise. "You're wishing back those words right now, aren't you?"

He couldn't help but laugh with her. "Maybe, but a promise is a promise. If I give you my word, I don't go back on it."

Frankie pressed her lips to his, a gentle kiss that slid and soothed. Her tongue teased his lower lip before her teeth tugged it into a pout. His hands were still useless, but he chased her retreat with his lips, craving more of her. Her taste, her texture, the sounds she made that reverberated through his mind as their tongues tangled. He was breathless and panting when she pulled back and braced her hands on his shoulders. It helped soothe his racing pulse that she looked as lightheaded as he felt.

"How about this? I'll let you free your arms, on the condition that you'll use them exactly how I tell you to."

"Fuck, yes. Deal." He stepped away from the wall and had his cuffs unbuckled and his shirts shucked before she could take it back. She giggled, and he grinned, holding out his hands to the sides and offering a slight bow. "I'm yours to command."

She ran a hand down his bare chest, and he shivered. "Do you have condoms with you now?" she whispered in his ear, chasing her words with a sucking bite to his neck.

"I do."

"And would you like to use them with me?" she purred as she ran her hand over the length of his erection through his pants.

"I would." He closed his eyes and fought for control.

"Uh-uh. Keep them open."

Jake snapped his eyes back open and focused on hers, waiting for her next command.

"Unbutton your jeans."

Slowly, he leaned back against the cold concrete and reached for his buckle, enjoying the way she watched him with open lust in her eyes.

"Now drop them. Show me the tool we're working with."

He obeyed and dropped his jeans and boxer briefs to his knees. His cock jutted out toward her, actively reaching for her touch. Gratified by the way her eyes widened, he started to toe off his shoe, intending to strip down completely, but she stopped him.

"No, leave those on. It's not safe to be barefoot on a construction site."

"Oh, but it's okay to be bare-assed?" he teased.

"We'll have to be careful." She patted his ass cheekily. "Wouldn't want this to get hurt. Where are the condoms?"

"In my pocket."

Frankie knelt down in front of him and tucked her hand into his scrunched-up pocket down near his ankle. Her mouth was inches from his groin, and her gaze stuttered as she got a good look. He tried to hold still, but his cock bobbed toward her on each pulse. As she stood with the condom, she closed her lips around his thick head and licked the moisture that had gathered at the tip of his cock. His eyes rolled back and closed as pleasure swamped him, before he remembered her request and opened them again.

"That's right," she said. She tucked the condom into her tool belt, which she was still wearing and which he found sexy as hell. "I want you to watch every second of this and tell me if it was as good as the video you erased. Now show me."

"Show you what?"

"Show me how you touched yourself when you watched the video."

He paused. That wasn't what he'd expected. She stepped closer, but still didn't touch him. His cock leapt at her nearness though, desperate for more of her.

"Show me how you like it when you're all alone and aching.

You watched me grind my pussy against your lap and come apart in your arms. Were you imagining me touching you when you came?"

Jake shook his head. She moved to his side, her breasts barely brushing against his arm, and she whispered. "Were you imagining fucking me?"

Jake closed his eyes, his memory taking him back to his frantic orgasm in the production trailer, and he nodded. He sat down heavily on the stairs and spread his legs wide. Her rough, callused hand gently gripped his wrist and moved his hand to cover his cock.

Without another thought, he gripped himself firmly and stroked hard. "I watched you take your pleasure. You were so fucking beautiful, sitting on my lap, riding me. I couldn't look away from your face in the video."

"Tell me more," she crooned, sitting next to him on the stair, still not touching any of the places he'd expected her to. She leaned on his shoulder like she had at the hospital, but this time she kept her eyes open and trained on his lap. "What did you imagine in your office?"

"I imagined your jeans were gone, and that instead of rubbing against you, I was deep inside you, thrusting to meet each grind of your hips." His hips were twitching again, just like they had the other day as he mimed the motion he'd use to fuck her. "Do you want me to come like this?" he rasped out.

"Not yet. Stop before you come."

Jake gave himself a few more tugs, but stopped as directed before things got out of hand.

"That was fast."

"It was the other day too. It doesn't take too long to take care of it."

"It can if you're doing it right."

So many different ways of *doing it right* danced through his head that he had to drop his hand completely or risk missing that opportunity. "I haven't had someone stick around long enough to do it right in a long time. Most women just get what they came for and move on."

"Is that why you thought it was okay to leave? Because I got what I came for?"

He shrugged. That was part of it.

"You must really mean that. You didn't even laugh at my terrible pun." She shifted her hand to replace his and stroked him hard and slow, her grip like firm fire.

He hissed his breath in between clenched teeth and fought to keep his hands off her.

"That's their loss, because it looks like you could really do it right…"

"Tell me… Tell me to touch you. Please, Frankie. For the love of God, let me touch you."

"Maybe I'll make you wait…"

Jake groaned and dropped his head back against the stairs.

"…or maybe I'll tell you to touch my breasts and make them feel good." The grin on her face was fucking powerful and hot.

"Is that what you're telling me to do, Frankie?"

"That's what I'm telling you to do."

His hands shot up so quickly that they got tangled in her bra. Fighting to get free, he popped a strap before reaching behind her and quickly freeing her as well. He palmed her small breasts, earning an arched back, before smoothing over her pebbled nipples with his thumbs. "Is there anything else you'd like to tell me to do?"

"Your tongue. Use your mouth," she moaned.

"Mmmmh." His reply was muffled against her skin as he eagerly tasted her, pulling her sensitive tits with his lips, rasping his soft beard gently against her chest, making her shudder.

"Oh, Jake! That feels so—" Her shudder cut off her words as he blew a firm breath over her wet nipple. She stood and tugged at the catch on her tool belt before dropping it to the ground. "Fuck going slow. I need you, Jake. I need you to touch me everywhere."

He helped tug her jeans down to the tops of her steel-toed boots before lowering her to sit on the stairs.

Sliding his fingers up her thighs, tucking his thumbs into the crease between her legs, he found her warm and wet. He pushed her thighs apart so he could see her, licking his lips. Her sweet pussy was begging him to taste her.

"Tell me to taste you, Frankie."

"Yes. Yes, use your mouth on me."

Jake gripped her ass to hold her steady and Frankie melted back onto the stairs as he set about learning her with his tongue. Her clit was incredibly sensitive, and she jerked every time he passed directly over it. No wonder she'd been able to come just by humping him on the bar. He teased around it, licking her lips, her folds, and deep inside her, but avoiding that particular spot until she was writhing, trapped by her clothing and his desire.

Her thighs were beginning to quake where they squeezed against his shoulders. It wouldn't be long until he gave her what she wanted. He felt the surge of smug power rising, until she abruptly shoved his forehead back and he stumbled to the wall behind him.

"Did you think this was going to be that easy? I believe I said something about doing this right…"

Kneeling in front of him, she took his thick length into her mouth and proceeded to turn him inside out. The feel of her lips, her tongue, her sweet heat sliding down to meet her firm hand on the way up, fuuuuck, it all felt way too good. When he pumped his hips up to chase the pleasure, she slapped his ass. He tried real hard to obey, but when she smacked his ass a second time, he jerked forward in reaction, pushing deep into her throat.

She pulled back and used her hands to anchor his hips to the wall. He tried to stay still, but she dragged her tongue from the base of his cock all the way up over the tip before rimming her lips around the head. Instinct took over and he pushed forward a third time. She took her mouth away and he gasped. *No.*

She sat on her heels, her mouth empty and closed, proving to him that she could and did hold the power even in this moment. Finally, she broke into a grin.

"You can't seem to stay still, can you?" Frankie teased. Jake shook his head with chagrin. "Well then, I guess I'll have to make you move."

She reached for her tool belt, and he flinched. What the hell was she getting? A hammer? Her tape measure? He'd move. He'd fucking move right up the stairs.

His panic must've shown, because she was shaking with laughter when she stood and tossed him the condom. "Put that on and get up here."

She leaned forward, bracing her forearms against the wall. They both still had their jeans around their ankles, and there was something sexy about still seeing her in work gear, her bare ass presented for him. That image was going to haunt him on set. He sheathed himself in latex and stood to await his next orders.

"Are you ready to do this right?" she asked, her breathy voice shooting straight through his chest.

Jake stepped forward, aligning his cock with the tight entrance of her pussy, waiting for the words to set him free. "I'm ready whenever you want me."

"Please, Jake. I need you."

Sliding her back on his cock was like sliding home. Despite every awkward thing about this encounter, this moment felt spectacularly right. She arched her back to meet his thrusts. Harder. Faster. He slid in and out, gripping her hips for balance, desperate to give her the orgasm she'd demanded. When she reached a hand down to touch herself, he gasped. She began twitching almost immediately, and he growled in approval.

"Yes, Frankie. Yes!"

Her hand was flying and he bit his lip, trying to distract himself from his own finish so she could come first. He could feel her sheath contracting around him, and she muffled a scream against her arm as she came apart in his arms. He kept thrusting steadily through her aftershocks, even though he'd already come at her first peak, wanting to prolong her pleasure.

When her head dropped limply against the wall, he leaned into her, pinning them both upright, and exhaled deeply. *God, that was good.*

"It sure was."

Fuck, was that out loud?

"Yep." She chuckled at his flustered outer monologue. "Don't steal another one of my orgasms, or I'll have to teach you another lesson."

"Is that a threat or a promise?"

"Both."

He kissed her tenderly on her swollen lips, chafed by his beard. "Then it's a deal."

They were back to awkward as he pulled out and they put themselves back together, pulling up jeans and turning shirts right-side out. He tucked the used condom into his jeans pocket and smiled over the fact that he'd have messy jeans for the second time that week and accepted it as the new normal. He was floating in a bubble of bliss.

Fun. It had been fun.

He followed her up the stairs, feeling good about tackling the rest of his day now that they'd put their troubles behind them. They could talk about it and set expectations later.

"Shit."

His feel-good bubble wobbled. "What?"

"I can't get the slab to move. We're locked in here."

His bubble popped.

CHAPTER 18

FRANKIE TURNED BACK down the narrow stairs and Jake took her place at the top. He frantically pushed at the slab of quartz, trying to shove it back along its tracks, but it wouldn't budge.

Neither would the hidden door, in spite of his shoulder bump, because it was held in place by the mechanism under the countertop. He pounded his fist against the wooden panel and yelled, "Hey! Anyone! Get us out of here!"

No response. Silence.

He reached for his phone, but Frankie already knew what he would find.

No bars. No service. No way.

They were well and truly stuck. Frankie broke the tense silence with a pulse from the percussion drill. She shifted and braced it again, drilling another anchor hole. If they were stuck, she might as well make the most of it. Her orgasms always left her with a strange buzz of energy, and she needed to burn some of it off or else she'd jump him again, lack of condoms be damned. She also wanted to catch her breath before they attempted the conversation that lingered unspoken between them.

The muscles in her arms shifted and tightened as she switched bits on the heavy drill and caught him staring. "What are you looking at?" she asked.

"A very sexy woman using power tools. She's riveting."

"Ha ha. I see what you did there."

Jake came down the stairs back into the small space, seeming to take up more room than he had before.

"We're stuck," he pouted.

"I know, genius. That's why I got back to work. Either someone will hear the drill or I'll at least get this project done."

"Need a hand?"

She paused at that, looking at his hands, judging their likely ability. "Sure."

He rolled up his sleeves and plucked the hammer out of her tool belt.

"Whoa, whoa, whoa. Easy there, big guy." She took the hammer and dropped it back into the appropriate loop before handing him a spirit level. "Let's start with something easy."

"Easier than a hammer?"

"On a project that doesn't require a hammer? Yes."

"You know, I've watched hours of these projects. I can handle this." He braced his hands on his hips, cocky and assured.

She chuckled. Of course he thought he could do this. She did her job and made it look easy. "You and every other viewer at home. That's the appeal, right? But if everyone could do this, I'd be out of a job."

"Okay, then walk me through the common mistakes people might make." Jake whipped out his phone.

"You're seriously going to film this with your phone?"

"Why not? As you said, you can handle your tools. I'll handle mine."

"But I look..." She ran a hand through her sex-tousled hair

and tugged out her ponytail. On autopilot, she pulled her hair back again and licked her lips. "I'm not even wearing lipstick anymore."

"I won't apologize for that. You look gorgeous and competent. Just walk me through the basics of this project."

Usually she was fine on camera, but this, informal and stripped down, had her nerves fluttering. She could feel the aftershocks of that orgasm still rippling under her skin. There was no way anyone watching this wouldn't know what she'd just been up to. And that wouldn't bother her if she and Jake were an established couple, but they weren't. They hadn't even had a conversation about it yet. But also, she was not ready to have that conversation yet, so she'd give this a go if it meant delaying the inevitable a little longer.

"Okay, fine."

Jake raised the phone and framed his shot. "Go for it."

"Before you start any installation project, it's important to lay it all out. Read all of the directions through to the end, and make sure your tools are in good working order." Jake snorted, and Frankie struggled to keep a straight face but pushed on. "This may seem tedious, but I can't stress enough how important it is to be prepared."

She made eye contact with Jake, and he blushed. She smiled at her discovery, both that this perfectly composed man was capable of blushing and that it made him look softer, younger, more approachable. *Note to self: make Jake blush.*

"This will be a wine rack, and because we are in a small cellar in earthquake country, proper anchoring is important. I'm drilling holes directly into the concrete so that I can sink anchors and mount the rear braces directly to the wall."

Jake tried to contain his laughter and failed. Another snort escaped, and he lowered the phone.

"What's so funny?" she asked with mock sincerity.

"You said drilling holes and mounting and rear bracing in one sentence." Jake chuckled again and tucked his hand into his pocket, shrugging his shoulder. "My sense of humor stopped developing at the age of twelve." He pulled his hand back out and grimaced. "Ugh. Do you have a wipe?"

Frankie stared at him like he'd lost his mind. If she was being honest, seeing him out of sorts made her want to grin like a loon. She had the power to make him lose control, and she liked it. Now that she understood why he'd left her, it made her even prouder that she could get him to loosen up. His fancy clothes and carefully coiffed hair were just a mask he showed to the world, and she had the power to take it off. Who would she find underneath?

"Do I look like the kind of person who carries baby wipes?" She chuckled at his obvious discomfort.

"No, but a guy can hope." Mouth pursed, he wiped his hand on his back pocket before adjusting the front placket of his jeans, pulling down and away. She'd bet anything he was the kind of guy who showered after sex.

Frankie set down the beam she was holding and crossed the small space to him. He watched her warily as she got right up into his personal space. "You seriously can't handle getting a little dirty, can you?" She gripped the edge of his shirt and untucked it on just one side. How long could he tolerate the disarray? "Are you always this uptight?"

"I am not uptight," he protested, tucking his shirt back into his pants.

Frankie countered by ruffling his hair against the part and laughing. He raked a hand through his hair to smooth it, and she untucked the tails of his shirt again.

"Sure you aren't. Do you iron your jeans yourself, or do you send them out with your shirts to the dry cleaner?"

"It's more efficient. I don't have time to do laundry."

"Hmm." She stepped closer, running her hands under the shirt she'd freed. "You know what I think when you walk on set, looking all polished and professional?" She caressed his pecs, pinching a nipple before pressing her lips to the pulse at his throat. She smiled against his skin when she felt him purr beneath her lips. He was so damn fun to tease.

"No. What do you think?" he rasped out.

With a little bite that made him shiver, she released him. "That it'd be awfully fun to mess you up. You know what else?" She glanced over her shoulder as she turned away. "I was right."

She crossed back to her tools, watching him out of the corner of her eye. He tucked his shirt back into his jeans, wincing. He ran his hands through his hair and fastened another button.

"It's fascinating watching you do that."

"Do what?"

"Put yourself back together. I can almost see you pulling your shields back into place."

"Do it often enough and it becomes second nature." He straightened his collar and began to unroll his sleeves.

She placed a hand on his forearm, stopping him. "Leave them. Explain."

"I've been in the public eye since I was a kid. You learn really quick that everyone is looking for a story. The next juicy bit of gossip. The next compromising picture. You learn to keep your weaknesses hidden. Only show them what you want them to have."

Frankie thought back over her life. The pranks she'd played as a kid, the stupid boys she'd dated as a teen, the occasional wild night out as an adult. And none of it had ended up splashed across the cover of a tabloid. How would her life have been different if she'd had to constantly filter herself? "That sounds like a terrible way to live."

Jake shrugged. "If you can, you keep your outer shell flawless. People tend to believe what they see."

Frankie touched a hand to his face, lifting his gaze from the floor to meet hers. She had so many questions. "Do you really have it all together all the time?"

"Irrelevant. I seem like I do, and that's what counts."

It's relevant to me. She began to see his choices and motivations more clearly.

"No wonder you like being a director now. You get to be in charge of crafting what everyone sees."

He nodded, eyes wide and solemn, as if she was the first person to ever see that. "Exactly. And after a lifetime of practice, I'm damn good at it."

"We wouldn't have signed another contract if you weren't," she said matter-of-factly.

"Thanks for that."

"Thank you, for explaining. I'd never have guessed that was the reason."

"I guess it's become more a part of me than I thought."

"But in private? Like now, when no one else is watching? Do you ever loosen up?"

"I'm willing to try."

She gripped his bare forearms and pulled him back in for a kiss. "Good," she murmured against his lips. "Because getting you a little dirty is a massive turn-on." She rubbed a dusty thumb over his cheekbone and he shuddered.

"Hmmm," was all she heard as she kissed him again, pouring all of her excess energy into him. She needed to reward his honesty. She wanted more kisses for herself. Win-win.

Letting him go, she handed him the level again. "Come on. You're so good at staying balanced, this should be a piece of cake. I'll line up the holes, and you can check the level before I screw it in."

Jake snorted again.

"You really are twelve, aren't you?"

"No, just my sense of humor. The rest of me is all grown up."

Frankie gave the bulge at the front of his jeans a cheeky and appraising glance. "That I can confirm. Now get over here and help me finish."

As they traded tools and innuendos, laughing and teasing each other, the wall of wine racks took shape. Frankie's wit, forged as the baby of the family, was sharp enough to keep Jake on his toes. He took out his phone along the way, recording more snippets of her competence and humor. She wondered how he juggled all of the seemingly random footage into a coherent episode. Just thinking about organizing all of that made her brain hurt.

When the last screw was tightened and all of the tools stowed, they sat side by side against the blank wall still waiting for the back-ordered shelves and admired their handiwork.

"You want your ten minutes now?" she asked. The elephant crammed into the tiny room with them needed to be addressed. She might as well pin him down while he couldn't walk away.

Jake nodded and picked up a leftover screw, turning it end over end between his competent fingers. "I've been trying to work this out." He waved his hand between them.

"Yeah? How's that going?"

"Not great. I like you, Frankie."

"That doesn't sound not great." She couldn't see where he was going with this.

"I'm only here through the end of the show. I've got to get back to LA to capitalize on the gains I've made here. I've been away too long."

Frankie's mind zoomed ahead. He was desperately trying to find a reason to stay away from her and maintain his precious control. If she could give him anything, she wanted it to be the knowledge that it was okay to lose control every now and then. She wanted to be that safe space for him, even if it was temporary. She'd just have to keep her heart in line. The alternative—ignoring this growing attraction—left a bad taste in her mouth. She was real tempted to kiss him again and cleanse her palate.

"I see. So now that we've established that I'm not too young, it doesn't matter that we work together, and you're not the asshole you seemed to be, distance is going to be a problem? You are working real hard to throw these roadblocks up, Jake."

"The last thing I want to do is hurt you. And thinking things through helps avoid that."

There's that need for control again. It must be exhausting to constantly be ten steps ahead.

Frankie reached over and stilled his hands. "I have an idea." She waited until he made eye contact with her before she continued. "I want you, and you want me. With me so far?"

He nodded.

"And we both need this show to succeed, agreed?"

He nodded again.

"That will be easier to manage if we have a smooth working relationship instead of bickering all the time, don't you think?"

"Sure."

"In an unrelated observation, orgasms make me super energetic and easygoing, which will make me much nicer to be around." Jake chuckled and pulled her into a side hug. "I'm just saying, I think we should take advantage of wanting each other for as long as we can by screwing ourselves silly."

"I couldn't have said it better myself." He covered her hand with his and kissed her on the forehead with a tenderness that almost made her cry.

She looked at the token he'd left in her hand. Yeah, she was screwed alright.

A loud scraping noise overhead sent them scrambling to

their feet. She looked at her phone. They'd been down here for nearly five hours. She needed to get home, but she did wish they'd stayed trapped a little longer. At least long enough for one more big O. She was destined to be disappointed on that front.

Within moments, the countertop slid back and the door panels swung open, revealing a concerned Enzo.

"Frankie? Oh, thank God! There you are!"

She climbed out first and gave her brother a hug, hoping she didn't smell too much like Jake's cologne. "Enzo! How did you find us?"

"Us?" Enzo peered down into the dark cellar.

Jake stepped out of the shadows and joined them in the light of the nearly finished kitchen. Enzo gave Jake a thorough head-to-toe glare before Frankie cleared her throat and spoke.

"How did you know to come looking for us? I thought for sure we'd be stuck until morning."

"Buster was going nuts and you weren't answering your phone. You always call if you're going to be late," Enzo said, his eyes never leaving Jake.

Jake's phone began to chime now that it had regained its signal and was downloading all of his missed messages.

The quiet had been nice, Frankie mused, her own phone buzzing away in her hand. "No cell reception in the cellar." Frankie grinned and looked at her phone.

"Yeah, that makes sense. So I called Seth because I knew he'd been over here. He told me about finishing the cellar racks. Some idiot moved the rest of the racking in here when it arrived and leaned it against the island." He pointed to where several large boxes were now tipped against the far cabinets, pinned by the sliding island countertop.

"That explains why it wouldn't budge," Frankie concluded. "Well, thanks for the rescue, big brother." She patted Enzo on the chest. "Who knows what would have happened if we'd been stuck in there all night!"

Frankie strolled from the kitchen with a smug glance at Jake over her shoulder to confirm that he was biting back a laugh. Twelve-year-old sense of humor, indeed.

CHAPTER 19

Frankie stood from where she'd been laying flooring and stretched her back. It was mid-afternoon on Thursday, July second. She and the crew were staring down a four-day weekend, and everyone was anxious to get to it.

She strolled from room to room, satisfaction at a job well underway filling her chest, and told each crewmember to go ahead and pack it in. They had been pulling late shifts for months, trying to meet the insane filming demands on top of their construction goals. Her guys had earned every minute of these four days. She was happy to let them start it a few hours early.

The build site settled into stillness, the quiet profound after so many days of busy noise. She touched the textured walls, smoothed a hand over the built-in cabinetry, and marveled at how far they'd come. She could see her parents turning this beautiful space into a warm and inviting venue for wine tastings and events.

She was watching the sun filter through the new energy-efficient double-glazed windows when Jake stepped up behind her.

"Everyone gone?"

She nodded, and he wrapped his arm around her waist and pressed a kiss to the side of her neck. "Gah! I'm a sweaty mess."

"Don't care. I've wanted to do that all day." He tugged playfully on her ponytail and she turned to face him, grinning like a loon.

It'd been like this for weeks. Ever since their quality time in the wine cellar, they'd been careful to keep things professional around the crew. But in private moments, Jake was remarkably tender with her. As someone used to being one of the guys, it made her knees melt when he reminded her that she was indeed a woman. A woman with needs he'd been fulfilling better than anyone ever had before. "Oh really?"

"Yeah, and that's why I can't be too mad about you letting the crew go early." He leaned in and pressed a firm kiss to her lips, one that said, *I missed you.*

"They've earned it. I was just going to walk through and set the alarms. Do you want to do dinner later?"

They'd fallen into a nice pattern of sharing their evening meal a few nights a week, either out at a restaurant or ordered in at his place. It felt cozy, like a warm blanket on a cold night, just the right amount of comfort. Other guys had wanted her around all the time, suffocating her like a warm blanket tucked into the bottom of the bed so her feet couldn't get free. Others hadn't wanted anything but easy hookups, leaving her out in the cold, no blanket at all.

This thing with Jake felt just right. God, and now she sounded like freaking Goldilocks.

But it was true. They spent time together, but had their separate time too. They were each holding up their commitment to making the show a success, and still taking the time to get to know one another better.

ROUGHED IN

"Sure," he said. "Where do you want to go?"

"Why don't you come to my place? I'll make something." Frankie wasn't sure what prompted her, but all of a sudden it seemed right that he should come to her place. He got along great with Buster on the jobsite, and she didn't want him to think he wasn't welcome. True, she'd avoided her apartment in their early weeks together because she didn't need Enzo breathing down her neck about it. The joys of living near family... But things were going so well that she didn't care if Enzo found out.

She didn't miss the hesitation before he replied. "Okay, but I thought you didn't cook..."

"I can pull together a simple meal. Just don't expect my mom's red sauce. How does six sound?"

"Perfect. Listen, there's something else I wanted to talk to you about. What are you doing on Saturday?"

"This Saturday? The Fourth of July?"

Jake rubbed a hand over the back of his neck. "Uh, yeah."

"I was planning on watching the fireworks with my family and enjoying Ma's barbecue. Why? Are you looking for an invite?"

Frankie couldn't believe Jo hadn't already invited Jake to the annual family cookout. Maybe she'd forgotten with all of the new and tiny distractions in her life.

"Actually, no. I've got an invite for you. Come with me to LA."

She stepped back to see if he was joking. "What?"

"The president of the network is hosting a Fourth of July party on a private yacht. I wasn't planning on going, but she specifically sent me an email and asked me to bring you. She wants to meet you."

"Me? Why on earth would she want to meet me?" Frankie's mind leapt into panic mode. "On a yacht? With, like, the entire network of people?" Oh God, what would she talk to them about?

What would she wear? How would they get there? Who would watch Buster? The questions swirled faster than she could ask them. Jake took both of her hands in his and raised them to his lips, which helped anchor her in the moment. She hauled in a deep breath and focused on his eyes.

"It would just be a few hours on Saturday night. We could spend the rest of the weekend together. I could show you my real apartment, take you on a proper date? Think of it as a romantic three-day getaway with a little work meeting in the middle. Please? At least think about it."

"Okay. I'll think about it. Can I let you know at dinner?"

"Of course. I'm going to put in another few hours on edits. See you at your place at six, right?"

Frankie nodded as he strolled away, without a care, as if his words hadn't just thrown her entire weekend into chaos.

⁓

THIRTY MINUTES later she was knocking on Natalie and Enzo's door, with Buster pulling his leash in the opposite direction. "Behave!" she muttered as she tugged him to heel.

"Who is it?" asked a high and happy voice.

"It's Zia Frankie, Daisy. Can you let me in?"

"Did you bring Buster to play?"

"I did. And I need to talk to your mommy."

"Okay. Just a minute."

Frankie heard a scraping noise and the locks clicking. Moments later the door swung open and her seven-year-old soon-to-be niece stood there grinning and holding a step stool.

Shoving the stool out of the way, Daisy dropped to her knees and opened her arms. "Come here, Buster!" Her pup wasted no time snuggling into that offered hug and covering her face with enthusiastic kisses. "We gotta be quiet because Dad is sleeping with the twins."

It still squeezed Frankie's heart every time she realized that her big brother was a dad now. He was so good with Daisy, and now that Laurel and Ash had arrived, his daddy skills had begun to bloom.

Frankie let Daisy take Buster's leash, and he happily followed her into her bedroom. Peeking into the master-bedroom-turned-double-nursery, Frankie grinned. Enzo was passed out cold in the old recliner she'd helped him carry in there, a baby curled up on each shoulder. She eased the door shut behind her, and walked back through what was now a family room to the doorway they'd opened up between Enzo's apartment and what used to be Sofia's. They hadn't had a chance to tackle the major renovations, like removing the second kitchen to expand the playroom for the kids, but at least they had easier access to the other side of their new four-bedroom apartment.

"Nat? Are you in here?" Frankie called out, walking through their living room/kitchen combination.

"I'm just finishing up a tutorial. Come on back! And bring a big glass of water, would you?"

Detouring into the second kitchen, she filled a pint glass with ice and water, steeling herself for the favor she needed to ask. Drawing in a deep breath, she walked the water back in to Natalie.

Nat took the glass in two hands, rubbing it over her forehead before downing half of it greedily. "Nursing for two has turned me into a camel. Thanks. So what's up?"

"Can't I just hang out with my favorite almost-sister-in-law?" Frankie picked at the tear in her jeans.

"I'm your only almost-sister-in-law, and most conversations begin with one person inquiring about the life and times of the other. But most hang-outs don't leave you looking like you're about to toss your cookies… Oh my God! Are you pregnant?"

"What? No! Jeez, I know you and Fi have babies on the brain, but not everyone is leaping into parental bliss!"

"Well, it has been speculated that there's something in the water and someone in your bed, so it's not so far-fetched. But okay, not pregnant." Natalie eyed her carefully, like she could see inside to Frankie's soul. "Just nervous, then. Spit it out. What do you need?"

"I need girl lessons." Frankie's cheeks heated, and she was sure her normally olive skin had flushed dark red.

"Girl lessons? I thought we had established that you are not pregnant."

"But we have also established that I have someone in my bed."

"Right now? Girl, why are you even here? Go!"

Frankie laughed and the tension she'd been holding on to dissolved. "Not right now, but I'd like to keep him there."

"There are all kinds of girls in this world. And you are the one he's choosing to be with, just the way you are."

"I know. I just…I need to know how to do the girly things, you know, all those things you are a professional at doing. I need to be able to put on the polish from time to time. Sofia tried to teach me when we were younger, but I didn't care back then so I didn't pay attention."

"And you care now?"

"Well, he invited me to a thing, and I need to look professional-level girly."

Jake always looked so put together. It was clear he valued order and image. After what he'd told her in the cellar, she could understand why. She'd never had that kind of public pressure. With the show taking off, she tried to grab a clean T-shirt instead of a dirty one when she ran out to the grocery store.

Now, she was going to be stepping into that life, even if it was temporary. She wanted to make a good impression at the network. But more than that, she wanted to show Jake she could thrive in his natural habitat.

Could he picture her in his life? Beyond the end of their show? The closer they got to the end of construction, the more she realized she didn't want their relationship to end with it. Happier than she'd been in years, Frankie wanted this to work. She wanted Jake to want that too, and if it took a little eyeliner to make that vision more attractive, well, she'd put in the effort.

"Well then, my skills are your skills, but you've got to let me film it. It'd make a great series, and you'll never remember it all without it."

"Deal."

Frankie approached the salon chair Natalie had tucked into the corner of the master bedroom in front of a stage mirror. It was still set up for filming her popular online makeup tutorials. Her flawless face and the scattered cosmetics meant she'd just finished a new one.

"We don't have to do this now if you're tired." Frankie took half a step in retreat before Natalie tugged her into the white swivel chair and spun her around.

"Nonsense. I'm fine." Natalie checked her watch. "I've got an hour before the little ones need to eat again. Plus I get another episode without having to scrub my face off, and you get a copy you can watch again later."

Frankie could admit that would be helpful when she tried to do this in LA.

Natalie draped her with a salon cape and steamrolled right ahead, not allowing any doubt to root in Frankie's mind. "Sit right here, and we'll get started. Were you thinking glam or more natural?" Natalie bustled around her, straightening her pots and sticks, wiping down brushes and setting the phone up to record.

Frankie shrugged. "It's a Fourth of July thing, but fancier? Maybe?"

"So mostly natural, but we can vamp up your eyes a little bit. Okay, here we go."

Frankie fidgeted through Natalie's opening patter. This had seemed like a good idea in her head, but now it felt like it was spiraling out of control. Story of her life, lately. First the build, then the party... Now even a simple favor was turning into a production. She took a deep breath and tried to calm down. She was grateful to have Natalie's help, even if it meant sitting in front of a camera again.

"Hello, friends. As you know, our motto here is 'Makeup doesn't make you beautiful. It lets the beauty inside shine.' You might recognize my soon-to-be sister-in-law, Frankie Valenti, from her hit show Million-Dollar Starter Home. She's more likely to be covered in plaster dust than powder, but today we are going to help the outside match her inner beauty. She's been so busy filming her new show, Valenti Vineyards, that she needs a little pampering today. We are going to start with this special cooling avocado mask, and then we'll move on to a look guaranteed to knock that special guy flat on his ass."

Frankie smiled for the camera as Natalie began to smear a cold, goopy, glittering green gel over her cheeks. It reminded her of the time Gabe had wiped a booger on her face when she was five and wouldn't quit pestering him. She valiantly resisted the urge to cringe and wipe it all off.

"So what's the occasion?"

"A Fourth of July party. I want to show him that I can clean up nice."

"Well, if you're talking about who I think you're talking about," Natalie turned and winked at her phone, "it shouldn't be too hard to grab his attention."

"I don't know. He's so out of my league."

"Um, other way around, sister."

"That's sweet, but look at me!" Frankie gestured to the mirror, where the green jelly was starting to dry and look like alligator skin. "I'm the creature from the Black Lagoon!"

"Well, obviously you're not going to show him this look." Natalie chuckled. "When he sees you at karaoke this week, his jaw will drop."

Wait, what? Karaoke? Jake never came to karaoke. Frankie held up a hand to block the camera and whispered. "Who do you think we're talking about?"

"Rico? I mean he's a little goofy, but he's the most eligible guy on the crew and kind of cute if you can get past the cocky—"

Frankie folded in half, shaking with laughter. Her belly ached and the thin, itchy drying mask crinkled around her eyes and her cheeks, giving her the wrinkles of a ninety-year-old. Sucking in a hard breath, she tried for words. "Nat. No. Just no. I'm not… trying to land…Rico." The giggles kept interrupting her attempts to correct the situation.

"If not Rico, then who?" Natalie asked, crossing her arms over her chest, resting them on top of her belly bump. "Because if you try and tell me that glow in your cheeks isn't from getting laid on the regular, I'll call you a liar."

No. No way was she spilling her guts in front of the entire internet.

"Will you delete this part?"

Natalie leaned over and tapped off the video. "Now spill. Who are you dating?"

"I've been seeing Jake."

The eyeliner that Natalie had done on herself really highlighted the way her eyes bugged out of her head. "Wow. I mean, I know I've been off set for months, but wow. I did not see that coming."

"Neither did I, but so far, so good."

"If you're happy, then I'm happy. Just...be careful. He can be a whole lot. That's all I'm going to say." Natalie hugged her from behind, careful not to touch the goo setting on her face. "So what's this thing you're going to?"

"He invited me to a network thing in LA this weekend. On somebody's yacht?"

"Ooooh, the Fourth of July cruise? Swanky! Okay, so we need to glam it up a bit more than I had planned."

Frankie grinned as Natalie turned the camera back on. She liked Nat because her brother was going to marry her. She enjoyed the snarky conversations they had shared on set. But she loved that Natalie was becoming a sister as well. Only Fi had ever talked about boys and relationships with her. And years of training behind a salon chair had likely honed Natalie's relationship diagnostic skills to a fine point.

"I bet you'd all love to know what she just told me, but my lips are sealed! Let's get this makeover started, shall we?"

Natalie peeled the mask off. The light tugging pulled the film off her face and left a tingly, clean feeling behind. Nice, but not worth dipping her face in guacamole on the regular.

Frankie sat back and tried to find the relaxation so many women claimed to feel being "pampered." And failed. She did manage not to squirm in the chair, but she flinched every time Natalie touched her face with some new texture. Cold, creamy, ticklish, poky, wet, sticky, ugh. She tuned out what Natalie was saying for the audience. She would try and figure it out from the video later.

How did women do this every day?

Had she thought she'd gotten better at enduring this with the makeup Natalie did for her on set? Clearly, the makeup artist had been taking it easy on her. No way could she keep this up. Jake was so far out of her league. This attempt to fit into his life was a joke. Her confidence retreated farther and farther into her chest, leaving a hollow feeling where it had swelled before.

When Natalie switched to wedding plans and slight tweaks to the build plan, Frankie didn't have the heart to push back. The paved platform patio and adjustable arched pergola would be great long-term additions to the property but they would also add another ten thousand to an already stretched budget. She'd figure it out though. She wanted to give them the wedding of their dreams.

After one more last spritz of god-knew-what that felt like one of the babies blew a raspberry in her face, Nat spun the chair and made her a little dizzy with her eyes squeezed shut.

"Open your eyes."

Frankie opened her eyes and dropped her jaw almost simultaneously.

"Frankie, look at that woman in the mirror."

"I am. Who the hell is she?" Frankie raised a trembling hand to her cheek, only to hover there, afraid to touch.

"She is one of the strongest, most confident, most beautiful souls I know. I can make your hair curl and your eyes pop, but that doesn't change who you are on the inside. No one worth loving would ever be ashamed to be seen with you."

The kind sincerity in Nat's voice almost undid her hard work as tears welled up in Frankie's eyes. She lowered her hand to rest on Nat's which was still gripping her shoulder as if she could will Frankie into having faith. Frankie chose her old standby, humor, to deflect facing the rising emotion in her chest.

"Is that glitter on my face?" She squinted at the mirror comically and poked her cheek.

Natalie laughed on cue. "No darling, it's just a little shimmering BB cream. Your skin is too gorgeous to cover up. Just a little tinted moisturizer with an SPF thirty built into it."

"Oh, I use SPF fifty every morning."

"Is it made for your face or the beach?"

"There's a difference?"

Natalie covered her face with her hands and let out a little scream, before turning to the camera and speaking directly to her viewers. "We are launching a new series. I'm calling it 'Educating Frankie,' where I will go over the basics for our new viewers just dipping their toes in the makeup game."

The look on her face dared Frankie to argue, but Frankie couldn't. She looked back at the polished and pretty version of herself in the mirror.

She'd spent years learning the foundations of building and now she was damn good at transforming basic houses into gems. Maybe a little education and practice would help her fix her own curb appeal.

"It's a date."

Frankie's head was still spinning when she retrieved Buster from his tea party and made her way back up to her apartment to get ready for her actual date. He nudged her hand with his snout, and she looked down and laughed. She unhooked his leash and stowed it before wiping her hands over his brow.

"Did you get a makeover too, big guy?" She'd have to tell Natalie that Daisy had a stash of blue sparkly eye shadow and pink lipstick that Buster was currently trying to lick off his muzzle. "That must've been some tea party."

She refilled his water bowl and stretched her back. How was she this exhausted from sitting still for half an hour?

As she walked back to her bedroom to change clothes, Frankie's mind raced. Not only had Natalie nailed the laid-back sexy look, but she'd nailed Frankie with her list of requests for the event space. She had until the October weddings to figure out how it would all happen, but her brain insisted on starting now.

The list of changes to the vineyard plans spun through Frankie's filter of building plans and codes and deadlines as she swapped outfits. Fresh black T-shirt and clean jeans in place, she double-checked the mirror to make sure she hadn't screwed anything up. Fluffing the big, sexy curls Natalie had coaxed from her normally dead-straight dark brown hair, she conceded. It was a fair trade. She'd figure out how to make it all work. The plans. The deadlines. This thing with Jake.

She'd just keep working at it until she figured it out.

CHAPTER 20

When Jake opened the door for dinner, Buster greeted him first with paws to his gut and kibble-scented kisses.

"Oh God! Down! Get down, Buster! Off!" Frankie called out as she hustled in from the kitchen.

Buster dropped to all fours and began to aggressively sniff Jake's crotch.

Frankie was trying to get a grip on his collar but was laughing too hard to be effective. Jake handed her the wine he'd brought and grabbed Buster's collar himself so he could save his junk from the ardent puppy love.

"He's feeling frisky. He just finished his dinner." Frankie turned back to chopping veggies.

"How much time before our dinner is ready?"

"Maybe forty-five minutes?"

"Okay, I'll be back. I'm going to take him for a—"

"Don't say it!" Frankie blurted.

"W-A-L-K."

Buster jerked free from Jake's grip and began sprinting in excited circles around the living room, barking loudly every time he passed Jake.

"Jesus Christ! Your dog can spell?"

Jake watched Frankie's shoulders shake as she collapsed into another fit of laughter, bracing herself against the kitchen counter.

Something about her carefree laugh squeezed around his heart momentarily. Her happiness radiated from her, and he felt its warmth wash over him, the small hairs on his arm prickling to attention. He stepped closer and almost got taken out at the knees by the still-racing Buster.

She reached into a drawer and retrieved a leash and a handful of poop bags from their hiding spot, tossing them to him. "If he can see them, he pulls them down and chews on them until you take him out. And yes, in addition to being his personal stylist, Daisy has been teaching him to spell. Knowledge is power and all that."

"Great. What other words does he know?" Jake asked as he blocked one of Buster's laps long enough to grab his collar and get the leash clipped.

"Bed, vet, food, and water so far." Frankie opened the door and Buster lunged, nearly pulling Jake over the couch in his enthusiasm to get outside. "Good luck!" she yelled after them as he got pulled down the stairs.

"I'm gonna need all the luck I can get," Jake muttered. Dog walker wasn't on his résumé, but if he could wear Buster out enough to let them eat in peace, he'd do it.

Jake followed Buster's lead down the stairs and around the front of the six-flat apartment building the Valentis owned and partially occupied. He pulled up short when he literally ran into Natalie and Daisy walking hand in hand, with Enzo behind pushing the twins in a double-wide stroller.

"Hi, everyone! Out for a walk?"

Of course they are, idiot. Jake would've slapped his forehead if he'd been able to let go of the leash. But he needed both hands to keep control of Buster, who started up his happy circles again, this time while tethered—which spelled disaster for Jake's ankles.

"Sit! Stop! Stay! Fuck!"

Nothing he said seemed to have an effect on the dog, but the humans were laughing hysterically.

"I don't think you want him to learn that last one." Enzo chuckled and wiped tears from his eyes. "I don't think I've ever seen you unable to wrangle something under control."

"Sorry. Daisy, don't learn that one either."

Natalie wrapped her arm around the front of Daisy's shoulders and pulled her back out of Buster's way.

"We were just going to get some I-C-E C-R-E-A-M. He knows that word too," Daisy whispered. "He can't spell it yet, but I can."

Natalie grinned. "So, um, what are you doing over here?"

"Frankie invited me for dinner and to talk about the show."

"Dinner. Really?" Enzo paused before adding, "Good luck with that."

Jake suppressed a smile as he tried not to think of just how lucky he'd like to get tonight.

Natalie's eyes crinkled with mischief. "So what did you think?"

"Think of what?" Did she guess? Did she know? Enzo surely suspected after freeing them from the cellar. Had Frankie told anyone about them? What had she said? How long had he stood here silently staring? Man, this relationship business was hard. That was why he generally avoided them. Well, reason number forty-two…

"Sheesh, Jake." Natalie shook her head in disgust. "You didn't even notice?"

"Notice what?"

"Do yourself a favor when you go back up and open your freaking eyes."

Natalie's advice rubbed him the wrong way. What had he missed?

Enzo clapped a hand on his shoulder, breaking the tension. "Well, don't let us keep you from your..."

"Don't say it!" Jake tightened his grip on the leash.

"...stroll," Enzo finished with a grin.

Jake laughed in relief. "Thanks for that. You too."

He watched with a faint tug of envy as the little family unit turned as one and walked—no, *strolled*—toward a sweet treat. Had he ever done that with his parents? He couldn't remember. He added ice cream strolls to his list of grievances to air with his future therapist.

Before he had a chance to go down that rabbit hole of disappointment, Buster took off after a squirrel and nearly yanked his arm out of the socket.

"Okay, you big mutt, let's get our stroll on."

He took Buster around the neighborhood, letting him mark every bush, fence post, and hydrant in a two-mile radius. Once the poor dehydrated pup was panting, Jake turned his steps back to Frankie.

As he was mounting the stairs to her apartment, his phone rang. He looked at the screen and sighed. Brian. Jake debated answering it for half a second, but Brian would keep calling back until he answered. "Hello, Brian. What can I do for you?"

"I can't just call to check in on my favorite showrunner?"

Jake bit back a snort at that blatant bit of flattery. "On the eve of a holiday weekend? What do you want?"

Frankie opened the door. She took Buster's leash and stepped back into her apartment. He followed her in and accepted the glass of wine she offered. Buster lapped at his water like a camel at an oasis.

"I saw that you are coming to the yacht party after all. Will there be good news to share with Madame President?"

"The show is moving along at a good clip. I've got the first two segments for each show through to final edits. I'm just waiting on construction to finish so I can…"

Frankie leaned against her counter and sipped her wine while she waited for him to finish his call. There was nothing he'd like more than to end this conversation, but Brian wouldn't let him go until he got what he called for. Instead, Jake ran through his show update without taking his eyes off her. Now he understood Natalie's cryptic remarks. Frankie looked different, and he drank her in over the rim of his wineglass.

Her hair was down over her shoulders, curling around her face. He'd only ever seen it yanked back in her trademark severe ponytail.

"Jake. Cut the shit. You know what I'm asking."

Brian's reprimand abruptly pulled his attention back to the point of the call. The money. All Brian cared about was getting to tell his boss's boss's boss that they were going to get money back on one of their productions.

"Construction is still ongoing."

"Which means no. I'm sure you can appreciate the position I'm in. If you want to continue making shows for us…well, I'm sure you'll pull it off, Jake. You always do."

"Understood, but don't—" He didn't bother finishing that sentence because Brian had already hung up.

The sun was low in the sky behind Frankie, shining in the window, creating a halo around her head, but that wasn't the only reason she was glowing. She'd done something to her skin. Her lashes were darker. Her eyes luminous. Even as he noted the details with his director's eye, the combined effect stole his breath. Why would she have gone to all this trouble just for a dinner at home?

"What was that all about?" Frankie asked.

"Just business." His answer was more curt than he intended,

but he was on the defensive and didn't really want to explain what Brian had wanted.

"Speaking of business, I need to talk to you about some changes Natalie wants to make, but that can wait until dinner. More wine?"

"Sure. Did you do something different with your hair?"

"I did. Do you like it?"

"I do, but I'm confused."

"Confused about what?"

"Why did you get all dolled up for this?"

"Oh, it's not for tonight. Well it is, obviously, tonight, but I thought if I go to LA with you I should be able to blend in. I didn't think a bare face and a ponytail would cut it."

"No, you sure wouldn't blend in."

Frankie's face fell, and he tipped up her chin so she couldn't hide from him. "And that's not a bad thing. Frankie, you are one of a kind. You will always stand out in a crowd to me."

"Says the man who won't be on display Saturday."

"That's what you think. So you'll come?"

She went up on her tiptoes to snag a kiss. "I sure hope so."

The innuendo in her voice had him leaning in for a deeper exploration of her slick lips. She tasted like wine and strawberries. By the time he came up for air, he was hungry for the next course.

"So what's for dinner?" he asked.

"Oh God! Dinner!"

Frankie sprinted out the door and downstairs to the grill. Jake didn't follow, but he could hear her inventive curses from here. He carefully wiped all traces of laughter from his face as she climbed the stairs with a plate of very dark steaks.

"Not a word, Ryland. Not a word."

"I wouldn't dream of it."

He wisely bit his tongue as she turned her back on him and

began to carve the steaks, carefully cutting away the charred exterior. When her shoulders began to shake, he felt horrible.

Jake stepped up behind her and placed a hand over hers on the knife, halting her shaky progress. "Babe. Hey, come here. Don't cry." He tried to pull her into a hug, but she stepped back.

"I'm not crying." She turned so he could see her face. She *was* crying, but they were tears of laughter. "The look on your face..." She put the knife down and braced herself against the counter as she lost the battle with belly laughs.

Jake let his laughter free and they propped each other up until the worst of the giggles had passed. He held open his arms, and his world shifted when she stepped into his circle, accepting his hug. He would say it tilted off its axis, but it felt more like he'd been going through life at this crazy angle and had only just now had his balance righted.

Her arms locked around his waist, anchoring him to her, and she pressed her head against his chest while her chuckles calmed down. How could he have reached the age of thirty-six and not have known that there was a woman who fit perfectly in his arms? He pressed a kiss to her forehead while she rambled.

"I'm sorry I burned dinner. I'm so not a cook. Ma and Sofia can do dinner. Usually I'm solid on the grill, but then you walked in all hot and bothered, and I got distracted..."

Frankie was running her hands up and down his sides and he was trying to pay attention, but half his brain was being pulled along on a string by her wandering hands.

"So I distract you?"

CHAPTER 21

FRANKIE CAUGHT the blatant satisfaction in his voice and grinned, eyes dry. She raised her hands to his shoulders and squeezed against his muscles full of stress. He melted into her, and she rolled them again.

"Do you like that?" she teased. "Knowing that you walk into a room and all I see is you? All I think is how much I want to ruffle you?"

"Ruffle me?"

"You walk onto the set all crisply combed, buttoned up, and ironed down."

She slid her hands down his chest, smoothing the wrinkles from his cotton shirt. She thrilled at the way his heart leapt beneath her fingers.

Her hands climbed back up around his nape and squeezed. "And there I am, covered in drywall dust or who knows what muck, and I just want to get you a little dirty. Bring you down to my level."

She ran her fingers up into his hair, giving him a good tousle. She was building his anticipation, touch by touch, and he was hooked.

"I really, really like ruffling you," she murmured, her lips still brushing his, light enough to tickle.

"I do like knowing that I distract you. It seems only fair, since you distract the hell out of me."

"Oh really?" Frankie bit her lower lip coyly, and he growled.

"Do you know what I want to do when I see you?" His voice rasped in his throat like he'd just run five miles.

She leaned back and waited.

"I sit for hours every day, watching you on-screen. You walk around the jobsite in complete control. The guys on the crew jump to do your bidding."

Frankie tried and failed to see where he was going with this.

"You are so powerful. So competent and in charge. Nothing ever fazes you."

She swallowed hard. He brushed her curls back from her face and pulled them into a ponytail in his fist.

"And this ponytail. God, I just want to pull it, just to remind you that I can. That I'm the man who gets to kiss your neck and make you shudder." He punctuated his words with a tug and a kiss that made her knees tremble. "The man who gets to kiss these lips until they go limp." She leaned into his body as he took her mouth. "The man who gets to make you lose control."

When he gripped her hips and lifted her onto the countertop, she leaned her head back against the cabinets, unable to keep her spine straight.

"Let me take control tonight. Let me take care of you, Frankie."

She nodded, unable to speak past the lump in her throat. When was the last time a man had wanted to take care of her?

"You work so hard. I think you deserve a little pampering."

A giggle slipped from between her lips and she clapped a hand over her mouth to stop others from joining it.

"What's so funny?"

"I think I'm going to like your pampering more than I liked Natalie's."

"I guaran-damn-tee it."

With a grin, he stripped off her T-shirt and tossed it onto the kitchen floor, already forgotten. His strong hands firmly traced her contours, as if she was the clay and he was the sculptor. It was just as well, because she felt as soft as putty. She so seldom got to be soft...

If this was how he reacted to seeing her in makeup, she had a new incentive to practice.

He put his lips and hands to work on her breasts, kissing and licking, plucking her nipples between his thumb and forefinger, making her gasp. When Buster jumped and put his paws on Jake's ass he fell into her and cursed. Before Frankie could get the giggle under control, Jake had tossed the steak she'd trimmed onto the floor and picked her up around the waist. She wrapped her legs around him and let him carry her back into her bedroom.

He kicked the door closed and dropped her on the bed. But then he paused and looked back at the door. "Buster can't do door handles, can he?"

She laughed so hard that her lungs were aching by the time he got her jeans tugged off. When he knelt in front of her and set his mouth to her, she was gasping for air. Then he added his fingers, and she stopped breathing.

After her first orgasm, he stripped his own clothes and donned a condom before joining her back on the bed to continue seducing her.

He pushed her up to her knees and took her from behind, pulling her hair back until she felt every thrust all the way up to her scalp. He braced her arms against the headboard and whispered about how he wanted to take her like this against the door of the production van. He rolled them to their sides, until they were spooning as they fucked, so he could touch her arms and shoulders, her back and neck, praising her strength even as he made her weak. She was content to follow his lead.

Every kiss, every groan, every whispered word of praise pushed her further from control until she was a shaky, sweaty mess, shuddering beneath his heavy body, reveling in the feel of his thick cock pulsing inside her. His weight pressing her into the bed was the only thing keeping her from floating away. She buried her face in his shoulder and treasured the sensations ricocheting through her.

When he lifted himself from her with a wince, she saw her mascara smeared across his shoulder. Frankie raised a hand to her face and tried to wipe away the damage. Nothing sexier to find in your bed than a smudgy raccoon. She grimaced at that image and tried to wipe the remains of her lipstick from his neck.

Jake put a hand over hers. "Stop. Leave it."

"But—"

He moved his hand to her lips, cutting her off. "You are so beautiful," he said. "With or without the makeup, you slay me."

The intensity in his eyes scared her, like he could see straight into her soul. She wasn't ready to share that part of her, so she reached for her shield. "I bet you say that to all the girls you fuck blind." She'd intended to tease him, but the minute she said it horrible images of who those other women must have been danced behind her clenched eyes.

"Nope. Only you, Francesca." He kissed her closed eyelids.

"Don't call me that. It makes me feel like I'm in trouble."

"Maybe you are." Jake matched her teasing tone and poked a finger into her ribs, tickling her into opening her eyes.

"I can't quite figure you out." She ran her fingers through his hair again, and he damn near purred.

"Good," he grunted.

"Why is that good?"

"Because I've seen you tackle problems. You don't quit. If I make myself enough of a problem, you'll have to keep figuring me out forever."

Her heart clenched at that word. *Forever.* Was that even possible? And why did she suddenly want that so damn badly?

∼

AFTER ROUND TWO, Frankie pulled herself into the kitchen and made them instant ramen for sustenance. She was getting lightheaded, and it felt safer to blame that on a lack of food than on her unsteady heartbeats. Plus, Jake needed to keep up his energy. She even made an effort to garnish with frozen corn and peas. With a grin, she dropped a few baby carrots into Jake's bowl.

She felt ridiculously proud of her prank when he fake gagged and picked the offending orange vegetables out of his soup with his fingers and tossed them at her. His laughter followed her into the kitchen as she went back for the wine. They cuddled on her couch, wrapped in her favorite throw blanket. Buster was passed out on the floor, snoring, his belly distended from his feast. There wasn't a scrap of that steak or any carrots left on the floor. No wonder he was comatose.

They watched a movie that she didn't pay attention to, and Jake told her about the people she would meet down in LA, and all the places he wanted to take her. When she was sleepy, he snuggled her close and let her doze with his heart pulsing steadily under her ear. It was all so cozy that his request for forever seemed perfectly reasonable as she drifted off to sleep.

∼

In the light of morning, Frankie looked at herself in the mirror and cringed. Scrubbing her face, she washed away the last traces of that glam girl and slathered on her new sunscreen. See? She could learn. She pulled her tangled curls into a ponytail and brushed her teeth before tucking her toiletries into a travel bag.

She tossed the bag of products Natalie had given her into her suitcase, along with a pair of jeans and her Chucks. A few T-shirts and fresh socks and underwear got tossed on top. When Jake came into the bedroom with a steaming mug of coffee, she was still staring into her closet.

"Why the frown?" He kissed the back of her neck. "When I left, you were limp and grinning."

"Yeah, well now I'm awake and trying to figure out what the hell to wear tomorrow. All of my yacht wear is so last season."

"Or…" He nibbled on her ear and sent a shiver down her spine before he continued. "You can just pack what you'll be comfortable in."

"I don't want to embarrass you, and you've seen what I am comfortable in. Somehow I don't think torn jeans and a band T-shirt is going to pass muster."

"Why don't I take you shopping when we get to LA? You'll get a new outfit as a souvenir."

"And what will you get out of this deal?" Frankie asked suspiciously.

"An extra thirty minutes this morning before we drop Buster with your parents and leave for the airport. Hmmm, how to put those minutes to good use?"

Frankie laughed and gasped when he put down his coffee and took her back to bed. She could worry about tomorrow, tomorrow.

∼

"Is this really your apartment?" Frankie dropped her suitcase by the door and toed off her gym shoes. The creamy marble floors were pristine, and nothing was out of place. That might be because he hadn't lived here for months, but she didn't think so. Jake seemed like the kind of guy who liked his things to be in order and under control.

"Home sweet home. I bought this the day after I turned eighteen and made it my man cave. When I turned thirty, I called in a designer to help me renovate it into the 'beach chic oasis' you see before you." Jake punched in the code to turn off the alarm and dropped his keys in a basket by the door. "Come on in. Make yourself at home."

"I'm afraid to touch anything." Everywhere she looked there was another detail that told her exactly how expensive this condo was. Inlaid marble trim braided around the edge of the room, linen couches that wouldn't last five minutes with Buster, a freaking custom driftwood sculpture in front of a burbling wall of water.

Jake took her hand and placed it on his chest, and she leaned into him. "See? You're not afraid to touch everything. It's just an apartment. This is the living room, kitchen is through there, and there are three bedrooms and two baths in the back. Relax. This is supposed to be a vacation."

"How the hell am I supposed to relax when I'm nervous about breaking something priceless? That is capital-A Art on the wall." Frankie pointed and stepped back into a side table, causing a mounted piece of coral to teeter precariously. "Fuck!" She grabbed for it and caught it before it fell.

Jake just laughed. "If you break something, you can just pay me back in kisses. Deal?"

Frankie didn't answer. The reality of his home opened her eyes to just how wide the gap was between them. When he was living in a hotel in Silicon Valley or inhaling free coffee at the craft services table, it was easy to forget that he was ridiculously wealthy.

This was a mistake. She shouldn't have come down here. Maybe there was another flight she could catch and be home in time to take Buster for his walk.

"Frankie, look at me." Jake gripped her shoulders and her spinning thoughts quieted. "It's just stuff. It doesn't change who I am or who we are together."

"Sure, yeah, of course." The lies just spilled from her mouth until he kissed her quiet. The kisses turned to caresses, and he backed her down the hallway into his bedroom.

Frankie happily followed him. He pushed all of the worries out of her head, replacing them with pleasure and whispered reassurance. She matched him beat for beat, kiss for kiss. Here they were equals. They came together in a quick frenzy of need. And she kept herself present. He gave, and she gave, and they sprinted together over the edge of anticipation into bliss.

This was the part of their relationship that made the most sense. Falling into bed was so much easier than falling into love.

In the sweet, sweaty aftermath, Jake rolled onto his back and starfished on his bed.

"I have wanted to do this for weeks." He made an abbreviated snow angel in his twisted sheets.

"What? Burrow into your own bed?"

"Yes, with you." He traced a finger down her bare arm. She curled into his side like a kitten and snuggled in, running her fingers through the dark hair on his chest. "I've wanted to share this part of my life with you."

Frankie didn't say anything to that, not wanting to spoil the lovely mood, but she still wasn't convinced there was space for her here, despite the ocean of taupe satin she was currently lounging in.

"You're still nervous about tomorrow, aren't you?" This was more statement than question, so Frankie didn't offer up an answer. He sighed when she sat up and began to put her clothes back on. "Okay, okay. I get it. Let's go find you a dress."

CHAPTER 22

JAKE FOLLOWED Frankie up the gangplank and only stared at her ass once. He'd gotten distracted by her hips, and then followed the bare curve of her spine from her waist to her shoulders. She'd kill him if he kissed her there, at that spot where her neck curved into her hair. They were at a work function, and she was still nervous. He wasn't about to add to that by broadcasting their relationship. But he'd kiss that spot twice later to reward his restraint.

He was so gone for her. It was getting harder and harder to do his job around her. He found himself easing off on the challenges he threw in her path on the jobsite. He had the bulk of them filmed already anyhow. It was really hard to watch her struggle, but it was going to make her triumph all the sweeter. And he had no doubt in his mind that she would triumph.

She was the most determined person he'd ever met and had the skills to pull it off. The show was going to be a hit once they finished the last bit of filming. Juggling one build over six different episodes was challenging, because everything was going to be done at about the same time, so he couldn't put any of the episodes in the can until they were completely finished and had filmed the reveal. He couldn't wait. In a few short weeks, all of his hard work would pay off when he could show the network that they had been right to trust him.

Frankie fiddled with the strap of the gown they'd found yesterday. With the help of a stylist he'd worked with in the past, they had settled on a red backless calla lily number with thin straps and a plunging neckline. The long slit up the front turned her leg into the stamen of the lily, while the dress formed the curled petal. Frankie's thin frame played off the barely there maxi-dress beautifully. The true genius though was the long skirt. It rippled and rolled as she walked.

She'd fought him on heels. He'd wanted to see her legs in them, even if stilettos were banned on deck. She could have worn the wedges. Frankie argued that being in a dress *and* on a boat were challenges enough, and that she needed to be able to walk. The bohemian tan leather sandals she wore gave the dress a more laid-back vibe. Just the right approach for a party like this. Put together but not trying too hard. His director's eye and his lover's heart were in agreement.

She was confident beauty in motion as she strode onto the yacht and joined the line at the bar. And he was the lucky fuck who got to stand by her side.

Jake grinned as she came back with two flutes of champagne and handed him one. Life was good.

He scanned the growing crowd on board, seeing fellow showrunners and executive producers he'd worked with in the past. There were a few "talents" mingling as well. Nobody too outrageous. He could just swan through the next five hours, glad-handing and small talking, and then he'd have the rest of the weekend to hole up with Frankie.

Jake wondered if he should make reservations at his favorite brunch place, or if that would be presumptuous. He toyed with the idea of taking her up to the Getty. Would she like that? She literally tugged him from his thoughts, her grip tightening on his arm.

"Is that Wilder Malone?"

He followed her gaze through the crowd, and noted the baseball-star-turned-home-designer. "It is indeed. He's doing a show where he creates sports-themed man caves for guys and surprises them with celebrity visits. Want to meet him?"

Frankie whimpered and turned her back on the guy. "I. Can't. Do. That," she hissed.

"Of course you can. I'll just ask him to come over—"

She gripped his button-down shirt up by the collar and pulled him down to her level. "Don't you dare." Her glare was furious but he saw the fear beneath it.

"Frankie, listen. I know you feel out of your depth here, but I'm going to let you in on a little secret. You are a talent too. People here will want to meet you because they've fallen for you on TV. They are waiting anxiously for this new show. You one hundred percent belong on this boat as much as anyone else does." He clinked his champagne to hers. "You're a star, baby."

Frankie shook her head and laughed. "You're crazy, you know that?"

"Crazy for you." It scared him a little to think how much he meant that. He caught himself right before he leaned in to kiss her.

"Hey, hey! If it isn't J.R. Hudson!"

Great, Fowler is here.

"Very funny, Greg. You know I go by Jake Ryland now."

"I'd heard...but I'm not looking for Jake. I need J.R."

Greg Fowler was a new hotshot showrunner whose style was all flash and little substance. Jake turned away, intending to dismiss the asshole, but the man grabbed his arm.

"Don't you even want to hear my proposal?"

"Not particularly, if you can't even get my name right."

"Fine, *Jake*, here's the idea. We renovate an actual house to recreate the set of Hudson House in honor of the twenty-fifth anniversary. We get actual items from the set plus whatever recreations we can afford. Then we list it on a home swap site and charge people a mint to stay there."

"Trying to cash in on nostalgia? Good luck with that."

"I don't need luck. I need you. To be the host."

Jake's blood froze, but Frankie stepped up and took his hand in hers.

"That's a nice offer, but Jake doesn't act anymore. Besides, he's way too busy on our shows to take on another one."

Frankie's free hand rubbing his bicep would look like a gesture of comfort to anyone else, but she was restraining him from tearing this asshole a new one. And he could appreciate the wisdom in that. Even if the asshole deserved it.

"That's not what I heard." Greg leered at Frankie. "In fact, I put in to be his replacement myself, but I guess they went a different direction."

"Well that's a blessing." The last thing Jake wanted was to hand over his projects to this jerk who would make them loud and obnoxious. "As for the Hudson House project, Frankie is right. I don't work in front of the camera anymore."

"Come on, Jake, don't be…"

Jake didn't catch the rest of Fowler's argument because he'd tugged Frankie's hand and they left, weaving through the crowd. It was a slow escape because every few feet someone stopped to talk to one of them, but at least Greg took the hint and didn't pursue them. Frankie carried conversations with laughing good humor and teased their way across the dance floor. It felt effortless, the way she worked the room. She fit right in, and he was grateful for her support. She was amazing.

Frankie nudged him into the line at the open bar. She handed him another glass of champagne. He sipped deeply while she accepted a fresh one from the bartender. Then she turned to him, eyes earnest and full of questions.

"What did he mean?" she asked.

"What did who mean?"

"What's-his-name Gary? Gray?"

"Greg. Greg Fowler. Fellow showrunner and general pain in the ass."

Frankie nodded and sipped slowly before she spoke. "He said he'd applied to take over for you?"

Jake rubbed a hand over the back of his neck, which was suddenly prickling. Had he developed a Spidey Sense for when he'd done something that would piss Frankie off? That could come in handy...

"Yeah, I'm more of a development kind of guy. I get shows up and running for a few seasons, you know, work out the kinks. Once the format is solid, I hand it off to someone else."

"And when are you planning on handing us over?"

Jake looked at the ground as he answered. He didn't want to see the look in her eye. "Season three will be run by someone else."

There was a long pause before Frankie spoke again. "Do you know who it will be?"

"Nothing has been finalized but I've made some requests. It all depends on who is free when Adrian and Fi are ready to start up filming again." He dared a glance at her then and saw her fighting to be stoic. Her jaw clenched and unclenched as she managed to stay calm in a room full of high-profile strangers. Damn, she was impressive. "Trust me. I won't leave the show with just anybody. And it sure as hell won't go to Fowler."

"What will you do next?" This came at nearly a whisper.

"I don't know yet." It was the truth. He'd had several projects pitched his way, but nothing had felt quite right. He hadn't been able to think clearly about it since they'd gotten together. "You know I have to go back to LA..."

Frankie just nodded and sipped her champagne, but her eyes were unusually shiny. "It just hadn't hit me that the show would be run by someone else. And that you'd be so happy to leave."

He didn't want to think about this. He didn't want it to be over. Not when he and Frankie were just hitting their stride... But it was inevitable. Her life was up north with her family, and his was wherever the next challenge took him.

A few weeks ago, he'd have told her that whatever they had was temporary. In fact, he had. But now he wished things could be different. They wouldn't be, but he wished it all the same. He wanted to take away the tears in her eyes and the tightness in his chest. But he couldn't lie to her. If there was one thing his life as a child actor had taught him, it was that for better or worse, everything came to an end.

CHAPTER 23

"Jake! How are you?" A short woman with a silver-gray blunt bob latched onto his other arm, interrupting his search for something to say to make everything okay again.

He turned to hug her and patiently received her air kisses. Lila Finch was a powerhouse in the industry. President of their network by age fifty, she had a career path he admired the hell out of and would love to emulate. This was her party. "I'm well. Lila Finch, let me introduce you to—"

Lila beat him to the punch. She stretched her hand out toward a rapidly blinking Frankie. "Frankie Valenti. It's a pleasure. I'm so glad Jake was able to convince you to come. You're quite the sensation."

"Lila is the president of the network. This is her boat and her party," Jake explained.

Lila laughed. "This *is* my circus and these *are* my monkeys."

"Well, thank you for inviting me, and for taking a chance on the Valentis."

"I knew the minute I saw Adrian and Sofia on-screen that I'd made a good investment."

Frankie nodded and looked down into her glass. Jake wanted

to pull her into his side, but he didn't think she'd appreciate it. He supported her with words instead. "The whole cast has really pulled together to make it a success."

"Don't get me wrong. I really love how your character has developed, Frankie. You are fresh and funny. And your version of the pilot for Valenti Vineyards is testing really well. Is everything on track to finish on time?"

"Um, yes. We'll be wrapping soon," Frankie answered hesitantly.

"Excellent. What's next for you?"

"I'm, uh, not sure." Frankie blinked rapidly, and Jake placed his hand at the small of her back, the only socially acceptable physical support he could offer.

"Well, I hope you consider continuing to work with us. We can shuffle the talent to cover hijinks on MDash if you want to keep doing solo projects. There are a few other rags-to-riches workups I've got sitting on my desk. We are very interested. I'll have my people send you a pitch." Lila turned her attention back to Jake, so he couldn't focus on making sure Frankie was okay. "You've done quite well for yourself, Ryland."

"Thank you."

"You've got a good eye for story and a deft hand. I'll be looking for your next proposal on my desk. Enjoy the rest of the party."

"Yes, ma'am."

She strolled away and Jake held himself real still until she was out of sight. Then he pumped his fist and growled, "Yes!"

"I take it that was good news?" Frankie asked dryly.

"Lila Finch asking for proposals? Yeah, that's the best news. That's what I've been working for. I'll finally have a chance to choose my own projects." The potential he read between the lines made him giddy. His mind was swirling with possibilities.

Frankie stepped back and crossed her arms. "I'm sorry that working on our little show has been such a trial."

She was mad? Now? Years of effort were coming to fruition, and he could hardly think straight himself. "Come on. You know it's not like that, Frankie."

"Sure. Of course it's not. I must not understand how this all works."

"Frankie—"

"I need some air. I'm going out to catch the fireworks."

What could he do but let her walk away?

He tucked his hands in his pockets and was watching her go when someone tapped him on the shoulder. He turned around and was instantly taken back twenty years. "Brittani! Hi."

She stepped into his offered hug but didn't squeeze him tight like she had when she'd played his little sister on Hudson House. Her limp arms felt all wrong. The years hadn't been kind, but she still had that innocent look about her eyes that had won her a place on the show and in the hearts of their fans. "Hey, Jake."

"How are you? How have you been?" His surprise pushed inane questions out of his mouth.

"I'm good. I'm good." She said it with varying emphasis, as if she was trying to convince herself of that as well.

"Okay..."

"No, that's a lie. I've been better, but I'm getting better. One day at a time." She stepped back from his hug and took a deep breath, like she was steeling herself to talk to him.

He remembered the days when they'd run around the set together, laughing and playing, sharing secrets and pulling pranks on each other, even being each other's official first kiss. How had they gotten from that to this?

"I'm sorry to ambush you, but after you wouldn't talk to your agent, I figured the odds were even worse that you'd take a phone call from me."

The reunion show. Of course. She wasn't here to catch up or reminisce about old times. She had only come to find him because she wanted something from him. Typical. "How did you know I would be here?"

"I didn't. A friend of a friend was coming and I begged my way into being her plus-one in hopes that you would be here. And here you are."

"Here I am." Jake sipped his champagne and wondered if Frankie was okay. His palms had itched to pull her into a hug, but he couldn't in front of all these business colleagues. He scanned the wall of windows that opened onto the deck, hoping for a glimpse of red that would reassure him.

"This was a mistake." The quiet words held a wealth of disappointment. Britt's eyes glittered with sadness and something darker. Shame? Guilt? Resignation?

"Britt…"

His use of her nickname seemed to straighten her spine.

"No, you don't get to call me that if you can't even hear me out. Out of everyone, I expected you would understand. We were friends once."

They had been closer than friends. They'd been the sibling stand-in for each other, growing up together under the watchful eye of millions. And losing her had hurt like hell. He had no desire to revisit those memories. "I just think it's time to move on."

"What do you think I'm trying to do? I did what you did and transitioned to older roles. I'd aged out of cute little sister parts, even though I was still technically a kid, so they sexed me up and threw me to the wolves. And my big brother wouldn't even talk to me anymore."

"What's that supposed to mean?"

But Brittani was on a roll, anger pushing her past the sadness. "You know what that world was like. I saw you at the parties, even when you gave me the cold shoulder."

Jake was stunned by that comment. It had been the other way around. His show family had disappeared on him just when he'd needed them most. What was she talking about?

Brittani pressed on. "The booze, the drugs, the men who don't care that you're sixteen and high as a kite. I lost everything that mattered, so I leaned into the things that could make me forget. It seemed easier than fighting my way back to a world that didn't love me."

"Britt, I had no idea. Why didn't you talk to me?"

"When exactly was I supposed to do that? When you never showed up at Martin's barbecues? Or when you wouldn't take my phone calls? Oh I know, maybe I should have talked to you on the reunion shows you refused to do."

Jake was reeling. Her words punched him in the solar plexus and left him gasping. Years of pain and abandonment issues pressed on his chest, making it hard to breathe. "What? There weren't— No one ever called— What?"

She was looking at him like he was crazy but he didn't care. When the show had ended, everyone had said all the things people say at the wrap party.

Let's do lunch.

I'll call you.

Can't wait to work with you again.

But none of those things actually happened. None of it had been real. To find out they had been meeting all these years without him cut to the quick.

"You have no idea what I'm talking about, do you?" Brittani asked carefully.

Jake just shook his head, still unable to breathe properly, let alone speak.

"How could you not know?"

When Jake had left that set, it had been worse than any

breakup. It had felt like he was the sole survivor of a car crash. He hadn't just lost a girlfriend; he'd lost his entire extended family in one fell swoop. The people who had been closer to him than his own screwed-up family, just...poof, gone. But in a way it was worse than a car crash, because no one was dead. They'd chosen not to love him anymore. Unlike the fairy-tale life he'd led on-screen, when this story reached the end he'd been back where he started with his washed-up alcoholic of a father and his hyper-controlling, ambitious mother.

That's when it clicked. His mother. She'd had every reason to want to isolate him and keep him dependent on her. She'd pulled his strings personally and professionally for years for her own gain. He coughed to clear his throat of the lump that had lodged there. *So much lost time.*

"I swear, I didn't know about any of that stuff. I thought...I thought you guys had abandoned me. I missed you so damn much. That's why I didn't want to do a reunion. It would have hurt too much to see you and then lose you all again. But I'd bet money on my mother being the one running interference. God, I wish I had known."

He opened his arms and Brittani stepped back in for another hug, this one longer and truer than the first. This was the hug he remembered.

"God, I missed you guys," Jake whispered against her hair.

"I'm so sorry I didn't push harder. I didn't know. Then again, there were a lot of years that I wasn't aware of a whole lot."

He leaned back to look at her—her eyes clear and full of emotion, body thin but strong. He hoped the past tense meant she had battled her demons and won.

"How are you now?" he asked.

"I'm good. I've got one year of sobriety coming up."

"I'm glad to hear that. I wish I had been able to help sooner."

"Well you can help me now. This reunion, I'm planning it in

honor of my first sober year. I want to raise awareness of what I went through, and raise money for the group that saved me. I need..." Her voice cracked and she swallowed hard. "I need to take a positive step back in front of the cameras that tried to break me. I need to know that I can. And more than that, if I can help someone else avoid my path or see a way out of it, I need to do that too." She squared her shoulders as she spoke, making her pitch and standing up for herself.

Puzzle pieces that for years had refused to make sense were still shifting and settling into a complete picture in his head. But he knew in his heart what the final picture would be. If there was a chance his family hadn't abandoned him, then he had years of catching up to do. And this cause, this triumph of will, was the perfect reason to push past his own insecurities and try again. The idea that he might regain what he'd lost and had spent a lifetime trying to replace was tempting as hell.

"I have two questions. One, when do you need me? And two —" He hesitated as she hugged him with a happy squeal. "Do you think they can forgive me?"

"One, we're filming next weekend. And two, there is nothing to forgive. Listen, when I was at my lowest, I didn't turn to my parents. I called Martin. He picked me up, opened his home to me, helped hook me up with the Sisters of Solace. He said he was glad I had turned to him, and that he would always be there for me. I know he still loves you too, Jake. Come to the reunion show and find out."

"I will. You can count on me. I know I haven't shown it, but—"

She cut him off with a finger to his lips. "We've lost enough years to regret. To fresh starts." She tapped her glass of club soda against his flute and grinned.

"To fresh starts."

ROUGHED IN

FRANKIE LEANED ON HER ELBOWS, champagne going flat and warm in the glass she held suspended over the railing. She'd been doing so well. After three hours of small talk and fake smiles, she had managed to stay on her best behavior. For a split second, she'd let herself believe she could fit into his world.

She had tucked away observations to laugh over with Jake later. She hadn't tripped on her freaking dress or spilled her wine. When Wilder Malone had stepped behind her in the buffet line and complimented her comedic work on MDash, she'd returned the favor, gushing over his Hall of Fame chances and quoting his career stats. When he'd suggested crossover opportunities between their shows, she kept her cool and said she'd think about it. Why had her words deserted her with the president of the freaking network?

She knew. The reality of Jake moving on had punched her right in the heart and shattered her inner composure. She was happy he'd be getting what he'd worked so hard for, but damn, it sucked for her. She'd gone and fallen for him. She loved the asshole, and he was thrilled to be moving on.

It was her own damn fault. She should've kept her walls up.

She turned to see the first of the fireworks bursting over the marina. The bright explosions of gunpowder and patriotism did little to calm her inner battle. The way each blast rattled through her chest was oddly satisfying though, if only because it distracted her from her aching heart.

She was so focused on ignoring what was going on inside that the hand on her shoulder startled her, and she did spill her champagne. Right down the front of her dress.

"Damn it!" She brushed ineffectually at the stain spreading down the bodice of the gown that had cost half of her rent.

Jake laughed. "Shit. I'm sorry. I didn't mean to scare you."

But he *was* scaring her. She'd thought she could trust him. She'd all but handed him her heart on a platter. This evening, seeing him in his natural habitat, had her doubting her judgment there.

"Did I see Wilder talking to you?"

"Yeah, he came by to say he loves the show and wants to do a crossover episode."

"That's great!" Jake gushed, and then paused, searching her face for clues. "Isn't that great?"

"Sure, it's great." Frankie tried to muster enthusiasm, but clearly failed because Jake was still staring. "I mean, I don't know why you'd be excited about it. It's not like you'll be around to set it up." She watched his face as she tossed in that last bit. It *looked* like pain on his face. Back home, she'd probably have believed she had truly hurt his feelings. But seeing him here, surrounded by all of these fake people he called friends, she wondered instead how good an actor he still was. Was she being played? The rest of his words were drowned out by the fireworks.

Frankie deliberately turned her attention back to the violent bursts of sound and light. Better to keep her thoughts on the ones turning the harbor into a stunning watercolor than focus on the ones exploding inside her chest.

As the patriotic display reached a crescendo, so did the sob she'd been trying to keep trapped in her throat. Quiet tears chased down her cheeks. All of her earlier bravado gone, she pressed her palms to her face and tried not to think about anything at all.

In the quiet after the cacophony, she finally faced Jake.

"I want to go home."

CHAPTER 24

AFTER THE LONG WEEKEND, Tuesday morning was brutal. Everyone was dragging. Half the crew showed up late or hung over. Frankie couldn't even call them on it because her own head was threatening to split in two after indulging in a wine-and-Netflix binge late Monday night to try and stop her brain from spinning things out of control.

She had flown home solo from LA, needing some space after that overwhelming party. Jake had stayed behind to take care of the meetings he'd scheduled around their trip. He'd explained, but she hadn't been listening. Too intent on retreating to lick her wounds, she'd barely paid attention to the conversation they'd had as he drove her to the airport Sunday morning.

He would be here today. Frankie hoped they could work through the weird vibe that had settled between them after the party. Could they get back to the place where she trusted him?

Something about the thousands of conversations she'd had was niggling at the back of her mind. Some little tidbit she felt like she should have paid more attention to.

She walked into the production trailer hoping to find him.

Lorena sat at one of the bays of editing monitors, scrolling video back and forth, but Jake was nowhere to be seen.

She looked over Lorena's shoulder, curious about what she was working on. A scene of her dealing with the latest snafu of broken tiles played in forward and reverse as Lorena moved her mouse back and forth.

"Whatcha doing?" Frankie asked, laying a hand on Lorena's shoulder. She bit back a laugh when the woman jumped in her chair and whipped her headphones off.

"Jesus, Frankie. You scared the crap out of me."

"Sorry, I thought you heard me come in."

"I can't hear a thing with these noise-canceling headphones on."

"What's this?" Frankie hadn't paid too much attention to the actual process of making the show.

"I'm trying to decide which version of the tension trigger works better here, you discovering the broken tiles or the guys finding it and reacting by not wanting to tell you."

Frankie's brain poked her hard. "What do you mean by tension trigger?"

"That's what I call the point in each episode that ramps up the tension, you know? Makes the viewer think, 'Can she really pull this off?'"

"There's one in each episode?" Frankie felt like she was walking through mud, struggling to make the connection. "How do you make sure you get something for each show?"

Lorena just looked at her like she couldn't possibly be this slow.

Oh my God. How could she have been so blind? Frankie had thought this build had more than its fair share of disasters. Because they'd been staged on purpose! Her mind walked back over every setback, every snag, every sleepless night she'd spent worrying about how to get it all done and not go bankrupt.

She'd been sabotaged.

She needed to see how badly she'd get slammed in the actual show. Was this going to kill her reputation? If she looked like a fool who couldn't run a build site, why would anyone trust her to run Valenti Brothers?

"Lorena, can you pull up the pilot for me?"

"Which one?"

That Lila lady had said that her version was testing well. Maybe it wouldn't be too awful if people were liking it. "My version?"

"Sure thing. It's not quite done yet, but here's what we have so far."

With a few clicks, Lorena had pulled up the first episode, and they watched it in silence. Frankie had to admit the story flowed. It was the kitchen episode, and there was just enough give-and-take, just enough humor to balance the serious drama of the missing racks and the delayed concrete.

She desperately tried not to think of what else had happened in the wine cellar, but when the footage Jake had filmed with his phone popped up on the screen, she had no choice. It was emblazoned across the screen. Her face was softer, happier. Her post-coital bliss there for everyone to see. She had trusted him with so much. The magnitude of her error was becoming more and more clear with every frame.

Thankfully, it switched to a stupid drawer pull contest she'd suggested and cut off right before the reveal. It was good. Damn the man.

But something was still prickling in the back of her mind.

"I've got to hand it to him. Jake is a genius at getting those shots to land. You come across as a fun, funny, and damn competent narrator."

"What's in the other version?" Frankie asked, her brain finally catching up.

Lorena's face blanked and she looked back at the screen. "Oh, I think it's just some backup rolls..."

"Lorena. Don't bullshit me. Play the other one."

"Shit," the other woman muttered, but she still clicked open the other file.

As Frankie watched a recut of the show she'd just seen, her rage jumped from simmer to boil. The "tension triggers" she could almost understand from the viewpoint of the show. She hated that he'd put her in compromising positions, but she could see why he'd done it. But this... This lit a fire in her gut.

On the screen were most of the same shots she'd just watched, but they were interspersed and overlaid with clips and voice-overs of Dom, mansplaining the process and every "mistake" she'd made.

As the episode unwound, Frankie felt each scene cut to her father like a lash.

Lorena was no idiot. She was picking up on the tension radiating from Frankie and tried to alleviate it. "These were just insurance rolls for the production office."

"But if they didn't like me, these would be the other choice."

Lorena's voice and shoulders fell. "That's right."

As more of the episode played, Frankie's worst nightmare came to life on-screen. She looked like a bumbling idiot. She knew that television often spliced together misleading clips to create a story, but all of these things had happened. She had tripped over the pile of two-by-fours, and thrown her hammer during demo only to have it bounce uselessly off the wall.

Hearing her father's criticism overlaying the damning video solidified that kernel of doubt she'd harbored in her heart. She fought the voice in her head every day, that voice that said maybe she couldn't handle the pressure. Maybe she wasn't ready to take over the family business. She certainly didn't need to be battling for her pride in the court of public opinion as well. The more she watched, the harder it was to keep the tears trapped inside. Her own father didn't think she could pull this off.

He didn't trust her skills or her judgment and had deliberately made a deal that would keep her working off her debt to him forever. Each word Dom spoke slashed her confidence and pride. It didn't reach her heart though.

That was already shredded by Jake's betrayal.

She'd opened herself up to him, and he'd exploited that trust.

Frankie slapped at the keyboard to make it stop and pushed away from the console.

"Where are you going?" Lorena warily leaned back in Jake's chair.

"To go kick some asses."

SHE WALKED the property hunting for Jake. Crewmembers dodged out of her way and averted their eyes. No one wanted to be the one to catch the anger that was flowing through her like hot lava. She could only imagine what her face looked like. The smashed boxes of glass tiles on the pallet that had been delivered yesterday only fueled her angry rampage.

She strode toward the event space where half of Enzo's crew was working on landscaping around the new platform patio. Jake stood next to Trina, talking quietly while she captured the physical labor that went into making a space beautiful on camera.

As Frankie passed a bit of brush they had cleared, a telltale hiss and crackle of dried leaves alerted her. She looked down just in time to see a snake slither across her path. She squeaked and jumped back a solid three feet, before grabbing a rake from one of the guys. Stunning the snake with a smack to the head, Frankie then scooped him up on the rake and launched him into the vineyards down below.

"Not fucking funny, Ryland," she yelled as she kept walking toward him. Trina now had the camera pointed firmly on her.

"Oh, come on. I didn't have anything to do with that snake." Jake laughed.

"Sure you didn't. I told you I hate snakes and all of a sudden one crosses my path while you're filming. Fuck you. I may be gullible but I'm not stupid."

"I never said you were stupid or gullible. Maybe you could stop yelling at me and tell me what set you off."

"You want to know what set me off? This bullshit." Frankie waved her arm to encompass the whole house.

"What bullshit? You'll have to be more specific." He actually grinned at her, as if her rage was funny.

Frankie dropped the reins on her temper and let it have its head. "Your list of bullshit is that long, huh? You need a refresher? Let's start with this." She chucked the rake at him, and he dodged. "What other little 'tension triggers' did you set up for me to stumble into?"

Jake's face pokered up. Frankie's mind was clicking, connecting the dots, and she didn't like the picture forming. Piece after piece fell into place until she couldn't deny the final image. She'd happily played the fool. A pitfall of being cast as the clown.

"The concrete delay wasn't an accident, was it?" Frankie crossed her arms and glared. "And the changes to the schedule? And the back-ordered shelves? Jesus, Jake! What the hell? Are you trying to make me look like an idiot?"

"No, I'm trying to make this show a success. Each episode needs a conflict for you to overcome, and you're too damn efficient for me to rely on you regularly screwing up on your own." Jake held his face carefully blank.

So, he was going to hide behind his actor's mask. No fucking way. Frankie needed him to bleed emotion like she was. "So now it's my fault for being too good at my job? That's rich. Do you know how hard I had to work to fix all those things?"

"I do. And so will America when these shows air."

"Will they? Which version are they gonna see?"

Jake winced as that accusation landed. Good. She didn't want to be the only one taking punches today. She kept swinging.

"You know what? It won't matter which one they see. You forget, Jake, I'm a woman trying to make it in a man's field. They'll see an incompetent contractor who can't get out of her own way. No one will want to hire me, let alone trust me to run a company."

"Frankie, I'm just trying to make a good show. Surely you knew there would be some work that goes into that."

"That's all this is to you? Work?" A horrible idea wormed its way through the rage. "Oh…oh my God." She clutched at her stomach and fought against the urge to throw up.

Jake stepped forward, but she stopped him with an outstretched arm. She couldn't handle his fake concern right now.

"The guarantee. That's what this is about. You want me to miss my deadlines and budgets so I have to pay you back. Then you get the show and a hundred grand. I'll be bankrupt and working for my dad forever to pay him back."

"Frankie, I—"

She cut him off, bile churning in the back of her throat. "Is that why you slept with me?" she hissed. "To keep me willing to jump through your hoops?" She gagged on that last thought. She looked around at the crew who had all gone silent. The guys were all looking away, trying not to listen. Even Trina had lowered her camera. *Great. Just great.*

He opened his mouth to reply, but she could not listen to more of this trash. And if she was going to be sick, she wanted to do it in private. She was gasping for breath, trying not to cry. She meant for her voice to be calm and forceful, but it came out as a scream.

"Get out! Get out of here! I can't… Just go!"

Jake tried to reach for her, but she dodged his grip and danced away from him and the nasty thoughts he put into her mind.

Jake raised his hands in peace. "Let's just talk about this."

"I said get out. This is my property, and I want you off it."

"You won't even let me explain?"

"I'm sure to your mind everything you did was completely rational and in service of the show. I'm the idiot for not realizing that the show would always come first for you. You'll be leaving as soon as you possibly can, and you think I'm overreacting? You are only threatening my future livelihood, deliberately spiraling me into debt, and breaking my heart. Gee, Jake, I can't imagine why I don't want to talk right now." Her sarcasm slashed like a knife as she struggled to defend herself. It didn't help that she was as angry with herself for falling for this as she was at him for pulling it off in the first place.

"That's not true," Jake said quietly.

"What part of it is a lie, Jake?"

He stared at her, silent.

"That's what I thought. Get off my site. Now."

She turned her back on him then and stormed off, her fury unabated.

CHAPTER 25

When Frankie found her father, sitting in his truck in the driveway of the vineyard property, laughing at his phone, she decided to keep the rage ball rolling. She knocked a knuckle on his window.

Dom rolled it down, still chuckling at some stupid meme on his social media. "Hi, baby. What's up?"

"I'm not your baby." Frankie's voice shook with anger as she tried not to unleash the tantrum that would prove her a liar.

Dom's grin faded. "What do you mean? You'll always be my baby girl."

"Is that why you went behind my back with Jake? To keep me your little girl and close to home forever?"

"What are you talking about?" Dom's face crinkled around the edges, years of laughter and frown lines pulled up in confusion.

"You set me up, Dad, and I'm calling bullshit." Frankie slapped her hand on the hood of his truck.

Dom swung his door open and stepped out of the vehicle. He wagged a finger at her, his own hair-trigger temper catching right the hell up. "You watch your language, young lady."

Something inside Frankie snapped.

"This is some god-damned-fucking *bullshit*, and I will say that however I want to say it! Did you plan to take over the show before or after you put me on the hook for a hundred grand?"

The confusion lines on her father's face deepened beneath the red bluster. "What are you talking about? I'm not taking over any show. God, after that first week, we all know what a disaster that would be."

"Then why are you filming critiques of my work for Jake?"

"I didn't. Jake said he needed some reaction shots to talk about how things go wrong on work sites, since I have more experience there than you. He's not even using them. Did you see the pilot?"

Frankie desperately wanted to believe that her father hadn't been in on the plot to screw her over. She felt her anger softening. "Yeah, both of them."

"Then you know. I'm not anywhere in it. It's you handling it all on your own. Made me damn proud."

So Jake was manipulating her father too. "Then you don't think I'm doing a terrible job?"

"No, Frankie. Despite working on a jinxed jobsite, you've got it under control. I love the plans you kids came up with for your mother. I'm impressed."

"So you think I'm ready to take over the company so you can retire?"

"I think between you and Adrian, I am leaving it in capable hands. I meant what I said. Once he and Fi are back on their feet, I'm done."

Frankie soaked up her father's approval. She'd been chasing it for so long. To have it acknowledged loosened the knot around her lungs that had constricted her breathing since she'd taken on responsibility for the project.

She had finally done it. She'd kept her promise to Gabe, and the weight of that slid off her shoulders as well. She was damn close to floating away. Dom's next words brought her firmly back down to earth.

"Back up a minute. What's this about 'both' of the pilots?"

Frankie took a deep breath and braced for a blowup. "There are two versions of the pilot. One featuring me running the show, which it sounds like you've seen, and one interspersed with clips of you narrating and criticizing my work. The execs apparently didn't trust that viewers would buy into a woman as head contractor, especially not after I'd been the comic relief."

As she explained, she watched her father's anger rise to match her own. At least she came by her temper honestly. His face turned redder and redder, and she was afraid he'd have a stroke if she laid too much more into Jake.

"Well, that *is* some bullshit."

"Also, the jobsite isn't jinxed. It's been deliberately sabotaged for dramatic effect, in spite of the fact that I could lose all that money. Actually, because I could lose all that money."

"That slimy bastard. When I get my hands on him…"

Frankie put a hand on her father's shoulder to bring him back down. "Dad, no. It's my build, my problem. I'm on it."

"But no one messes with my little girl and gets away with it."

"You're right about that, but your little girl is going to be the one to put him in his place."

Dom's face contorted for a full minute as he bit back all of his arguments and frustrations before nodding. "Okay, but I'm right here if you need me." He cupped her face in his callused hand and stroked a rough finger over her cheek. "He doesn't deserve you, angel."

"Thanks, Dad. I'll let you know how it goes."

Frankie was already walking away with her phone in her hand, heading back up to the house.

"Hi, Bill? Yeah, this is Frankie Valenti… Yes… Yes, I'll tell him you said hi. I'm calling about the sea glass tiles we ordered for the vineyard project. We had an accident here on site, and I need to rush pick up three more boxes. No, no, everyone is fine. Do you have that in stock?... Great, I'll send Rico by this afternoon. I also need you to add a note to this file. No one makes changes to the orders except me. No one... Yeah, it's a long story, but thanks. You're a lifesaver."

She hung up the phone and scrolled to their next supplier.

Jake thought he could outmaneuver her? *Think again, asshole.*

∼

FRANKIE WAS SITTING in her truck, thumbing through the paperwork she had tucked on the dash to see if she'd missed any suppliers in her flood of phone calls, when Jo pulled into the drive.

"Hi, Mom! What brings you out here?"

"My senior group went to a garden walk hosted by the local winemakers association down here. I thought I'd stop by on my way back and see how everything is going. Got a minute to show me around?"

"Of course I do. You won't believe what happened this morning..."

Frankie took Jo for a walk through the least finished areas, pointing out what things would be and describing details that hadn't been installed yet. She didn't want to spoil the surprise of the reveal. When they got to a back bedroom that had been drywalled and was waiting for paint and therefore not rigged for filming today, Frankie spilled her guts.

"I found out that Jake has been lying to me. For months!"

"About what?"

"The show and all the things that have been going wrong around here. He's been manipulating all of it to create tension for the show."

"It seems like that is pretty standard for reality shows, isn't it?" Jo pointed out in the reasonable tone that had driven Frankie nuts as a teenager.

Frankie pushed back. "It seems dishonest when you are doing things to trip up the person you're sleeping with, especially when the shit he pulled could have cost me a hundred grand." His behavior was not okay.

"That is a valid point. Men." Jo sighed. "Always putting payment before people. If I had a nickel for every time someone else's kitchen remodel took precedence over my needs, I'd be a wealthy enough woman to pay off the debt he's driving you into."

Frankie knew her mom was talking about her dad. She tried to understand how that must have felt. A kitchen wasn't worth missed birthdays, and yet she knew her father had done exactly that. Was that a legacy she would have to take on if she was running the company? She didn't like the answer she saw before her.

"Jake put his job first every time. He continually set me up to fail. It's a miracle I didn't veer off budget long before now."

"That's not a miracle. That's your own hard work. You've done wonders with this place on a shoestring. It's going to be beautiful." Jo took a deep breath and stopped to face Frankie. "You know I don't like to interfere in your love life, but I have to say this. Be very careful about falling for a man who will put his job before you. It's painful to always play second fiddle to his ambition."

Too late.

"I thought I did love him, Ma. I thought what we had mattered. But now it all feels false. If he lied to me about this, what other lies did I fall for? How can I trust anything he says?"

"Broken trust is the hardest thing to repair, even for someone as skilled at fixing things as you. Do you still want him?"

Frankie hated her heart that sped up at that question. "I don't know, Ma," she forced herself to say. "I want the him that only I get to see when we're alone. I want the him he is away from here."

"Darling, you don't get to have just one part of him. You have to take him as a whole. The good, the bad, the ugly. Is dealing with his ugly worth it for a shot at his very best?"

Frankie mulled over that as they walked out the side door onto a partially finished patio that overlooked what would become the parking lot for the commercial space once construction was done. Jo turned around and gasped as she took in the views of the rolling vineyards and the mountains that came right down to the edge of the property. The drought-dry brown grass and shrubs that covered them met with the green of the grapevines and created a beautiful contrast. It would show even better in the spring when everything was lush and green from the snow runoff.

"This is beautiful, Frankie. I'd like to come back and see this place once it's up and running. This land is like a little slice of heaven, and the work you've done is turning it into a masterpiece."

Frankie grinned, proud that her mother was loving the space that would one day be hers. "I think that can be arranged."

They walked back around the exterior of the house toward Jo's car, Frankie's thoughts shifting once again to Jake.

"Ma, how will I know?"

"Know what, darling?"

"How will I know if I can trust him again?"

"You'll have to see how he handles this blowup. Watch what he does and what he says. Try and figure out why he's making the choices he's making, and then decide if you can live with that."

"Thanks, Ma. I love you."

"And I love you, baby. I'm going to stroll over to craft services for a coffee before I hit the road, but I don't want to keep you. Will I see you at dinner Friday?"

"I'm planning on it."

"Good."

Frankie watched Jo walk off toward the food and beverage tables with a grin. How on earth did her mother always know exactly when to show up for a heart-to-heart?

CHAPTER 26

JAKE LEANED against the craft services table in the shade of a pop-up tent with his fresh cup of coffee, trying to figure out what his next move should be. He always knew what came next. It was always laid out in his head, like a clear path from where he was to where he wanted to be. When he'd started this project, his aim had been to prove himself as a director and to keep his crew family employed and together as long as possible. He hadn't expected to have the bedrock of his beliefs about family and his sense of not belonging shaken. He hadn't expected to be welcomed into the Valenti fold or to find out that his lost childhood had been a sham.

And now his goal was tangled and cloudy, and it was all Frankie's fault. He wanted the show to succeed and he wanted her to earn Dom's approval. But he also wanted her to love him. And he seemed to have lost his shot at that last one by chasing the first goal too hard.

"I think that's the first time I've seen you with coffee in your cup but not drinking it."

How long had Jo been standing there watching him moon over her daughter? "Hi, Jo."

"You really stepped in it this time, huh?"

"I see you ran into Frankie."

"Yes, I came by to see my daughter and check out how the build was going. She mentioned that you sabotaged things to make the show more interesting."

"Every challenge only makes the show better, which is good for both of us. But she won't even let me explain."

"So, she's pissed because you made her life harder on purpose, and you're upset that she won't let you mansplain to her why she's wrong? Interesting stance."

Jake dropped his head and stared at his coffee, hoping it would give him the right words. "That's not what I meant."

"No, but it's what you said. Words matter, Jake, and actions matter more. You should have told her."

"This is just how reality TV works. My God, Jo, she's been on MDash for two seasons. How could she not know?"

"Because she isn't some Hollywood actor who grew up playing the game. She put her dreams and her heart in your hands, Jake, and your lie betrayed her on both counts."

"I never lied to her. I never told her I wasn't doing it. She didn't ask."

Jo gave him such a look that he dropped his head in shame.

"Oh, so we're using four-year-old logic now. A lie by omission hurts just as much."

Jake flushed. She was right. He knew that. He should have been more open with Frankie about what he'd been doing behind the scenes. A hot summer breeze whipped up off the valley floor and blew past, scorching them both, but his shame burned hotter. Jake couldn't tell if he was sweating from the heat or the panic that he'd screwed this up forever.

"I never meant to hurt her."

"And yet you purposely made her job harder, knowing what she stood to lose if she failed."

"But she hasn't failed. She's brilliant, smart and funny, and a damn good leader on the site. This show is only going to showcase her strengths."

"Can you guarantee that? I heard about the multiple versions of the pilot. Can you promise me that only the good one will get used?" Jo propped her hands on her hips, and Jake shrugged his shoulders up toward his ears.

"It was never going to air, Jo. My execs were nervous about trusting so much responsibility and money on an untried woman who had shown them nothing but humor and hijinks on the other show. I had to cut together a backup version with Dom's voiceovers so they would move forward with the show. But I edited that version so closely. No offense to Dom, but it's nowhere near as good as Frankie's solo pilot. She shines on-screen, solving problems and getting things done."

"But at what cost? She has put the rest of her life on hold. She's made sacrifices on the build and called in favors to make it all work. Personally and professionally she put herself on the line for this. You stole that time and energy from her."

"She would have worked this hard on the project anyway." He wiped away the sweat on his brow. Definitely panic this time.

"Exactly. You didn't have to manipulate her to get her effort."

"I didn't manipulate her, I tweaked the situation." Jake couldn't help the defenses that flew from his lips, even as he knew he was the one in the wrong. Had anyone ever called him to account like this? Certainly his own mother hadn't, and no nanny had cared enough to try. It was damn uncomfortable, but he was also strangely touched that Jo was taking the time. It felt like something family would do, and his goals got even cloudier.

"Don't you try semantics with me, young man. I know bullshit when I smell it. Imagine how it feels to know that a person you've worked with has been scheming behind your back the entire time, knowing it could ruin your career and your financial stability. Now imagine how much worse that is coming from someone you're in a relationship with. You should have told her before you slept with her."

Heat flashed to his cheeks and he burned with mortification. Had Frankie told her mom they'd had sex? Was he blushing? *Jesus.* He ran a hand over his mouth, his beard rasping in the sudden silence. He glanced around then, grateful that most of the crew had taken refuge inside where it was air-conditioned. There was no one but Jo to witness his embarrassment. "I, uh, I didn't mean to—"

Jo silenced him with a mom glare. Jake decided to shut up.

"Don't finish that sentence. I hope you meant to, and I hope you treated her with respect. If you haven't, you need to fix that."

"How do I fix it if she won't talk to me?"

"Well for starters you could apologize. And I don't mean this rambling defense of inexcusable behavior that you've just trotted out for me. I hope you've gotten that out of your system, so you don't spew that crap at her. The best apology is only three words long, but you have to mean them. I. Am. Sorry." Jo ticked off the words on her fingers. "Next, you need to back those words up with actions. She needs to see that she can trust you again. And it won't happen overnight. But I happen to know my daughter is pretty special. She is worth the work and the wait."

Jake nodded and let those words roll around in his head, like the child's puzzle game with the silver balls. He tried to get his thoughts and dreams and plans to settle into those small, precarious holes, while Jo cracked open a soda. If he could hold his past, present, and future just right, he might still manage to win.

This woman who'd just read him the riot act was Frankie's role model. She might think she was more like her father, but Jake could see Jo in the way Frankie didn't back down and met every problem head-on. And Jo cared enough about the people in her life to have the difficult conversations that made things better. Frankie would be used to that. How on earth was he going to convince her to have one of those conversations with him? How could he show her he was sorry?

Jo pulled him from his musings with a firm grip on his shoulder. She stood in front of him now, and he met her eyes through his regret. The compassion he found there almost buckled his knees.

"In spite of all this, I think you could be good for each other. Play it straight, Jake. Apologize for what you did wrong, acknowledge your fault, and tell her how you'll change. That's what you do when you love someone."

He nodded, but his heart stuttered over that word. *Love.* Love? Did he love her? How could he know? He'd had precious little of that over the course of his life to compare this feeling to. He didn't readily recognize the signs. He did know he'd never cared this much about another person's reaction before. He needed to get himself straight before he tried again.

Frankie had told him to leave. He would do that, honor her wishes, and figure out how the hell to fix this. He lifted his head to thank Jo, but she wasn't looking at him anymore. Her gaze had shifted over his shoulder and softened.

"Ryland! We need to have a talk."

Dom. Great. He braced himself for more parental condemnation, but Jo surprised him.

"Dom, don't beat the boy up. He knows what he did is wrong and he's going to fix it."

Dom pulled up short, confused. "But...but... Did you know about the...?"

"Double pilot? Yep." Jo linked her arm through Dom's elbow and turned him away. "Come walk with me through the vines, Dom. I need to talk to you." Dom was still blustering, but he allowed her to lead him toward the gravel drive. She called back to Jake as they were about to turn the corner. "Don't mess this up, Ryland. I like having you around."

Her approval rested warm in his chest as he gathered his things and left.

~

JAKE RETURNED to set Wednesday morning, no clearer on how to fix things but willing to try. After an enforced afternoon off, he was at least well rested and ready to get back to work on making the show a success. The best thing he could do right now was make an excellent show that proved Frankie's suspicions wrong.

He walked into the empty production trailer.

Maybe he could show her more footage. Surely then she could see that all of his maneuvering was for the good of the show. He hadn't done anything she couldn't handle. Hell, the fact that she was such a professional at handling these crises was going to work in their favor.

It was just business. Some shows needed more external molding than others. Maybe he could show her the story maps he used for each show. If anyone should understand the concept of following a blueprint, it should be Frankie! He usually kept his work close to the vest to maintain the aura of reality for the talent. But Frankie was more than that. He wanted her to be more than that. Maybe he could let her behind the curtain. Maybe he didn't have to be the man pulling levers all alone.

Rising from his desk with his still full mug of coffee gone cold, he went to find her. Maybe he could talk to her about his remaining planned conflict points for the final episode. Could she fake frustration? He had to try something. He couldn't lose her.

He strode past craft services, forgetting his excuse of a refill, and headed straight for the last spot on the filming schedule, the back bathroom, site of the tile massacre. On the way he pulled up the tile guy on his phone and called.

"Hi, Bill. It's Jake on the Valenti project. I wanted to check the status of those replacement tiles."

"Um, I'm not at liberty to give you that information."

"Excuse me?"

"You'll have to check with Frankie." And then the man hung up.

Jake's pulse throbbed at his temple. What the hell was this?

"Problem?" Frankie asked as she stood, arms akimbo, blocking the bathroom door.

"Did you tell the tile supplier not to give me information?"

"No."

Jake's relief was intense but brief.

"I told all of our suppliers not to talk to you. I am point on all of those accounts, and I will be sending them business long after you leave town. The Valenti name still means something, at least until you drag it through the mud with this show."

"Frankie, the Valenti name will always mean something in the Bay."

She took his elbow and pulled him into the back bedroom that was already half staged for the reveal, away from the prying eyes and curious ears of her crew.

"Even after you make me look like a prize idiot? Even after you make me look so incompetent that my own father can't find a kind word?" she hissed and shut the door behind her, closing them in.

He wished that she had a quickie in mind for this private moment, but he feared those days were gone for good. He had to convince her if he was ever going to get back to that place of trust. "Frankie, you know that's not true. That's not how you will look. I can show you—"

Frankie cut him off with a wave of her hand, brushing his

words aside. "I thought I knew what was true and what was fake, but now I wonder just how good an actor you really are."

"I never acted with you. Everything with you was real," Jake said softly, his heart on his sleeve.

He watched her lip tremble, but then she firmed it resolutely. "Tell me, Jake, if they had decided to go in the direction of Dad's pilot, would you have let it go to air?"

Jake paused to think about that. All along he'd been so sure of his vision, of her skill and screen appeal, he'd never truly considered that the network wouldn't see the obvious choice. In his mind, it had never really been a choice. Before he could figure out how to say that, Frankie leapt into the silence.

"And there's my answer. You once told me that this show was a stepping-stone for your career. I didn't realize that the stone would be on my back or how heavy it would be."

She pushed past him before he had a chance to defend himself. Honestly, he didn't know what else to say. She didn't get it. The pressure, the expectations, the money—they were all parts of how the Hollywood game was played. But he hadn't intended to fall for her. He never would have used their relationship against her. Her lack of faith and trust slashed at his heart, but he could see where she was coming from. He just couldn't figure out how to fix it.

Arguing was not the answer. She wouldn't listen to him explain it right now. One thing he knew for sure: trying to reason with a woman at the height of her temper was never a good idea.

"All-crew meeting in ten minutes!" She opened the door and bellowed the command at full volume to a chorus of "Yes, boss," replies. She tapped her phone, presumably sending the message to the outbuildings too, before she glanced over her shoulder at him. "Stick around, Ryland. You're going to want to hear this one."

Oh Lord, now what? Jake stomped after her out into the

kitchen. She'd already cut him out of the supply chain. She'd questioned his integrity and slapped back his attempts to talk to her. This couldn't be anything good.

He took a sip of his coffee and grimaced. He'd forgotten it was cold. He'd lost sight of everything but her today. He was positive he'd have to completely redo the raw editing he'd put in, but he'd stay and hear what she had to say. And then he'd get his head back on straight. He had a show to run.

Crewmembers filed into the kitchen from all over the property, subcontractors and employees alike, and gathered around Frankie, who commanded the room from a step stool like a queen. Her troops gathered for battle, and she was their leader.

"Thanks for coming together so quickly. I'll keep this brief because I know you all want to get out of here on time. Number one: all subcontractor and supplier changes will be communicated directly from me. If you hear something different than the original plans from someone else, I expect you to double-check it with me before you act on it. Number two," she looked directly at Jake, eyes burning with fury, "anyone caught tampering with or altering supplies or plans will be slapped with trespassing and vandalism charges so fast his head will spin. The good thing about the show is this place is crawling with cameras. I'll be adding a few of my own, and I'm sure Jake will be only too happy to cooperate if the police need evidence. Isn't that right, Jake?"

"We always cooperate with local authorities. It won't be necessary."

"Excellent." She smirked. "My goal is to curtail the troubles plaguing this build and get caught up. I'm offering gift cards to anyone whose work passes first inspections under deadline. Any questions?"

"No, boss."

"Got it."

"We're good."

The affirmatives circled the room.

"Good. Let's wrap it up for the day and start fresh tomorrow. Clean up your tools and head out."

The room swelled with the cheers of men about to get off work an hour early. Jake poured his cold coffee in the sink and watched his hopes of getting things back to normal swirl with it down the drain. He almost didn't hear her as she walked past him.

"You're not the only one who can manipulate a situation."

~

By Friday, Jake was at his wits end. Now that she was on to his game, she was constantly one step ahead of him. He hadn't been able to set up any of the scenes he still needed. The last episode was going to fall flat if he couldn't figure something out.

The suppliers weren't budging. Her guys were watching him like a hawk while working like fiends, determined to win their rewards. He should have known that the youngest Valenti would have serious management skills. Trina and Lorena were tiptoeing around him in the production trailer. Even Dom was giving him the stink eye and refusing to go on camera.

The family he'd found on set was crumbling around him, and it was all his fault. He often worked with the same crew of people, sharing a language and a history with people he liked. He did what he could to keep his merry band together from project to project, but he'd always held himself a step apart, ready to walk away with his feelings intact when things ended.

He hadn't managed to keep his distance from the warm and welcoming Valenti family, and that had lowered his boundaries across the board. To have his people pull back from him instead of the other way around left him cut to the quick with his defenses down.

Even worse was that Frankie wouldn't speak to him without Trina or Rico present. She wouldn't give him a chance.

He'd never been in a situation he couldn't talk his way out of. He needed to explain. He wanted her to respect his job and his skills as much as he respected hers. Didn't it just suck sideways that the first woman he'd fallen for in years was the one person who wouldn't listen to him?

Jake sighed and packed it in at noon. He told his crew to leave and get an early start on the weekend. He had a flight to catch, and a different on-screen family to contend with. He'd told Brittani that he'd be there for her, and he did not intend to be made a liar. Maybe, just maybe, he'd regroup enough to figure out how the hell to make this right.

CHAPTER 27

WHAT WAS HE PLAYING AT?

Frankie had been wondering this all afternoon, after Jake had uncharacteristically let his half of the crew leave early.

She was no fool. Sensing an opportunity to solidify loyalty, she'd let the construction guys go early as well. After less than one week of zero delays, they were actually ahead of schedule. These guys had been busting their asses for weeks, and were already working at peak efficiency. They had earned a break.

Work on the outbuildings was moving along fine now that she was no longer trusting Jake the Snake. Monday was soon enough to finish.

But now, all alone at the vineyard, doubts and second-guesses plagued her. Had he let everyone go so they would fall behind? Was this another trick? Waiting for the other shoe to drop was exhausting. She couldn't shut off her paranoia, so instead of heading back home for Friday dinner, she was knocking things off the punch list for the nearly finished areas. She refused to give him ammunition to make her fall behind again.

Frankie had started measuring and cutting for the decking out back, but the dry, sun-scorched wind whipped her hair around and brought tears to her eyes. Already too close to tears for comfort, she abandoned her Skilsaw and settled for interior work. She dutifully went from room to room screwing faceplates on every outlet. She squinted as she finished the last one. The room had gone dim while she worked.

Frankie reached for her phone to call her mom and apologize for not making it to dinner, but the display made her pause. It was only four thirty. Why the hell did it look like dusk?

Frankie walked into the kitchen to check the bay window over the sink that looked out over the vines. A chill raced down her spine.

Gray billows of smoke rose from the back of the hills behind their property.

Fire.

One word guaranteed to strike fear into the hearts of Californians.

The hot, dry summer meant that the hills in the backcountry were covered in kindling. They were still months from the potential cooling rains of winter. A wildfire could spread fast and furious if not caught early. And judging by the size of the plumes, this one had caught hold.

Gratitude that the work site was clear of people raced through her head as she sprinted from the house and out to her truck. She called the fire department on her way back to check out the blaze. She parked her truck at the ridge that marked the high point of their property and climbed out. She had to see it. She had to know what she was dealing with.

The heat was already brutal, and gusting updrafts blew past her on the crest. The fire was creating its own weather. That hot and fast wind would drive the fire quickly. Right toward the vineyard.

She knew Enzo had taken precautions with the landscaping,

but he wasn't finished. She also knew that nothing would stop a fire determined to burn.

Coughing from the heat and particles of ash already swirling her way, Frankie turned back to her truck. She wasn't going to let this fire take her family's legacy.

They had protected the existing vineyards as best they could with wide gravel firebreaks around the edges, and grapevines had been known to survive a burn.

But they hadn't cleared the areas around the outbuildings yet. With the babies coming earlier than expected, Enzo hadn't had a chance, and Frankie had pushed off the landscaping to focus on the buildings. And now she could lose it all.

She looked in the rearview mirror, and the rolling gray clouds were tinged with red reflecting from the flames. She was driving away from a hellscape, and it was chasing her.

This was no small fire. This could take everything she'd been striving for and burn it to the ground in a heartbeat. This house held the combined hopes of all her siblings. It held the promise she'd made to Gabe. It was the promise of the future she'd dreamed for herself. It held her father's promise of a new adventure for her mother.

She refused to let it all go up in flames.

Not on my watch.

She pressed the pedal to the metal and tore back up the drive, spewing gravel from her tires. Parking in front of the house for a quicker getaway and to avoid potential explosions of her gas tank from the heat, she leapt from her truck. Then she tossed a ladder against the front of the house, cranked the hose on high and tucked it into her tool belt for the climb.

She climbed over the peaked roof of the house and looked out over the field of vines that stretched toward disaster. So much promise, so much potential. She couldn't let it go without a fight. She squeezed the nozzle and sprayed down everything she could reach: shrubs, decking material, the sides of the house, the roof she was standing on. Just a few more minutes. Just a little more water. Then she'd climb down and get the hell out of here.

Her phone buzzed in her pocket and she ignored it. No time for Jake's bullshit right now. She hadn't answered his calls in days. One might think he'd get the message.

Frustrated with him, she yanked the hose to make it reach the far side of the house and heard the metallic clang of metal hitting wood.

No.

If her hands hadn't been filthy, she'd have slapped her forehead. She'd made a rookie mistake and stranded herself on the roof by knocking down the freaking ladder with the hose.

Idiot.

She couldn't let her family down. She wouldn't let their dreams go without a fight. But she'd never intended to put herself in danger.

From her vantage point on the roof, she watched the fire creep closer. The blue oak trees along the far ridge were going up like kindling.

The glowing smoke was brighter now, and Frankie turned the hose on herself for a minute to cool down, before she remembered her phone in her pocket. She pulled it out to check it and cursed. It was dripping. Before she could turn it off, it rang again.

Jake.

The screen flashed his name and that electric pulse fried her phone. Water damage complete.

She was well and truly fucked now.

She thought of all the camera equipment and the money already invested in the project. She reluctantly aimed the hose toward the production trailer. The amount she'd owe them if it burned made her throat tighten up. Or maybe that was the smoke she was inhaling.

The wind was picking up and blowing right toward her.

He'd wanted drama. He was certainly going to get it. Those ugly thoughts from before rose to the surface again.

Could he have done this?

He'd cleared out his crew early, and made sure hers had gone too. He probably expected her to be sitting at her mother's dinner table. Surely he wouldn't have jeopardized the project like this. Unless he truly didn't think it was going to succeed with her at the helm and was trying to cut his losses.

No. Jake was from California. He knew how easily a fire could get out of control. No way would he put so many people in danger.

But that niggling doubt lingered in her mind. After everything she'd learned this week, she couldn't just blindly trust that he hadn't been involved. Regardless, she gave the production trailer a good soaking. If she could save the equipment, she would. One less thing he could charge her for.

Exhausted, Frankie crouched down on the edge of the roof, like a gargoyle, and did her best imitation of a garden sprinkler. She waved the nozzle back and forth and contemplated her options.

She couldn't jump. It was too high, and if she broke an ankle on the fall she'd be useless trying to get away. In hindsight, she was wishing she'd said yes to the upper story balcony that had been in the original plans. She could try and shimmy down the drainpipe, but she was less than optimistic about her ability to cling long enough. She would give the fire department a little longer to arrive before she attempted idiocy.

Wiping sweat and ash from her forehead, she reached for comfort.

"Gabe, if you can hear me, I could use a little help right now."

She often had conversations with Gabe in her head, but this

one found its way out of her mouth. It seemed like the right moment to put voice to her fears.

"I haven't forgotten my promise or our plans. But this...this is scary. I'm afraid we're going to lose everything. My chance, the business, the vineyards, Mom and Dad..." Tears she'd willfully held back for weeks now streamed down her face as she unburdened her heart to her big brother.

She told him about the show and Jake's betrayal, and the pressure she felt to make this property perfect for everyone, for weddings and for a marriage, for her own hopes and dreams. She poured her heart out to her dead brother on a soaking wet roof as a wildfire crept even closer. She closed her eyes against the acrid smoke.

"And now I have to wonder, was it worth it? I've worked so hard to have it all go up in smoke, and it feels empty."

She could hear the snapping and sparking of the fire now as it flanked the back access road.

"Gabe, if you've got any pull up there, I could really use a hand right now. And if you don't, well, I guess I'll be seeing you soon. I'm so sorry I let you down."

She eyed the drop to the ground and her head spun. Or maybe that was from dehydration. Either way, it was now or never. She gathered her courage to try the pipes, but paused when she heard something else.

Sirens.

She ran over the roofline to the front of the house. God bless the cavalry. Two red fire trucks, lights blazing, were racing their way up the curving front drive.

"Thanks, Gabe." She smiled and waved like a fool as the professionals piled out of the trucks and got to work.

CHAPTER 28

JAKE PRESSED his phone to his ear, desperate for things to be different this time.

But she still wasn't answering. No surprise there. She hadn't taken his calls all week. It hadn't gone straight to voicemail before though. He'd always gotten a few rings in before she hit ignore. Somehow knowing she knew he had called made him feel better.

He'd reached a new low. He was dissecting the probable cell phone actions of a woman for clues about how she felt about him, while sitting in an airplane waiting for the doors to close. He'd wanted to tell her why he was going to LA. He'd wanted to share his nerves and his excitement over the reunion project. He'd wanted her to care.

Pitiful.

Where was the confident king of the Hollywood teen scene with girls falling over themselves to be noticed by him?

Oh yeah. He'd left that asshole behind years ago. And good riddance.

But he could use a bit of that confidence walking into a room of people he'd thought had left him behind. He turned his phone to airplane mode for the hour-long flight. He'd just have to muscle through this on his own.

He was thankful that Britt had arranged it so they would have a private reunion at Martin's home first, instead of meeting for the first time on set again. His stomach was in knots and his heart beat thickly in his chest, anxiety setting him off his rhythm. He'd been a good actor, but he doubted he'd be able to cover his nerves if this first meeting was going to be televised.

∼

WALKING up the path to Martin's palatial estate, Jake felt about twelve years old again. He shoved his hands in his pockets and hunched his shoulders against the feeling of helplessness and insecurity he'd thought he'd gotten past.

It wasn't too late. He could still walk away. He could still maintain the illusion that everything was fine.

But he wasn't fine. He desperately wanted the family he'd lost to be magically waiting for him behind that door. The desire to be welcomed and loved by people who knew him was strong. His parents hadn't been capable of this. He'd come close with the crews he'd built, but they only stuck around as long as the show did. It was too tenuous. He'd thought he'd been building that with Frankie and the Valentis, but that had all gone sideways.

The people he'd see tonight had known him his entire childhood. If Brittani was right, and they did still care… Well, that was worth this risk of walking through that door.

He rang the doorbell. As the chimes echoed off the terracotta tiles, cold sweat beaded on his forehead and he straightened his cuffs compulsively.

Ever since he'd talked to Britt, he'd been beating himself up for not seeing it sooner. It had been ridiculously easy for him to believe the worst in them. He was positive his mother had kept them apart, pushed them away, all so she could maintain her control over him and his career. Swamped with shame and regret, Jake saw that he'd been the one to leave them, and he hadn't even realized it.

Today was his day to make amends.

The door was opened by a small woman in a well-tailored uniform.

"May I help you?" she asked.

Jake wanted to bolt, but her kind eyes kept his feet still. "I'm here for the barbecue?" His voice shook as he forced the words out.

A deep voice that made him feel twelve again boomed down the hallway.

"Jake? Is that you? Mary, let him in! Britt said you were coming, but"—Martin Milton, his brawny frame attesting to his continued popularity as the aging hero in action films, pulled him into a bear hug—"I couldn't believe it. How the hell are you, son?"

Martin had been a pivotal role model for Jake. He'd talked to Jake like a person, not just a kid, and he'd offered friendship and counsel while Jake's actual father had been largely absent. He'd been the one to suggest that Jake had the brains and the eye to make it behind the camera as well as in front.

Jake thought of how much he'd missed because of his mother's interference and his own stupidity, and wanted to throw up. He hugged Martin back as tightly as he could instead, as if he could transmit his apology through his arms.

"Martin, listen, I'm so sorry." His voice rasped as he spoke through the grateful tears he'd managed to trap in his throat.

"I'm gonna stop you right there, Jake. Britt explained everything. Your mother was a viper back then, and by all reports is even more so now. You were just a kid. You're supposed to be able to trust the people who love and raise you. We're going to put all that behind us."

"Just like that?"

"Just like that. I've been following your career. I'm proud of you. Come on back to the grill and tell me about your next project."

Those words—words his own father had never spoken—washed away the last of the fear in his heart. He hadn't completely screwed things up. His shoulders dropped in relief, and he felt the migraine pulse start to recede. Just like that. Could forgiveness really be that easy? Jake would forever remember the kindness of this man in this moment.

That meeting set the tone for the others as people began to arrive for dinner. Sadly, his mother from the show, Brenda Milliano, had lost her battle with breast cancer five years back. But Brittani and her best friend from the show were there, as well as their on-screen neighbor, Jake's schoolmate, and the guy who ran the diner on the show. He couldn't believe that everyone welcomed him back so readily. But he wasn't going to jinx it by asking too many questions. He was going to put in the time and effort and get these friends back for real. He was livid that his mother had kept them from him in the first place. The smell of roasting tri-tip and barbecued chicken swirled through the air on the eddies of decades worth of conversations flitting back and forth.

"So, Mister Up-And-Coming-Showrunner, get us up to speed on the personal. Any special person in your life?"

Was Frankie in his life? Had she written him off completely? He sure as hell hoped not. He wanted to be able to count her among his family. "I'm working on that, but I sure hope she is."

He told them about the show, and how things had hit the skids between them.

"Well then, when you've fixed things, you'll bring her to a

barbecue. I want to meet the woman who's managed to get under your skin."

Martin ruffled Jake's hair the same way he had twenty-five years ago and Jake grinned. Thank God some things never changed. He thought back to the last barbecue he'd attended with burned steaks and scorched sheets, and his resolution to fix this firmed. Martin's optimism unlocked Jake's own. "That's a deal."

After the plates were empty and bellies were full, Jake pulled Brittani to the side with a hug around her shoulders.

"Thanks for this."

"It's nothing," she demurred.

"It's everything, and I think you know that."

"We're family." She shrugged it off, but Jake was not deterred.

"Exactly. So I'm going to ask you this like a big brother would. Financially, how are you? I know we're doing this show tomorrow to raise money and awareness for the sisters, but are you working on other projects?"

Again Brittani shrugged and looked away. "There's the money from the Hudson House syndication, but nothing I've auditioned for has come through. I guess people just aren't willing to take a chance on a has-been."

"You aren't a has-been. You're a will-be-again, and I've got a project to talk to you about if you're interested in hosting a home renovation show."

Jake laid out the pitch that Greg Fowler had approached him with. He'd had no interest in getting back in front of the camera, but Brittani did and she still had that America's Sweetheart glow about her. This could be the perfect launch pad for her next career, wherever that might take her.

"Jake, you don't have to make up things for me to do."

"I'm not. This isn't even my project. I just know they need someone from the show, and I think you'd be perfect. If you're interested all I will do is put Greg in touch." *And watch out for you on the network side*, he added silently. He couldn't bear the thought of his little sister getting taken advantage of again. Not while he had any say in it.

"I...I think I'd like to hear more," Brittani said, quiet hope blooming in her eyes.

"Consider it done."

CHAPTER 29

Jake walked into his LA condo, tired but at peace for the first time in years. He hadn't lost them. The people he'd loved and needed in his life had welcomed him back with open arms. Now if he could just convince Frankie that she belonged there too. He pulled his phone out of his pocket to see if he'd missed a call from her and realized he'd left it on airplane mode.

He clicked it over to accept phone calls, and his phone blew up in his hand. There were messages from everyone. Jo, Dom, Trina, Adrian... Everyone but her. His texts were still downloading when he listened to the first message from Jo and collapsed on his couch.

A fire?

He listened to it all the way through twice, just to hear the most important part again.

She was okay. There had been a fire at the vineyard, but Frankie was okay. Some smoke inhalation, but they'd let her go home from the hospital already.

He listened to the one from Trina. The event barn was a total loss, and some external cameras had melted. A few acres of the vines would be impacted, but the main house was untouched. And Frankie was okay.

The call from Dom was to the point.

"Frankie is fine. But this had better not fall on her shoulders with the network. I'm trusting you to stand up for her."

He needed to double-check the contracts.

He needed to hear her voice.

He called her and it went straight to voicemail.

"Hey, it's me. Jake. I just heard about the fire. Please call and let me know you're okay. I'm in LA, and I will take care of everything. I promise. I...I miss you." He'd almost slipped and said I love you, but no woman wanted to hear that for the first time in a voicemail.

He searched for news on his phone. The fire was only fifteen percent contained and still moving, but the wind had shifted, blowing the flames farther down the valley. The mountains were creating a natural funnel. But Frankie was okay.

He could fix everything else as long as she was okay.

It was more important than ever to make things right. He'd spent too much time bending over backward to make the production company happy. It was time to focus on what would make him happy. And that was Frankie safe and sound and back in his life.

Pulling up the available flights back to San Jose, he cursed. All of the flights that could get him there and back in time to film the charity fundraiser were booked. Maybe he could fly standby...

He began throwing clothes back in his bags, and called Jo.

"How is she?" he asked as soon as Jo answered.

"She's fine, Jake. She can't talk right now. Doctor's orders to rest her throat, but she's fine. Her phone got fried though, so if you need to tell her anything you should call me."

"Does she need anything? I'm on my way to the airport to see if I can catch a flight, but I can make some calls if I need to on the way."

"No, Jake. We've got her covered. Stay and do what needs doing."

Jake slumped against the door jamb, his overnight bag bouncing against his knee as he dropped it to the floor from his limp hand. He couldn't help but wish she needed him, just a little.

And then it hit him. She did need him. He could make sure she didn't have to worry about a thing. He would handle the network end of the fire and recovery in person, and she wouldn't have to deal with any of it.

"Okay. Tell her…tell her I called. Tell her I miss her."

"I will."

After a restless evening spent pouring over contracts, Jake finally fell asleep, but he was tortured by dreams of Frankie separated from him by a wall of flames. In the light of morning, he had a moment of clarity.

Normally, his pristine home brought him peace and comfort. Everything was exactly where he wanted it. He'd personally worked with the designer to make it reflect his taste. This was his oasis. Usually.

This time his home felt empty. The beach chic decor looked indulgent. His kitchen was quiet—no clicking claws announcing an imminent pounce, no cold nose from Buster trying to steal his dinner. He'd turned to comment on an email update and realized no one was there to hear him. His king bed that had so often been a refuge was empty without Frankie.

He hadn't even made coffee this morning.

This place didn't feel like home anymore without her.

Jake slouched on his couch and dropped his head back on the hard wood back rail, staring at the ceiling. He hated this. He'd finally found the woman who made everything click, and he'd blown it. He had to make this right.

True, he'd made a few accidents happen on set. No one got hurt. And every time he was able to show her being a badass boss and fixing it. He'd only done what any self-respecting reality showrunner would do. He'd gotten his shots.

But he'd lost the girl.

Yeah, because you put your show ahead of her needs. You made it all about you. You didn't let her in on any of it.

The smart-ass voice in his head had been unhelpful for days. But instead of wallowing in his failure, Jake picked up his phone. There was just enough time before he had to be on set to get the ball rolling with legal. He wasn't about to let her go without a fight.

∼

THE OLD FAMILIAR twisting in his gut and pre-migraine throb came back the minute he stepped into his old studio. They had recreated the living room from the set, and it was like climbing into a time machine. One that was guaranteed to spin him around and make him nauseous.

There, on portable bleachers, sat a live studio audience who had paid handsomely for the opportunity. There would be glad-handing and an autograph auction after the show, as well as a live bank of operators to take donations from viewers at home. Jake's mouth filled with cotton.

"Okay, let's get this show on the road!" Martin boomed. Then more quietly, "You okay, son?"

"That's been a long time coming, but yeah, I'm good."

"You look a little pale. Still get that stage fright?"

Somehow he felt better that Martin had seen that, even if he hadn't been able to help. "No. There was a fire yesterday at the vineyard. I'm just a little shaken up." His hands trembled, but his heart was steady.

ROUGHED IN

Jake was ushered to a high-perch leather chair by a production assistant who looked like he was bursting to tell someone about what he'd just overheard. So much for keeping out of the media spotlight. He'd just have to give them something better to talk about.

"Welcome, everyone. Today we have a rare assembly of the cast of Hudson House."

The moderator was one of the perennially perky professional hosts who could often be found lurking outside red carpet events and reality competition shows. He introduced everyone and quickly got down to business.

"It's been twenty-four years since Hudson House went off the air. As the youngest members, we'll start with you, Brittani and Jake. You were still kids when the show went off the air. Where did your paths take you?"

Brittani spoke first. "Well, Stein, I want to say that I will always be grateful for the start Hudson House gave me in this business, but when I left I think my fall from grace was pretty visible to everyone. I was pushed into roles that were too mature for me, you know, the teen vixen. And then I fell into that lifestyle for real. Underage drinking, drugs, sex. I was a predator's dream."

Brittani choked back tears and Jake took her hand for support. He squeezed it twice, and she squeezed it back three times. Their old code. A silent reassurance that they had each other's back in front of the cameras.

"There were so many times I wished I could come back home to Hudson House. When I hit rock bottom, Martin helped me find the Sisters of Solace. They gave me shelter and counseling while I detoxed. Without their generous help, I wouldn't be here today. That's the reason we are all here. I am so thankful that my Hudson House family could help raise awareness of the amazing work they do. Please give generously during the call breaks to support this great organization."

"And Jake?"

"I found myself in the same kind of space, pushed to play older than I was. But I think the teen heartthrobs probably have it a little easier than our female counterparts. I wish I'd been able to see it back then. What many people don't know is that I suffered debilitating stage fright. I was fighting to get out. Martin pointed out the path, and Billy Gene gave me the map by teaching me on this set what a great director can do. I'm still learning, but I'm infinitely happier behind the camera."

"What have you worked on since leaving the limelight?"

"I worked my way up, but I'm currently the showrunner for Million-Dollar Starter Home and Valenti Vineyards, an upcoming six-episode spin-off." His mind shifted back to Frankie and how she'd take all of this.

"And what's next for you?"

"That's still up for grabs at this point, but I'm hoping to make an announcement soon. It's not enough to be good at what I do. I should be doing good with what I do. That's why I am here, to support Brittani and the Sisters of Solace."

The conversation moved on, and Jake was hanging on every word. Getting these updates and finding out what his TV family had been up to in the intervening years filled him with simultaneous joy and regret. He'd missed so much.

When they did a brief "In Memoriam" section for Brenda, Jake bit back tears. He was included in stills with her from the show, and there was zero shame or chagrin. He realized that no matter what he did with the rest of his life, he was proud of his work on Hudson House because it had brought these people into his life. He didn't have to chase acclaim anymore. He was enough just as he was.

Frankie was right. He'd put his head down and pushed

through a bad situation to make something of himself. But that had been a reaction to having his family pulled out from under him. He hadn't wanted to be that vulnerable again, so he'd put himself in positions of control. And he'd done so with the skills he'd observed in his mother.

He didn't have to be that person anymore. He had his family back. He'd proven he was a capable director.

It was time to do some deep thinking about how he'd ended up here and where he wanted to go next.

CHAPTER 30

THE GROUND WAS STILL warm Monday afternoon. The heat rose through the soles of Frankie's steel-toed boots. She inhaled deeply, trying to tamp down her panic, but her throat burned, still raw from the smoke. She coughed harshly. The respirator mask she wore over half her face was choking her. She longed to rip it off, but the firefighters had warned them that dangerous gasses were still rising off the piles of smoking debris.

Although the main house and most of the vines had survived untouched, the barn and storage shed, along with all of the farming equipment they had stored in there, were toast.

The fire had been contained relatively quickly, all things considered, but not before burning a swath through the valley. Two other vineyards had sustained structural damage, and an entire mobile home park had been destroyed.

Frankie was helping with a volunteer effort to pick through properties for anything salvageable. She had the required safety gear, so she and a few of the guys from her crew had gone down to help. First stop was the mobile home site to sift through the wrecked remains of people's lives. Thank God everyone had made it out alive.

Water-damaged albums and books, closet safes too hot to touch, melted bicycles...entire lives worth of possessions reduced to rubble and ash.

The emotional toll of this work was more than she'd expected, but there was nowhere else she'd rather be. As she piled anything of value on the concrete pad that had been the driveway, she gave thanks again that no one had died.

But these families were going to be starting over from scratch. These families who could least afford it.

The enormity of starting over from nothing made her looming hundred-grand debt feel paltry. How did one replace a lifetime of memories?

As soon as the firefighters had given the county the all clear, she and a few of her guys had put on their steel toed boots and safety masks and waded in. It would take more than her little crew to clean up this mess, but it felt good to do something, no matter how small.

Her impulse to help was strong. It was practically ingrained in her DNA. Hell, the family motto was do good work, on time, under budget. This was good work.

How had they strayed so far from their original mission? If they'd kept it simple, they wouldn't have lost so much. She wouldn't be staring down a one-hundred-thousand-dollar debt she had no idea how to pay and a job that was still not finished. Then again, if she'd listened to Fi and clad the barn in stone... No, it still wouldn't have survived the fire unscathed, and they'd still have lost money and time.

She picked up a white album and flipped through someone's wedding photos. Some pictures would be salvageable, she hoped.

But Sofia wouldn't get the wedding she'd dreamed of. There was no way they could afford to redo all the work they'd already done on the barn.

No, she couldn't go back and wish things different. It was

what it was. She had to stay grounded in the now, or she'd be lost to regrets. She had to move forward from here.

And forward meant working off the debt to her dad, while getting back to basics. She would do what Valenti Brothers did best. Good work, on time, under budget, for people who couldn't afford chandeliers and wine cellars. She would keep her promise to Gabe. No more TV shows.

This thought did not buoy her like she'd hoped. It felt…empty.

She would just have to fill it up. She could work on projects for Adrian and Fi when the new season started, and try to convince her dad to give her another shot at running her own projects, this time off-camera and minus a saboteur. And she would donate her free time to helping rebuild down here.

That should keep her busy enough to forget about her failure.

Picking through the remains of a kitchen, Frankie set aside a cast iron skillet that had survived. The sound of weeping pulled her attention to the roadside where a woman had collapsed against her teenaged son.

She crossed to them and yanked off her mask. "Ma'am, you shouldn't be here. It's not safe to breathe the air."

"It's gone. It's all gone." Tears left bright streaks down her dirty cheeks.

"Mom, come on. You've seen it now. Let's go." Her son tried to turn her back to their idling truck, but she pulled her spine straight and stood on her own.

"No. I'm not leaving without them." With wild eyes she scanned the wreckage that Frankie had been clearing.

"Ma'am, was this your home?" Frankie stepped between the woman and the smoking rubble, forcing her to make eye contact. She nodded. "Are you looking for something in particular? I've got the gear. I can look for you."

The woman gripped Frankie's hand with a strength that

surprised her. "My rings. I took them off while I was washing the dishes after dinner. Mine and my husband's." She was worrying the bare spot on her left ring finger with her thumb repetitively. "I have to find them. They're all I have left of him."

"Ma'am, what's your name?"

Her son chimed in. "I'm Tyler, and this is my mom, Sylvia. My dad died last year. I told her we couldn't come down here, but she wouldn't listen."

"It's okay." She turned back to Sylvia and gripped her shoulders. "Listen, it's not safe for you to go through the pile right now. You could get hurt, and Tyler needs you. Tell me exactly where you left them. What do they look like?"

"They are gold. Mine had a diamond. I put them in the little blue bowl on the shelf by the sink. I...I can't see it." Sylvia was still craning her neck, trying to see past Frankie.

"I'll go look. Here's the stuff I did find." She handed the woman the photo album of her wedding and pointed to the small pile of items on the slab. "Why don't you go through it and see if you want to keep any of it? Hey, Rico, can you grab two N95 masks from the truck?"

Frankie got them sorted with the masks and gave Tyler a stern look. He nodded, but his mother seemed subdued, flipping through the ruined pictures.

Wading back into the mess, Frankie returned to the area where she'd found the pan. Lifting a wall panel, she found the metal sink and tangled pipes. She began to sift through the broken porcelain and glass near it carefully, looking for any shard of blue. So many fragments of a broken life slid between her gloved fingers. This was like looking for a needle in a burnt haystack.

But she wouldn't give up. These people needed her help. This felt real and concrete, unlike the last few months of all-consuming un-reality.

She lifted the metal sink and shifted it to the side. A sparkle caught her eye. She whipped off her glove so she could delicately pinch the golden rings from the ashes. She dropped them quickly onto her other hand and blew on them to cool them before returning them to their distraught owner.

"Oh my God! Oh, you found them! You're an angel!" Sylvia's tears fell fast and free, soaking Frankie's neck as she was pulled into a fierce hug. Sylvia tugged her son into the hug too.

"Okay, can we go now?" Tyler allowed the hug, but his voice was all annoyed teenager.

"Hang on a minute. Sylvia, did you have insurance?"

"We did. Brendan made sure we were covered before he deployed."

"What branch?"

Tyler piped up. "Dad served in the army."

Frankie felt the hair on the back of her neck stand up. Gabe would want her to help. Hell, *she* wanted her to help. She needed to stop hiding behind her big brother's larger-than-life image. She was going to make this offer, because it was what *she* wanted to do.

"I'm a builder here in the area. If you decide you want to rebuild, I want you to give me a call." She repeated her name and number for Tyler as he put it into his cell phone.

"You've already helped." The rings were already back in place on her finger, the smaller holding the larger one in place. "You gave me back the one thing I couldn't bear to lose. I've got my son and my health. Everything else is replaceable."

"Well, when you decide to replace it, I'd like to help. I can design something custom based on your insurance payout, and get it roughed in pretty quickly. I'll build your new home, on time and under budget. That's the Valenti way."

"We'll see." Sylvia and Tyler picked their way back to their car and drove off, leaving Frankie to ponder in the ashes.

Her offer felt right in her heart, unlike the churning stress of the last few months.

She put her mask on and got back to doing the hard work that made a difference for people.

She'd cleared another home with the volunteer crew when Jake pulled up in his fancy car. She hadn't seen him since he'd disappeared on Friday. Her mom had said he called to check in, but she'd been resting. All of the pain and frustration and sadness bubbled up in her chest, mixing with her new ideas and desires, into a toxic sludge that was just waiting to boil over and burn it all down.

He had a lot of nerve coming to find her here.

Perversely, it pissed her off even more that she was first seeing him while completely disheveled. He always made her self-conscious. He had no right. He'd missed everything with the fire. And she'd missed him, dammit, even though she hated to admit it.

She'd needed him, and he'd hadn't been there for her.

That had been a hard lesson learned.

"Frankie." The way his voice dropped when he said her name vibrated deep in her belly.

"Jake." She kept her voice hard as concrete.

"I was hoping to catch you at the vineyard. They told me you were down here helping out."

"Because that's what you do in a disaster. You stick around and help people out." She pushed her disdain into her voice. She would be strong. She couldn't let herself weaken before she'd gotten to the bottom of this.

"I was already down in LA when I heard about it. I had promises to keep, and Jo told me you were okay. I thought I could be more helpful putting out fires there, getting all the details sorted."

"Promises to keep? Is that code for 'I got you your money back. Where's my promotion?'"

"What exactly are you implying?"

"It's awfully convenient that you were in LA when your maneuvering finally came to fruition." Her temper was flaring high now, and the words coming out of her mouth burned through her filters.

His head reared back as if she'd singed him. "Do you honestly think I would endanger lives for a TV show?"

"I don't know! You've turned mine into a steaming pile of shit for the better part of a year. After all the crap you've pulled... I don't want to think you did, but how can I know for sure? Do you know how awful it feels to doubt your judgment of the person you're sleeping with?"

"Yeah, at the moment I've got a pretty good idea. Jesus, Frankie."

"You haven't given me a whole lot of truth to trust."

"Frankie, you want the truth? I went to LA to help my show-sister Brittani film a reunion and to support her addiction recovery. I reconnected with the family I thought I had lost forever. And it felt nice, but not quite right. Do you know why?"

Frankie crossed her arms across her chest and jutted her chin out, silent.

"Because you weren't there to share it with me. Because I wasn't here with you when you were hurting."

His words pierced right to her heart. Damn him for making her want to believe. She clutched her arms tighter.

"Do you know why I didn't come back on Sunday?"

She shook her head and focused on the embers at her feet instead of the ones burning in his eyes.

"Because I was pulling Lila Finch out of brunch to beg her for an extension on the show and to remove the penalty."

"It's a real shame you played that card. The barn burned to the ground. Even I can't tweak a budget that's already been spent. Your show is over."

"First of all it's our show, and second, it's not over until it's over."

"Jake, give it up."

"No, I won't. And I won't let you either."

"Look around you, Jake!" She was shouting now, and the other guys from her crew had stopped to shamelessly eavesdrop. "How can I work on a retirement vineyard when there are people left homeless?"

"Because you have a contract to finish it? Because you'll be jeopardizing your reputation, as well as Sofia's, Adrian's, and Enzo's." He ticked their names off on his fingers. "You'll scuttle Million-Dollar Starter Home's third season. You won't work in Hollywood again."

"Praise the Lord. Where do I sign?"

Her mouth was running, but she didn't truly mean it. She hadn't thought through how this would affect her family and the other show. They were counting on things working out. She was going to have to finish, dammit, but it left a sour taste in her mouth. She would resent every minute.

"Don't do this. Don't throw away everything we've been working for. How can you turn your back on all of this? On us?"

"What *us*? How can there be an us when you lied from the start? You don't deserve my time and energy. These people do! Do you think it matters if viewers like to watch me race to tear down a wall or do pull-ups from the rafters? No. What matters is getting Sylvia and her son back in a home."

The tears she so often concealed were flowing down her cheeks. *Fuck it. Let them flow.* She was done holding back.

"You want to make your mark on the world, Jake? You want people to think you're more than a pretty face? Why don't you try making something that matters? I'll finish out the contract.

Just stay out of my way. Starting now, Jake. I've got real work to do."

"I'll give you your space, Frankie. But I'm going to show you that I care about you more than I do about this show. You won't listen, but maybe when you see it you'll believe me. This isn't the end. This is just the beginning."

She turned her back on him and walked into the smoking wreckage, where Jake, in his Italian leather shoes, couldn't follow.

CHAPTER 31

Swish. Swish. Swish.

The repetitive motion was soothing. With each swish of the broom, more of the dirt was pushed away. More of the devastation righted. More of her frustration burned off.

It had been one week since the fire. The county had stepped in for recovery efforts and the trailer park build would be tied up in more red tape than she'd ever encountered. But it would just be another opportunity to learn.

In the meantime, she could tend to her own. Turning her attention back to the event space, Frankie cleared the rubble, salvaging what she could. She'd hauled barrow after barrow of charred wood to the dumpsters while the crew had kept working on the house. Finally, she was down to the concrete foundation slab.

Swish. Swish. Swish.

She used the time to chase the cobwebs of her dreams out of her mind as well.

Good work, on time, under budget.

She wouldn't forget again.

She wouldn't let her ambitions get away from her.

She wouldn't lose sight of her promise to Gabe.

She wouldn't let a man run her into the ground again for his own gain.

It wasn't working. Her decisions weren't bringing her the peace she craved.

Swish. Swish. Swish.

"Hey, baby girl. How are you doing?"

Dom stood on the edge of the slab with two bottles of water in his hand.

Sweat dripped down her face, and she wiped it away with the back of her raw leather glove. The relentless heat of summer beat down on her back and radiated up beneath her feet. "I'm fine, Dad. What's up?"

"Can't a man check in on his kid? Especially when she hasn't come up for air all day?"

"I'm just trying to keep moving forward."

"Sometimes we need to slow down and sit with the struggle, so it doesn't come back to bite us. Trust me. I learned this the hard way. Come sit down with your old man." Dom lowered himself to the edge of the slab and looked out over the charred hills where vines used to thrive.

Frankie let the broom fall and sat down next to her dad, guzzling half the bottle of water he offered in one long sip.

She sat silent for a minute, listening to the sounds of a busy work crew breaking through the day. A Skilsaw here. A nail gun there. Positive noises. Progress. So why did she feel this overwhelming need to apologize to her father?

"I'm sorry, Dad." The words were out before she could think to stop them, but they needed saying.

"Sorry for what?"

"Sorry for screwing up this project. For turning Valenti Brothers into a laughingstock. For letting you down." She didn't look up from the ground in front of her. She couldn't bear to see the disappointment on his face.

"You done?"

"For letting Gabe down." Dom raised her chin with a gentle finger and tilted it toward him. Reluctantly she met his eyes, but only found love and sympathy there.

"Let's start there. How do you figure you've let your brother down?"

"I promised him that I'd keep our plan to run Valenti Brothers the way it had always been run. I got blinded by the sparkle of this show idea, and I ran with it, right into the ground."

"Do we love Seth any less for wanting to run his own woodworking business with Nick instead of taking over Tony's share? No, of course we don't. Plans change. You get to live your life the way you want to live it. Gabe wouldn't shame you for reaching for something different, and neither do I."

"The business motto. I broke all of it to make this damn show work, and I still failed." Frankie picked at the callus on her hand.

"You haven't failed at all. You turned a dream I had for your mother into a reality more beautiful than I could have imagined. So what if it takes a little longer to finish it? Are natural disasters your fault as well now?"

"This show was supposed to prove to you that I am ready to take over Valenti Brothers. I can't imagine you would even consider it after all this."

"This was your first solo gig and you ran it while juggling a TV production schedule and sabotage on top of it. I'm damn proud. Do I think you have the experience to run the whole company yet? No. You're still young and I don't want this business to consume your life. Do I think you could take your place at the helm with Sofia and Adrian? Absolutely. If that's what you really want."

"What does that mean? Of course it's what I really want."

"Is it? After all this, the excitement of the show, the big budget to play with, the freedom to do what you want…"

"Dad, I failed."

"Quit saying that. In building, you only fail if you quit. The motto? That's what my brother and I got to after making a whole bunch of mistakes. But we were always honest and we didn't quit until it was right. Did we hit that motto every build? Hell no, but it was the goal. Are you quitting on this job?"

"No." Her voice wasn't as strong as she would like.

"Then you haven't failed. But I'm going to ask you again, now that you've gotten a taste of leading your own team, doing the projects your way, is this still what you want?"

"I don't know."

There was that small voice in the back of her head pushing her ideas for a new show forward, but she hushed them right up. She could help people on a smaller scale. She could keep her dreams smaller and still do good. She was committed to this. If anything, this crazy experience had taught her she was better off tackling projects she knew she could handle and keep under control. Her life would be so much easier if she just kept it simple, stupid.

"My dream is still to run this company the way you and Zio Tony and Gabe would have done it. And I'm going to earn your trust."

"You already have it, Frankie. I just don't want you to chain yourself to a promise to your brother and miss out on a bigger dream. I've seen the videos. You're really good at this show biz thing, says the guy who can barely string together two coherent sentences on camera."

Her father's approval warmed her heart, but no, she couldn't set herself up like that again. Bending over backward for the network had nearly killed her and their company. She definitely didn't want to do that again.

ROUGHED IN

~

THAT NIGHT, all was quiet in the Valenti Brothers' construction office. Everyone else was busy with babies and revamping wedding plans, but someone had to keep the lights on. She strolled from mismatched room to room, admiring everything her father and uncle had built. Everything she had helped build. She'd been pitching in on jobsites since she'd been old enough to lift a hammer. The current success of the business was definitely part hers.

She imagined sitting in Dom's office, running the various builds, paging through the stacks of job applications they had, leading the company forward.

Wandering into the kitchen, she poured herself a cup of coffee. She drank half the cup before she remembered she didn't like coffee. She'd been craving the flavor of it recently.

Dumping the second half down the sink, she rinsed the mug and went back to her office.

She vaguely started organizing her desk into neater piles, but her heart wasn't in it. This place that had been her second home for so many years felt different today. It seemed quiet, somehow small, and she didn't feel the usual hustle rise inside her when she came in the door.

Damn him for making her think about more. This was all Jake's fault. She picked up her phone to see if she had somehow missed a call or a text or even an emoji at this point. But no. He'd shown her a different life and then disappeared. True, she'd told him to go away, but now she didn't know how to get him to come back. It had been nearly a week without contact. Was she too late?

The jingle bells tied to the handle jangled along with her nerves as someone came in the front door. Her heart fluttered into her throat. It wouldn't be the first time her thoughts had made him manifest.

Frankie walked out front with a grin on her face. But it wasn't him.

"Sylvia? Tyler?" Frankie reached out to shake her hand and found herself pulled into a hug. "What a nice surprise! How can I help you?"

"We just wanted to come and say thank you again for all of your help. I was able to get a few of our wedding pictures cleaned up, and these rings mean the world to me. You were so kind to us. We had to thank you one more time before we left."

"Wait. What? You're leaving?" Frankie pulled them farther into the office and sat them at the consultation table in the main room. "Tell me everything."

"Well, the county said it would be weeks before they will even have the trailer park cleared and okayed for rebuilding. The current owner of the land isn't even sure they can afford to reopen. The firefighters gave us a gift card to help with immediate needs, and we have the money from the insurance, but I can't spend that on rent. I need to buy a house, and you know what the property values out here are like…"

Sylvia raised her hands in a shrug, and Tyler wilted in his chair as if each reason for leaving was an added weight on his shoulders.

"Tyler, do you want to move?" Frankie asked.

The teen shook his head. "I've got friends and I like my school here. I don't want to start over."

Before Sylvia could redirect him, Frankie asked her the same question. "Would you stay if you could?"

"Of course. I have a solid job here and Tyler is settled. Plus this is where we have our last memories with Brandon. I just can't see a way to make it work." Sylvia was near tears now, but Frankie was energized. She loved a good challenge.

"Give me ten minutes, okay? Can I get you water? Coffee? Soda?"

She settled them in with their drinks and raced to her office. She reached into the middle of the stack on the edge of her desk and came up triumphant with an unlabeled manila folder. She snagged her yellow legal pad and a pencil and tucked all three into her arms.

Sitting back at the table, she laid out her goodies.

"Okay. I have an idea. Hear me out before you decide anything." At Sylvia's confused nod, she opened the folder and turned it toward her. The sheet on top was a printed MLS listing. "Valenti Brothers owns this property. We bought it a few months ago, intending to update the kitchen and baths before we flipped it. The project moved to the back burner because of the vineyard project. It's in San Jose, and I realize that would add to your commute, but it would be a temporary housing solution. The rest of the building is in pretty good shape. I can rent it to you below market price, because you'd be doing us a favor by keeping it occupied while we wait to start renovations."

Sylvia's eyes had gone wide as she flipped through the pictures of the older home. "Why? Why would you do that for us?"

"Because Valenti Brothers has always been about getting people into the homes they need at a price they can afford. This is just an extension of that. And I think your community needs you as much as you need them. Now, if you think that will work for the short term, let's talk about long-term rebuilding. Let's make a list of all the things you would like to have in your next home."

Sylvia and Tyler spit out ideas and Frankie took notes and sketched out ideas, and at the end of two hours, had a tentative plan for a small home that could either be built on a mobile home base or onto a permanent foundation, depending on where they ended up putting it. Frankie made a mental note to contact the owner of the park and see if they'd be interested in selling.

Standing, she tucked everything back into the file folder. "So I think we have a good plan. Let it settle for a day or two, and then we can work out the paperwork and get you moved in."

Sylvia rose and pulled her into another big hug, tears running down her cheeks. "I am overwhelmed. I never thought I'd say this but the day I met you standing in the middle of our burnt-out house was the best thing to happen to us in a long time. You are our guardian angel."

As she walked them out and shut the door behind them Frankie smiled. She knew who the real guardian angel was. Gabe had set these people in her path, and she wasn't going to blow it. Maybe this was her way forward. She couldn't deny that she'd felt the thrill of seeing herself on TV, but if she had a platform like that she'd use it for something more important than everyday home transformations or large-scale vanity projects.

And it hit her. She did have that platform. Whether she came back and ran Valenti Brothers or not, Jake had given her this platform and positive momentum. For the first time since she was six and plotting to take over the world with Gabe from their tree house, she let her mind explore an alternate future. What would she do with her life if she could do anything?

Working out the details of Sylvia's new home had given Frankie a solid dose of clarity. Building homes for people recovering from disaster was the missing piece. She could still be affiliated with Valenti Brothers, but she couldn't go back to only working on kitchen and bathroom renos. She wanted to use her fame for good.

Frankie pulled up her social media app and watched the teasers the network had posted. Trina's camerawork was truly special, but it was Jake who had crafted it into a compelling story. A new video trailer had gone up, this one focused on the fire.

He'd pulled footage from the external cams, showing her on the roof with the hose juxtaposed with the rebuilding effort. Seeing the damage brought the pain and panic back, but even the minute-long teaser had been edited to evoke hope and renewal. He'd even added contact information for the California Fire Foundation.

Jake had opened so many doors. Yes, he'd been a jerk and thrown some obstacles in her path. But she believed that at his core he was a good man. Even after she'd pushed him away, he'd still created these breathtaking teasers casting her as the hero. She could almost believe that person really was her, or maybe just the best parts of her. What would that woman do?

She wished Jake was here to talk about options. Because in every image of her future that had raced through her mind, personal and professional, he was there. She'd let her temper get the best of her, and she owed him an apology. She just hoped he'd accept it.

If she wanted a different future, she was going to have to make it happen. Who was she to ignore a lightning bolt from fate?

CHAPTER 32

WHILE FATE MIGHT STRIKE with the swiftness of a lightning bolt, logistics hit with the force of a freight train at rush hour.

Her plans to apologize ground to a halt under the weight of her responsibilities to the show. They worked like dogs over the following weeks, hustling to get the vineyard build done and repaired. They had all agreed to wait on rebuilding the barn space. Her siblings had decided to have their weddings on the burnt-out slab. They wanted to keep the walls open to the view behind it and only put up enough framing studs to suggest the shape of the barn. The rest of the construction could come later. That suited Frankie and her budget, but it meant everyone else was scrambling to pull in their wedding plans by a month and a half.

It also didn't help her plans that Jake had to keep flying down to LA for end-of-series meetings and promotional opportunities. He was also hearing new pitches for shows, and Frankie hoped he didn't accept one before she could talk to him about hers.

Despite being absent, he'd asked Lorena to rope her into the end of the day conference calls where they reviewed footage and discussed strategies for how to craft the last bits of the show for maximum impact. For the first time, she really saw his genius. The way he crafted a story arc was masterful, and Frankie was grateful for the chance to be included in the decision-making process. She was less grateful for the fact that Lorena was always there so she never got a chance to talk to Jake alone.

It wasn't until the day of the final reveal and wrap party that she even managed to broach the topic.

Dressed and primped for the final walk-through, Frankie stood on the gravel driveway, flanked by Sofia, Adrian, Enzo, and Natalie. They were all going to greet Jo when Dom surprised her, and then Frankie and Dom would walk her through the house room by room. It was going to be torturously long, having to set up and break down cameras in each room to grab Jo's reactions from multiple angles, but it would be worth it. Frankie just hoped she could get Jake by himself for a bit so they could talk.

Even now, they were so close but so far. He stood just behind Trina's left shoulder as she kept her camera trained in tight on the siblings. But he hadn't looked up from the viewfinder screen once. He was taking his vow to prove himself with actions instead of words seriously. But she missed him.

This was her last chance, and she couldn't waste it.

Looking directly into Trina's lens, she let all of her longing and desire show on her face. She thought about how much she'd missed him and how sorry she was, and hoped it translated to her expression. She must have gotten some of it through, because Jake's head snapped up and stared straight at her.

I need to talk to you. She mouthed the words and he nodded.

Later, he mouthed back, but the tension around his mouth had eased a little. His lips relaxed and he tucked his hands into his back pockets.

She smiled with her own relief and was able to turn her attention to the car her dad was guiding up the driveway. Her mother sat in the passenger seat with a blindfold on.

Everyone held their breath as he parked and circled the car to help her out.

"Dom, what is going on?" Jo asked, exasperation and laughter coloring her tone. "Where did you take me?"

Frankie could see her dad's hands shaking from where she stood ten feet away, and prayed he could pull this off. He took Jo's hands in his and backed up until they were standing on the X of black tape someone had set on the driveway.

"My Jojo." Dom's voice cracked on her nickname. He held her hands in his as they stood face to face, inadvertently recreating the pose of their wedding photo that sat in pride of place on the mantel at home.

The symbolism hit Frankie hard, and she blinked back her tears.

"Josephine Valenti, do you remember back when we were young and newly in love? When we'd sit out at the beach bonfires and dream with a bottle of wine between us?"

Jo nodded her head and her smile dimmed a little.

"My dream was to own my own business. You stood by my side every step of the way while we made that dream a reality. You took care of the kids and kept the office running and the bills paid and gave more years than I ever had the right to expect to my dream. And I thank you for that. Because of your sacrifices, we have a legacy to pass on to our kids."

Jo's lips pursed, and Frankie was willing to bet there were tears being absorbed by that blindfold, but she still didn't speak.

Dom pushed on, putting his heart on his sleeve for the world to see. Frankie hoped it would be enough to bring her parents back together.

"I remember your dreams too. You were going to be a teacher, and when we retired we were going to drink wine and watch the sunsets over a plot of land in the country. Do you remember?"

His voice was thick with tears now, and Jo's shoulders were shaking as she nodded.

"You've taught our children how to be wonderful adults. I know that's not exactly how you pictured being a teacher, but you have to know the difference you made in all of our lives. I hope this second part shows our appreciation. I hope..." Dom cleared the emotion from his throat. "I hope it's everything you dreamed we could have."

He reached back to untie the blindfold, and Jo winced at the sudden brightness. But as her eyes adjusted and she realized where they stood, they grew round with wonder. "Dom, what are you saying? What does this mean?" She clutched his arm as he turned her more fully toward the house.

"It means this was all for you. For us. I'm walking away from the building business. I'm leaving it in very good hands," he said as he looked over his shoulder to where they all stood, watching.

For the first time, her mother realized she had an audience, and self-consciously wiped her cheeks. "Oh, Dom. This is too much. Is this what you've been hiding the last few months?"

"This, and a few other things I'll tell you about later. Do you like it?"

"I'm overwhelmed. It's beautiful, of course, but I never thought it would be mine."

"Well, it's fifty acres in the country, and I thought we could give making our own wine a go. I know you want to retire and travel and do all those things we dreamed, but let's be honest. You'll go nuts with me underfoot, and I'll go nuts without a project to tackle. This solves all of those problems, but still gives us the freedom to do those things we dreamed about all those years ago. Will you let me show you my dream for us?"

Jo looked up at him, and Frankie saw love and hope and pride written clearly on her face. That's what she wanted someday. She wanted to look at her man like that, and have it all be reflected right back at her. Frankie chanced a glance at Jake then, and he wasn't looking at her parents, or at the screen. He was looking right at her, and what she saw there weakened her knees.

They had a lot to talk about, but the expression on his face gave her hope that someday her dreams would come true, and he would be the man to help her make that happen.

Now if they could just get through this shoot…

~

FRANKIE HELD on to her patience as she showed her mother the great room that would be perfect for entertaining, the back bedrooms that could be rented for events, and the renovated bathrooms in what was the old farmhouse. Jo oohed and aahed her way through the kitchen, which made it easier for her to ignore her emotions as she showed her mom the in-ground wine cellar.

Those same pesky emotions threatened to overwhelm her when she took her mother into what would be the lower level tasting room, complete with distressed wooden bar. Jake was everywhere in this house. If they didn't manage to work things out, it was going to be real hard to carry on. But Frankie couldn't let herself think things like that. The camera picked up everything and today it needed to see joy and delight.

They walked the terraced decks that they'd installed at various levels to maximize the views over the vineyards and then crossed to the slab of concrete that had once been the barn.

Everyone grew solemn at the sight of the bare concrete and charred edges, an acknowledgement of the fire that had come so close to taking everything. Frankie had pressure-washed the floor and sealed it tight, but the smoke and fire staining remained. Personally she thought it would add character to the space for her siblings' weddings.

By the end of the day her feet were throbbing and her cheeks hurt from smiling. She would kill for a glass of red wine and a foot massage. Luckily, the wrap party was getting into gear so the glass of wine at least wouldn't require a body count. She leaned against the kitchen sink and looked out the window at the best view ever. Her parents were propped against the deck railing she'd built, arms around each other, watching the sunset over their vines. *Mission accomplished.*

Now she just needed Jake to get back up here from his production trailer. She wanted to talk to him about everything that had happened. She hoped for his advice on her plan and to tease him into laughter. He didn't laugh enough. He had laughed with her.

Oh, fuck.

Frankie blinked rapidly against the loss that twisted her gut into knots.

Jake tapped her on the shoulder and she leaped and yelped as if she'd been burned.

"Is now a good time?"

"Sure," she said and smiled tentatively as he led her to the wine cellar. It would be even harder to resist the memories with him there. The man sure knew how to set a scene to his advantage. Given that she was hoping for the same outcome, she didn't mind.

Hidden in the close space again—this time outfitted with full racks of wine and the sparkling mini chandelier—Frankie let the memories engulf her. She stopped on the last stair, bringing her closer to his height, and held out her arms. He stepped into them and gave her the crushing hug she needed. She'd been an emotional wreck trying to keep it all together, and damn him, she'd missed having him to depend on.

"Missed you too," he murmured against her neck, his head

resting on her shoulder. She felt the tension drain out of them both as they stood in the quiet, wrapped up in each other.

"I'm sorry."

Their voices twined through those simple words. She wasn't sure who said it first, but it didn't matter. She kept talking.

"I was angry about the manipulations and stressed from the fire, but I shouldn't have accused you of having anything to do with it, and I'm sorry. I can kind of understand why you did what you did with the tiles and stuff now that I've seen how you put together an episode, but it really hurt to find out you'd been putting me through hell while we'd been…whatever it was we were doing," she finished lamely, not wanting to put names to actions just now.

He took half a step back and moved his hands to cup her face. "You don't have to apologize. I made this job harder behind your back, because that's how these shows work. I never expected to fall for you. Once we were together, I should have told you and worked out a better solution. You were right to be mad. I was wrong, and I am sorry."

She let his words sink in, and it helped fill in a few of the cracks he'd made on her heart. A little apology spackle went a long way.

"During the reunion, I had this epiphany that all the while I thought I was being independent, I was really just keeping people at arm's length so I wouldn't get hurt when they inevitably left me. Turns out it still hurts. I don't want you to leave me. My home doesn't feel right because you're not there. My head doesn't think straight for wondering what you'd say. And my heart… My heart tells me I'm a complete idiot daily since we've been apart." He pulled his arm tighter around her waist, dropping his forehead to hers.

"I don't want to lose you either, but how are we going to make this work? We are both stubborn, headstrong, and believe we know how best to get things done," Frankie pointed out.

He hesitated a moment, and she didn't breathe until his hands slid up into her hair.

"Figuring that out will be part of the fun. I think if we keep doing this honesty thing and the talking thing, this other thing will be just fine."

"Oh, and what's this 'other thing'?" Frankie whispered, close enough to feel her lips brush against his.

"This falling in love thing," he replied before taking her lips in a soft and quiet kiss.

Frankie tightened her arms and pulled him flush against her, needing to feel him, needing to believe this was real. "God, I love you too."

They kissed as if it was the first time. They kissed like it was the last time. Like new lovers, and old friends. She never wanted it to end.

But there was a party happening, and they needed him too. She could share for a little while longer. She made herself pull back from the kiss, and was gratified that it took him a moment to compose himself as well.

"So where do we go from here?" she asked.

"Back up those stairs with two bottles of prosecco for your mom."

"Ha ha. I'm serious."

"So am I. We go up there and celebrate like crazy with your family. There will be plenty of time for us to work things out. I'm not going anywhere. Let me prove to you I've changed."

"I'd like that."

CHAPTER 33

Jake popped open the prosecco, and it fizzled over as the cork flew into the yard. Everyone who'd gathered on the back deck cheered and passed around cups.

"Speech, speech, speech!"

Frankie cleared her throat and raised her glass. Jake watched her command the crowd's attention effortlessly.

"To the best damn crew in California. You took a chance on me, and we couldn't have finished this project without your dedication and skill. You all are like family now, and I'll…" She choked up a little before pushing through it. "Thank you. For those of you who passed first inspections, your gift cards are here inside your final paychecks."

She waved a stack of envelopes and grinned.

"Season three of MDash starts filming at the end of month. So, eat, drink, and be merry while you can! Cheers!"

Literal cheers erupted again, and Frankie started handing out envelopes and backslaps.

Jake raised his glass, and cleared his throat obnoxiously until everyone quieted down again. "What she said!" Everyone laughed. "Seriously, both crews did amazing work. Thank you."

Enzo cranked the music back up and the party lurched into high gear.

Jake looked around at the house full of family, friends, food, and fun, and realized he had a part in this. These people were his family as well. They'd brought this place back to life for its next adventure. *Mission accomplished.* Though it also meant he needed to get moving on his next adventure as well.

His eyes scanned the crowd to find Frankie again.

She was watching Jo and Dom snuggle in the porch swing she'd hung for them, looking like newlyweds who couldn't bear to be apart. This was Frankie's model for grown love. He realized it had become his as well. And he wanted that with her.

Jake stepped up behind her and startled her by taking her free hand and tapping her glass with his. "Congratulations, Ms. Valenti. A job well done."

"It's amazing what we can accomplish when we finally start working together."

He smiled at that and kissed her hand where their fingers entwined. Had she read his mind? "Walk with me."

They strolled down the gravel drive toward the framed-out barn where her siblings planned to host their double wedding in a few short weeks. Jake still couldn't believe they'd asked him to stand up as a groomsman.

He walked, hand in hand with her where the aisle would be, and helped her sit down on the edge of the slab. He flicked on the fairy lights she'd strung and joined her as she stared out over the blackened hillside.

"So," she said.

"So." He mimicked her tone for tone.

She bumped her shoulder into his and asked the question he had been struggling with for weeks. "What's next for you?" He could hear the nerves in her voice.

"I'm not sure," he said honestly.

"That's not like you."

"I know, but see, I've got this person in my life now, and I need to plan with her instead of making the decisions on my own."

"Learned that one quick, did ya?" She chuckled.

"What about you?"

"I'm not sure either. I thought I knew. I had it all planned out, but now…"

She shrugged and he leaned back, bracing himself with one hand behind so he could wrap an arm around her shoulder and pull her into the comfort and support of his hug. "Talk me through it."

She rested her head heavily on his shoulder and sucked in a deep breath before she spoke. "I don't want to run the company," she whispered.

"Whoa. That's a big shift."

"I know." She slapped her hand playfully against his thigh. "And it's all your fault."

"My fault? How do you figure?"

"Everything was fine and dandy. I was all set to carry out Gabe's legacy, take over the company and let my dad retire. Adrian and I could handle running the place and keep the family motto going. Good work, on time, and under budget. It would have been enough."

She shifted farther into his embrace and touched his cheek with her fingertips until he turned to look at her.

"And then you showed up and made me see bigger possibilities. Now those old dreams feel small. I need to rough in some new dreams, but I don't know where to start, and I need your help. Can I pitch you an idea?"

"Sure."

He scooted sideways so he was facing her, one leg crossed in front of him, the other dangling over the edge. She mirrored his move, but she was looking at her hands, fidgeting with her cuticles. He put one of his over hers to calm her nerves and nodded for her to start.

"What would you say to another show, one where we help rebuild homes for people who have been struck by tragedy? We could travel all over, or stay close to home here, helping people get back on their feet by fixing or rebuilding their homes and their lives."

Jake thought about it for a minute. Logistics, scheduling, funding, casting, red tape all swirled through his mind, distracting him momentarily from the point. Pushing all that aside, he realized this woman was handing him what he'd been looking for. A way to do good in the world, and a way to stay involved in her life.

He gathered his words carefully. "You said something the other day that really stuck with me. I should be using my powers for good. I have the influence, the name, the money. I should be doing more for the world than just making an entertaining reality show."

Frankie smiled shyly, as if she was afraid to believe this was real. "I thought the drama could come from the already existing tragedy. No more manipulations, at least not without talking about it. We could be a team."

"I like the sound of that."

"I still feel like I'm letting Gabe down a little." Frankie looked out across the burned fields, searching for forgiveness she could only give herself.

Maybe he could nudge her in the right direction. "Let me ask you something. Do you think Gabe would stand in the way of you making a difference in the lives of all these people? Or would he be the one encouraging you to take the risk and chase your dream?"

She couldn't answer beyond a nod, because those tears were choking her up again.

"Valenti Brothers is in good hands. Adrian and Sofia will keep it the family business it's always been, and you won't ever lose that. But we could do so much more."

"Do you think the network would go for it? Especially after everything that went wrong here?" she asked.

"I think they'd jump at the chance, but I don't want to offer it to them."

Frankie's eyes snapped to his. "Why not? What are you plotting?"

"I was thinking maybe we start our own network." He wasn't sure if Frankie's silence was good or bad, so he kept talking, hoping to sway her. "I'm tired of jumping through their hoops just to prove I am good at what I do. They were a stepping stone."

She laughed at that. "You've got a lot of those."

Jake cringed. "Yeah, I'd been thinking about one day running my own production company, but having my own network is even better. I have the funds to get us started until we find investors. And now I have the motivation and the guiding purpose for it. All I need is a partner to help me bring it to life."

"One show does not make a network. How would we fill the rest of the roster?"

"Some syndicated shows, some original content. Once people see what we are doing, I'm sure I'll get pitches from other runners and creatives. I know this great family who might want a more flexible production schedule now that everyone has babies, and a makeup artist who wants to grow her show bigger by doing real-life makeovers for deserving people. Her husband is tackling these large-scale landscaping projects that could be cool to film. And there's this singing carpenter who likes to hang out with this amazing camerawoman. Even Britt was pitching me ideas last weekend. If we build it, people will come... You're awfully quiet. Look, I know it's risky, but—"

Frankie held up a hand, and he bit back his next words. He was still learning to listen, but he'd like to think he was getting better at it.

"My head is spinning. I'm excited, but this is a lot to take in. It's exactly the kind of project I wanted to tackle. And it would keep us moving in the same direction. We'd be partners?" she asked.

"Yes, full partners."

"Making decisions together in the best interests of the company? Open, honest communication?"

"I like the sound of that." He tucked her hair behind her ear, and marveled at how much this fierce and brave woman had changed his life.

"Partners, in all ways? At work and at home? I need you all in or I'm out, I'm afraid."

"All in. You are my heart, Frankie. I can't do this without you by my side."

"Okay."

"Okay?"

"Yeah, okay. Let's do this."

As the sun set over the black hills, painting the sky a fiery orange, they planned a future from the ashes, together. Head to head, heart to heart, hand to hand.

It was always risky exposing dreams to the light, but with this partner in his corner it wasn't scary anymore. Everything he'd ever wanted was within reach. A meaningful life. A lover to share it with. A family who truly cared for him. Picking up the Valenti project was the best decision he'd ever made.

"I love you, Jake." Frankie's words were soft in the cooling air, but he heard them and they warmed him to the core.

"I love you too…" Jake leaned in for a kiss, but a cold nose to the neck made him yelp and pull back.

Frankie laughed and threw her arms around Buster.

Jake grimaced, but rubbed Buster's head anyway. "I love you too, you big troublemaker."

Buster barked and licked his face.

"Aww, he loves you too. We're gonna be one big, happy family," Frankie said in her puppy-talk voice, but Jake was dead serious in his reply.

"Yeah, we are."

EPILOGUE

Dom tugged at the bowtie that was attempting to strangle him. He hadn't worn one of these rigs in years. The fact that Jake had taken him out to get fitted for it meant it was a good one, but he was still uncomfortable as hell.

"Daddy, knock it off." Fi slapped at his hand and straightened the tie herself.

"I can't help it," Dom groused. "Damn thing is trying to kill me."

"No, it isn't. It's making you look handsome." Jo stepped up behind him and gave him a brief hug of support. She knew how nervous he was.

Today he was sending a daughter and a son off into wedded bliss. He had the privilege of walking both brides down the aisle. He was terrified he'd screw it up.

This was worse than having to film those crazy shows. This was real life and it would go down in the annals of family lore for decades if he tripped or stepped on someone's hem. Jo's hand between his shoulder blades helped center him. She knew what this was really about.

They'd started seeing a couples therapist in addition to their own separate sessions, so she had a better idea of where he was struggling and vice versa. It was the most they'd talked about things that really mattered in years.

It had come up last week that Dom was struggling with the regret that Gabe would not be at the wedding. That there were all these family triumphs he'd missed. That there was a person out there who would have been perfect for him too, who would never get to know him. The futility of Gabe's death still weighed heavy on his heart all these years later, and the load got heavier to carry around major life events.

"Remember, breathe through it, babe." Jo repeated their therapist's advice. She held her bouquet in front of his face. "Focus on the now. Smell the roses. The girls need you."

Dom hauled in a deep breath, grounding himself in the rich scents of the flowers and the soothing haven of his wife's voice. He nodded. "You're right. I've got this."

He looked around the master bedroom at the vineyard that had been converted to bride central. Natalie was getting her hair curled and tucked into some fancy mess low on her head. Frankie sat with her eyes closed and a drape over her blush pink dress, and some lady with purple hair was doing her makeup. Sofia, hair and makeup finished, was beginning the process of donning her gown. Even little Daisy was here, walking slowly around the perimeter of the room in her miniature version of Frankie's dress, practicing her flower girl walk. Thank goodness they hadn't put any real furniture in here yet, or they wouldn't all fit!

Jo stepped over to help zip Sofia into her dress, and one of the photographers Jake had referred to them began snapping pictures he knew would make Jo cry later. His baby was becoming a bride before his eyes. His heart pinched so he focused on his wife instead. She stood beside her daughter, a

ROUGHED IN

dress of shimmering champagne hugging every curve he loved to touch. He'd make sure to show her that later. Maybe in that fancy wine cellar in the kitchen...

Clearing his throat, Dom resisted the urge to tug on his tie again and looked around his feet to make sure there wasn't anything fragile or fabric before he stepped toward the door.

"You ladies seem to have everything under control in here. I'm just going to step out for some fresh air and see how the boys are doing."

Before they could protest, he was out the door and hustling down the hallway. He turned left at the stairs and went down to the tasting room, which had been designated as the gentleman's prep area. The bar had been stocked just for the occasion.

"Dom!" Adrian called from his seat at the bar. "How's my bride doing?"

"She's stunning and almost ready to go."

Enzo held up a bottle of beer and a red Solo cup. "What can I get you, Dad?"

"I'll have the beer. Thanks, son."

Jake turned from where he'd been talking on his cell phone and tucked it into his pocket. That boy never quit. Always hustling. Since he'd turned that hustle in service of his family, Dom couldn't complain. Hell, he'd been the same way. Trust Frankie to fall for someone just like him. Dom's chest puffed out with pride as he assessed the men in the room. He took a sip of beer to wet his throat that had gone suspiciously dry.

They were all wearing tuxes that seemed to effortlessly fit. Dom knew from his own fitting with Jake's tailor that it was anything but effortless. He also knew the ladies were going to swoon when they saw this crew standing up by the altar.

These men fate had brought into his life... Enzo, his son, always true to himself. Adrian, a son in his heart and today son-in-law, solid and trustworthy no matter what. And Jake, the man he'd trusted to solidify his legacy, bring the Valentis to the world, and now marry his youngest child.

Those damn tears pressed against his closed eyelids when he thought about Gabe, the fourth man who should have been standing at that bar. He would have joked with Adrian like they had back in the day, talked Enzo into taking a dare. And Jake? Well, Gabe would've kept an eye on Jake, just to make sure he was treating his best girl Frankie right.

As these men joked and kept their own nerves at bay, Dom just let the conversation flow past him, caught in his own thoughts.

When the fire had taken down the barn they'd been planning to use for the weddings, Dom had been worried about how Natalie and Sofia would handle the loss. They'd spent months making it perfect, just to have it go up in flames... All that was left was the concrete slab overlooking the terraced vineyards.

But instead of panicking or delaying, these women had rallied. They had actually moved up the date, while juggling new babies and maternity leaves. They had adjusted expectations and come up with a new plan that made Dom proud to call them all Valentis. Sofia and Natalie had pulled together a joint outdoor ceremony, at the vineyard, on the slab, fire be damned.

Good work, on time, under budget.

It made him smile. He set down his beer, practically untouched, and let himself out the double doors that would eventually be the main entrance to the winery. He'd just go check and make sure the space was all set.

Hands tucked in his pockets, Dom circled around the property and climbed the slightly graded path that took him to that slab.

Frankie had constructed an open frame where the barn had

been, leaving the roof and sides open to the view of the charred landscape as requested. Enzo and Adrian had pitched in, laying a fresh gravel path and hanging fairy lights and Edison bulbs to create a starry ceiling.

The large marble countertop that Frankie had salvaged from the rubble of the event space sat all cleaned and shiny atop two carpenter's horses as a makeshift altar. A central aisle was flanked by rows of white chairs that were filling with family and friends to celebrate this double wedding.

His children wanted their weddings to be a symbol of new beginnings and new births, like a phoenix rising from the ashes. They planned to come back next year and recreate their wedding photos with a very different backdrop.

They had also reached an agreement with the network to film it as a two-hour special that would run as a telethon for the California Fire Foundation's relief efforts. He knew Jake had been instrumental in making that happen.

Trina was helping check the camera setup, and Winston, Rico, Seth and Nick were helping people get seated. Everything was perfect, down to the sun just beginning to sink into the western sky in front of them.

"Dom? Dom!" Jo's voice cut through the chatter. He turned and saw her standing on the deck behind the house, calling to him.

His partner, his wife, still had the power to make his heart want to beat out of his chest. He was a blessed man indeed.

"Dom, it's time! Get up here."

He climbed the stairs and found all of the ladies had moved to the kitchen, ready to go. Daisy bounced beside Dom and grabbed his hand, distracting him from his melancholic thoughts.

"Come on, Nonno, we gotta go smile and throw flowers." The seven-year-old tugged him forward, gossamer fairy wings fluttering behind her as she skipped toward the florist who handed Daisy her basket of rose petals.

Frankie carried a gorgeous but heavy bouquet of blush tea roses, coral dahlias, and pale green and blue succulents. Natalie and Sofia stood side by side in their gorgeous and unique gowns, each holding a bouquet that matched their personalities. Enzo's florist friend had worked wonders given the newly shortened time frame. Sofia's rosé bouquet was perfectly balanced with bright pops of darker pink and burgundy, while Natalie's was more whimsical and dreamy with champagne roses and an asymmetrical drape. Even Dom could see that the flowers were perfect for each woman who carried them and ideal for the vineyard wedding theme. He made a mental note to send the florist a tip.

Both brides were beaming. They had such bright futures ahead. He couldn't help but think back over his own marriage. It hadn't been all sunshine and roses, but in the seasons when it bloomed, it was a paradise worth every sacrifice.

He wanted that for them, the challenges and the triumphs. A life lived in love.

The music that had been playing in the background stopped.

"That's our cue, everyone." Jo bustled toward Dom. She wiped away the tear he hadn't realized was running down his cheek. "You okay?"

He nodded, incapable of words. She tucked herself into his arms. He sucked in a shuddering breath, trying to get himself under control.

"It's okay, babe."

"It is. It really is." He squeezed her tight. "Thank you for everything."

"Don't get us started again. Sentimental watering pot," Jo teased, a tender smile creasing her cheeks. She ran a hand down Dom's cheek and kissed him.

"Ewwww, Moooooom! My eyes!" Frankie gagged and covered her eyes like she had when she was ten and thoroughly embarrassed by parental displays of affection.

Dom chuckled. It felt so normal. Finally.

"Go line up smart-ass, and take Daisy with you." Jo led Dom over to the brides who each tucked a hand into his elbow for their walk down the aisle.

Once everyone was arranged, Jo ducked out to take her seat, and Pachelbel's "Canon in D" began to play.

Showtime.

Dom cleared his throat again. "Ladies, this is a privilege. I'm so proud of both of you. Let's go get married."

He made it down the aisle without tripping. A few tears had escaped, but he was only human. Anyone would have cried at the sight of his boys' faces when they first saw their brides. And maybe a few more tears were shed for Gabe, who should have been there, maybe with a wife of his own, his babies giggling with the others being tended by various grandparents. But he wasn't, and he never would be.

Dom knew that he'd made mistakes, that he'd hurt the people he loved with his knee-jerk reactions to his grief. Jo's acceptance and forgiveness was his first step to making things right. He hoped that the fact that all of his children had found their people because of his impulsive decision would weigh in his favor, also. Realistically, he'd never hear the end of it over Friday dinners, but that was fine. That was family.

He also knew that though Gabe was gone, he'd never be forgotten. Dom would keep his son's memory alive for the generation currently swaddled in the front row. He'd work to let go of the loss, but keep every bit of the love. That looked more attainable with Jo back firmly by his side.

He turned at the end of the aisle and sat literally by her side, and Jo magically produced a tissue for him. It was a blessing to be with someone who knew him inside and out, even if they'd gotten a little lost along the way. Rebuilding that knowledge of who they were now was a challenge he was ready to tackle.

This was a happy day.

Dom wouldn't remember most of the ceremony. That was just words spoken by a preacher. He would remember the way Jo had rescued baby Laurel from Seth, swapping her flowers for the baby so that she would calm down. She swayed at the side of the aisle, rocking Laurel in that instinctive rhythm she'd used for their own babies, while their children spoke their vows. Abuela Cici had brought Baby Gabe over to join them, and Brandy had carried Ash asleep on her shoulder. So much love for so many babies.

He would remember the way Adrian's sisters had thrown flower petals at their new sister Sofia as they'd walked back down the aisle with shrieks of laughter, and the way Adrian had scooped her up at the end of the aisle, triumphant.

He would remember clearing the chairs to turn the slab into a dance floor and watching Enzo and Natalie share their first dance with Daisy and the twins. Never had "My Girl" seen so many spins and giggles.

He would remember ducking into the kitchen for more wine, and catching just a glimpse of Jake slipping a ring on Frankie's finger before ducking back out empty-handed.

He would remember dancing with his wife, while Winston serenaded the crowd with an acoustic version of "Thinking Out Loud." Holding her in his arms, while the song spoke of loving her until they were seventy. They were nearly there. Maybe they should change that to eleventy...

He chuckled and pulled her closer. He was grateful to have been given a second chance with his amazing woman. He danced her onto the path and into the darkening night towards the future they'd build together. It wouldn't be exactly the same as they'd dreamed all those years ago, but it would be full of love and family and laughter. A dream come true.

Keep reading for Jo & Dom's love story in Reclaimed Dreams.

RECLAIMED DREAMS

EVA MOORE

CONTENT WARNINGS

This is a marriage redemption story. Over the course of forty years, this couple has experienced miscarriage, the death of an adult child in the military, and near divorce. Please read safely.

CHAPTER 1

5 years *ago*

THE EVENING HAD BEGUN like every other Friday night in recent memory. Jo Valenti had turned her Alfredo sauce down to low and dropped the fettuccine into the boiling salty water. Dinner was almost ready. Sofia was on the phone in the living room. Enzo and Frankie were already curled up in the family room in front of the TV. She sighed and looked at the one chair at the table that would not be filled tonight. Maybe Christmas, he'd said on their last call.

When Gabe and her nephew, Seth, had joined the army together, she knew they'd be stationed far away for a few years. In the end, she'd sent them off with hugs and smiles, because she knew what it was to have dreams that needed chasing. So even though her heart was breaking, she'd pushed her fears aside and given what was needed. The fact that the cousins were as close as brothers and wouldn't be going alone had brought a small measure of comfort.

But that didn't mean her heart didn't still pinch when she

looked at Gabe's empty seat. She still set his place, because often his high school friends or army buddies would drop by for dinner. Her Friday dinners were famous among her children's friends. Others might sit in it, but it would always be Gabe's spot, waiting for him to come home.

The doorbell rang, announcing guests, and when Dom walked in to the kitchen with two men in uniform, Jo assumed they were friends of Gabe's, come for dinner. Her son usually tried to give her a heads-up when people were going to drop by, but it wasn't always possible due to his deployment. He was currently stationed in Iraq, and to say it was remote was an understatement.

She turned to the sink to fill a pan with water to steam the vegetables and called into the living room. "Fi, come add some places to the table. Welcome, boys. I hope you're hungry. Did Gabe send you?"

The two servicemen stood silent in her kitchen, hats in their hands. Dom waved a hand toward the table.

"Come, sit. Can I get you boys a drink?" he asked.

"No, sir. Thank you. Maybe you and your wife should take a seat."

Jo registered the serious set of their faces and slowly lowered herself into the nearest chair. It would occur to her later that she'd chosen Gabe's chair.

"The Secretary of the Army regrets to inform you that your son, Gabriel Valenti, was killed yesterday in the Ninewa Province, Iraq…"

Her ears stopped working after that. She could see the man still talking, as though his words hadn't just shattered her world. She saw Dom collapse into a chair and cradle his head on the table, shoulders shaking. Sofia, Enzo, and Frankie came running, and when the taller soldier spoke to them, they burst into tears and circled the sibling wagon into a tight hug. The shorter soldier stepped close and placed a hand on Jo's shoulder. His lips were moving, but she couldn't hear anything over the buzzsaw in her head. Her baby, the boy who'd made her a mother, was dead. What more could he say?

The child she'd held in her heart had died, and Jo felt the severed connection pulsing through every vein in her body. Part of her was dying along with him, and it burned.

Jo closed her eyes. She couldn't bear it. She didn't want to hear this. She didn't want to see this. Even the feel of the hard wooden chair against her back overwhelmed her. Everything was too much, too real. But how could any of this be real? She opened her eyes to double check and the two soldiers were still sitting at the table. The soldier that she wanted to see wasn't ever coming home.

It was too horrific to be a nightmare. The pain of this new reality was too much to handle all at once. Jo felt a little click in her brain as it shifted to protect her, a brittle wall forming around her heart, containing her emotions so they couldn't swirl out and level the room like a hurricane. Numb was the only way she could get through this day. Later, she would let it all out, but this grief was too raw, too painful to share.

She had to do something, so she did what she always did. Jo pushed herself up from the table. She pulled a tray of cheese and salami from the fridge and placed it on the table in front of the men. She filled water glasses for everyone. She dumped the overcooked pasta into the strainer and filled the pot with fresh water.

Step by step, she pulled herself into her reality by doing the next right thing. The things she did every day of her life. The things that formed the structure and routine of her life. The things she could do without thought.

She allowed her mind to stay far, far away from the unreality that Gabe was gone.

By the time she served up warm noodles in a scorched

Alfredo sauce, the two men had gone and the rest of her family sat stone-faced around the table, completely still as if movement would make them all shatter. She understood that stillness. It felt like a kind of death in itself. It mirrored the feeling in her chest.

No one ate.

No one spoke.

The spark had blown out of her family.

~

THAT NIGHT IN BED, she let the tears come. She cried as memories of Gabe's too-short life cycled through her head like a highlight reel. She wept for all of his present moments she'd missed with him so far away. She sobbed for the memories she would never get to have. She'd never dance at his wedding, hold his children in her arms, or even just see him walk through her front door again. They wouldn't be together at Christmas this year or any year. He wouldn't take over Valenti Brothers. He wouldn't watch Sunday football with Dom and his siblings. He wouldn't wrap her up in a bear hug and tuck her head under his chin ever again.

Tears soaked her pillowcase as her brain tortured her with loss after loss. She turned to Dom for comfort, but he had already escaped into sleep.

She was alone with her thoughts and prayed for oblivion. She also prayed for God to watch over the child he'd taken home again too soon. God had made a mistake. Jo knew it, just as she knew it was blasphemy to think it.

So little time... Nothing was guaranteed. She had planned on having years and years with her family to experience all of those milestones. But she could die tomorrow.

Would she be content with her life's highlight reel if that happened?

No.

She was proud of the family she'd raised, but this had just proven how fragile it all really was. What had she done beyond tying shoes and packing lunches? All of the goals and plans she'd once had, all of them had slipped to the side as her family had needed her. She'd accomplished nothing. Now, when grief was weighing heavily on her heart, she had nothing, no life raft, no buoy to lift her back up. She sank deeper and deeper under the weight of her thoughts, until sleep finally claimed her.

∼

Dom lay on his side in the dark pretending to sleep. He'd heard Jo turn to him but hadn't rolled over to face her. He couldn't. He wanted to be strong for her, but his foundation had been deeply shaken in a heartbeat. He wasn't structurally sound anymore. He could barely support his own grief let alone anyone else's.

He'd sat stunned at the table, long after the soldiers had left, unable to speak or move. What could he say? How could the world just keep on turning? How had Jo managed to pull together dinner? He'd had barely enough strength to stand and get himself to bed. For the first time, he hadn't been able to push through the pain to be there for his family, and he felt that failure deeply.

His firstborn son. His baby boy. His hope for the future. Gone.

Gabe was supposed to take the reins of Valenti Brothers, of the family, of everything. Dom knew that sounded old-fashioned, but of all his kids, Gabe was the most like him. Loud, brash, fearless, and strong-minded… It had been a challenge to raise him. But usually they were in lockstep, in line with each other. Gabe joining the army was the first big thing they'd argued about.

Dom understood the impulse to serve his country, but he'd had plans that involved Gabe being home. He'd recognized that stubborn set jaw though, and had eventually come around on the whole army plan. Hell, he'd even helped convince Jo that everything would be fine. He wished like hell he'd fought harder, found the right words to convince Gabe to stay.

God, how could he face her now? Did she blame him? He blamed himself.

It was all he could do to listen to Jo cry and not hold her. Having been part of the reason Gabe left, he couldn't imagine Jo wanted his cold words of comfort. He didn't know if he even had those in him right now.

How could he support his family if he was this weak? He'd never felt so powerless in his entire life.

He'd find a way. He'd have to be stronger, harder than before, but he'd find a way. Dom could make them all strong enough to survive this. He just needed to be more forceful, more in control. *If I'd been stronger, would Gabe be alive today?* Regret and guilt gnawed like rats in the pit of his stomach.

He'd do everything in his power to keep the rest of his family safe.

Soon.

Tomorrow.

CHAPTER 2

2 YEARS ago

Jo PULLED the lasagna from the oven with a little shimmy of her hips. Tonight was the night. Dom had been hinting all week that he had big news to share at the family dinner this week. She couldn't wait.

After losing Gabe, Jo had fallen into a deep depression. She'd stopped working, stopped going out of the house at all. It had been a difficult time, but she'd clawed her way back to the land of the living. God bless grief counselors and modern medications. One core realization from that time had really stayed with her: time was not guaranteed.

She'd vowed to make the most of whatever time she had left. She had embraced a "seize the day" mentality and hoped that Dom would finally join her. She wanted to seize their future together. They weren't getting any younger, and Jo was done being tied down to the family business. Now was her chance to finally chase *her* dreams. It was past time to sell it or let the kids take it over. She'd already stepped down as office manager and had put her real estate business on hold.

And tonight, Dom was going to leave Valenti Brothers as well.

Daydreaming of the future, Jo glanced at the clock. She automatically pulled a few marinated mushrooms off the antipasti tray for Sofia, who was running late, before putting the tray out on the counter. Jo hated that Fi had basically stepped in to fill her shoes at Valenti Brothers. She wanted so much more for her daughter than the fate she'd had, stuck in a job she was good at but didn't love. Maybe tonight would free them both. She took the tray into the family room where the horde descended like a pack of wolves.

She returned to her sanctuary in the kitchen, sipping her favorite wine, the Montepulciano Dom had suggested she open tonight. Her mind wandered back to the cold California beach where she'd fallen in love with the wine and the man. She remembered that night like it was yesterday.

I love you, Jo, and we'll figure this out. I'm not going to lose you.

He'd given her the words then, and she'd learned the truth in them over the many years of their marriage. He'd worked so hard to keep that promise. Yes, she'd made sacrifices for the family and the business too, but they'd made their lives work together.

Her mind continued to wander as she chopped veggies for the salad. If she could do anything now, what would it be? The list was long, but where would she start?

Travel was at the top of her list. She wouldn't lie. Seeing Tony and Elena jaunting all over Europe made her wild with jealousy. She pictured Dom at her side on the balcony of an Italian villa, sipping red wine and watching the sunset. She wanted that reality. She was sure she could get him through his fear of flying for at least one trip.

Then she wanted to come home and actually spend time with the Dom she fell in love with. She hoped he was still in there somewhere, buried under the years of fatherhood and breadwinner stress. He'd gotten quieter and quieter since…well, since things had changed. Maybe having fewer responsibilities would bring the man she'd married back to her.

And she wanted to work with kids again. She'd never forgotten the joy she'd felt in her classroom, helping a child learn to read. She wasn't quite sure how she planned to recapture that feeling now, but she'd figure that out.

She glanced at the clock again. Sofia better get her butt through that door soon or Jo was going to burst from anticipation. She was beyond ready for Dom's announcement!

As if summoned by her mother's anxiety, Sofia arrived, Seth in tow, razzing her.

"I was getting worried. You should have called."

"I got caught up at the office." Sofia leaned in to kiss her cheek in her habitual greeting.

"That office… Enough, I won't get into that now. I hid some mushrooms in the fridge for you." Jo patted Sofia on the back and nudged her toward the kitchen.

"You are the best mother ever. I am sorry I was late. Last-minute snag on the Chu project that I had to untangle."

"Bah! Nothing is more important than family. Come. Sit." She turned and yelled, pitching her voice toward the raucous family room. "Time to eat! Everyone washes."

Jo pushed aside her guilt at having left Sofia holding her old job and hustled everyone to the table. She listened to their conversation with half an ear as she loaded the table.

"Hey Seth, where's Zia Elena and Zio Tony?" Sofia asked.

"They decided to extend their European holiday by a week. Apparently Spain was too tempting to miss," Seth replied.

"And Brandy?"

"She's working the evening shift at Flipped to cover for someone out sick. She's sorry to miss this."

"You'll take her a plate." Jo scooped a square of lasagna onto a plate, setting it aside, and caught Seth wiggling his eyebrows.

"Yes, ma'am. I sure will."

"I will call her tomorrow to ask how it was."

His tone dropped comically like a scolded child. "Yes, ma'am."

"God, Ma. This is delicious." Sofia closed her eyes and moaned.

"Thank you, sweetheart. I wanted to do something a little special for your father's announcement." She raised her glass with a secret smile for her husband of forty years.

"So, Ma, made any travel plans lately?" Sofia teased.

"You know I won't go anywhere without your father. But I was talking to Elena the other day." She switched her gaze to Seth as she spoke of his mother. "She was filling me in on all the details of their time in Italy. She was quite taken with all the vineyards. It sounds beautiful in the summer. We'll see."

Dom cleared his throat, immediately drawing the attention of everyone at the table. "I'm officially calling this family meeting to order. You all know that Jo and I have been talking about retiring for the last few years."

Jo let her smile escape and stretch wide across her face. *Here we go!*

"I'm not convinced that the business is in a strong enough position for me to walk away. People come to us because of the reputation Tony and I spent our lives building. If we just leave, I worry that the work will drop off."

"But Dad, the Valley is booming!" Frankie's outburst was cut off with a firm slice of his hand.

"I also can't see a clear successor to take over running the business. So I've decided to kill all the birds with one stone. We're doing a TV show."

Jo set down the wineglass she'd raised in preparation for a

toast. "What do you mean a TV show?" Her voice was shrill, but she was beyond caring.

"A producer approached me a few weeks ago."

Jo's temper flared. "A few WEEKS? You've been thinking about this for weeks and didn't see fit to discuss it with me? Does Tony know?"

Dom turned to the rest of the table, ignoring her question, shutting her out. Jo sank into a cold silence as he kept explaining the plan to their children, as if her concerns didn't matter. She held her silence while her children jumped into the conversation with their usual chaotic zeal. Her heart held its tongue as her mind struggled to find a way to excuse this disrespect. Again. But she couldn't.

She couldn't make another excuse for her husband who had so clearly locked her out of the decision-making process.

It wouldn't be until much later, after the kids had gone and the dishes had been washed and her house was quiet, that she would realize the gift of running out of excuses. It meant she'd also run out of fucks. He'd cut her out? Fine. She'd stop making her decisions with him in mind. He refused to join her? That was fine too. She'd stop waiting.

∼

29 YEARS ago

NURSE THE BABY, change her diaper, feed the toddler, clean up the mess left by the toddler, convince the toddler that peeing out in the yard was fine for dogs but not for little boys, nurse the baby again, put everyone down for naps, fold three shirts out of the laundry pile that had consumed her couch before someone started crying, pull the toddler out of the baby's crib, wonder how the hell he'd gotten in there in the first place, soothe the baby, distract the toddler, feed everyone again.

Jo was slowly losing her mind.

Her days had been reduced to a simple loop, managing tiny dictators' bodily functions. Eat, poop, sleep, repeat.

Jo never thought she'd long for the days of organized chaos in her classroom, but here she was. At least everyone there had been able to wipe their own butts! She rubbed her chest to erase the guilt that scrawled across her heart. How could she be anything but happy with her two beautiful children?

After their first loss, they had tried so hard for baby Gabe. It had taken a few years, and then they'd immediately started trying for another, afraid it would take just as long to get pregnant again. But it hadn't. And now she had an infant and a toddler. How could she wish for even a second of the life she'd had before? These babies were miracles. But Jo couldn't deny that the days of eating hot food and showering regularly looked real tempting.

Dom had been working so hard to make this year of her staying home from work possible, while still trying to save money for their company, that she felt ungrateful for complaining. Having two babies in three years had really strained their finances, and he was making so many sacrifices to give her something she suddenly wasn't sure she wanted. The ingratitude smacked her in the face, so Jo kept her frustrations to herself.

Even Elena was constantly reminding her how lucky she was to stay home with her children. Maybe she'd feel that way too if they'd start letting her sleep through the night.

She looked up at the clock, willing it to move faster, but it stayed stubbornly pointed at three. Three more hours and a dinner to prepare before she'd get a breather.

Dom tried to help. He always scooped up the babies after he'd showered off the day. But the scant fifteen minutes of quiet she got before it was time to start the bedtime routine weren't cutting it.

Fussy cries called her back into the nursery. Sleep-tousled blonde curls stuck out like a halo around Sofia's head as she let her discomfort be known. Gabe slept on through her petulant tears, for which Jo was supremely grateful.

"What is it, baby girl?" Jo whispered. "Do you need your diaper changed?" She lifted Fi from the crib and gave her a quick nuzzle before laying her back on the changing table to remove the offending diaper. With one hand on Sofia's belly, Jo reached for a fresh diaper, only to discover that the bag was empty. She managed to toe the backup pack out from under the table and open it one-handed. Well, teeth were involved, but she did it without letting go of the baby and that still counted as a win. A feral win, but a win all the same.

Flush with her success, she turned her triumphant smile back to Sofia, who was wearing a happy grin of her own....because she'd managed to pee *and* poop on the changing pad in the meantime.

"Oh, come on!" Jo muttered, barely managing not to swear in front of the baby, although would she really understand anyway? Still, it was better to not break that seal, or Gabe's first sentence would have to be censored from his baby book. Switching back to her baby-soothing voice, she crooned, "Was that what woke you up?" She cleaned up everything as best she could. Sofia fussed at the cold wipes but settled once she was in a fresh and dry onesie.

Jo picked her up, hoping she'd be able to put the baby back down for the second half of her nap. On the way up to her shoulder, the real nap-stealing culprit made its appearance as Sofia let loose a deep burp and spit up all down the front of her new onesie and Jo's shirt.

Near tears, Jo opened the dresser drawer to find it empty. *Shit.*

The bad news was all of the baby's clothes were either dirty or on the couch. The good news was so were Jo's clean shirts.

She carried Sofia at arms length into the living room and stripped her down over the hardwood floor before whipping her own shirt off as well, tossing all of the wet clothes into the dirty basket on the floor. She'd just gotten the baby clothed again and situated in her bouncy chair when the front door slapped open.

Jo screamed and covered her bare chest, startling the baby back into crying.

"Jo? Jo!" Dom didn't even seem to notice that she was half naked as he ran to her and spun her around in a circle.

A few years ago, seeing her topless would have stopped him in his tracks. My, how times had changed. Would her body ever start to feel like her own again?

"Babe, you'll never guess what happened today!"

"It's three thirty in the afternoon. Is everything okay?"

Dom barked out a laugh and kept dancing her around in a raucous circle she was sure the neighbors downstairs were loving. Gabe toddled out of the nursery, rubbing his eyes, and Dom released her and scooped him up into the dance. Jo tugged on an inside-out T-shirt and picked up Sofia to soothe her.

"John wants to retire!"

Jo's heart fell into the pit of her stomach. John ran the construction company Dom and Tony worked for. If he was retiring and shutting down the business, they'd lose everything.

"Oh my God! Dom, what are we going to do? That's our only income."

Dom cut her off with a kiss. "He wants to sell the business to me and Tony!"

"Oh! That's...can we afford that?"

"I don't know yet. We'll figure it out, but this puts us years ahead of our goal with established customers and bids in the queue. Babe, this is the break we needed!"

CHAPTER 3

29 years ago

Dom danced Gabe into the kitchen and pulled a beer from the fridge. He was on cloud nine. He'd busted his ass to learn the business and save for his own startup. To have that hard work and sacrifice recognized and rewarded felt damn good. And after so many financial setbacks, he and Tony were finally catching a break.

He respected the hell out of John as a boss and a friend. He'd learned a lot from him in the years working on his crews. To have John approach him about taking over the business took away a lot of his worries that he wasn't ready. If John thought he was, he was. The money part would work itself out. Maybe they'd even pay him out over a few years. The opportunity was too good to pass up.

Gabe patted his cheek, grinning, and Dom leaned in to blow a raspberry against his cheek, teasing giggles from his son.

"Someday I'll hand this business down to you, Gabriel."

"Slow down there, Daddy. One retirement at a time," Jo teased.

Dom sat Gabe down in front of his hammer and pegs, set his beer on the coffee table, and pulled Jo in for a kiss. The kind of kiss that said, *Damn, you're sexy when you bust my chops, and I'm so glad you're mine.*

The kind of kiss that often led to *Let me show you what I do with what's mine* kind of kisses.

The kind of kissing they didn't have a lot of time for these days.

Just as Dom felt Jo sinking into the moment, Sofia started crying, and Jo pulled back. She picked up the baby who immediately stretched her arms out for him and tugged on his beard when he swooped her over. Who could resent the interruption when it came in the form of his golden-haired little princess? Snuggling her into his chest, he pressed a kiss into her milky sweet curls and grinned at his good fortune.

Beautiful children, a wonderful wife, and a dream opportunity landing in his lap wrapped up with a fucking bow. It didn't get better than this. He was a lucky man.

"Just think, Jo. Stepping into an established business gets us past the lean startup years. You could stay home with the kids instead of having to go back to work in the fall." Dom bounced Sofia on his hip and only caught a flash of Jo's back as she ran from the room crying.

"What did I say?" he asked Sofia, as if she held the answers behind her bright blue eyes.

She spit up on his chest in reply.

∼

2 years ago

. . .

Dom climbed into bed next to his wife, who hadn't spoken a word since dinner. He punched up his pillows and huffed as he settled in, but Jo didn't turn over. He let out another aggravated sigh. He didn't know why she was being so difficult. They had talked about him retiring and how he still felt shaky.

When Jo fell into her depression, responsibility had fallen heavy on his shoulders. He had thought he understood just how much she did to keep their family running, but he'd had no idea until he tried to step into her shoes. Keeping everything under control had kicked him into overdrive, and now he couldn't turn it off.

He felt compelled to make sure that the kids and the business were in a good enough position that they wouldn't ever fail. When he thought about retiring, a cold sweat broke out on his forehead and his arms trembled.

Dom thought back to John's retirement so many years ago, and wondered how the hell he'd known Dom was ready. He truly couldn't see the path forward yet.

So he'd found another solution. One that would make their company and the kids strong enough to survive. He didn't understand why Jo was so upset. He was working toward their goal.

He rolled to his side to face her, but her back rose and fell slowly as he stared at it, willing her to turn toward him, even if it was just so they could have the fight he knew was brewing, clear the air, and get some sleep.

But she didn't.

She must have already fallen asleep. It would have to wait for morning, but he'd explain and she'd see that he'd done it for them.

But morning came and went, and with it went Dom's confidence that he'd be able to bring Jo around. He explained over coffee. He cajoled over scrambled eggs. He ranted over lunchmeat sandwiches, and Jo still hadn't uttered a word. How was he supposed to argue with her if she wouldn't say anything?

After lunch, she'd just calmly picked up her purse and walked out the door. That click as it closed behind her reverberated through his chest, and Dom couldn't help but feel a door had been closed permanently between them.

As days turned to weeks of silence, Dom's anger grew. Why couldn't she see what he was trying to do? Losing Gabe had dropped a bomb into their lives, explosive, painful, and completely unexpected. Dom's life—past, present, and future—lay in broken shards on the ground, and he was desperately trying to fit them back together, despite knowing that crucial pieces were missing or mangled. He was terrified of what failure would mean.

He had to be sure the future was as secure as possible before he could even think about relaxing. *A Valenti builds to last.*

Tony had retired, Gabe was gone, and the rest of the kids simply weren't strong enough to tackle running the business on their own. This show would toughen them up and make them the faces of the company. They'd stand on their own reputation, and he could rest easy knowing his legacy was secure.

Every decision, every hour of overtime, every yes when he wanted to say no, all of it had been for her and the family they'd built. How could she not see that?

But clearly she didn't see, because she still wasn't talking to him. And she didn't want to see, because every time he tried to explain again, she left the room.

She was leaving a lot these days, at odd hours, going God knew where. She wasn't sharing that with him either. Home had become a lonely place, and he didn't like it. But for the first time in his career, he couldn't see the blueprint for how to fix it.

15 years ago

"So, what do you think?" Jo shielded her eyes as Dom stepped up beside her on the curb. Dom, the man who was never quiet and never still, stood and stared, silent. The frown on his face said it all. Jo tugged his arm and pulled him up what would be the front path to the six-flat apartment building that had seen better days.

"Oh, come on. It's not that bad. Let me walk you through it."

Real estate license newly acquired, Jo was eager to make her first sale. She had worked hard, studying at night and taking tests on weekends, to make this new dream a reality. Going back to teaching was impossible as long as Dom needed her help in the office. So she'd looked for opportunities she could schedule around her office work and the kids. She could sell real estate on the side, and the extra cash would go a long way. And most importantly, it was something just for her. She'd given up so many of her dreams already, she wasn't going to let this one go without a fight.

"Look at the potential income here. Most of the units only require basic updates and a few repairs." She opened the door on a ground floor unit, and managed to suppress a gag at the smell. Why wasn't that skill on the real estate tests?

"Minor repairs? This place is one inspection away from being condemned. How long has it been vacant?" Dom grimaced, not hiding his disgust.

"Six months. The old owner died, and they haven't found anyone willing to do the updates required to bring it up to code."

"Did he die in here? It reeks!" He leaned his head into the open doorway and peeked around her. "This place is a money pit, and the upgrades are probably going to cost a fortune. There's no way..."

"Dom. Block of salt. Give it a chance."

She left the door cracked for ventilation and started the spiel she'd practiced, flinging up windows as she went.

"There's a good-sized living space, and the kitchen is here on the right. We might consider opening this wall to make it feel larger as long as we have the walls down to fix the wiring."

Dom's jaw dropped. "The electrical needs to be replaced?"

"Yes, but we won't have to pay an outside contractor to do it. Back down this hallway are two decent bedrooms and the bath. The tile is in pretty good shape, under the filth. I don't think we'll need to replace more than the fixtures."

"And all the walls." He had his arms folded tight across his chest.

Jo hated when he got stubborn, but she knew her husband well. "Dom, listen. Will it cost more to fix this than it will to buy it? Yes. But once we're done, that's six units of income every month on a property we will own outright instead of just a one-time sale. I know you're used to building from scratch or redoing someone else's mess, but I think there's something to this renovation and rental model. Fifteen hundred a month times six is nine thousand. Which means $108K a year. In three years, we've recouped our investment, and it's pure profit minus maintenance and taxes."

Dom's arms were still crossed, but he'd unclenched his teeth, so Jo reached for her trump card.

"Gabe graduates from high school in two years, and the others aren't far behind. Our chicks are leaving the nest. We'll be paying for college times four. The extra income wouldn't hurt, and wouldn't it be nice to offer them a branch to rent close to home when they're done?"

Dom's arms dropped to his sides. "You really want to do this?"

"I do. I think it's a solid investment."
"I'll think about it."

~

Dom was still thinking about it that night in bed. His head was dizzy from the teeter-totter of pros and cons that had run back and forth in his mind all day, and he still hadn't settled on an answer.

Life was changing too quickly for his liking. His eldest was learning how to drive. His little girl was starting to date. His wife kept adding job titles to her résumé. Office manager, realtor, property manager. He felt like everyone was moving past him, away from him, and he was stuck. He didn't know if he could change along with them.

But he couldn't deny that the money made sense, and he trusted Jo's planning ability. Keeping his kids close to home was definitely appealing, and guaranteed income made a lot of sense.

But were he and Tony ready to become landlords? In the early years, profits had been lean, but with Jo's help they'd survived and gotten everyone paid. Even though they no longer kept a "playroom" at the offices, his kids were comfortable there. All of his kids knew their way around a job site, and he was damn proud of that. One day, Gabe would take over Valenti Brothers. Did Dom want to mess with a business model they'd finally gotten working?

He and Tony were doing just fine, but they did have five kids combined to put through college soon. He wanted to pass them a legacy, not a pile of debt.

That meant they needed more revenue, and that meant adding new lines of business. To be honest, Jo was probably onto something with this flipping real estate or developing rentals idea. It took a lot less time to do a few renovations than it did to build from scratch. But it hadn't been a path he'd considered before now, because he'd largely kept the business the same as it had been when John passed it over to them. If it ain't broke, don't fix it.

He rolled over in his bed and kissed Jo's shoulder.

"Mmmhhhh," was her response. He kissed her again, and she rolled, pulling the blanket up higher.

"Babe," he whispered. "I think we should do it."

Jo groaned and muttered over her shoulder. "You always think we should do it. I've got four kids to prove it."

Dom laughed, and she rolled back to face him. He would never get tired of seeing that face. Even sleepy-eyed, grumpy, and not interested in sex, his wife was the most beautiful woman alive. Add to that her grit and brilliance, and he was a lucky man.

"I meant the apartments. I think we should do it."

A sleepy but satisfied smile spread over Jo's face, and he felt a tick of pride over making her happy.

"I knew you'd see it. You won't be sorry."

"Now do you wanna do it?" he teased, and she slapped his arm.

"No. Go to sleep. We can talk about an offer in the morning."

"I've got an offer for you right now," he said, tickling her neck with his whiskers and making her laugh. When she turned into his arms and kissed him back, Dom grinned. He really was a lucky man.

CHAPTER 4

2 years ago

Jo should have been having the time of her life. She'd joined an active seniors group for their program that matched volunteers with after-school programs around the city to help cover tutoring and childcare gaps. The fourth graders she'd been assigned to help were delightful. She hadn't laughed so hard at kid antics in years. She actively ignored the melancholy that came when she thought of her own kids at that age.

One boy, Lanh, had a bright, mischievous smile that reminded her so much of Gabe. Some days were hard, but others were filled with laughter and boisterous hijinks. She was able to help with homework, and she got kid hugs at the end of the day. She hadn't realized how much she'd missed those. With one raised hand at a meeting, she'd added joy and purpose to her daily routine.

She'd also added friendship. Once upon a time she'd had friends. A few from college still exchanged Christmas cards. The mom friends she'd made through her four kids had drifted away as the kids grew older and started driving themselves to soccer practices. She'd heard from a few at the funeral, but she imagined no one wanted to listen to her go on and on about the death of her son. Since that had been all she'd been able to focus on for months after the funeral, she'd stopped reaching out. Elena was the only friend she spoke to regularly, but with her and Tony gone on their multi-month European jaunt, Jo was lonely.

When Jo had gone to her first Late Bloomers meeting, she'd been overwhelmed by the options and had signed up for a little of everything. Coffee chats (where she learned how delightful a mocha could be!), book clubs (so many good stories she'd missed!), salsa nights (who knew her hips could still do that?)... Her calendar was suddenly filled, and faces were becoming familiar. And these people liked her for her. Not because she was so-and-so's wife or mother or business colleague. But because she was witty, smart, and outgoing. Feeling valued and wanted was heady indeed, and so she'd kept signing up for more events.

It also didn't hurt that it was easier to keep up her silence if she wasn't constantly around Dom.

One face in particular was becoming very familiar. Alessandro was a widower the ladies at book club referred to as The Silver Fox, due both to his luscious full head of bright gray hair and his propensity to flirt with the ladies.

He approached her first at one of the monthly mixers.

"Widow or working?" he asked with a smile.

"Pardon me?" Jo paused in the act of selecting a glass of wine from the open bar at the informal mixer.

"Are you a widow? Or a working woman who never married? Most of the ladies here fall into one or the other."

Jo picked a glass of red and turned to face him. "Neither. I married, and had a career and a family."

"Ah...divorced?" The blatant hope in his voice made Jo laugh.

"No. Still married."

"Hmm, so you're here for…"

"Friendship. I could really use some friends," Jo said firmly.

"Then here's to new friendships and where they might lead." He clicked his plastic wineglass to hers and stayed politely by her side, introducing her to people he knew and keeping a conversation flowing.

It was disconcerting. Give her a muscle-bound meathead and she knew what to do. Hand her a suave gentleman who could talk circles around her and she was lost. Which was how she ended up agreeing to ride to the Winchester Mystery House tour with him. The man was certainly persuasive, and she couldn't deny it felt good to have someone care enough to persuade instead of just assuming she'd comply.

At least she'd had the wherewithal to suggest meeting him at the coffee shop after her date with Sofia. She didn't think Dom would take well to another man picking her up from the house.

But she was done caring what Dom thought, she reminded herself firmly. It was time to put her dreams first.

∽

25 YEARS ago

"Hey, Dom! Where's the invoice for the Shue project?" Tony lifted stacks of paper from Dom's desk, rifling through them before slamming them back down.

Dom walked into his office, tossed his hard hat on top of the mess, and tapped his temple. "I've got it right here. Why do you need it?"

"Mrs. Shue called to confirm something and I need to see it. Damn it, Dom. We talked about this. We need to have things written down."

"It takes too much time. I'm always on the job site. Besides, I know what we did on that job. Just ask me."

"No, Dom. Make me the fucking invoice."

"Come on. I'm about to leave."

"Yeah? So was I, until I got this call, and now I have to wait because you didn't do your job!"

"Tony, Jo is on her way to pick me up with all the kids in the car because my truck is still in the shop. I'll do it in the morning."

"Bullshit! You'll do it now."

"But—"

"I told her I'd have an answer for her tonight, and we don't disappoint our customers."

"You can be a real asshole, you know that?" Dom growled as he walked around his desk and flopped into his chair.

"So you've been telling me since you were five and learned your first swear word. Write the invoice," Tony said on his way to the door.

"Fuck," Dom muttered under his breath, shuffling papers on his desk, trying to find a blank invoice sheet. "This is a load of crap."

Whirling, Tony shouted. "You know what's a load of crap? Getting down to five hundred dollars in the bank after payroll because I can't send out invoices to get paid if they're IN YOUR FUCKING HEAD! Pull it out of your ass, Dom, and look around. This is a business, and you're driving us into the ground."

"What?" Jo asked from over Tony's shoulder as she hitched Frankie up on her hip.

Shit. He'd tried to protect her from their struggles, both financial and emotional. Hell, the first few years of a business were always rocky, right? And he and Tony were brothers. It was natural that they'd fight a bit. Jo had enough on her hands taking care of the house and the babies. She didn't need one more burden. He could handle this.

"Nothing, babe. It's nothing."

"You're right about that." Tony stormed out past her, and Dom took out his frustrations on the papers on his desk.

He swiped everything off his desk with a roar. "Shit!"

As papers fluttered to the floor, Enzo peeked around Jo's leg. Wanting to play, he grabbed some papers from the floor and tossed them into the air, gleefully yelling, "Shit!"

Dom dropped his head into his hands.

"Gabe, come here." Jo handed her youngest to her oldest, who propped the toddler on his hip like a pro. "Take Frankie and Enzo to the samples room and build a fort."

With squeals of joy and laughter, they took off for their favorite place to play.

"Spill it, Domenico. What was Tony talking about?" Jo crossed her arms and leaned on the doorjamb.

"It's nothing." He scrubbed his hands over his face. "He's just pissed I didn't have some paperwork he wanted."

Jo walked farther into the room, placed her hand firmly on the now-clear desk in front of him, and waited silently for him to make eye contact. He hadn't thought he was a coward, but the challenge of facing his wife just now was proving him one. She might have left the classroom, but her teacher look still worked just fine.

"Dom, do not treat me like I'm an idiot. I heard what Tony said about only five hundred dollars in the account. What is going on?" When he didn't answer quickly enough, she slapped her hand on his desk and he jumped. "Start talking."

"Business is good." Dom shrugged. "We've been cruising along, juggling so many projects, that we got a little behind on the billing. It'll all be fine."

"We?"

"I...I got behind on putting together invoices, but seriously, there wouldn't be anything to invoice if I hadn't—"

Jo held up a hand to stop him. "And being fine depends on you doing paperwork?" Her voice fairly dripped with sarcasm.

"You don't have to say it like that." Dom's confidence was taking a beating left, right, and center today. He was a damn good builder, a good father and husband. Why couldn't that be enough?

Jo checked her watch. "How long do you need to put together the thing for Tony?"

"Half an hour?"

"Okay, I'm going to go pick up Fi from ballet, and when I get back we're going to talk."

Dom hated the promise of a lecture in her voice. He hated feeling stupid in front of his wife. He would have argued with her, but she was already gone, rounding up their crew and hustling them back into their minivan while listening to excited descriptions of their fort and drying temper tears over being torn away from it.

Dom sighed, but he got busy.

∽

Jo carried the four happy meals in from the van, trailing behind four kids who were anxious to get back to their fort construction at Valenti Brothers.

"Dinner first!" she called out, dropping the boxes on a demo counter. These kids needed to eat or she'd have a nuclear meltdown on her hands. And when Dom said thirty minutes, he usually meant an hour minimum.

Jo did some quick mom calculus. She had at least another half hour here keeping the kids occupied, plus the drive home, plus bath time and stories for all the kids to get through. Not to mention four loads of laundry that needed folding before she could finally sleep.

She'd be lying if she said she didn't resent Dom a little bit right now. She had given up so much to keep their family functioning. Her hopes, her dreams, her body, her personal space and time. All so Dom could chase this dream of owning a business with his brother. And he couldn't even get the bills sent out!

Kids distracted by cheeseburgers and cheap plastic, Jo began to set the office to rights. She was here anyway. Might as well be useful, and the space was a mess. Did they see clients with it looking like this?

After tackling the pile of dishes in the sink and sorting the mail, she got the kids cleaned up and back to work on their fort. Enzo was laying a path of tile samples to the door, and Sofia was coloring on copy paper to make art for the walls. Gabe dove inside with Frankie hot on his heels and their giggles and laughter lifted her heart.

"Do you think I drew a good tree, Mommy?" Fi asked on a yawn.

"It's beautiful, baby. Take some tape and hang it up inside."

Jo checked her watch again. She had to get these kids home and in bed or tomorrow was going to be a nightmare.

"Ten minutes, crew. I'm going to round up Daddy."

As she left the sample room, Jo found Tony and Dom back at it, albeit quieter because of the kids.

"We can't do business like this!" Tony whisper-shouted.

"I don't know how else to make it all work!" Dom hissed back.

Jo cleared her throat, and the two of them separated like she'd rung a bell to end the round.

"Thanks for cleaning up. I've been meaning to get to that for a while now. Do you want a job?" Tony joked, trying to break the tension in the room.

Jo chuckled, playing along, but not really finding it funny. This was NOT her job.

But Dom didn't laugh. Instead he got that look on his face that said he was thinking.

Shit. What now?

"That's not a bad idea."

"You don't need to hire me to wash coffee cups, Dom."

"No," he glanced over at Tony, "but I think it's clear there's too much work for just the two of us. We need help running the office. Neither of us are here enough to handle the phones and paperwork reliably."

Now Tony had that thinking look. Jesus, it was scary to be caught between these brothers when they were tossing ideas back and forth. Jo felt like she was about to get knocked over the head by one.

"It would certainly solve the problem of getting the invoices out so we can get paid." Tony rubbed a hand over the scruff on his chin, itching as if the idea was scratching him from the inside.

"She's brilliant at managing."

Jo let Dom's words soothe her ego at the slight recognition of all she did for their family, before his next words slapped at her pride.

"And she's family so we wouldn't have to worry about trusting her with accounts and collecting money. After things went down with Chad, I've been wary of hiring anyone else."

She watched, mute and fuming, as the brothers spitballed the idea back and forth in front of her as if she wasn't standing right there, with ideas of her own in her head, none of which led to her becoming their gofer.

Part of her wanted to tell them where they could shove this "idea" and bundle her kids home to bed. Gabe still had spelling homework to do. Her hands were full enough. And despite a sometimes desperate desire to get out of the house, she did not count cleaning up her husband's messes in a different location as a break.

Frankie toddled out from the fort and raised her arms in a silent demand. Jo tucked her against her chest, and her last baby snuggled her head into the crook of Jo's neck and popped her thumb into her mouth. Jo inhaled deeply and knew she was stuck. Her anger faded to resignation.

All of their eggs were in this basket. It wasn't like they could afford daycare for her to go back to work. And her babies needed to eat and have a roof over their heads. Which meant Valenti Brothers could not fail. And without her, these two knuckleheads wouldn't stand a chance.

Damn it.

She was going to have to step up and do this.

"Dom, we've got to get these kids into bed. I'll come back tomorrow after the school drop and we'll see if we can figure something out. I want to talk about what you'd need me to do."

"That's my girl!" Dom's voice boomed, and he planted a jubilant kiss on her lips, quite pleased with himself.

She smiled, but her heart tightened inside her chest. She felt her dreams slide even farther out of reach.

For better or worse. She'd said the words in a church in front of God and her family, and she'd meant them. She just hadn't expected to be so thoroughly tested.

CHAPTER 5

2 YEARS ago

JO ENTERED the coffee shop and walked up behind Sofia, dropping a hand on her shoulder. The poor girl nearly fell out of her chair.

"Whoa! Easy. I didn't mean to startle you."

"I was daydreaming. Can I get your latte?" Sofia smiled.

Was she really that predictable? "No, darling. I'll have a mocha."

Fi's eyes widened but she didn't comment. "You look lovely today. What's the occasion?"

Jo bristled. True, she'd fallen into years of jeans and flannel, but that was because she'd worked in a construction office. She knew how to dress nicely, but between the kids and the job site, she didn't often get the chance. To have her daughter point out how nice she looked with surprise rubbed her the wrong way.

She didn't need a reason to look nice. She could put on lipstick and a nice top just because it made her happy. And if she happened to be meeting up with her new friends today, well, that bit of confidence boost wouldn't go amiss.

"I don't need a reason to do the things that make me feel good. No time like the present."

"That's true."

Sofia rose to order their coffees, and Jo's anxiety rose. Why had she told Alessandro to pick her up here? She wasn't ready for the questions it would generate from Sofia. Jo hauled in a breath and reached for calm. It would all be fine. She didn't have to do or say anything she didn't want to.

Sofia passed her the chocolate-laced coffee and settled across from her. "So, how've you been, Ma? You haven't come around the office lately."

The office. Why should she have to go to the office to see her kids? She had washed her hands of the whole damn thing. Why should she care how it was doing? Her temper began to flicker to life, and she didn't try to keep it from her voice.

"I'm not giving that place one more minute of my life."

She'd already given it her hopes and dreams, her husband and her children. She had nothing left to give.

Jo's phone buzzed in her hand while Sofia said something about the show Jo was actively pretending didn't exist. "That's nice, dear."

The text was from Dom.

D: Where are you?

OH, now he cared about where she was? He thought he should get to know her plans after not particularly caring about them for years? That was rich. She didn't need to justify a damn thing to him, since he didn't feel the need to do it either. The flicker of temper flared and burned at the base of her throat as she typed a one-word reply.

J: Out.

SENSING THAT FI had gone quiet, Jo tuned back in. Right, the pilot was done. Whoop-dee-freaking-do. "You know what I mean. I'm sure it was challenging, and I'm glad it's done now. I didn't know how you were going to juggle everything. But honestly I hope the show doesn't get picked up."

Her phone buzzed again.

D: What do you mean out?

THAT LOW BURN grew into a ball of rage and she broke and replied.

J: Why do you care? Shouldn't you be celebrating your precious pilot?

D: I wanted to celebrate with you.

J: Not something I care to celebrate. It doesn't concern me, and I've made plans.

. . .

How dare he? It would serve him right if she gave him a taste of his own medicine. She'd just make her decisions for herself, screw the consequences, and see how he felt about it.

"Are we still on for family dinner next Friday?"

Sofia's question pulled her back to the conversation and reality. Dom might have pissed her off, but she couldn't just abandon her kids. Before she could force the anger away, her phone buzzed again, this time with a message from Alessandro. "Yes."

A: *Leaving now. See you soon. :)*

"Can I bring Adrian along?"

Jo sighed and turned her phone facedown on the table so Fi couldn't see the texts. Sofia probably wanted to celebrate the successful pilot, and she really didn't want to have to put on a happy face for company, even if it was just Adrian, a man she'd known and worked with for years. "I wish we didn't have to bring business to the table, but I suppose it's fine."

"It's not business, Ma. I'm seeing him."

Jo snapped her head up at that. Oh. *Oh no.* This was unexpected and not at all what she'd hoped for her daughter. True, Jo had needed to get the hell out of that office after Gabe had died, and at the time she'd been grateful that Sofia had stepped in to help. But she'd never intended it to be permanent.

She'd thought Dom would see Sofia struggling and hire someone else like he should have done years ago. But no, her tunnel-vision husband hadn't noticed or hadn't cared, and now her daughter was caught in the same trap she had been. Dating their crew chief was no way to get out of it. But Jo couldn't say any of that without giving in to her own guilt and regret, so she stayed silent.

Besides, Fi was a grown woman and didn't need her permission to date whoever she liked. Jo settled on a nod. She took a sip of her coffee that now sat sickly sweet on her tongue.

"So what have you been up to lately?" Sofia broke the tense silence with a desperate question.

Jo was happy for the change of subject. "I've joined a group for older adults that plans outings to local sites of interest. It has been so fun! We got in for a tour of Moffett Field and the Rosicrucian Museum. We even helped prune back the roses at the San Jose Rose Garden. I've learned so much!"

Jo's discontent receded as she shared her new interests until her daughter made an innocent assumption.

"Did Dad like being put to work on his day off?"

Jo didn't look up from her mocha and flicked the lid with her thumb, desperately trying not to snap at Fi. "He didn't come. He was too busy."

Jo picked up her phone where it buzzed on the table.

A: Five minutes out.

J: I'll be ready.

SHE TYPED her reply before turning back to Sofia who stared at her wide-eyed.

"In fact, I'm heading out for a tour of the Winchester Mystery House in a little bit, so I'm afraid I can't stay long."

"Oh. That's okay. I just missed catching up with you."

"You're so sweet. How are things outside work?"

Jo tried to get this conversation back on familiar ground, but Sofia stalled as if she didn't know how to answer that softball question. Jo hadn't realized it had gotten this bad. She tried to stay quiet and not offer her opinions where they weren't wanted, but this struck too close to home. She had to say something.

"Judging by your silence, I'm going to assume you're still working your fingers to the bone for that damn place." Jo leaned forward and gripped Sofia's hands tightly. "Listen. Don't do what I did. Nothing—no company, no job, no man—nothing is worth sacrificing everything for. I gave that place thirty years of my life. I don't want to see you trapped in the same pit."

And what had she gotten for her years of dedication? A silent, angry bed, years of dreams put on hold, and a husband who didn't think she should be consulted about major life plans. She was sick of it. Jo could feel her pulse behind her eye and knew she needed to get out of there before she said something she'd regret.

"That's easy to say when you're the one who walked away and left me holding the shovel," Sofia said.

"I never said you had to take over the office work."

"Who was going to make sure the bills got paid? Who was going to send out invoices and keep the place afloat? Who was going to make sure our employees still got their paychecks? Dad? Enzo? Frankie? No. I was the only one stepping up." Sofia's voice quivered with frustration.

The teen years had been the last time Fi had triggered Jo's defensive temper so quickly or deeply. All of her filters were already stretched far too thin. Jo's guilt and fear and anger squeezed her throat tight, and she lashed back. "You always do this. You tear people down with all these questions. I don't answer to you, Sofia. I did what I had to do, and I don't regret it. No one is making you stay and do those things, Sofia."

"I am, Ma. I want my design business to be an integral part of Valenti Brothers. We have the reputation you all worked so hard to build, the opportunity to expand our brand through the show, and I am finally getting to do what I love. I can't walk away from the business side and let it all fall apart before I have a chance to succeed."

Jo pulled her hand away and checked her phone again before tucking it inside her purse.

D: Well you can plan to come home to an empty house. I'll be celebrating at the office.

WHAT WOULD he do if she just didn't come home? Exhausted from the roller coaster of emotions in just the last half hour, Jo considered it. She could just leave it all behind. Never had running away looked so good.

"I wish it would burn to the ground," she whispered. Why couldn't he see that this fucking show and that damned company were tearing them apart? Why did he keep putting it first? No, she couldn't go back to those thoughts now that she'd broken free. She was an independent woman who could do as she pleased.

She could walk away from everything. Giddy rage filled her head with ideas she'd never contemplated before. But she sure as hell was thinking them now.

Sofia sat silent, so Jo pushed on.

"He will never leave that company unless it is gone. I didn't want to bring this up, but you should know. I am considering leaving your father."

Saying it out loud scared her a little, but her filters were fully gone, burnt up in her temper and rage.

"What? Does Dad know about this?"

"I don't know what your father knows. We haven't spoken

since he announced that ridiculous television show. He knew. He knew I needed him, and he put that company first again."

Jo finished her too-sweet coffee gone cold in one gulp and gathered her things. There was little left to say, and Alessandro was waiting.

"So he could leave it in a strong position for the rest of us." Sofia tried to explain, but Jo wasn't having it.

"Don't be naive. He won't leave until a backhoe loads his casket into the ground."

Jo looked over Sofia's shoulder and saw Alessandro getting out of his car. She couldn't handle this meeting between her daughter and her friend and the questions that would follow. Not with her filters lying in ashes on the floor. Who knew what else might pop out?

"I don't want to see what happened to me happen to you too. I love you, Sofia. It's just not worth it. My ride for the excursion is here. I've got to run. Thanks for the coffee. Give my love to Enzo and Frankie."

Jo kissed Sofia's cheek and prayed her daughter would listen to her advice as she hustled out the door.

"Sorry I'm late. I was having coffee with my daughter."

Alessandro brushed away her apology and opened her door with a flourish. "Nonsense. Family always comes first."

∼

14 YEARS ago

JO SWUNG in through the front door, hair wild and flannel shirt hastily thrown over her pajamas, having barely made the school drop-offs in time. Tossing her purse and keys on the table in the foyer, she sprinted down the hallway toward the kitchen. In precisely fifty-three minutes, she had a showing for a client looking at homes in Los Altos and still had to pull herself together. She also had to get the kids' baseball uniforms through the wash before their games tonight, start dinner in the crock pot, and pick a bag of lemons for Mrs. K as a thank-you for picking up Frankie from practice this week.

As she rushed past the piles and messes created by her lovely family, a million different tasks crowded her mind, making it hard to hold on to just the ones she'd prioritized for this morning. She'd have written them all down except she didn't even have time for that, nor to deal with the resulting overwhelm of an eight-page to-do list.

Dom had already headed out to the job site. Jo could catch up with him at the office this afternoon, assuming the showing went well. There were a few potential flip properties she wanted to run by him, maybe see if he was interested in letting Gabe do some more involved work this summer, now that he was seventeen. It would help to have extra hands and would keep the labor cost down even more.

Spinning into the kitchen, Jo opened the cabinet to grab her favorite to-go mug that Sofia had gotten her last Christmas. Not seeing it, she whirled to the dishwasher. It had to be here. Yes, the mug was hot pink and said *Mom* on the side in purple glitter, but it was her lucky mug. The dishwasher was empty. Dom must have emptied it before he left.

She smiled at the thought. He might strike out in the cooking department, but he was solid batting cleanup. Too much baseball. Between Enzo and Gabe both in different school leagues, and Frankie playing softball, she was drowning in sweaty stirrup socks and dusty sliding pants.

Her watch judged her inability to caffeinate effectively, taunting her with the minutes flying past as she searched for her mug. Frustrated, Jo yanked a random mug from the shelf, one of Dom's that looked like caution tape.

Refusing to believe this would jinx her, Jo turned to the coffee machine and stopped midstride. There was her mug, already filled with coffee and a little milk, just the way she liked it. She couldn't fight the grin that spread across her face. That man.

Jo sipped her still-hot coffee with a sigh of appreciation. Perfect. This might be the only still moment she got all day, and Dom had taken the time to make sure it was right. She might want to strangle him from time to time, but he came through when it counted.

She glanced down at her watch. Forty-six minutes left. She took another bracing sip before gathering beef stew ingredients from the fridge and dumping them into the crock pot. Coffee rapidly disappearing, she crossed to the laundry room and tossed all of the dusty uniforms into the washer.

On the floor, Dom had shed his favorite pair of work jeans, beat to hell and covered in all kinds of dirt. Feeling gracious and blessedly awake, she tossed them into the wash as well so he wouldn't have to wait a week to wear them again. It was the little things they did for each other these days that showed their love. No one had time for big romantic gestures with four children, but they had time to take care of each other.

As the washer filled with water, Jo finished her coffee and headed up to hop into the shower. It would likely be cold, but she'd keep it quick. She'd have to be quick to make it to Los Altos in time. In and out, hair washed and body scrubbed, she had perfected the five-minute shower when her babies were little. The skill still served her well because with six people showering there was never enough in the water heater to go around.

Wrapping up her hair in a towel, she rushed to dry herself and put on lotion and minimal makeup. She hoped her black suit didn't smell too bad, because she hadn't managed to catch the cleaners while it was open yesterday, and the funeral suit was the only option still here. She turned toward her closet, and again pulled up short. The dry cleaning was hanging in a bag on the bar with a yellow receipt stapled to it. Her husband's Sharpie scrawl caught her eye.

Jo- You've got this. Knock 'em dead. Love, Dom.

Bless that man. He hadn't always known how to support her, but he'd learned along the way, same as she had.

Instead of reaching for her reliable cotton underwear and nude bra, she pulled out the satin set before tearing into the plastic bag and donning her red power suit. Today was going to be a good day. And tonight Dom just might get lucky. He'd given her a boost this morning without even being there. She could return the favor tonight.

Feeling like she could conquer the world, Jo strode back out into the world with her head high, lemons in a grocery bag, and three minutes to spare.

∽

2 YEARS *ago*

ALESSANDRO WAS VERY attentive as the group toured the Winchester Mystery House, built by the widow who'd inherited the gunmaker's fortune and spent years trying to outrun the ghosts created by his invention by building the most confusing house in the country. The idea of never-ending construction on her home sent an honest-to-God chill down Jo's spine. How had that woman lived with all of the hammering and dust?

Jo could not imagine willingly choosing to do that if she weren't married to a contractor. Which led her to thoughts of

Dom and their failing marriage. But Alessi distracted her from her melancholy.

Small touches at her back as they rounded corners, allowing her to go first up the bizarrely shallow stairs. Always right next to her, ready to laugh at her sarcastic comments. He was a perfect gentleman.

So why was she so annoyed?

"Jo, can you imagine? All this space by herself? It's wild."

"It's sad. It needed a family and friends and visitors. She didn't have any of that," she replied. She tried to imagine a life without her bustling Friday dinners and crazy family Christmases. A deep sadness chilled her, and she couldn't blame it all on the haunted house.

After the tour, Alessandro invited her to go across the street to Santana Row for a late lunch. "I'll take you to my favorite. You'll love it."

Jo nodded, distracted by her unease, and followed him.

She sat down at a place that served "California cuisine" and cost more than it had any right to, being a casual lunch spot.

"We'll have a bottle of the chardonnay, an artichoke to share, and I'll have the steak frites. Jo, you should try the Cobb salad here. You'll love it."

Jo nodded to the waitress and handed off the menu she hadn't even finished reading. It was his money. He could spend it how he chose, even if artichokes in restaurants were always oversteamed and served cold. She hated chardonnay though, and put her hand over her glass when the waitress came back to serve them.

"You don't want wine?" Alessandro asked.

"No, I don't care for chardonnay."

"I wish you'd said something before I ordered a whole bottle."

That's when it hit her. She was doing it again. Going along

with what a man wanted and not speaking her mind. No. Never again. She was stronger than this.

"I wish you'd asked me what I wanted to drink before you ordered."

Alessandro cringed and changed the subject. "Fair point. So what did you think about the house?" he asked, sipping the wine he clearly preferred.

"It was so sad. Think of her living all alone in that great big house, afraid of the legacy her husband left behind."

"Yeah, kind of crazy, huh?"

"I didn't say she was crazy. I said it was sad. She lived her whole life unsettled and alone because of something her husband did."

"Yes, but who spends millions of dollars based on the advice of a psychic and isn't a little crazy?"

"A woman who felt guilt deeply." Jo looked at the salad as the waitress set it down in front of her. It was deconstructed into little piles with artfully drizzled blue cheese dressing and looked ridiculous. She hated blue cheese. Why the hell hadn't she spoken up? What was she doing?

She'd thought this was what she wanted. An attractive man paying attention to her, interesting experiences, good food and wine… It was everything she'd wanted for her retirement. Except she was sitting across from the wrong man.

Even as frustrated as she was with Dom, she missed him. When he ordered wine, it was always because her favorite was on the menu. When he suggested a dish, it was because he knew her taste. She didn't want to fulfill her dreams with just anyone. She wanted the man she still loved to pull his head out of his ass.

Moreover, Jo wanted a chance to start exercising her voice and her will with him instead of against him. She regretted her years of silence and capitulation. She was part of the problem. She should have said something sooner. They would have argued, sure, but he would have taken her needs into account. She'd always just assumed that her needs weren't as important, because she hadn't been the breadwinner for so many years.

But that wasn't true. She was just as valuable a member of their marriage as he was. Sadly, by the time she'd figured that out, they'd been too far down that road to change course.

But she wasn't ready to give up. Her reactions to Alessandro today confirmed it. She didn't need to waste any more energy on trying to replace what she already had. She needed to figure out how to fix it. And this emotional ping-pong was giving her a headache.

"Alessi, thank you for lunch, but I really should be going." Jo reached for her purse and secured it on her shoulder.

"Wait, what do you mean? You've barely touched your food."

"I need to head home." She pushed her chair back.

"Is this about the wine?" he asked.

"No, it's about my husband."

"I thought he was out of the picture."

"He's moving back into the frame." She rose and he stood, awkwardly looking for their server.

"I see. Do you need a ride home?"

Jo stopped him with a hand on his shoulder.

"No, I'm fine. Stay and enjoy your lunch. I can take care of myself."

Now to figure out how to do that...

CHAPTER 6

43 years ago

Domenico Valenti got what he wanted. Confident and outgoing, he led with his charm. If that didn't work, he put his shoulder into it and pushed until it gave way. At the ripe old age of twenty-one, the world was his oyster. He had a strong back and a sturdy if sometimes stubborn mind. His future was bright.

So when he walked into the bar for the blind double date with his brother and saw *her*, he had no doubt she'd be his. Across the smoky bar she smiled and laughed, and he couldn't stop staring. Everything else fell away. Tony elbowed him to get him moving again. But even as they walked past the bouncer, Dom couldn't stop staring.

As he made his way to the bar to order his beer, he kept an eye on the mystery girl hanging out near the pool table. She clinked her bottle with Elena, Tony's girl, and his hopes rose. If she was his blind date, he'd take back every gripe about driving Tony to see Elena.

When he finally approached her, it was with the confidence

that life had given him as a favored son. He leaned against the wall behind the pool tables and watched her.

It wasn't the curve of her hips or her breasts that drew his attention, although those would have been enough for a second glance. No, it was the curve of her mouth that pulled him in. The flash of teeth, the glint in her eyes, finding delight in a dive bar, her smile open and amused and so fucking sexy he couldn't take his eyes off her. Her joy was infectious. He wanted to know what she was smiling about. Hell, he wanted her to be smiling because of him.

And yet, he'd been standing there for ten minutes, and she hadn't even made eye contact. Dom wasn't used to being ignored.

Tony had abandoned him, cuddled up in a booth playing tonsil hockey with Elena. No help there. Dom straightened his collar and tucked a hand in his pocket. He leaned forward and placed a small stack of quarters on the edge of the pool table.

"I'd like your next game."

She twirled her cue and looked him up and down. "I'm meeting someone," she demurred.

"I'm someone. Dom Valenti, nice to meet you." Dom grinned and held out a hand.

"Nice try, but I don't think so." She kept her hands firmly on her stick.

Dom wasn't going down without a fight. "How about we play a game before you decide if you're meeting me too?"

The friend she'd been playing abandoned their game and waved her off with a smile. He reached past her to grab a cue from the rack. Close enough to touch, but he didn't. Close enough to smell, and God help him he did. Her scent, deep and sultry sweet jasmine, cut through the smoky bar and swam through his senses like a drug, temporarily stunning him.

She stepped around him and began expertly racking the balls, while he tried to shake himself from his intoxication.

"So are you going to tell me your name?" Dom asked.

"Depends. If you win, I'll meet you. If I win, you'll leave me alone." Her lips kicked up on one side and the dimple that appeared in her cheek charmed him. "Your break."

Lining up the cue ball, he shot and broke the triangle with his usual straightforward power shot. She nodded with reluctant admiration as the two ball fell in the pocket.

"Solids." He crowed and thumped a hand on his chest. "Just like me, solid, dependable."

That smirk he wanted to taste showed up again.

"Yeah, you look a little thick. Although if I were you, I wouldn't be so proud of claiming the blue ball."

Did she just drop a double dick joke into the mix? My God, she's perfect.

"I sure hope that's not how tonight ends up," he said and lined up his next shot.

"Well, I'm not one to argue with a sign."

That was good. She wouldn't argue when he explained that the universe had aligned tonight to bring them together. Wrapped up in imagining how that conversation would go down, Dom missed his shot.

Gentleman that he was, he stepped back and let her have the table. He didn't even check out her ass in those jeans when she leaned over the table. Well, he glanced, but he didn't leer.

She sank the ten easily.

"There, now all the blue balls are off the table." She winked at him and assessed her options, scoping out her next shot.

"Does that mean I'll get to meet you later?"

"Hmm. The game is young. It'll depend a lot on the next five minutes."

"What's going to happen in the next five minutes?"

He didn't have long to wait for an answer.

She twisted her long brown hair and tucked it over one plaid-covered shoulder, the thin cotton of her western-style shirt stretching taut over her chest. Then she sank the nine ball. She leaned over the table directly across from him, giving him a shadowy glimpse of her cleavage, making him long to pop the pearl snaps covering the rest. She frowned as she busted him for looking, and sank the twelve. Without breaking eye contact.

Grinning, she boosted her jean-clad hip up on the table, stretching to line up her shot and untucking the edge of her shirt in the process. The flash of golden skin made his mouth water, and he looked away and took a sip of beer to hide his swallow of lust.

The sharp clack of balls bouncing and two muted thumps drew his attention back to the scrubby green felt. He had to count the table to see that she'd sunk the eleven and the thirteen on the same shot.

He was sunk too. She had him hook, line, and sinker, and she knew it. She was just playing with him now. He leaned back against the wall, propping a foot behind him, and watched her take him to town.

She moved with confident grace, a knowing smile on her face. She'd held control of this game from the moment she'd accepted his quarters. She was a pure pleasure to watch as she cleared the table, leaving only the lonely solids. He was openly grinning as she sank her last stripe.

His opportunity to convince her to give him a chance was rapidly disappearing. Dom pushed away from the wall and stepped into her path on her way around the table toward the eight ball. "Before you call that last shot, can I ask you a question?"

She gripped her cue like a wizard holding a staff and nodded. "Shoot."

"Where did you learn to play pool like that?"

"It was my father's game. I used to sneak down to the pool

hall to play with him. When I was twelve, my nickname was 'The Ballbreaker.'"

"I'll bet it was."

She moved to walk past him.

"Wait, I have to know. Are you going to give me another chance to meet you?"

"I don't know. I don't like being ogled."

"I'm only human. When a beautiful woman leans over a pool table…" Dom held up his hands in surrender to stop her protest. "And cleans my clock, it's hard to look away."

"I'm more than a pair of tits and a nice ass."

"You sure as hell are. I came on this blind date as a favor to my brother. I stayed because I want to get to know all those other things about you."

"Hmmm."

That hum of contemplation crawled right under his skin and made every goose bump stand at attention.

"Eight ball, corner pocket." She turned and tapped the table, dismissing him.

She had a beautiful clear shot, and he'd blown his. He felt something monumental slipping through his fingers as silkily as the cue slipped through hers.

Dom held his breath as the white ball hit the black and rolled across the green felt. The eight ball dropped cleanly into the corner pocket, taking Dom's heart with it.

But as he watched, a miracle happened. The cue ball followed right behind it. She'd scratched. On purpose. It had to be on purpose. She was too good to miss that shot on accident.

Dom tore his eyes from the table and caught her laughing at him.

"The look on your face is priceless."

"You scratched," Dom said. His brain had short-circuited and spit out the obvious.

"I did. Oops." She shrugged and held out her hand. "I'm Jo."

He took her hand in his, touching her for the first time. Her hand fit perfectly in his, pale gold against his dark tan. He had a flash of insight that he'd be holding this hand for the rest of his life, for better or worse, and everything in between.

"But I'm really not the person you're meeting tonight."

"You lost." His brain still hadn't moved past stating the obvious, but he was desperate to keep her talking.

"Ah, but you didn't win." She looked over his shoulder and smiled. "And my actual date just walked in. Thanks for the game." She pulled her hand from his and racked her cue.

"This isn't over."

"It is, judging by the daggers Elena is staring into your back right now. Who's the redhead?"

Dom glanced over his shoulder to where his brother and his irate girlfriend were sitting with a pissed-off stranger, who was likely his blind date. He'd been wrong. Or maybe he'd been very, very right. "Shit," he muttered. He turned back to tell Jo he'd ditch the blind date if she bailed on hers. But she was already gone, walking toward the door of the bar and pulling her actual date into a hug.

This couldn't be right. This wasn't how fairy tales were supposed to end.

Dom frowned. That could only mean one thing. This wasn't the end yet.

∼

JOSEPHINE BERTELLI CLIMBED the stairs to her dorm slowly. Her feet hurt from the stupid boots she'd worn to impress Daniel. Her hair smelled like cigarettes, and between Daniel's uninspiring kisses and the cheap red wine, she couldn't wait to brush her teeth.

The bad wine she'd been prepared for. The bad kisses had been a disappointment. She and Daniel had been friendly for months, gradually moving closer to more. She'd been looking forward to tonight for weeks. Their first date.

But all it had taken was one pool game with Mr. Tall, Dom, and Handsome, and she'd lost interest in Daniel's kisses. His pissy reaction to being beaten three games in a row had killed any residual attraction. The memory of Dom grinning as she'd run the table on him just made letting go of her hopes for Daniel even easier.

Dom had captured her imagination. She had no idea if the reality of him would live up to the fantasy she'd crafted about him over one game of pool. But the potential had been high enough to bump Daniel right out of the running.

This was crazy. She didn't even know where to find the guy. That girl from her dorm had been draped all over a guy who had to be related to him. Broad shoulders, trim waists, dark haired, and cocky. She'd bet they were brothers. Maybe she could go back to the bar next weekend...

Jo rounded the corner of her hallway as she walked to her dorm room, still toying with plans for running into the man who was taking up serious mental real estate. Her steps faltered when she realized "that girl," Elena, was lounging against her door, arms crossed and eyes narrowed.

"Uh, hi."

"Hi. Good date?" Elena asked, her voice carefully neutral.

"Not really. Yours?"

"It was great until Dom came back to the table all grouchy. What did you do to him?"

"I just kicked his ass at pool. I swear." Jo held her hands up in defense.

"Well, you sure made an impression. A fact that did not go unnoticed by his actual date, Peggy. I spent the whole evening listening to her bitch at Dom for watching you instead of having a good time with Tony."

"I'm sorry, but I truly didn't do anything."

"Oh honey, I'm not mad. I think you're the key."

"The key?"

"The key to the mystery of the perfect date for Dom. Here's the deal. Tony and I have been going together since high school. Now that I'm here at college, he's got to drive up to see me. He's got no car, so his brother Dom gives him a ride in return for a date setup. Peggy is the fourth friend I've lost over this. But he seems to like you, probably because you're the first girl who isn't falling all over him. So what do you say?"

"Was there a question in there?"

"Come on. You said your date was a bust. Dom will be back in two weeks. Be his blind date. It'll be fun."

Maybe it wouldn't be so hard to find him after all.

"I'll think about it. You can tell him I said that." Jo shared a smirk with Elena before she slipped into her room alone.

∽

2 years ago

DOM WALKED through the build site where Million-Dollar Starter Home was filming that week. He generally tried to stay out of the way, keeping the builds that weren't being filmed running smoothly. After his brief stint on camera, never to be repeated —*thank God*—he wasn't needed on set. Who knew he'd have stage fright?

At first he'd been miffed about being excluded from his own show, but after seeing the footage, he'd quickly realized Jake was right. He was better off behind the scenes. Besides, he hadn't anticipated the nerves or stage fright being as debilitating as it was.

But as owner of Valenti Brothers Construction, at least for a little while longer, he had a vested interest in making sure the build was progressing to his standards. He knew only too well how rushing, in this case to meet a TV production schedule, could lead to errors and shoddy construction. This show was supposed to solidify their reputation, not demolish it.

Dom strolled from room to room, checking wiring and framing, growing more and more impressed with what his crew had accomplished. Adrian and Sofia made a good team when they managed to stop sniping at each other.

He checked out the chandelier in the dining room and wondered how far over budget it had set them. He could admit it made a statement though. Sofia was certainly displaying her talent on these projects.

As if summoned by his thoughts, his eldest daughter's voice drifted to him from the kitchen around the corner.

"Have you noticed anything strange about Mom lately?" she asked.

"Other than the fact that she's still royally pissed at Dad?" Frankie replied. "Not really. Why?"

"We met for coffee, and she just seemed…off."

Dom knew he shouldn't be eavesdropping, but if something was wrong with Jo, he needed to know, and she still wasn't speaking to him.

"Like what?" Frankie asked, helpfully.

"Well, first she ordered a mocha—"

"GASP! Not a chocolate coffee!"

"Would you please take this seriously? Have you ever seen her drink anything other than drip coffee with milk or a skim latte?"

"No, but a change in coffee order doesn't exactly make me panic."

"She was so angry about everything, and she couldn't put her phone down for five minutes."

"Again, I'm not seeing anything..."

Sofia cut her off. "She freaked out when I asked about bringing Adrian to a Friday dinner as my date, and said she didn't want to see me go down the same path she had."

That comparison felt like a misfired staple gun to his chest. She didn't want Sofia to have a marriage like theirs? He didn't have time to ponder that because Fi's next words smashed into his heart like a sledgehammer.

"And then she said she was considering leaving Dad."

"What the hell? Way to bury the lead, Fi!"

"I'm worried, Frankie."

Dom was trying to figure out how to breathe with this new gaping hole in his chest where his heart had been. It wasn't going well.

"No. No way. I mean I know she's mad, but she wouldn't really leave, would she?"

"I don't know... She left with some dude with slick silver hair and a slick silver car to match. She said it was just a trip with her seniors' club, but I don't know why that would make her so jumpy..."

Dom's mind went to static at that last revelation. She'd already replaced him? He'd always known deep down that Jo was out of his league, and that she deserved so much better, but he'd never expected she'd have reason to go looking for it.

Despite the fact that he couldn't feel his feet, Dom had to move. He couldn't stay and hear another word of this. He stumbled backward out of the dining room as quickly as he could. He made it into his truck and just sat there, immobilized by doubt.

She wanted to leave? The question played on a loop in his head, each repetition hitting his brain with the force of a nail gun, leaving a stabbing pain in its wake. He'd thought he had time. Time to fix things. Time to win her over. Time to figure out how to give her what she wanted.

Maybe she had a point with all of her "seize the day" and "the time is now" jabs.

He had known she was pissed that he hadn't consulted with her before starting the show, but he hadn't known how close she was to the end of her rope. The idea of life without Jo was untenable. His battered brain quite literally couldn't even picture that reality. He didn't ever want to know what that would feel like. He couldn't let her go, not without the fight of his life.

When his hands began to ache he realized he'd been clutching the steering wheel so hard that his fingers were white. Dom hauled in a deep breath and released the wheel.

Pull yourself together, man.

He would fix this. That was his job, and he'd never met a problem he couldn't solve with a good idea and a bit of elbow grease. It was the idea bit he needed to come up with right now.

What did Jo want enough to convince her to stay? She wanted him to retire, but what on earth would he do then? Endless empty days stretched into his future, which cranked his anxiety up to eleven. No, he had to find something to do, or he'd drive them both to divorce anyhow.

How did the heroes do it in her books? He'd picked up a few of them over the years, out of curiosity. There was always some big reveal or grand apology when the hero screwed up.

Mistakes had definitely been made, and Dom knew a good grovel would help, but he needed more than that, something big.

His mind went back to the conversations they'd had when they were young and in love and flat broke. Jo had always wanted to travel. His fear of flying had put a damper on that plan, and then they hadn't had the money to spare to do it with the kids. Maybe...maybe he could bring the travel to her...

His mind, eager to escape his earlier meltdown, now kicked

into high gear. He started scribbling in the project notepad that lived in his pocket. An idea formed on the page, taking shape around the idea of recreating a trip to Italy here and needing a project to keep himself busy. Details and logistics swirled as he sat in his sweltering truck, oblivious to the heat, and tried to save his marriage.

Yes, he'd screwed up, and yes, he needed to make up for it, but he'd be damned if he lost her without a fight. He could do this. He had to make it work.

"This is not how this ends," he muttered to himself. He'd spent thirty years developing his skills. It was time to use them to rescue his marriage.

He just prayed it wouldn't be too little too late.

CHAPTER 7

23 YEARS ago

"Good, now use the hammer." Dom grinned as Gabe picked up the hammer Dom had given him last Christmas—over Jo's protests on behalf of her walls—from the messy pile of tools in his bucket. He'd told her he'd give the boy something appropriate to use it on, and the idea for the tree house was born. When Gabe began driving nails with a quick and sure three taps each, Dom just sat back like the proud papa he was and watched.

Together, he and Gabe had drawn up plans and framed out the whole tree house. Frankie had demanded a role, and Dom watched as she worked the block of sandpaper he'd given her over the scrap hardwood floors he'd installed. At four, she was already showing signs of inheriting his stubbornness, and she might as well learn how to channel that energy for good. Sofia had gone with Jo to pick out paint colors they could all agree on, and little Enzo was practicing his knot skills making the rope ladder and spreading tan bark around the base of the tree.

This tree house was a testament to what the Valenti Family

could build together, and it warmed Dom's heart. Sitting in the corner, watching his firstborn wield a hammer like it was a natural extension of his arm, Dom began to dream.

Someday, he'd pass Valenti Brothers down to his children and his nephew, Tony's boy, Seth. The cousins would take the stable foundation he and Tony had laid and build to even greater heights. And Gabe, the oldest and most like him of all the kids, would be at the helm.

"You know, some day you're going to be one of the brothers in Valenti Brothers. You're learning so many skills today that you'll use forever."

"I'm gonna build houses, just like you, Dad."

"That's the plan."

"Only mine are going to have kick-butt slides that go from the second floor to a pool and trapdoors and secret rooms..."

"They can have whatever your client pays for, but we still aren't putting in a pool or a waterslide. Nice try."

Gabe hunched his shoulders into a pout and hammered hard enough to bend the nail.

"Do you remember what to do?" Dom asked gently.

"Yeah, I'm not a baby like Frankie." Gabe's lips pressed into a sullen line as he turned the hammer around to remove it before tossing the bent nail out the window and starting another.

"Hey, watch it!" Enzo yelled from below.

"I'm not a baby!" Frankie argued from her spot in the corner.

"Baby, baby bay-beeee," Gabe taunted.

Frankie threw the wooden sanding block at Gabe's head with the speed and accuracy of a child who'd been forced to sit through too many little league games, and screamed at a decibel and pitch reserved for maligned four-year-old sisters. "I'M NOT A BABY!"

"Ow, Frankie that hurt. Fine. You're not a baby."

Pacified, she crawled into Gabe's lap for a hug, which her big brother automatically gave. Dom's heart swelled in his chest to see the bonds forming so clearly between his children.

"Dad! We're back with the paint!" Sofia yelled from below.

"Hey, don't drag the ladder through my wood chips. I just got them level!" Enzo protested.

Did four kids under eight create an unholy amount of noise and chaos? Yes.

Did they fill his heart to bursting, this wild crew of misfits he was raising? Also yes.

"Come on, Frankie. Let's go paint." Gabe was already sliding her out of his lap and heading for the stairs, hammering up the plywood walls forgotten.

"No, I'm gonna stay and help Daddy." She picked up the hammer Gabe had dropped in his haste, and went to the wall. With one even swing, she sank the nail Gabe had left hanging. "Another!" Frankie giggled and bounced, delighted with herself.

Dom started another nail for her and smiled.

A house by Valenti was built to last.

∽

2 YEARS *ago*

DOM CROSSED the parking lot toward Enzo as he tucked his phone in his pocket. He grinned and waved to get his attention, since that boy looked lost in thought.

"Lorenzo, wait up!"

Dom had come in early on purpose, hoping to catch his son before he got busy. He needed Enzo's help on a secret project so he was trying to be discreet. Admittedly, not his strongest suit.

"Hi, Dad. Jim Hamilton sends his best."

"What are you talking to him for? Looking at buying something?" Dom asked. Since Jo had hung up her realtor license, Valenti Brothers had gone back to working with Jo's mentor and longtime friend who'd sold them their first house. Dom felt a slight twinge that he hadn't asked Jim to help with his plan, but he knew he needed to keep the surprise a secret. There was no way Jim wouldn't let something slip to Jo.

"Nope, just helping a friend. What's up?" Enzo ran a hand over his neck and stretched until it cracked.

"I need to talk to you about a project."

If things worked out as planned, this project would fix things with Jo. And God, he needed to fix things with Jo.

"Is it for the show?" Enzo sighed and looked back at his phone.

"No, it's—"

Enzo cut him off before he could explain. "Then I don't have time, Dad. I'm slammed with my regular clients on top of the show. That's why I'm already here and getting down to business at seven a.m."

Dom swallowed his frustration and tried again. "Just hear me out. I'm tackling some new construction in south Santa Clara county."

"Dad, we've been over this. I'm not interested in building. I wasn't when you asked me last month. I wasn't when you asked me last year. I'm not Gabe. Stop trying to make me take his place."

Dom froze. Was that what his son thought? That he was trying to turn him into Gabe? Words deserted him as he struggled to free his mind from the clinging cobwebs of grief and memories. Hurt that his child could think that he was trying to replace one son with the other, Dom struggled to pull his shields up.

"Listen, Dad, I—"

Dom raised his hand, blocking Enzo's words and apologies. "No. You're busy. I get it. Don't let me keep you."

Dom turned and got in his truck, but instead of starting it, he just sat there. He stared out the windshield and let the feelings flow. By now he knew that trying to keep pushing through them was not a thing that worked. Had he really screwed up so royally?

True, he had a distinct plan for how Valenti Brothers should operate. His vision was the only reason the company even existed! If it hadn't been for him, they never would have made it out of their first year. But maybe he'd been blind to the vision others had for the company.

He started the truck and shifted into reverse, backing his way out of the tight spot.

This Million-Dollar Starter Home project had really opened his eyes. He'd badly misjudged how he saw Sofia fitting into the business. The truth was he had little use for design. Build the wall, install the cabinets, let the homeowner worry about what it looked like. It had worked just fine for them for decades.

Besides, he'd needed help when Jo had walked away. He knew that the business side of things was not his strong point. So when Sofia had stepped in to handle the accounts, he'd been grateful.

And when she wanted to shift into design for the show, he'd panicked at the idea of changing again. It was one more piece of control being taken away from him, and he'd responded by coming down hard. He was proud of Sofia for chasing her dream anyway. She'd helped him solve the office problem by hiring her friend, who seemed to be working out. And he couldn't deny that the homes she was designing for the show were stunning.

She really was building her own reputation within Valenti Brothers, which had been the whole damn point.

When he hit the highway, his thoughts shifted to Enzo blowing up at him today. What missteps had he made there? Yes, he'd always envisioned the company passing on to Gabe, but it belonged equally to the rest of his kids. He just needed to be sure they were ready to handle the responsibility before he handed over the reins. So he pushed them. Wasn't that what fathers were supposed to do?

Nobody got anywhere in this life without a little hustle, and he needed his kids to hustle in the right direction so he could do what Jo was asking him to do. He couldn't just walk away from the business he'd spent decades building with his blood, sweat, and tears. So he wanted his son to take a bigger interest. Was that a crime? He was just as talented as the rest of his crew. Dom would never understand why the boy seemed content to keep mowing lawns. He had hoped that Enzo would help him assess the property he was going to see, but apparently he'd just have to handle it by himself.

He sat stuck behind a semi, morning traffic slowing Highway 101 to a crawl. He hated feeling boxed in, and it seemed impossible to escape these days.

His thoughts turned to his youngest child, Frankie. That girl was entirely too confident. She thought she could tackle anything if she ran at it hard enough. His pride rose in his chest as he saw his own persistence reflected in her. But she hadn't had to work for what she wanted. Most things had come easy to her as the baby of the family. Would she buckle at the first sign of struggle? She needed to get some more experience at running jobs and failing before he'd feel comfortable giving her more control.

Eventually, he reached his exit and pulled off the highway onto a quiet back country road. Remote and rural, it was the perfect spot for what he had in mind. God, this had better work. His throat tightened and his chest resisted breathing as he let himself spin out what could happen if he failed. No. Failure was not an option.

By the time he drove past the *For Sale* sign at the gate, he had collected himself, at least enough to present his usual jovial front to the seller's realtor.

"Hi there Mr. Valenti. I'm Rosa Velasquez."

She was an attractive woman in her late forties, and Dom noticed the way she assessed him, but felt no desire to return the perusal. He wanted his wife back, damn it.

"Hello, Mrs. Velasquez. I'm so glad you were able to meet me on such short notice."

"No problem at all. Let me tell you a little about the property while we walk."

She showed him the sprawling ranch house, the dilapidated barns, the gravel drive around the side, but the part that caught his imagination was the vines. Acres of established grapevines sprawled into the distance. In the early morning sun, the rust-colored leaves glistened with morning dew. It looked just like the pictures Tony had sent from Italy.

Fixing the house, landscaping the grounds, that could all come later. That was what he did. But this—the view and the future it promised—couldn't be fixed. It had to feel right, and it did. He could make this work for Jo.

He let Rosa finish her script on the house before he interrupted.

"What kind of grapes are these?"

Rosa checked the listing. "Mostly Italian varietals that like the heat. Sangiovese, Nebbiolo, Montepulciano…"

He stopped listening. There was his sign. He was going to buy this property, and win back his wife, and make her favorite wine, and live happily ever after.

"So, Mr. Valenti, you'll let me know if you'd like to see any other properties in the area. I have several others if this isn't to your liking."

"That won't be necessary," Dom said, still staring out over the vines.

"Well!"

He caught the affront in her voice, and chuckled, holding up a hand. "Because I'll be buying this one. Let me get things rolling with the bank, and we can figure out an offer." He wished Jo were here to handle the real estate wrangling. He hated paperwork and contracts, but he'd do them if it meant he could keep this a secret.

Rosa's demeanor instantly shifted back to all smiles. "You had me worried there for a minute. Of course, I'll pull together all of the disclosures and contracts."

She chatted about details but Dom was back in his daydream, sipping wine made from his own grapes, sitting on that back patio with Jo perched in his lap. That was a retirement dream he could get behind.

Now he just had to do what he did best: build a dream into reality with a solid foundation and sturdy walls. A house by Valenti was built to last.

～

27 YEARS ago

"YOU'VE GOT TO BE KIDDING."

Jo stepped through the front door of the house Dom had found. Their realtor, Jim Hamilton, was due any minute, but they'd arrived at the open house before him and decided to wander.

"Grain of salt, babe," Dom said under his breath.

"Grain of salt? I'd need a block of the stuff. Is that…broken glass? On the front porch?" She shifted Enzo more firmly on her hip. A hip that was rapidly disappearing as her body grew to accommodate a fourth baby. A baby that needed more space than they could manage in the tiny bungalow they were currently renting.

A new baby, a growing business, and a small inheritance from her great-aunt meant the time to invest in a home had arrived. But this house?

"Who doesn't at least clean up vandalism before an open house?"

"Well at least they aren't hiding anything."

"Don't jinx us!"

Jo walked farther into the house, holding Gabe's hand tightly in hers. "Dom, keep a hand on Sofia, please."

Who knew what other surprises this house would hold?

"Dom, what made the holes in the drywall?"

Dom wandered over to peek through with his flashlight. "Hmm, not sure. I wonder what kind of pipes it has..."

"Hey there, Dom! Jo! Good to see you." Jim Hamilton bustled in the door behind them. "Sorry I'm late."

"Not a problem. How are you?"

"Oh, you know, just living the dream, every day. Let's talk about your dream."

"I'll be honest, Jim. I've barely made it into the living room, and this feels more like a nightmare."

"I hear you, but I'll be frank. Finding a five-bedroom house in this area in your price range is a stretch. When this came onto the market, I immediately thought of you."

"I don't know if I should be insulted or not." Jo cringed.

"It's a compliment. I know it's in rough shape, but you have a very handy husband and an eye for what makes a house a home. You could give this house the second chance it deserves. Just keep an open mind as we walk through."

Jo sighed but did as she was asked. The fact that there had been a break-in while the house was vacant could account for the broken glass as well as the damaged hardwoods and holes in the walls. The poor eyesight of the eighty-year-old previous owner explained the navy blue living room, army green kitchen with black countertops, and a crimson wall in the bedroom. It also explained the general lack of maintenance around the house. On a fixed income, actually fixing things could be prohibitively expensive.

"Sofia, please get up off the floor. Dom, are those mouse droppings on the carpet?"

A lot of mouse droppings. A skittering in the wall made Jo wonder exactly what was living in them and which had come first, the holes or the rodents.

While she pondered this, Gabe darted for the open back door and the freedom of the backyard. Between Gabe and a young boy's paradise of overgrown bushes and low-branched trees lay a rickety, rotting deck with no handrail and a three-foot drop. Jo's heart jumped into her throat.

"Wait!" She tried to lunge for him, but holding Enzo slowed her down and her belly protested the sudden movement.

Dom picked Sofia up onto his hip and raced after his son, scooping him up with an arm around the waist moments before he would have taken flight off the edge of the deck. With carefully placed steps, he crossed the deck and deposited the kids inside the house, sliding the door shut behind them.

A death trap. Her husband wanted to buy a death trap.

"Let's go upstairs and see the bedrooms."

Jo was unconvinced anything she saw upstairs would impress her, but she was wrong. Her children scattered and claimed their rooms, and she could see how much they all needed their own space. The layout of four smaller but decent-sized rooms along the hallway, with a large suite for her and Dom at the head of the stairs, would definitely work for her growing family.

"This one is going to be mine." Sofia did a little pirouette in the middle of the Pepto-Bismol pink bedroom, and Jo smiled.

Every kid would have a space to make their own. After years of trying to get babies to sleep in shared bedrooms, this would give them all a lot more nighttime peace.

The promise of eventual sleep opened her mind further to the potential of the space. Back downstairs, instead of focusing on the ugly color of the kitchen, she could appreciate the way it opened into the back family room. Instead of seeing the gouges in the floor as an impediment, she welcomed the chance to sand down the grimy floors and stain them to her liking. The beautiful woodwork around the trim and doorframes added a Craftsman charm that she could reclaim from beneath layers of white paint.

Standing on the staircase, she could see it gleaming in the background of prom photos. The living room, with its original fireplace and large windows, was just screaming for a family at Christmas to gather around a tree and open presents. Jo walked over to the beautiful carved wood mantel and ran her fingers over it. Hidden under the layer of dust were little nail holes. Six of them, evenly spaced, along the front edge. Perfect for hanging stockings. This house had been loved once, and it could be loved again.

With a little bit of vision and a whole lot of hard work, likely provided by her husband and his brother, this run-down house could become a real home for her family. The challenges started to fade as her mind began to mentally fix things, creating a warm, inviting space to raise her children and welcome friends and family.

They walked back out the front door to stand in the driveway. Looking back at the house, Jo could see the beauty in its bones. She could make this work.

Jim picked up his pitch, stepping into the silence.

"So, this is a five bedroom on a large lot under market price because of the level of work that needs to be done. It's a great school district, and you've got established neighbors. I think it's a steal if you can do the work for cost yourself."

"Jim, the size and price are right, but I don't know if we're up for this challenge. With the baby and the kids..." Dom had Gabe tossed over his shoulder and set him down to run around. Meanwhile, Sofia was standing on his foot with her arm wrapped around his leg.

"If you need to think about it, take a few days, but I think it will move pretty quickly if developers catch wind. And then all of this old charm will be lost."

"Gabriel Valenti, what are you doing?" Jo shouted at her son who was standing suspiciously behind a bush planted along the edge of the house.

"What? I had to pee!" Gabe shouted back.

Jo shook her head and sighed. She would never understand boys. "Well, he marked it. I guess we have to buy it now."

Dom's jaw dropped, and Jo couldn't help but laugh. Her impulsive husband, stunned by her decision? About time he got a taste of his own medicine.

"Do you mean it?" he asked.

"I'm thinking about it. Can you handle a renovation this extensive?" Jo teased.

Dom shuffled over to her, Fi still clinging to him, and kissed her deeply. "Anything for you, love. If you can see it, I can build it," he said when he came up for air.

"Then I think we should do it," Jo said. "Jim, we'll need to make a list of fixes and see the disclosures and school data, but if the price is right, I think we can make this house our home."

The life Jo envisioned in this home would be full of laughter and love, and she was confident there was no one better than Dom to help her build that.

She turned back to him, face held in mock censure. "But Dom, I'm not moving in until you get the rats out of the walls."

CHAPTER 8

27 YEARS ago

DOM LEANED his sweaty shoulders against the fireplace so that he wouldn't leave a wet print on the freshly hung drywall. After three hours, he'd just finished hanging the living room. Only eight more rooms to go. Wrists on his knees, he dropped his aching head in the space between, stretching his neck and his patience.

He'd hoped to be farther along, but between working at the end of already long days and doing everything by himself, it had taken months to even get this far. Little Francesca had her crib wedged into a corner of their bedroom in their rental, because Jo rightly didn't want to move an infant into a construction zone.

He was busting his ass, but it wasn't good enough.

True, he'd finished the electrical rewiring and had swapped out the old galvanized plumbing for copper. At one point most of the walls in the house had been missing, which allowed him to see exactly which nests belong to the rats and which ones were the squirrels before he cleared them all out. He had also rerun ductwork and replaced soiled insulation while repairing termite damage. He was determined that this house would be solid once he was finished with it. So likely they'd be able to move in by the time Frankie was five.

The sound of the front door creaking open snapped his head up. No one should be here this time of night. He'd be damned if he let another break-in happen on his watch. Picking up his screw gun, he slowly stood and moved behind the wall he'd just covered with plasterboard. Tentative footsteps crossed the foyer, and he jumped out in that direction, hoping to scare the burglar away.

Jo dropped the cooler she had in her hands and screamed. "Dom Valenti, what the hell do you think you're doing?"

He was laughing too hard to answer. She smacked him on the shoulder, and he dropped the gun and pulled her into a sweaty hug.

"You scared the life out of me! Let go! You're all smelly."

"I thought you were someone breaking in. I just laid all that copper pipe, and I haven't finished covering it all with drywall yet."

"Here I go out of my way to bring you supper, and this is the welcome I get."

"Come here, I'll give you a proper welcome."

Dom pressed his lips to his wife's, and despite the disarray around them, it felt like coming home. These quiet moments alone together were few and far between with so many little ones running around. He took advantage and reminded his wife just how much he loved kissing her. She blossomed for him, opening her mouth, seeking his tongue with her own, diving her hands into his sweaty hair, and reminded him right back how much she loved kissing him.

Some thought was trying to make itself known, but it struggled to get through the sudden onslaught of passion pulsing through his brain.

Dom backed Jo up to the staircase and walked her up a step so he could reach her better. On a normal day, he'd have boosted her up, hands under her ass, and pinned her against the wall, the better to ravish her, but she was still recovering from delivering Francesca. These were always the hardest weeks to stay away from her, because the end of celibacy was in sight but still so far away. He missed his wife, but he knew she had to heal and focus on the baby right now.

The baby. Right. The kids!

"Where's the baby?" he asked, pulling back from her puffy lips.

"Elena brought Seth over and offered to babysit so I could come help you, since Tony's out of town."

Dom finally got a good look at his wife, in her ratty painting T-shirt, overalls, and with a kerchief covering her hair. She was the cutest subcontractor he'd ever seen. "Are you sure? I don't want you to do too much. I can handle this."

"I know you can, but I want to know that I helped do the work too. And even I know that hanging drywall is easier with two sets of hands."

"Mmm, I know what I want to do with my hands." He slid them from her hips up over her breasts, where she tensed.

"Dom, so help me God, if you make my milk drop, I'm going to leave you here by yourself to suffer."

He held up his hands in surrender. "I guess we better put them to more boring use. Drywall it is."

For the next two hours they worked side by side, hanging panels in the kitchen and dining room before calling it quits. Jo spread a blanket on the floor in their dining room and handed Dom a container of chicken parmesan and a cold bottle of beer before collapsing prone on the floor.

He shoveled the now cold pasta into his mouth gratefully.

"Are we crazy to think we could do this?" Jo asked with her eyes closed.

"That we could renovate a house? Absolutely not."

"It's just with you and Tony working so much and the baby coming a little early, it feels like we're wading through neck-high mud. Are we ever going to finish? We've moved so many times. I just want to be in our forever home so we can finally settle in."

"Trust me, babe. Now that the drywall is going up, we're in the home stretch. It'll start looking more like a house, and we'll get you and the kids in here as soon as possible."

Jo rolled to her side and rested her head in his lap. "I do trust you. I'm just so tired of living out of boxes and not having a stable routine. I'm tired of being in limbo. So tired…"

She closed her eyes, and he felt her body go slack against his. This incredible woman had mothered four children all day and still come to pitch in on the construction. He knew her strength wasn't boundless, but some days it was easy to forget. "So impatient. Don't worry, babe. We're almost there."

Vowing to pay his guys out of his own pocket for a few days work to speed things along, Dom held his wife while she slept curled up on the newly sanded hardwood floors of their home.

∼

2 years ago

JO WALKED into a quiet empty house late Friday night. The charity dance had been a success at raising money for the local library, but the rest of the evening had fallen flat. None of her new friends could understand why she wasn't spending time with Alessandro anymore. Alessi himself was behaving like a petulant child. And to add insult to injury, the food had been mediocre and the cash bar laughable. She knew fundraisers typically tried to put the bulk of the money raised toward the charity, but really? Serving three-buck Chuck at an event in Wine Country, California?

She was annoyed, but mostly with herself. She'd signed up for the event, in spite of its Friday date, hoping that Dom would come with her. He'd barely taken notice when she'd told him about the dinner, too busy tapping away on his phone to even look up. How was she supposed to figure out how to repair her marriage with him if he wouldn't even listen to her?

She tossed her purse on the bench by the door and walked back to the kitchen for a proper glass of red wine. She drew up short at the pile of pizza boxes on the counter. The recycling bin was full of beer bottles, the garbage full of paper plates. They'd had Friday dinner without her. She poured her glass of wine and drank deeply.

She could admit that she'd deliberately not canceled with the kids, because she had wanted Dom to have to handle it. She'd hoped he'd talk to the kids about skipping a Friday because she had an event, and perhaps be guilted into going with her. Worst case, he'd flounder a bit and appreciate her a little bit more.

Instead, he'd ordered pizza and had a party with their kids without her.

This was what she could look forward to if she left. Family events split between them. Missing out on half of everything, because if she left, she didn't think she'd have the strength to be around him as a friend.

Was her protest worth it? She didn't want to give up the family she'd spent her life building. She didn't want to lose the closeness with her children or access to her grandchildren once they started arriving. She just wanted to move out of the rut she'd been in for too many years. There were so many things she wanted to do and see and try. Was it so wrong to want to be done working before she was too old and decrepit to enjoy things?

Pouring herself a second glass of pity wine, Jo picked at a piece of cold pizza. No. No, it wasn't wrong, or too much, or selfish, but sometimes rebellion was exhausting. If she didn't have everything riding on this working out in her favor, she'd choose to go back to the way things had been, as unhappy and empty as she'd felt. At least it would be a familiar pain, one she knew how to deal with, instead of this constantly feeling off-balance. But her pride and her stubborn streak wouldn't let her go backward.

She hoped to God Dom would catch up soon. She was lonelier than she'd ever been before. Finishing her slice and her glass of wine, she quietly climbed the stairs, dragging her hand over the railing she'd refinished with Sofia so many years ago. Turning away from the vacant bedrooms that no longer housed her children, toward the room she'd shared with Dom for decades, her chest felt empty too. Why did this house she'd worked so hard on no longer feel like home?

She tiptoed to her side of the bed and quietly changed into pajamas before washing her face and brushing her teeth in the bathroom Dom had built to her specifications. She held back a sob as she climbed into bed. Dom kept his back to her, but his soft words reached her anyway.

"We missed you tonight."

The words burned on her tongue in reply. I miss you too, she wanted to say, even though that wasn't what he'd meant. She wanted to roll over and feel his strong arms pull her close and his soft lips kiss her worries away. But she couldn't without giving up everything she'd been fighting for.

So she stayed quiet and let her pillow absorb her tears. She didn't want this life alone, but it seemed she couldn't have it with him in it either.

CHAPTER 9

2 YEARS ago

JO PULLED up outside the elementary school and waited for Daisy to come out. She still had on the makeup Natalie had done for her spot on the show this morning, and was riding the high of feeling beautiful, even if her husband had barely noticed.

The little girl came out of her classroom, and Jo got out of the car and waved. Daisy raced over, all smiles, clearly recovered from her tummy bug.

"Are you ready to bake some cookies?" Jo asked, grinning at the little girl who was nearly bouncing out of her shoes.

"Yes! I told Maddie that I was going to bake cookies today, and she said she wants one, so I said I would pack extra in my lunch for her tomorrow, so we gotta make enough, okay?" Daisy's enthusiasm turned her thoughts into one long sentence.

Jo grinned, buoyed by the giddy excitement Daisy couldn't quite contain. "We can definitely do that. Hop in! Is Maddie a friend?"

"I think so. She sits with me at lunch and asks me to play with her at recess."

"That sounds like a friend to me. How was your day?"

As the young girl regaled her with stories from the front lines of second grade, Jo was transported back in time to when her own children were full of this joy and energy. She missed this time with little people. She was excited about the prospect of grandchildren, and saw no reason not to indulge her Nana impulses with Daisy. She'd even pulled the magic bookcase out of storage and stocked it with her kids' old favorites in anticipation of having little readers in her house.

She'd been spending less time with the senior social activities, because they made her miss Dom too much. She had continued with the after-school tutoring, because it brought her such joy, but she could only do so much there.

This afternoon in the kitchen with Daisy was a gift. Jo got to share something she loved with a delightful little girl, and the little girl got to spend time with an adult who wasn't her mama and eat treats. Win-win!

She wrapped Daisy up in a too-large apron and snapped a picture to send to Nat. If her son had half the brains she thought he did, perhaps this little one would be hers to spoil long into the future, but until then she'd just stand in as a surrogate. Reaching for a brown banana, Jo offered it to Daisy, who shook her head in disgust.

"You know, I used to think the same thing. I hated bananas in my lunch because they always got squished. But then I learned the magic."

"What magic?"

"I'll show you."

While Jo pulled frozen bananas from the freezer, Daisy eyed her skeptically. Jo put the frozen bananas into the blender and let Daisy hold the button down until they magically turned the consistency of soft-serve ice cream. She scooped some into a bowl for Daisy and topped it with chocolate chips.

"See? Magic."

And the little-girl giggles that filled her kitchen were a special kind of magic indeed.

"What do you call this?" Daisy asked.

"I don't know what it's called," Jo replied.

"Banana Jo, Jo Banana, Jo Nana...JoNana! That's it! JoNana's magic ice cream."

"JoNana is perfect. I love it. In fact, I insist on being called JoNana henceforth."

"Fence, what?"

"It means from now on. Deal?" Jo held out her hand, and Daisy's sticky fingers clasped hers firmly and shook.

"Deal."

At the end of the afternoon, peanut butter cookies in tow, Jo brought Daisy back to what used to be Sofia's apartment.

"Really, I can't thank you enough for picking her up from school," Natalie said, rising from her perch at the table.

"It was my pleasure!" Jo ran a hand over Daisy's mop of dark hair. "I've always wanted to be an active grandma, but my children are proving to be remarkably slow in that department. If they don't get a move on, I'll miss my window."

"You strike me as a woman with a lot of life and love ahead of her," teased Natalie.

"Plans change, dreams fade."

Jo could hear the tired dejection in her voice but was unable to temper it.

Natalie plated the cookies, nodding at Daisy when she turned on the puppy dog eyes. "Daisy, why don't you grab a snack and read in your room? Jo, can I offer you some tea or coffee? Water? Wine?"

"I'm tempted by the wine, but I'll stick with tea. Story of my life."

Natalie puttered with mugs and the kettle while Jo sat at the beautiful kitchen table she'd helped Sofia pick out. She was glad her daughter had been able to help Natalie out of a tight spot. Her apartment definitely showed touches of the new residents though. Toys and crayons lay on Fi's coffee table, and there were little-girl socks scattered on the floor, but Sofia's signature style still shone through. That girl had talent. *God, please don't let her waste it.*

"I wanted to say thank you for letting Sofia rent me her apartment at your subsidized rate. I know how much this property is worth," Natalie said from the stove.

"Nonsense. You're doing us all a favor, keeping it occupied and paid for, and Fi can start saving for the wedding. Plus, the only reason you're in this mess is because of my husband's crazy scheme. We're happy to help."

Jo watched Natalie fuss with the tea and smiled at the nerves pouring off the girl.

"I'm sorry I don't have china."

"It's just how I make mine at home," Jo tried to reassure her.

"Do you take cream, sugar, lemon?"

"Just a little sugar, sweetheart. Relax." Jo covered Nat's hand and gave it a reassuring squeeze before she tipped a scant half teaspoon of sugar into her mug and neatly strained her teabag, before lifting her mug in a toast. "To mothers helping mothers."

Jo watched the tears gather in the younger woman's eyes and wondered why she'd had so little help. She wanted to give her a boost and looked for something positive to say…

"I know that parenting solo is hard. Hell, joint parenting is no picnic. It was the hardest thing I've ever done, and my kids are grown. Now that they are, I envy your freedom." Where had that thought come from? Now that she'd spoken it, she realized it was how she felt. Was her yearning for freedom now an outgrowth of her past?

"Freedom?" Natalie looked perplexed.

"I just think about how things might have been different if I had been the one to make all the decisions, to be the one in charge. I compromised on so many things that now I'm left wondering what I believe in anymore."

She'd forgotten what making decisions on her own felt like. What would have happened if she'd found her voice earlier?

"This isn't the ideal." The doubt over her sanity showed clearly on Natalie's face.

Jo could imagine that the responsibilities as a single mom were overwhelming. But she couldn't shake this thought. "I don't know. I wonder if we had done something different, would Gabe still be here? I don't regret raising my kids with Dom, but now that we don't have them holding us together, I think about freedom a lot."

Jo's hands gripped her mug tightly, as if that could hold her life together too.

Natalie covered one hand with hers, offering connection and understanding. "You two have raised some pretty amazing kids who are smart and independent. I'm sure Gabe was too. Are you really thinking about leaving Dom? You've invested a lot of years together. Would you really just walk away?"

"If he doesn't want to spend time with me, why should I stay?"

Jo stopped speaking, momentarily lost in memory.

"When I met Dom in college, I fell hard. So tall and strong. So handsome. I was putty in his hands. When the kids came along, I molded myself into the mother they needed me to be, and then the office manager Tony and Dom needed to succeed. That man is allergic to paperwork." She let out a watery chuckle and took a sip of her tea, fighting for control. "After all that bending and stretching to fit the needs of others, I'm ready to find my own shape again. I want to enjoy this next phase of our lives, but he won't let go of the past so we can stretch into the future together. I'm thinking I might have to reach for it by myself."

Jo exhaled a shaky breath as she released that heavy thought into the world.

"What would your next phase be? What's that new dream?"

"We were supposed to pick up new hobbies, spend time together, play with our grandchildren and finally relax. I've been waiting for years, letting Dom set the pace, but when we lost Gabe something changed. I'm not willing to sit back and let life pass me by. I don't know if I can make myself follow his lead anymore."

"There's nothing wrong with wanting something more or different for yourself. That's why I do my makeup tutorials. But have you thought about what you'd be giving up?"

"Some days it just feels like it would be easier to walk away and start fresh than keep digging at the pile of shit between us."

"I thought digging in shit was Enzo's job," Natalie teased.

Shared laughter broke the tension. Jo's shoulders shook before dropping back down from her ears.

"Just don't do anything rash."

"That's my line." Jo laughed, but her voice held no humor. "I've spent my whole life playing by the rules, and where did it get me? An empty home, a son in the ground, and a husband who dismisses my needs out of hand. Maybe rash is exactly what I need."

Jo still struggled with what-ifs, even though Gabe had been gone for years. Would there ever be a day she didn't wonder if she could have done something more or something different and have him still sit at her table every Friday night?

And what if she'd done something different with Dom? Would her marriage be falling apart now? What would the *something different* have been? Even though the idea of finding someone else had fallen away, Jo still couldn't see going back to the way things had been...

She let the fantasy of traveling Europe by herself fill her head. She'd drink tea in London and wine in Italy, stroll through the Louvre in Paris and the Uffizi Gallery in Florence, eat pastries in a French café and fish pulled fresh from the sea along the coast of Italy. Her list had grown over her thirty years of dreaming. Then when she'd rambled all her rambles, she'd come home to a tidy little apartment that she'd let Sofia design for her and live comfortably in a smaller place that wasn't so hard to keep up.

It was a nice dream, but it wasn't quite right. Something was still missing, some driving force. It frustrated her to be unable to see a solution. She was so tired of feeling like she didn't know how to live her own life, but she'd never shared that with a soul. She didn't know why all of this was coming out now, other than Natalie asked good questions and actually listened to the answers.

Jo gripped Nat's wrist. "Please don't say anything about this to my kids. I know you're friendly with them. I just needed to blow off steam and talk to someone who might get it. You're a very good listener."

"They teach us that in beauty school. And don't worry, beautician's code." She held up two fingers and snapped them like scissors. "Your secrets are safe with me."

~

43 years ago

Jo spread the ancient army surplus wool blanket on the dry sand next to a driftwood log, well above the tide line, and took out the cheap bottle of red she'd stashed in her purse. Dom sat on the blanket next to her and grinned. They were close enough to feel the warmth of the bonfire, but far enough away that they had the illusion of privacy from their rowdy group of friends celebrating the end of the semester.

It was December in California, and while only a fool would actually go in the water, the deserted beach was fogged in, perfect for a party around a fire.

Jo snuggled up against Dom's warm bulk, happy to let him block the brisk breeze coming in off the water, and handed him the bottle. He pulled out his Swiss Army knife and muscled it open.

"I can always trust that you'll have the right tool," Jo teased as she took the wine back and sipped a healthy mouthful straight from the bottle.

"You know me, always prepared. Wanna see the other tools I'm packing?" Dom tapped his pocket, and Jo grinned at the double meaning. He always had that pocketknife, and since they'd started dating eight months ago, he'd also carried a condom. Or two.

She might be a sexually liberated woman, but she sure as hell wasn't going to get pregnant right now because of it. The fact that he was on the same page and made sure he was prepared was a big mark in his favor.

She handed him the bottle and cuddled her face into his sturdy shoulder. This was the spot she claimed as hers whenever they were close. She felt safe and protected, maybe even loved.

They'd been dancing around the subject for weeks, but she was sure tonight was the night he'd say it. She watched his Adam's apple bob as he took several swallows of the wine. He held the bottle out to read the label.

"Montepulciano, huh? Italian wine? It's not bad," he said.

"California Italian. I like it. And it's three dollars a bottle."

"Can't beat that. Here, have some more."

They passed the bottle back and forth until Jo was comfortably warm inside and out.

"Beautiful night." Dom pulled her in closer.

"The weather? We're going to talk about the weather?"

"Beautiful lady?"

"Is that a question or a statement?"

"A statement?"

"Well, that sounds convincing." Jo chuckled.

"What do you want to talk about?"

This was just the opening Jo had been waiting for. Dom was sweet, but he needed someone to point him in the right direction. "Tell me about your dreams…"

"You want to hear about the blue sheep who stole my car keys and went for a joyride?"

Jo burst out laughing. God, she loved a man who made her laugh. She loved *this* man who made her laugh. She couldn't wait until she could tell him back.

"No, you idiot. I am one semester from graduation. I'm thinking about what comes next. What do you see in your future?"

"Hmmm, well, I've got the construction gig. It pays good, and I'm learning loads. Not like you are in college, but on the job. But Tony and me, we've been talking about starting a business together someday. We don't know when or how, but I know we're gonna make it happen. Valenti Brothers…" He waved a hand in front of him as if he could already see the sign in lights.

"I believe you. Is that all you see in your future?" she prodded.

"I see a family, lots of kids, a house with a yard. You know, the usual stuff. What about you? What do you see in your future?"

Jo looked up at the stars and poured out her heart.

"I want to travel the world and see everything I've only read about in books. I want to go on adventures. I want to watch sunsets over mountains and beaches in faraway places. And then

I want to come back home and teach. I don't think there's anything I could do more important than that. I'm going to be a great teacher, the kind who gets hugs and letters on her desk and who opens minds and hearts. Then maybe retire to the country for more sunsets and wine." Jo spun out her plans for the future, shapes she could see emerging from the blank fog of her future. No one else could do that for her.

"You've thought about this a lot."

"Um, yeah. Isn't that what college is for? Thinking about what you want to do and then learning how to do it?"

"I guess that makes sense. I wouldn't know. Never went to college. Never even been on a plane, and never will if I can help it. Is that all you dream about?"

"You know, the usual stuff, a family, kids, a house with a yard. A home built around love. I want that too. Maybe not right away, but yeah, I want kids."

Jo bumped her shoulder against him, and Dom just grinned and nodded. Jo pressed on.

"You know, Dom, in a few months everything is going to change. I'll be done with school and looking for jobs. "

"Hallelujah!" He chuckled. "If I had to keep driving up here every two weeks to see you..."

She hated bringing the mood down, but she had to be realistic with him. She didn't want this to end, but she also had to think about her future. "Dom. I don't know where I'll get a teaching job. I'm applying all over."

The big man next to her went silent for a long moment. Had she pushed too far? What if he said he wasn't willing to move? What if this was the beginning of the end? Panic clutched at her throat while she waited for him to say something, anything.

"I hadn't thought of that. I just assumed you'd get a job nearby."

"I've applied at the local districts, but I'm also looking at LA and Seattle," Jo said softly.

"Well." Dom turned and took a deep pull from the bottle of wine before he spoke again. "Do they build houses in LA and Seattle?"

Jo let loose the breath she'd been holding, and her shoulder relaxed into his chest again. "They do."

"Then we can figure this out. Let's not borrow trouble right now, but if it comes down to it, we'll decide together."

"What about opening the business with Tony?" Jo voiced the fear that bloomed in the darker corners of her mind. Was his bond with his brother stronger than this fledgling relationship they had? Would he put his family first?

"We'll have to turn it into a West Coast franchise."

Jo chuckled at Dom's bravado. He leaned down and pressed a kiss to the top of her head and mumbled into her hair.

Jo sat up abruptly, nearly knocking skulls with him. "What did you say?" She had to ask, afraid her ears were hearing what she wanted to hear from that mumbled mess.

"I said…" Dom sat a little straighter and looped an elbow around his raised knee until he was looking her straight in the eye. He hauled in a deep breath and started again. "I said I love you, Jo. We'll figure this out. I'm not going to lose you."

Giddy laughter rattled around in her chest, bursting joyously from her mouth as she tackled him to his back. She was grinning like a fool and quite possibly glowing from the heat flowing through her veins, but she didn't care who knew it as long as the man beneath her did.

"I love you too, Dom. And I'm not going anywhere without you."

She took his mouth with hers in a messy, tangled kiss. She couldn't stop grinning long enough to do it properly, but it accomplished what it needed to, turning words into action, sealing this vow between them. When Dom rolled her, settling his weight on top of her, the kiss took a different turn. Hotter. Needy. This big, gruff man loved her, needed her. And he'd said it first.

Jo couldn't feel the cold breeze off the ocean. She didn't care about the wine spilled on the blanket or the sand getting everywhere when he moved his hands to her hair. Her senses were consumed by love for this man.

Only the loud cheering from their friends by the fire broke through the magic of the moment, but she couldn't be mad. She loved and was loved in return, and wasn't that a marvelous thing?

CHAPTER 10

2 years ago

Dom had always loved Halloween. Getting the kids all dressed up, taking them around for candy, claiming a handful of their stash for taxes once they got home... Jo would always wear something witchy that made him hustle the kids to bed. He missed those days.

Seeing Enzo with Natalie and Daisy brought those memories racing back. His children were starting to build families of their own, and he was excited to get to experience all of the childhood fun through the lens of grandpa. He could see where things were going between Enzo and Natalie, and it wouldn't be long before Sofia and Adrian's bump became a baby. Soon the house would be full of children's voices again, and Dom couldn't wait.

So many pieces of his plan were falling into place. Now, if he could just figure out the thing with Jo and with the business, he could retire a happy man.

His living room was full of neighbors and family members who had banded together this evening to find one missing little fairy who was now safely tucked into a bed upstairs. The search party turned impromptu Halloween party was well underway when Dom finally found Enzo and offered him a beer.

"Good work in there." Dom tipped his own bottle to click against his son's.

"We Valentis do good work, right Dad?"

"Nailed it in one."

"Speaking of work, Dad, there's something I wanted to talk to you about."

"You've finally come to your senses and want to help run the business so I can retire." Dom said it flippantly, but immediately Enzo tensed up.

"Uh, no, Dad." Enzo sighed deeply and Dom could tell he wasn't going to like what Enzo had to say. "Actually, I want to talk to you about a plan. I need you to buy out my branch of the business."

"What kind of idiot plan is this?" Dom roared as the conversations around them fell silent. His reaction might've been over-the-top, but he'd already lost one son to a foolish decision. He was not about to lose another one.

"It's not idiotic. I've been thinking about it for a while, and the time is right." Enzo yelled right back, which startled Dom. Enzo was more the "walk away and fume" type. Dom couldn't remember the last time Enzo had stayed and fought.

Everything was changing, and Dom couldn't keep up. "The time is not right. Why the hell do you need me to buy you out now?"

"Because starting up my own landscape design and maintenance firm is going to cost money."

This was the first he'd heard of Enzo wanting to start his own business. What the hell was wrong with working for Valenti Brothers? Didn't he know Dom was depending on him to stay and help? He'd already lost years trying to function after Gabe left. Dom could feel his entire plan for the business, the shows, and his retirement slipping through his fingers.

He doubled down hard. "Money you don't have. So stay here and work for Valenti Brothers." He injected as much finality as he could into his words, but Enzo wasn't buying it. Dom panicked and racked his brain for counterarguments while Enzo pressed his case.

"I need to build my own, Dad. I need more than backyard gazebos and lawn care."

"This is a big ask, and we've got a lot going on right now. The show, the new project...I don't have the capital right now to indulge your whim."

Enzo's face flushed, and he snapped back. "Bullshit. You just don't want to slow down on your 'project.' You don't want to step back from the show. You, you, you. This is all about what you want to do. You are choosing those plans over my dreams."

"And why shouldn't I value concrete plans over speculative dreams? It's my business. I built it with my blood, sweat, and tears. Nobody handed me anything."

Who was this boy he'd raised to tell him he was being selfish? Didn't he appreciate the sacrifices Dom had made his entire life? Hell, the sacrifices he was still making for Enzo's welfare? He'd jeopardized his entire future with Jo because he'd been worried about the kids and the business.

Enzo's head snapped back as if he'd been slapped. "So the last decade of my blood, sweat, and tears, poured into growing this side branch of the business, doesn't count for shit? How much revenue did I bring in last year, that you are now pouring into this money pit in south county?"

"We are a family business. Everyone contributes—" Dom fumed when Enzo cut him off.

"But you are the only one who gets to make decisions and plans. I see. Someone just taught me the folly in that. You might want to rethink your strategy. Although this makes it even easier to walk away."

Enzo turned to do just that, and ran into Natalie coming down the stairs.

"Hey, how's she doing?"

"She's fine, still sleeping. Are you okay?" Natalie brushed a hand down Enzo's arm.

"I'll be fine. I had just hoped that my dad would support my dreams and respect what I've brought to Valenti Brothers. It's clear he doesn't, so I'm done."

"Now wait just a damn second!" Dom protested, but Enzo didn't turn. His son ignored him in favor of Natalie, enraging him even further.

"Why are you trying to sell out?" she asked quietly.

"Because someone I know is dead set on going back to LA. I've been dreaming of going out on my own for years, but now I've got a reason to put my solid plan into action. Relocating might even make it easier to pull off."

Dom was not done with this discussion even though Enzo had turned his back on it. This had gone from harebrained scheme to terrifyingly viable option in seconds. He had to pull out the big guns. "Why are you moving to LA? You'll break your mother's heart."

"More like your pocketbook," Enzo shot back without turning away from Natalie.

"I can't give you the cash right now. Just stay here and we'll work something out. Then next year we can talk about this."

Dom laid it out rationally and prayed that his son would see the reason behind it, but Enzo never looked away from Natalie.

"I can't do that, Dad. I'm needed in LA now. Like you said, you started from scratch and so can I. I've only got eight months to get myself established. I can't wait on a maybe. If my company doesn't do well right away, that's okay. I know how to work hard.

You," Enzo said directly to Natalie, making sure he had her full attention. "This dream we are building is more important to me than anything or anyone. Love won't wait."

Enzo pulled a crying Natalie in for a kiss, while Dom watched his carefully laid plans crumble around him. His son was leaving. His plan to retire and leave them solvent relied on the steady income from Enzo's landscaping and maintenance. It covered payroll between big jobs getting approved. Not to mention the fact that he simply didn't want his son to move away. It would break his heart not to see him every day, and he'd had enough heartbreak for a lifetime.

"Enzo, you don't have to…" Natalie spoke as she wrapped her arms around Enzo to return his hug.

"No, we are in this together. I'm not letting you run away. Wherever you and our kids need to be is where I need to be. What's it going to take for you to believe me?"

A chorus of gasps rose at the announcement. Jo quietly hustled everyone into the kitchen. Dom assumed she just meant to herd the neighbors away from family business. When she came back and shoved his shoulder, he stumbled from his spot propping up the wall. Taking advantage of his loss of balance, she aimed him at the kitchen doorway as well.

"Me?" he whispered. "We're not done discussing this."

"That was not a discussion. That was you bullying our son to get your way. And yes, you're done with that now," Jo hissed back.

"But—"

Jo clamped her hand over his mouth. "Look at them."

Dom looked again, the lens of temper clicking off, and he saw his son wrapped up in the woman he loved.

"Do you remember that, Dom? Do you remember when you looked at me that way? Did you want your parents watching? Now let's go. Get in the kitchen."

Dom let her push him toward the door and reluctantly followed. What did she mean, did he remember when he looked at her like that? He looked at her like that every morning. Didn't he? When had she stopped looking back to see?

Once in the kitchen, he leaned back against the counter and crossed his arms. As the impromptu party erupted into excited chatter around him, he stayed quiet. Jo stood near the door, shamelessly eavesdropping.

Did she really think he didn't love her anymore?

And that dig from Enzo about not respecting his work! Of course he respected what Enzo did. Would he like Enzo to move more into the building side of things? Sure, but that was just for the stability of the business model, and all right, a little selfish pride. What father didn't want his son to follow in his footsteps? Did Enzo really believe he didn't respect his contributions? Or worse, that he was trying to turn him into Gabe?

He simply didn't understand why Enzo needed to go out on his own to have success. Dom couldn't afford to buy him out, not with so much tied up in existing projects, and he didn't want to take over running that part of the business himself. Maybe Rico...

Dom was still ruminating on the ways he'd screwed up when Jo burst through the door to the hallway, pulling Enzo and Natalie into a big hug. He followed her to the doorway.

"Mind? You're already part of this family! Get in here and give me a hug! Oh, another baby! It's just so exciting! I hope you got all of that straightened out, because I stayed in that kitchen as long as I could. I want credit for my restraint."

"Noted." Enzo grinned at his mother.

"Can I have hugs too?" Daisy's voice piped up from the top of the stairs where she had snuck silently and clearly listened in.

And Natalie was pregnant? He was going to have another

ROUGHED IN

grandchild, but this one was going to grow up in LA? That was too far away! Family should grow up together!

Damn it! He had to fix this.

"Looks like we have more than one eavesdropper in the family," Natalie teased as Enzo held out his arms toward her little girl.

Daisy threw herself into the hug, and Natalie surrounded them both, pulling them both tight. Daisy tugged away and hugged Jo, pulling at Dom's heartstrings.

"Rule number one in big families: privacy does not exist." Enzo chuckled.

"Speaking of which, there are a lot of people in the kitchen who were very worried about you, little girl. Let's go tell them the good news." Jo drew them all into the kitchen where friends and neighbors had gathered around the table.

A cheer went up when Daisy came through the door. Sofia and Adrian had been on their way over to see Daisy's costume when they'd gotten the call about the excitement. Frankie had a standing Halloween date to mooch chocolate from the trick-or-treat bowl. A few neighbors who'd helped search had stayed for wine and beer once they'd found out Daisy was safe.

"Also, since I will soon be an official grandma, I will *henceforth* be known as JoNana to all of my grandchildren."

"Including me?" asked Daisy shyly.

JoNana pulled her into a side hug and grinned. "You most of all! You gave it to me. You've got the important job of teaching all these babies how to say it, seeing as you're the only one who can speak!"

Dom stood off to one side, watching his family officially welcome Daisy and Natalie with an ease he envied. He wanted to be happy for them, but he couldn't get past the pile of rubble created when his dreams had come crashing down. LA? Who wanted to live in LA? But he'd have to come to terms with it, because the thought of losing another son permanently was intolerable.

~

9 YEARS *ago*

"Make sure you get it square."

"I got it, Dad. Jeez, you'd think I'd never framed anything before. I know how to do this." Gabe balanced a level on top of the deck framing and raised his beam a quarter of an inch before sinking the screws that should hold it steady.

Dom lifted his hands and leaned back. "Old habits die hard. I've been teaching you for so many years, it's hard to stop."

"Well you could at least make an effort," Gabe quipped as he lined up the corner of the frame with the T-square. "No one would ever believe you trust me enough to hand over the company."

"I don't yet."

"I don't think you ever will, but that's okay. I've got time." Gabe sank two more screws and grinned.

Dom thought over the plans Jo kept talking about for travel and hobbies. "Not as much time as you think. Your ma is getting antsy."

"Well, I might need a few years before I'm ready to take over."

"Wait, what? What are you talking about?" Dom wasn't ready either, but hearing Gabe wasn't was news to him.

Gabe laid down the electric screwdriver and sat on the finished crossbeams, legs dangling into the space below. "There hasn't been a good time to bring it up, but now is as good as any. Seth and I enlisted."

"Enlisted what? A crew of able-bodied men to join the business?"

"We're the able-bodied. Joining the army."

"What the hell are you talking about?" Dom took off his safety glasses, as if that might help him see this situation more clearly.

"Dad, just listen. Seth talked about joining up, and I thought it was a good idea."

"Well it wasn't, but don't worry. I'll go down there tomorrow and get you unenlisted."

Gabe shook his head and grabbed his water bottle. He took a healthy swallow before tossing it back on the ground. "No, Dad, you won't. I'm going."

"This is stupid."

"No, it isn't. It's a rational plan. Let me explain."

Dom snatched up the electric screwdriver to anchor the frame to the supports sitting on concrete footers they'd laid out yesterday. The loud, repetitive whirring drowned out the words he couldn't bear to hear.

Gabe unplugged the drill. "Dad, listen. Please."

Dom crossed his arms and waited, formulating his argument to convince his son to back out of this idiocy. Every bone in his body was vibrating with the conviction that this was idiocy, pure and simple. Anytime you had to convince someone you were being rational, you likely weren't.

"College was expensive, and you're paying for three more besides. If I go work for the army for a few years, they can pay my room and board and salary. I'll save a bunch of money, pay off my college debt and have the GI Bill money to pay for business school."

"I saved enough. Between the rental income and the loans, you got through all right."

"Can you say you'll still have enough by the time Frankie goes through college if you're still on the hook for my loans and Fi's and Enzo's?"

"I've busted my ass for nearly thirty years. I kept you fed and clothed and safe, and it's still not enough. Your mother and I will make it work, and cover the gaps with loans. And what's this about business school?"

"Dad, I don't think we should go further into debt if we don't have to. We've talked about me taking over the business, but I don't know anything about managing people or running the financial side of things."

"That's your mother's job. She handles all of that."

Gabe just stared at him for a minute before rolling his eyes. "And you don't think Ma is going to want to retire along with you? You and Zio Tony have done just fine, but I want to do more than just run the business. I want to grow it. I don't want to always have to be the guy with sawdust in his hair, if I can also be the guy who wears a suit and tie. And if I have to wear a bit of camouflage to make that happen, I will."

Dom hated that he could see the logic behind his son's choice. He doubled down on his anger and ignored the persistent twinge of panic. "If it ain't broke, don't fix it. And if it is broke, Valentis fix it together. The company has run just fine this way for years. You don't have to go off to war to pay for grad school. We can find another way."

Gabe put his hand on Dom's shoulder. "I'm not asking you, Dad. I'm telling you what I've decided. I'm going in for three years, see a bit of the world outside California, and then I'll come back and take over the business."

"You've been outside California." Dom was grasping at straws to keep the conversation going until he could figure out the magic words to convince his eldest child to stay.

"We drove to the Grand Canyon when I was fifteen. That hardly counts."

Had it really been so long since they'd taken a road trip? Dom knew they hadn't taken a ton of vacations, but surely Gabe had forgotten some. Or else he'd inherited his mother's wanderlust spirit. She was always talking about the places she'd like to visit. In fact, a family road trip might be just the thing to distract Gabe from this nonsense.

"If you want to travel, we can travel. I'll pack up the car—"

"Dad, stop. It would still be too expensive and not get me where I want to be regarding school. Besides, I want to serve my country. You always said we should be proud to be Americans and to vote and take care of our community. Think of this as an extension of that civic pride."

"Who told you to listen so closely when I spout off on the Fourth of July?" Gabe chuckled but Dom couldn't find the breath to laugh. "I'm worried, son. This is a dangerous decision. The army doesn't just march around and do push-ups. They engage in active war zones. You could get hurt or worse. Also, you expect me to believe that you're going to listen to your commanding officer when you'll barely listen to me?"

"Dad. I'm a grown man. I can take care of myself, and yes, I know how to listen to a boss. I don't listen to you because you're my dad." Gabe said it teasingly, but Dom couldn't help feeling like it was more truth than tease.

He grappled with the thought that he wouldn't be able to change his son's mind. His plans for the future were falling through his fingers, and the tighter he gripped, the faster they slipped. Oh God, and what would Jo say about all this?

"Have you told your mother yet?" Dom didn't think Gabe had, because he'd have heard about it for sure. Jo was going to flip.

"About that…I was kind of hoping you could tell her?"

"How can you claim to be army strong and then be too chickenshit to talk to your own mother? Absolutely not. You tell her and break her heart."

"Hey, it was worth a shot. I will tell her. I just wanted you to know first. Will you at least back me up?"

"I make no promises. I'm still hoping she can talk some sense into you."

"Trust me, Dad. Everything is going to be fine. This is the plan that makes the most sense. You'll see. Didn't you ever long for adventure?"

Dom thought about that. No, he hadn't, because he'd had Jo. This life they'd built together had been all-consuming. "No. I had everything I needed right here."

"I will too by the time I come back, so I can build my life here knowing I did everything I needed to for our success."

It wasn't often that Dom lost an argument, but his charm had little effect on his son, and he couldn't use brute strength to change his mind, unless he tied him to a chair and forbade it. Though the image appealed, he knew it wouldn't work. Unfortunately, his eldest son was a lot like him, impulsive and stubborn as hell when he was convinced he was right.

Dom knew enough to know that if he continued to push, Gabe would just walk away and shut him out.

"I don't have what I need here. I'm not even sure I know what I'm looking for, but I need to go see for myself. I love you, Dad. I need to do this."

"Yeah, I'm getting that message loud and clear. I love you too. Just…just come back home safe and sound. I'll keep the business going until you're ready. Now, let's finish this deck for your mother."

As they fell into the easy repetitive flow of *measure twice, cut once, lay the spacer and screw*, Dom racked his brain for the argument to sway Gabe. But by the time they'd laid all the planks, Dom was still lost.

2 years ago

Enzo came over and leaned against the counter next to him, arms crossed over his chest, Dom's mirror image, albeit dressed as a life-sized woodland fairy.

"I can't buy you out. I don't have the cash," Dom said glumly. "But if you're bent on moving to LA, I'll see what I can do over the next few months."

"Nah, Dad. Nat wants to stay. She seems to like this crazy, rowdy bunch we call family."

"Oh thank God!" Dom's shoulders dropped and he released a sigh of pure relief.

"I'm still leaving Valenti Brothers. But it doesn't have to be right away," Enzo said.

"This is really what you want to do?" Dom asked. When Enzo nodded firmly, Dom looked his son square in the eye. "Then we'll make it work."

He'd lost Gabe, and when he'd left, there had been a wedge between them. For better or worse, all of his children had inherited his bullheadedness. Enzo was going to go his own way. And Dom refused to damage his relationship with another child.

"You mean it, Dad?"

"Yeah, I mean it." He wrapped his arms around his grown son and pulled him in for a tight hug, remembering a time when he would have lifted him and swung him around, filling the embrace with laughter and love. With a gruff laugh to clear the tears from his throat, he let Enzo step back. "Go hug your mother. You scared her with all that talk of LA."

While Enzo joined Jo around the table, Natalie came to stand beside him, and he dropped a heavy arm around her shoulder.

"Thank you," Dom muttered gruffly.

"What for?"

He looked at Enzo and cleared his throat. "For staying." He turned his gaze on his wife. "For giving her a reason to be happy." He swiped a hand across one eye. "For teaching this old fart a thing or two."

She leaned into the hug. "You big softy."

"Welcome to the family." He kissed her on the top of her head and stepped outside to compose himself.

CHAPTER 11

9 years ago

"What do you mean, you and Seth joined the army?" Jo's voice rose over the din at the Friday night supper table. Everyone else at the table quieted down, clearly stunned as well.

"Just what I said, Ma. We're going to serve our country for a few years, make the world a safer place, and then they'll pay for grad school. I've got it all planned out."

"No. No! Absolutely not. Dom, you'll get this straightened out Monday morning."

Dom's shoulders dropped, and he refused to look her in the eye. "Jo, he's an adult now. I can't stop him if this is what he wants."

Jo's jaw dropped as she stared at her husband. Was he serious?

"Mom, it's already done."

She swung her gaze back to her eldest son—the boy who'd made her a mother, who she'd worked so hard to birth and raise, now trying to go off to war—and then back to her husband who looked more defeated than she'd ever seen him. Her eyes filled to the brim. "Dom..."

"He's made up his mind, Jo."

Jo swallowed hard. Her imagination was busy spinning every possible worst-case scenario. How? How could Dom say they had to let him go? This made no sense. While her brain tried to make it make sense, her heart was breaking.

Her other children began to pepper Gabe with questions that filled in some of the blanks. He spoke of business school and grand dreams, paying off debts, and adventure. But to her mind none of it balanced the scale against the possibility of losing life or limb.

Shaken, Jo remained uncharacteristically quiet for the rest of the evening, even when she and Dom turned in for the night. She didn't understand how Gabe could have come to the conclusion that this was the right decision for his future or how Dom could be on board with it. Everything inside her told her to fight, to argue, to convince these two bullheaded men that they were wrong. And yet she bit her tongue. She knew it would be useless to argue once they'd made up their minds, and she couldn't bear to send her son off to war with angry words between them.

∽

2 YEARS ago

JO FOLLOWED Dom outside and sat beside him on the stairs of the deck he and Gabe had built for her years ago. He stared out into the darkened yard, his face full of regret.

"So, another baby..." Jo dropped her conversational gambit into the darkness between them.

Dom didn't reply. He just gripped his hands between his

spread knees and sighed. She let the silence deepen, giving him space to say what he was struggling to put into words.

"I really fucked it up this time, didn't I?"

Jo didn't say anything. She'd said all the things that needed saying months ago.

He pressed on. "You know, my whole life all I ever wanted was to make things good for you and the kids. Provide a good life, keep you all safe and happy, give you what you needed. And I failed."

Dropping his head into his hands, he pushed on.

"I couldn't protect Gabe. Sofia and Enzo aren't happy working with me. I haven't given you the life I promised."

Jo still didn't say anything, afraid that harsh words would slip past her filter and break the tenuous thread holding them together. But she put her hand on his shoulder and let him feel the weight of her support at his back. When he finally turned to look at her, tears in his eyes, she didn't look away. She held his gaze as tears filled her own.

"I'm not giving up," he whispered hoarsely.

"I'm not either," she whispered back.

"I was afraid you already had."

His shoulders relaxed under her hand. She wasn't ready to forgive and forget, but she could hold space in her heart for hope. Maybe this would be the wake-up call he needed.

"This isn't how it ends, but we can't go on like this." Jo dropped her hands to her lap, mirroring his stance.

"I know."

"So where do we go from here?"

"Let's figure that out, together."

∽

42 years ago

* * *

Jo sat at the hand-me-down dining room table they'd claimed from her parents garage, reading travel books and dreaming of the future. No sooner had the ink dried on the marriage license than Dom had gone back to work, taking as many hours as he could get on construction sites. It was summer in California, and business was booming. He was picking up overtime nearly every day. They hadn't had enough money to take a honeymoon and afford the security deposit on their apartment. The apartment had won out, and the trip was on hold until they could save up.

She had a classroom placement for the fall, but until then she was content to spend her days unpacking and setting up their new home, and her nights having as much sex with her husband as he could manage before he fell into exhausted slumber.

He was working his tail off, trying to get enough savings in the bank so that they could afford to take a trip somewhere fun before the summer ended. She was distracting herself from boredom and organizational labor with trip planning. She'd narrowed down her list to Italy or France, mainly so she could eat good food, drink good wine, and feel sophisticated when she got home and told everyone about their adventures. She'd dreamed of travel for so long, and now it was nearly within reach.

Her list of places she wanted to visit was as long as her arm, but she knew she wouldn't get to all of them on this trip. But if she had enough options, at least she'd get to see a few of them. The planning part of her brain was buzzing, and she needed more resources.

The library! That was what she could do—run over to the library and see if they had any more European travel books she'd missed.

She loaded her pens and journal and maps into her purse,

grabbed the keys to her ancient Impala, and despite the obscene gas prices, headed out.

When her car began to sputter halfway to the library, Jo sighed. Maybe she should have paid more attention to the gas lines. But when she glanced down, the tank was still half full.

"No...no, baby. Come on." She turned the keys in the ignition and the engine just clicked but didn't turn over. *Damn it! No!*

Yes, her car was almost ten years old, but she took good care of it. She hardly even missed her oil changes by more than a few months, and hadn't she just replaced the wipers? This car needed to last and get her back and forth to her school in September!

She slammed her fist against the steering wheel, accidentally knocking the horn and scaring the shit out of herself. She slipped the car into neutral and climbed out to push it out of traffic. She walked the rest of the way to the library so she could call Dom. Maybe the library had books on car repair.

They really couldn't afford this right now.

~

TEARFULLY, Jo put her journal up on the shelf in their bedroom. There was no point in planning anything more for this summer. Their little nest egg had barely covered the repairs needed to keep her car running. So much for a quick honeymoon.

The reality of one person working a school schedule and one person working a construction schedule was rapidly sinking in. One of them would always be off during the other person's busiest season.

She was still sitting on the bed, tears on her cheeks, when Dom walked in, filthy from a hard day building.

"Hey baby, you okay?" Dom hovered, wanting to comfort her but not wanting to get her or the bed dirty.

"Just sad about the trip. Who knew repairs would be so expensive?"

"About that..."

Jo glanced up sharply at that. "Oh God, what now?" Panic laced her voice and she gripped her hands together, bracing for bad news.

"I've got a surprise for you. I'm going to hop in the shower. Put on that sexy dress you bought for our trip." And without another word, he began stripping off sweaty clothes on his way to the bathroom.

What on earth had he done? Jo's curiosity piqued, she changed, did her makeup, and didn't call him on the trail of dirty laundry he left on the floor. As she slipped into her espadrille sandals, Dom emerged from the steamy bathroom in a towel. She lost track of the straps when he moved said towel from his waist to his hair.

God, her husband was a handsome man. Beads of water gathered on his firm chest, and her fingers itched to brush them away. Taut muscles rippled in his arms as he vigorously dried his hair. And lower, her favorite part of him twitched as he caught her peeking. She reached for the tie on her wrap dress, intending to convince him to delay whatever plan he had in mind.

"No, don't look at me like that, Josephine." He pulled on briefs and an undershirt. "We have reservations." He pulled his blue suit out of the closet. She'd never seen him wear it outside of a friend's wedding.

"Fine, but I reserve my right to convince you later. Wouldn't want to wrinkle your suit. Where are we going?"

Dom just shook his head. "You do understand what surprise means, yes? Come on, we'll be late."

They climbed in her traitorous car and he drove her into the city. San Francisco glowed in the evening mist, romantic and cool. Jo shivered in her warm-weather dress, unprepared for the change in temperature at the coast. Dom snuggled her close as they made their way up the block to Original Joe's.

"Right this way, *bella signora*."

"Hmm, *grazie*."

He led her to a romantic booth in the back where a dozen roses waited and her favorite red wine was already opened and breathing on the table.

"You paid a corkage fee for a four-dollar bottle of wine?"

Dom shrugged. "It's your favorite."

He poured her a glass and then filled his own.

"A toast. To my beautiful bride. I may not be able to take you to Italy for our honeymoon, but I will always do my best to give you what you need to be happy. Tonight, I am hoping that a nice dinner at an Italian restaurant with your favorite wine and dancing later will soothe the sting. Tomorrow, I thought we could go to the Legion of Honor to see some statues and art."

Tears threatened Jo's fresh mascara. She felt like a watering pot these days. So many changes had tumbled together one after another, from finishing college, to starting her new job, to getting married, to moving into their first place together, to planning a honeymoon and then losing that chance. She could barely catch her breath. But two things stood out from the chaos with blinding clarity. One, she had definitely chosen the right partner to stand by her side through these challenges. And two, he was getting laid tonight.

She smiled at him over the table and clinked her glass to his. "To my handsome husband, for making every day magical. I love you too."

CHAPTER 12

$\iff$

2 years ago

JO'S HEAD WAS SPINNING. A real nightmare before Christmas was playing out in her living room and it was all her fault.

She'd had this crazy idea to have a big family Christmas, since it was the first they'd have with serious significant others for two of her children. She'd stressed for weeks over what to make and who to invite and a special surprise for Natalie. And it had all blown up in her face.

"Oh Enzo, what have we done?" She tucked her head against her son's chest.

Enzo just shook his head and chuckled. They'd screwed up Christmas good and proper.

"I feel like I pushed too hard for this," Jo continued. "I had this picture in my head of how things would be. But I was *so wrong*! Poor Graciela has barely said two words all evening because she had to be sedated to come here. Midnight Mass might push her over the edge. And that woman, Portia, she's a piece of work! Who brings her daughter's ex along for Christmas, and then proceeds to hit on every man in the room under forty?"

"I must have missed that last bit." Enzo laughed.

"I may have promised Seth extra tiramisu for tolerating her." Jo met Enzo's eyes, earnest regret swamping her. "Enzo, did I ruin Christmas?"

She had just wanted that feeling of a joyous Christmas back. It had been years since she'd been able to feel like Christmas wasn't missing something vital. Not since Gabe died. She'd thought with all the budding love stories and a child in the family again, this would be the year. Once again, she'd expected everyone to just fall in line with her plans and had forgotten to account for the fact that people had free will and messy emotions. God, she couldn't even wrangle her own emotions. She swiped at her eyes and cursed, forgetting she'd put on makeup.

"No, Ma. You can't ruin Christmas. It's still the day God sent his love to the world. All we can do is try our best to do the same. This try just backfired a little."

Jo pulled Enzo in for a mom hug, grateful he still allowed her to do so. His calm embrace soothed her ruffled edges, and she found a bit of her equilibrium.

"Those Sunday school lessons really sank in, huh? You're a good man, Enzo. Okay, let's go fix this. I'm going to thank Graciela for coming and ask if she wants to go home. I think Rey can probably drive her. As for Portia—"

"Leave Portia to me and Nat. I'm learning that when we don't work together, shit hits the fan."

Wasn't that the truth? She and Dom had forgotten that key lesson and look where they'd ended up. After his meltdown at Halloween, she and Dom had been taking tentative steps back toward each other, but it was hard to move past the months of resentment and her husband's continued adherence to his plan. He felt the responsibility to the show so strongly she worried he wouldn't be able to deviate. For the first time in months though, she had hope. "An important lesson to learn. Do you know what I've learned tonight? I am pretty damn grateful for our family."

"Me too, Ma. Can I ask two favors?"

"Anything."

He leaned in and whispered in her ear, and Jo grinned at her baby boy, delighted that some things never changed. Enzo wanted a plate of pizzelles Christmas morning, and winter followed autumn.

"Of course. It'll be ready and waiting first thing. And the second?"

"Will you kill me if I miss Mass?"

"Go fix things with Natalie. I'll consider that penance."

They'd had their ups and downs, but the way her children and the people they loved had handled the crisis she'd inadvertently created gave her great hope for the future.

"I love you, Ma."

"Love you too, baby. Merry Christmas."

∼

27 YEARS ago

THE TREE THREATENED to fall over under the weight of handmade ornaments. A tradition begun in scarcity had become overwhelming thanks to enthusiastic preschool teachers with a fondness for glitter and popsicle sticks. But the kids loved it. Gabe and Sofia chased each other around the living room with their candy cane reindeer ornaments, pretending to pull Santa's sleigh. Enzo was content to play with a wooden spoon and a pot at Jo's feet in the kitchen, while she juggled Christmas Eve dinner and making the pizzelles. Despite the cacophony around her, she managed. At least she knew where he was.

Thankfully, Francesca was still asleep up in the nursery.

It was their first Christmas in their forever home. She and Dom had finished the basic renovations needed to make it livable by September. Little by little they were tackling the rest as there was time and money available. And there hadn't been enough of either lately, so Jo was cooking in the ugliest kitchen known to man, made only slightly more bearable by a coat of primer to cut the army green walls. Someday she'd have the kitchen of her dreams. Until then, she'd make do.

She'd upgraded from the early years and purchased an electric griddle for her husband's favorite cookie, which made the process easier and faster. She'd also had over ten years of practice at this point and was a pro at making them.

As a parent of four little ones, she'd learned to juggle the details and still make the magic happen.

The first piping hot cookies came out of the press, and she transferred them to the baking tray to cool and get a dusting of powdered sugar snow. Stir the cioppino fish stew, add another round of cookies to the press, make the rice, throw fish sticks in the oven for the kids, remove the next cookies, shift cooled ones to a plate on the table, repeat.

Jo was a machine, churning out holiday magic, until a crash from the living room had her sprinting from her post.

As she swung through the antique wooden door she and Dom had refinished together, the sight of the toppled tree and two crying children greeted her.

"It wasn't my fault!" Gabe protested immediately upon seeing her face.

Fi just continued wailing, and Jo bundled them both into her arms.

"Are you hurt? Are you okay?" After assuring herself that the kids were fine, she asked, "What on earth happened?"

"We was playing reindeers," Fi murmured through her tears.

"Okay, you were playing reindeer, and…" Jo turned to Gabe, hoping for more details.

"Fi was chasing me, and the cord grabbed my leg and I fell."

Jo carefully kept her face neutral as her son tried to blame this accident on everything but himself. "Gabriel, I'm not mad, but try that explanation again. I…"

Eyes on the carpet, hands clutched together in front of his little belly, Gabe hauled in a deep breath and began again. "We were playing, and I tripped on the cord, and it pulled the tree down, and I'm sorry, Mama."

"That's better. Well, there's only one thing to do."

Gabe nodded, but the tears began to fall. "I guess we gotta tell Santa not to bring any presents, cause I was a bad boy."

"No, that's not the one thing." Jo pulled him in closer. "You did the right thing by owning up to what you did and apologizing. The only thing left to do is clean up this mess!"

Jo stood and righted the tree, tightening the base and moving it closer to the wall.

"No more running behind the tree, okay?"

Fi nodded and wiped the snot from her face with the back of her hand.

Jo grabbed a tissue and wiped her down again. "Can I put you two in charge of redecorating?"

Her babies nodded vigorously. As she headed back to the kitchen, she heard Fi directing Gabe.

"No, dat one goes here, at da top!"

With a smile, Jo pushed through the door and froze.

The kitchen was quiet. Too quiet. And the floor was empty. Jo raced to the stove. Nothing burning. She ran to the pantry, one of

Enzo's other favorite spots. Empty. It wasn't until she heard his little baby giggle that she turned around and looked higher.

There he was, sitting on the kitchen table, covered head to toe in powdered sugar, happily munching on the pizzelles. Apparently, chairs made excellent ladders. She hadn't realized he was strong enough to climb. Parenting had just leveled up on her, again.

Lifting him from his feast set off wails until she put a half-eaten cookie back in his hand. He'd put quite a dent in the pile she'd made. Time to double that recipe again.

That was how Dom found her: smelling of fresh pine sap, covered in glitter, and holding a sugar-sweet baby on her hip as she made the green beans.

"Hmmm, looks like someone got into my cookies."

"That would be this little Houdini over here." Jo grinned and handed him Enzo, before turning back to the stove.

"Looks like he got a little on your face." Dom set their son on the ground and took Jo's face in his hands, gently brushing his fingertips over her cheekbones. "So sweet," he murmured as he raised a hand over their heads, holding up a fake green sprig of holiday fun.

Dom took her lips and took her under. The soup boiled over. The cookies burned. And Jo kissed Dom under the mistletoe. When Jo finally came up for air, Dom put his arm around her shoulder and pressed a kiss to her forehead.

"Merry Christmas, babe."

Enzo clapped and giggled. From his perch on the table. Double-fisting the pizzelles.

CHAPTER 13

2 years ago

Dom stared at the nativity scene he'd started for Jo's first Christmas with him and added to over the years. Each piece he'd lovingly carved, and as each child joined their family, he'd added a special piece just for them. It had been a long time since he'd made a new figure for it, and he was glad to have the work again. His kids used to always fight over who got to put baby Jesus in the cradle at midnight. This year, there would be no arguments, despite the figure being added this morning. It was Daisy's turn. Christmas morning had arrived, and Jesus needed to rest.

He called the sleepy little girl to the table. "Daisy, come here. I have a very important job for you."

As he explained the tradition, Daisy's face took on a solemn glow as she recognized the importance of the job she'd been given. He pointed out who everyone was in the scene. She took special delight in the little shepherd boy he'd carved once upon a time for Enzo.

"Go find your mom, Daisy. I've got an early present for you two to open."

The little girl ran off, and Dom couldn't help but think that Enzo would have his hands full, envying him that a little bit. His son was going to make him a grandfather soon enough, and then Dom would have children's laughter back in this house. It couldn't be soon enough, to his thinking. But he really needed to fix things with Jo if they were going to enjoy grandparenting together.

He ducked into the den to get his current pieces and ran into Seth, dozing on the couch, with Brandy fast asleep in the recliner.

"Don't tell me it's morning already!" Seth protested. "I'm exhausted. That woman wore me out."

Dom chuckled that Brandy might take offense at that, but he knew what Seth meant. Natalie's mother was a real piece of work. Inviting her extended family had been a mistake, but it had been one made from a place of hope and love. Most of his recent mistakes had come from decisions born of fear. It was a pattern he needed to break.

"Seth, I've been meaning to ask… Do you think… Maybe, next time… "

While he struggled to find the right way to approach his nephew about the sensitive subject on his mind, the younger man rose to stand next to him. In the end, putting hope ahead of fear unfroze his tongue.

"When you came back, after Gabe died, you talked to someone, right?"

"I did. I got referred through the VA."

"Do you think they'd be able to talk to me?"

"I know they have veteran family sessions. I'll ask if that extends to parents. If they can't, I can find someone who can." Seth clapped his hand on Dom's shoulder and pulled him in for a hug. "I'm glad you're ready. I'm happy to help in any way I can."

"Thanks, Seth. You let me know."

Daisy peeked her head around the doorframe and Dom hid the small figurines behind his back.

"Now I've got an early present to deliver. Excuse me." Rubbing the heel of his hand over his eye, his precious cargo tucked in the other, he waded back into the chaos of the living room.

"Look, Mommy! I got to put baby Jesus in his crib. Now they are a real family."

Dom stepped up next to his granddaughter-to-be and opened his hands. "Here, Daisy-girl. Add these to the scene."

He handed her a delicately carved little girl holding a flower and a figure of a mother cradling her pregnant belly.

"Did you carve these, Dom?" Natalie asked.

"It's just a hobby. Everyone has a special piece in the nativity." Dom looked away from the wonder in her eyes, his cheeks blazing, intent on the reaction from Daisy.

"So these are for me and Mommy?" Daisy asked quietly.

"They sure are. You're part of the family now," Dom replied just as quietly, but with a certainty that reverberated.

Daisy hugged Dom around the waist, and his tears ran over. He reached for Natalie, pulling them both into a hug that was probably too tight. He couldn't be happier that his family was expanding to include these two angels. Swiping his eyes, he released them and coughed.

"Will you make ones for the twins next year?" Daisy asked.

"You bet. Now let's get this show on the road. Jo!" he bellowed toward the kitchen. "Are you ready?"

"Almost!" came her hollered reply.

Moments later, Enzo appeared, bearing a tray of confections.

"What are those?" Natalie asked.

"The first pizzelles of Christmas." Enzo glared a warning at Frankie and Fi, whose ears had perked up at the mention of the treat. "Don't even think about it, you two." He turned back to Natalie. "Someone once told me that I looked at you like the first pizzelle of Christmas, hot off the griddle. That's when I knew this was serious. So it seems only fitting that you get the first this year."

Natalie grinned and took exaggerated care in picking one and biting in. "Mmm. That's delicious."

"Come here and give me a taste."

Dom took the tray and set it down on the coffee table while Enzo kissed his woman, so the horde could comfortably descend. He claimed his spot on the couch and sat back to watch the fray.

Jo came in with a tray of sliced panettone and coffee cakes, and set it down on a side table before sitting down next to him on the couch. Dom looked at her in surprise. It was the first time she'd willingly sat so close to him in a very long time. Her nearness felt like a gift in and of itself. He'd missed this physical nearness to her with an ache he'd dared not look at too closely.

But when Jo dropped a hand on his knee, he put his arm around her shoulder and pressed a kiss to her temple before wiping his eyes again, gratitude flowing through his body, bringing deadened nerve endings tingling back to life.

Christmas miracles were unfolding everywhere he looked, and the sweet scent of hope was in the air.

~

42 YEARS ago

JO SAT on the floor of their apartment surrounded by tiny wrapped packages and homemade Christmas cards. It was the last day of school before break and also Christmas Eve, and the world felt magical. She sipped the celebratory glass of prosecco she'd poured herself in honor of making it through her first semester of teaching. Her students had sent her off with lovely little gifts as well, which made the space under the tree feel festive and bright.

As for proper presents, she and Dom had agreed to homemade gifts this year. The August Impala episode had been the tip of the iceberg of disasters. A sprained ankle had slowed Dom down at work for a bit, and they'd gotten behind on their credit cards. Jo had also had to buy a bunch of supplies for her classroom and that had eaten up what little savings they'd managed to scrape together. Back at zero, they were being responsible this Christmas and paying down debts instead of buying big gifts.

But Jo was determined to make their first Christmas together memorable. She'd pulled out the aluminum foil and was folding origami stars to decorate the Charlie Brown tree she'd salvaged from the Christmas tree lot that was closing down for the season. They didn't have any real ornaments, so Jo was going old-school. The big bowl of popcorn was waiting to get threaded into garland. Jo was also eating said popcorn with her prosecco, so it might be a short garland, but it would be festive, damn it.

"What are you up to?" Dom asked, surprising her. She wondered how much wine she'd had if she missed hearing her husband come in behind her.

"Decorating the tree!" She handed him the biggest foil star she'd crafted. "Here, you're the tallest so you get to put the star on top."

"The tree is only three feet tall, Jo."

"And I am currently two feet tall, and I have no intention of standing up. Go ahead, big guy."

Dom set down the plastic bag he'd carried in next to her knee and gingerly took the star. With exaggerated care, he crimped the foil around the very tip and stood back, arms spread wide in triumph.

Jo clapped and laughed outrageously. "Bravo! My hero!"

Dom took a mock bow and snagged a handful of popcorn on the follow-through.

"Hey! That's for the garland."

"Sure it is. That's why the bowl is two-thirds empty and the string has ten kernels on it." He crunched his booty loudly.

Jo turned her attention to the bag. "What's this?"

"Just a little something I picked up."

"I thought we agreed that we wouldn't buy any presents this year."

'It's not a present. I went by my mom's house on the way home and asked for a string of the bubble lights. It's not Christmas without them. She added a few ornaments too."

Jo started to tear up as she opened the bag and picked through the assorted decorations.

"Babe, I'll take them back. Forget I said anything." Dom reached to take the bag back out of her grasp, but she clutched it to her chest.

"Don't you dare! That was so sweet of her! I'll have to say thank you at dinner tomorrow night. I should ask my mom for some when we see my parents in the morning. Something old, something new, something borrowed, something blue," she said pointing to the blue bubble light. "Looks like we've hit the highlights. Let's get these on the tree and heating up. If you can take over trimming, I'll go start dinner. And no peeking!"

"That's a deal. I'm starving."

Jo retreated to the kitchen with her wineglass, groaning as the feeling came back into her legs. Luckily, she'd started cooking earlier in the afternoon and the kitchen was redolent with tomato and garlic and wine. It was her first cioppino, and if it tasted as good as it smelled, she'd make the fish stew every Christmas Eve.

Dinner was basically done except for the rice, so while it

steamed she began on her gift for Dom. Pizzelles. She'd gotten the inside scoop from Tony that Dom loved the wafer-thin cookies coated in powdered sugar. So she'd scrounged up a pizzelle press from her aunt and had figured out how to make the dough. One small ball of dough at a time, she pressed the cookies flat and cooked them over the range. Say the Hail Mary, flip, repeat, remove and cool. This was going to take all night! But it would be worth it to give her husband one of his favorite things.

The first one stuck and split in half when she opened the press. The second one burned. The third one came out raw. The fourth one oozed over the edges and set off the fire alarm.

Jo lost her battle with tears as she waved a dish towel frantically trying to get the damn thing to stop beeping. The prosecco buzz was starting to hit her too, and it always made her weepy. Of course that was why she was crying, not the impending doom of failing at Christmas.

"Everything all right in there?" Dom asked, inching the door open.

"If you value our marriage, do not open that door. Everything"—*sniff*—"is fine!"

The door swung closed.

"Okay." His reply was muffled by the door. "Let me know if you need any help."

"Come on, Jo. You can do this." The timer buzzed for the rice and she took it off the heat to set. "Just get one damn cookie right."

She scraped off the press, coated it with oil, and pressed a smallish ball of dough between the iron plates. She set it over the medium flame and began to pray.

"Hail Mary, full of grace, please bear with me. Blessed art thou amongst cooks, and blessed is the food from your kitchen, cookies. Holy Mary, baker of sweets, pray for this sinner now and at the time to flip the pizzelle. Amen."

She flipped the cast iron plates and sang a verse of Silent Night instead.

With a whispered plea of "Come on, baby!" Jo eased apart the two sides of the mold, and inside lay the perfect golden brown pizzelle. Using her fingertips, she ignored the heat and gently transferred the cookie to the cooling rack where she doused it with powdered sugar. While it cooled, she scooped two bowls of rice and stew and poured more wine. Gently, she folded her one successful cookie into a Christmas napkin and put it on a plate between them.

"Come and eat, babe."

"Just a second." He tucked some tinfoil into a brown paper bag and came to the table. "Merry Christmas, Jo."

"Merry Christmas to you, Dom." She nudged the plate toward him. "Go ahead, open it."

"No, you first." He handed her the brown bag.

Jo reached in and pulled out the foil. "Nice wrapping paper," she teased.

"Just as nice as yours," he teased back, lifting the corner of the red poinsettia napkin.

In slow motion, Jo watched her perfect cookie fall from its protective cover, hit the table at just the wrong angle, and break.

Her gasp was so sharp it felt like she'd swallowed knives.

"Oh shit! I didn't know that it would fall out!" Dom collected the pieces of his cookie onto his plate, his face ashen. "It's okay, I'll just go get another one."

"There isn't another one!" Jo wailed. "I only managed to get one perfectly cooked."

"It's still perfect, babe. Please don't cry." Dom wiped the tears from her cheeks. "Look, it's even better now, because I get to share it with you."

Dom handed her half of the broken cookie and held up his own.

"*Salute.*"

Jo took it and tapped it to his, releasing a shower of sugar all over the table. Laughing, she replied, "*Buon Natale*," and took a bite. The crisp anise and vanilla cookie fairly dissolved on her tongue, and Dom groaned in appreciation.

"Jo, this is delicious."

"Maybe if you're a very good boy I'll make you another one next Christmas," she teased.

"I'll always remember my first. It's delicious, Jo. Thank you. Now open yours."

Jo reached into the brown bag again and her fingers closed around four small wooden figures. Pulling them out, she immediately recognized Mary, Joseph, Baby Jesus and the manger.

"Dom, these are wonderful. Did you make them?"

"Yep, I carved them on my lunch breaks. They could use some stain or paint, but I just finished Jesus this morning."

"No." Jo brushed her fingers reverently over the whittled figurines. "They are perfect, just as they are. I love them, Dom. I'm going to put them next to the tree."

"I was thinking I could maybe do more next year, to fill out the scene."

"Another new tradition. I love that idea." She stood and leaned over him to give him a kiss, which turned into kisses, which turned into fun under the Christmas tree and a very belated Christmas dinner just in time to head out to Midnight Mass.

CHAPTER 14

1 YEAR ago

DOM SAT behind his massive desk, feeling like someone had set a steel I-beam on his shoulders and told him to carry it a mile. He raked his hands through his hair and pondered the last time he'd showered. He was just so damn tired. Christmas had renewed his hope, but the New Year had rung in more struggles.

Keeping up with his commitments to the show, getting the vineyard ready, and picking up the slack for his crew who were all ready to pop out babies, he hadn't had a chance to show Jo that he was serious about retiring. He'd hoped to be able to prove to her that he'd heard her needs and was working on them. It was all just taking longer than he expected, and overruns always pissed him off.

The other thing that was sitting heavy on his soul was the therapy appointments he'd begun in January. He hadn't been making good decisions, and had started seeing a guy Seth had recommended. He was easy to shoot the shit with, but when they dug deep about Gabe's death and Jo's abandonment, it was real work. The emotional hangover was brutal.

He just wanted to be done already. Done with fighting Jo, done with the vineyard, done with work, just done. But he couldn't walk away from any project half finished, especially not one as important as his marriage. That wasn't how Valenti Brothers operated. So here he sat, waiting for Jake to show up.

Jake strolled in from the hallway with a chipper "Good morning, Dom! Ready to sign some papers?"

"Is this going to work?" Dom knew he should sound more excited, but this morning he was full of doubt. He needed a bit of the younger man's enthusiasm to carry him through.

"Of course it is. The network is very excited." Jake leaned back in the chair and crossed his leg, ankle to knee, the very picture of a confident male.

"I don't give a shit about the network. Is this going to fix things with Jo?"

Jake grimaced. "How do you see this fixing things with Jo?"

Dom cradled his head in his hands, elbows propped on his desk, and sighed with frustration. Overwhelmed, he let the truth flow. "I want my wife back. I want her to talk to me, like we used to. I want her to want me again. I wish I fucking knew what to do."

"What does this have to do with the vineyard, Dom?"

"Jo kept talking about wanting to go to Italy and eating the food and drinking the wine. Well, what do we need to fly to Italy for? We've got all that right here. Giving her a little slice of Italy here at home seemed like a good compromise." Dom ran his fingers through his hair again and pointed his finger at Jake. "And the property was a steal. It's a solid investment. Jo is going to be great at running a winery. Hell, look how she kept this business going for years." Dom outlined it all with his hands, painting a picture with his gestures to make it clear to Jake that his plan was a good one.

Dom could hear the skepticism in Jake's voice as he asked his next question. "What has Jo said about the project?"

"She doesn't know," Dom said simply.

He needed it to be a surprise. He wanted to give her a grand gesture that would both solve all their problems and soften her heart toward him again. He knew he'd botched the delivery on the whole television show adventure, so he had to do something equally as grand to make up for it.

Except in the back of his mind he was worried this was an impulsive mistake too. The last time he'd surprised Jo with something big, he'd broken her trust. Would this heal it or tear it even further? His doubts plagued him, and he desperately needed some reassurance, even if it came from the reality show director who only cared about his shows.

"Don't you think you should tell her about it before you invest all this time and money?"

"It's a surprise, to celebrate our retirement."

Jake sighed and looked at the contracts in his hand, but before Dom could press him, Frankie popped her head in the doorway.

Her smile narrowed to a frown when she spotted Jake. "Hey, what's going on in here? You okay, Dad?"

"I'm fine, baby girl." Dom waved his youngest in for a hug. "Just talking through some business with Jake here."

Frankie pulled back slightly from her father's hug to skewer Jake with a glare. "What kind of business?" She perched on the arm of his desk chair and crossed her arms, settling in for a fight. Sometimes he wished she wasn't quite so exactly like him.

"We're signing contracts for the Valenti Vineyards project," Dom said.

"Dad, we talked about this—"

Dom slapped a flat hand against his desk, cutting her off. "You and Sofia are treating me like a child. I am still head of this company, and I don't need anyone holding my hand through a simple contract signing!" He slumped back into his chair, exhausted by the extra effort arguing cost him. He was literally running on empty.

"So you've read through the contracts? Sent them off to our lawyer Cousin Giulia for a read-through?"

Dom just stared blankly at his desk.

"Dad, do you know what you're signing?" Frankie's sharp tone snapped Dom's head back into the game.

"I'm sure it's the same as the contracts for Million-Dollar Starter Home," Dom argued.

Frankie muttered under her breath, "Yeah, and those contracts weren't a problem at all." She turned to Jake. "I'm staying."

Dom groaned. He recognized the set of her chin. He saw it in the mirror most mornings. The meeting just got at least an hour longer.

"Okay. Do you want to walk through the agreements?" Jake asked.

"No," Dom said.

"Yes," Frankie said at the same time.

Dom tried to head off the battle he could see coming, but Frankie had the bit between her teeth now. There'd be no turning her.

Frankie laid a hand on Dom's shoulder. "Humor me. I haven't heard it yet."

Dom knew a losing battle when he saw one and gave in, and Jake set the contract in front of them.

"Basically, you all agree to participate in this six-part miniseries featuring the renovation of Valenti Vineyards. The network will assume..."

Dom's attention began to wander to what the vineyard would look like when it was finished. He could picture Jo sitting out on the patio, a glass of her favorite red wine, this time made from their own vines. He'd sit beside her in their Adirondack chairs made from old wine barrels and look out over the acres at sunset. It was a good dream. This had to work. It just had to. He was out of options.

"No, we won't."

Frankie's sharp reply pulled him back into the conversation.

"Elaborate," Jake said.

"Similar format, fine, but we will not stick to the current roles."

Frankie turned to him to plead her case.

"I've got ideas about how the property should be developed. I know what Ma would want, and I'm not giving up control to some suits." Whirling back to Jake to drive home her point, Frankie drilled her index finger into the desk. "Saving my parents' marriage is more important than a silly show."

"No one said you wouldn't be involved. You'll still do your thing."

"My thing?" Frankie spat. "What exactly is my thing? The comic relief?"

Jake shrugged, and Dom cringed. One did not simply shrug at a Valenti woman. The man had a lot to learn.

Frankie moved to sit on Dom's desk, turning her back on Jake. "Dad, listen. I want this project. Sofia can help me with the details around what I've already laid out. But with all the babies coming, no one else is going to have time for this. Plus, what better way to prove that I can handle taking my place in the business than by running this project by myself?"

Dom smiled at the thought of grandchildren, and his mind started to wander to all the ways he'd spoil them rotten. Having little ones running wild around the property once again was just what they needed. He couldn't wait. "Imagine, me getting to be a grandpa to three babies all at once. The only thing that would make it better would be a trifecta." Dom lowered his chin and sent a heavy glance Frankie's way. He loved to tease her.

"Dad, please. I'm not even dating anyone. Besides, right now I want this company with Adrian. Let me prove I can do it. Go play with babies and fix things with Ma. Let me be the head contractor on this job. Please, Dad?"

Anyone would think Frankie was wrapping him around her finger, but he knew exactly what he was doing. He trusted his daughter, but she was still largely untested. He knew the only way to prove herself was experience, but there was so much riding on this build that he had to be careful.

"This is a big job," Jake interjected, trying to get them back on track. "I'm not sure this is the time—"

"I know exactly how big it is. I've got schematics and timelines already figured out," Frankie tossed back. She turned back to her father and stared him down. "If not now, when? I'm twenty-six, I got the degree you said I should have, and I've been working with you on job sites since I could walk. Don't you trust me, Dad?"

Dom mulled it over. She made excellent points, but she was still his little girl in so many ways. Giving up control was not something he did easily, and ceding it to his youngest daughter stuck in his throat. He was sure Jo would give him shit for that, but he'd spent too many years planning to give the company to Gabe and Seth to pivot easily.

But like him, Frankie never backed down from a challenge, and she pulled out her final stop in her argument, the one she knew he couldn't refute.

"Dad, listen. I'm going to run this company because I promised Gabe I'd look after it while he was gone." She paused to swallow hard. "No one expected him to be gone forever, but a Valenti keeps her promises. You taught me that. I'm not going to let him down. Consider this a dry run. If I can handle running our largest renovation to date, not only will you have proof you can trust me, but you and Ma can have that dream retirement she's been planning."

Jake cut off her monologue. "What if you fail?"

Frankie looked at him blankly, as if the possibility hadn't even occurred to her. "Excuse me?"

Dom still hadn't spoken, but his attention bounced between them as quickly as their words. He wanted to see how she handled herself. If she was going to run things, she had to be able to stand up for herself during confrontations.

"Hey, let's invest half a million dollars in a project run by a twenty-six-year-old woman with no track record. It'll be fine. Is that what you want me to sell my executives?" Sarcasm dripped from the younger man's voice.

Dom didn't appreciate it. Neither, it seemed, did Frankie.

"I don't give a flying fuck what your executives—"

Jake stood and cut her off, slapping a hand on Dom's desk, getting in her face. "Yes, you do. If you didn't care about the show being a success, you wouldn't be in here fighting to lead it."

"Of course I want it to succeed. Why would I want anything with the Valenti name on it to flop? I just don't care that your network doesn't think I can handle it. Or is it really that *you* don't think I can handle it?"

Jake dodged the jab and leaned in even farther. "Where is the money coming from? Their approval is the only way this show gets green-lit and funded. If you want the money and exposure from this, you need to get them on board, baby. Cold selling the class clown as the project leader is going to be damn near impossible. Give me something to work with."

"And whose idea was it to make me the clown in the first place?"

"You wanted a bigger role—"

Dom cleared his throat, breaking through their bickering. While they'd been arguing, he'd been figuring out the angles. She was right. He had to give her a chance sometime, and it was now or never. But she also needed to feel the weight of ownership. He also had to juggle the needs and responsibilities of the rest of the crew. And, despite her protests, they needed the network backing to make any of it work.

"Frankie, you will be head contractor on the show. All designs will go through Sofia and will be done before the baby comes. Adrian will help with the local builds off camera so he can be flexible for Fi. Our architects will approve any structural changes. You will run the build crews. Enzo's crews will handle the outdoor design as we've already agreed on a timeline that works around the twins. Jake, you will tell the network that she has my full support and oversight. And if we fail to hit production deadlines, we will pay back twenty percent of their seed money."

"Dad! That's a hundred grand!" Frankie blanched, but he stood firm.

"I know, and you'll be the one covering it. You want to run the business for real, you've got to have skin in the game."

"I can sell that." Jake was quick to agree, which meant Dom had found the right path through the negotiation.

See? He hadn't needed a babysitter after all. Sometimes going with his gut *was* the right decision.

"I'll do it." Frankie shook hands with Jake to seal the deal.

"It's a deal." He left to adjust the contracts to reflect what they'd agreed on, leaving Frankie and Dom alone in the office.

"Dad, I promise you won't regret this."

"I hope *you* won't regret it. This is a big step, baby."

"Dad, how could I regret chasing the dream I've had for so long? I would regret *not* stepping up more than trying and failing." Frankie edged toward the door. So confident. So sure she wouldn't fail.

He couldn't deny that she knew how to work hard, but as the baby of the family, things had always come easier for her, it seemed to him. He needed her to see the realities here. "I want you to remember that if you end up working for free for a few years to pay down the debt."

That stopped her in her tracks. Turning back to him with her hands on her hips, she stared. "Wow. Thanks for the vote of confidence, Dad. You really think I'm going to fail?"

Dom pushed back in his chair and met her annoyed glare steadily, calm now that he'd settled everything to his liking. "I didn't say that. But I've been in this business long enough to know that sometimes things don't go according to plan. You've never held all of the cards before. I think it's going to be more challenging than you expect."

"And I know I am up to the challenge. In fact, I'm going to clear a few things with Sofia so we can hit the ground running."

Frankie turned once more to leave, but Dom stopped her again, this time with a gentle hand on her wrist, his voice low and thick with concern. He had to make her understand. "Francesca, you know I love you. It's hard not to want to protect you from the ugliness of the world, especially now."

"Playing it safe doesn't get you anywhere good. Did you and Zio Tony play it safe when you built this place? Or did you make sacrifices along the way to grow and thrive?"

He thought back over the years of sacrifices, the years he'd gone without so the kids could have what they needed, the marriage he'd nearly lost, the compromises along the way, and sighed. "I did those things so you wouldn't have to." He turned his hand into hers and squeezed three times.

"But what if I want to, Dad? After all, I learned from the best." She squeezed back four times, kissed his forehead and left.

One more project, one more risk and sacrifice to take, and then things would be better. He just hoped Jo could hold out until it was done. He prayed what was left of their marriage was strong enough to last until he could fix it.

CHAPTER 15

1 YEAR ago

JO LOOKED AROUND THE PARTY, glittering with Edison bulbs and laughter, in celebration of a season well done. Million-Dollar Starter Home had wrapped. Everyone from the cast and crew was there, decked out to the nines.

She had hoped this would be a celebration of the end of this madness, but Dom had signed on for another six-month stretch of a new series. She'd had time to come to terms with it, and she couldn't deny that the show had brought many blessings with it. She'd made her peace, with the show if not with her husband. Seeing Jake standing by himself, she decided to deliver the apology she'd come prepared to make.

She sidled up behind him and spoke. "You know, it's okay to join in the fun."

She surprised his beer into going down the wrong tube. He coughed and wiped his face, tears in his eyes.

"Sorry! I didn't mean to startle you." She tried, and failed, to hide her laughter.

He waved away her apology and laughed along with her. "Enjoying the party?" he asked once he could speak.

"We never get into the city. It's nice to have an excuse."

Her eyes sought out and fixed on her husband. She tried not to be resentful that the show was the thing that had brought her into the city on a pretty spring night. She tried not to feel bitter that this was exactly how she'd pictured their retirement date nights, minus the thirty other people milling around, and she'd yet to be able to enjoy one with her husband. She tried not to feel angry that she and Dom were still not back to where they had been five years ago, despite celebrating the end of the second season of the show he'd claimed would solve everything. She failed on all counts.

She had no idea what of that cocktail of emotions showed on her face, but it had Jake staring at her. No matter how complicated her feelings were surrounding her husband, she'd been unfair to take them out on this man and his professional obligations. "It's good to have something to celebrate."

"I'm glad you came." Jake sipped his beer with exaggerated care, giving Jo the moment and the laugh she needed to collect her thoughts.

"Jake, I want to apologize." Jo fiddled with the rings on her left hand, while she stared at his shoes and tried to find the right words.

"Jo, there's no need—"

"No, let me get this out. I'm sorry I haven't made more of an effort with the shows. You might have noticed my husband can be impulsive. When he signed on for these, I was ready for us to retire. These shows seemed like a hell of a lot more work."

"They are," Jake said, but Jo held up a finger. She would not be deterred from getting this all out. Like lancing a wound, she had to get it all out at once, so it could heal clean.

"I hated you and this show for taking Dom farther away from me."

"Ouch." Jake rubbed his free hand over his chest. "Tell me how you really feel."

"I'm trying to." Jo chuckled. She hated to admit it, but the show really had done some wonderful things for her family and the business. Part of her could admit that Dom's plan was working, even as the other part of her wanted to cry that it was taking so long. "Over these two seasons, I've seen the changes that have come to our business and to Dom's state of mind. Your project has strengthened them both. He needed something to work on to get him through the worst of his grief, and the business is booming. My kids have found love and are starting families. Your work on this show played a big part in that."

Jake held his tongue, and Jo pushed on.

"I won't say I understand why Dom needs to renovate a vineyard for someone, but Frankie is very excited for her chance to run the build. You've done so much for my family. So, I don't hate you anymore. I still want Dom to retire, but for the rest of it, thank you, and I'm sorry. If you need more from me on the vineyard project, I'll try."

Jake chuckled. "I will keep that in mind, though Frankie has things pretty well in hand. I might ask you for some design help once Sofia is out with the baby."

"Whatever you need." She was surprised to find she meant it. She'd learned valuable lessons from her "break." She'd discovered that she still wanted to be married to Dom and still wanted the family they'd built together, especially now that grandbabies were on the way. She still wanted her retirement dreams, but she'd learned they'd lost their luster without Dom by her side. Christmas had renewed her hope that Dom was taking this seriously, but here it was early spring, and they were launching a new show. She'd learned that she could be mad at Dom and not sabotage the rest of her family. If she could help Fi and Adrian or Enzo and Natalie ease into parenthood, she'd be there.

"Thank you, Jo."

"Tell me more about this vineyard. I know Dom bought it to flip for a client, but I don't have any of the details."

Jake suddenly found everywhere to look but at her. For an actor, he wasn't very good at lying. What on earth was he hiding?

"We are still nailing them down. That's probably why he hasn't told you anything. Actually, you just reminded me. I need to talk to Frankie about something. Have you seen her?"

So he was going to use Frankie as his get-out-of-jail-free card. "She stepped outside for some air."

"Great, thanks. And thanks for what you said too. It means a lot."

"I'm trying to own my mistakes better, and I think I was wrong about you, Jake Ryland."

Jake turned and headed for the door, rubbing a hand over the back of his neck.

Jo watched as he walked outside to find her daughter. She saw him steal a sip from her Ghirardelli cup and steady her when she stumbled on the cobblestones. *Interesting.* The fact that Frankie took his arm willingly and arrived back at the bar laughing was another point in his favor. She recognized the look in his eyes as more than collegial. More than friendly. As they chatted near the bar, Jo followed her hunch. "You found her."

"I did. Hot cocoa run." Jake was distracted, still watching Frankie as she schmoozed some execs.

"Did you get your question answered?"

Jake turned his attention back to Jo and grimaced. "I think so."

"You should come to Friday dinner soon."

Jake stuttered in surprise. "Um, yeah, sure. I'd like that. Can I bring anything?"

"Just your patience and a sense of humor," Jo replied. She hugged him briefly before rejoining the party.

Dinner would be soon enough to test her theory. She didn't want to push too hard, but Jake seemed like just the kind of man Frankie could stand up to but not resist.

∼

27 YEARS ago

DOM HAD WALKED IN, after a six a.m. start on-site and a busy day in the office, to absolute chaos at home. They were still packed into a too-small rental with the kids doubled up so the baby could have a crib in a nursery that she refused to sleep in. Soon they'd be in the new house, but for now everyone was just making do.

Laundry consumed the couch and abandoned toys littered the floor like a minefield. Gabe, Sofia, and Enzo sat on pillows that Dom was pretty sure Jo preferred to keep on the couch, clustered around the TV for afternoon cartoons. A box of Ritz crackers lay torn open on the ground, and each of his children was steadily consuming a separate sleeve. War might break out over that fourth tube, given their blank stares and feral feeding frenzy.

He'd tiptoed back to his bedroom, where he found Jo curled up around a sleeping Francesca, tears running down her cheeks.

"I think she has a cold. She's so stuffy that she couldn't breathe. She's finally asleep, but she fussed all day and wouldn't eat, and I'm so engorged, it's painful. I'm exhausted."

"Don't worry. You rest and pump or sleep or whatever you need to do. I'll handle dinner and bedtime."

Ignoring her skeptical eyebrow, he went back out to the

kitchen to figure out dinner. Pasta. Boiling water. He could handle that.

Pot out, filled with water, on the stove to boil.

Hitting his groove, he pulled a package of spaghetti out of the pantry and looked for a jar of sauce. He moved every can and box in that pantry, before realizing that Jo only ever made sauce from scratch. He pulled out a small can of tomato paste instead and reasoned that he could make his own as well. Starving, he also pulled out a dried salami and some parmesan cheese to snack on. He contemplated getting the fourth sleeve of crackers from out front, but decided he liked having his fingers attached to his hands.

No sooner had he dropped the pasta in the water than he heard the news theme song from the front room. *Damn it!* Cartoons were over. Sure enough, his three little rascals came strolling single file into the kitchen looking for sustenance.

Each of them comically stopped walking when they saw him at the stove.

"Where's Mama?"

"What are you doing?"

"Daddy!" That last was from Enzo who toddled to Dom with his arms outstretched, demanding to be lifted and perched on a hip. Dom was pretty sure he couldn't handle juggling a baby and a pot of boiling water, so he gave Enzo a quick snuggle and then set him back on the floor, where he promptly began to fuss.

"Are you all hungry? Do you want some sausage or cheese?"

"I don't like that sausage, Daddy. Do you have some fruit?" Sofia complained.

"Fruit. Sure, fruit. I'm sure there's some around here." He poked around the fridge and came up with a wrinkled apple and a brown banana.

Sofia wrinkled her nose.

"Never mind."

"Nana!" Enzo cried, reaching for his favorite snack. The cold, soft banana was his teething treat, but Dom had to cut it up. He got out a small bowl and a spoon and began slicing it up.

"I'll take the apple, Dad. Can I have it with some peanut butter?" Gabe asked, reaching for the butter knife like he could cut the apple himself.

Dom took the knife from his hand and sliced the apple himself before scooping peanut butter into a bowl and adding the apple. "Do you want some of this, Fi?"

His little princess shook her head. "I don't like it. I want grapes."

"I bet you want them peeled too," Dom muttered under his breath. "How about some raisins? I think I saw some in the pantry."

"No. I want grapes."

"Raisins are grapes that have a suntan."

Sofia giggled. "No, they aren't, Daddy. You're making that up."

"Don't you know? I heard it through the grapevine…" Dom began to sing and swirled Sofia up into a boogie toward the pantry. She had no idea what he was singing about, but she was always game for a twirl. He got out a little box of raisins and handed it to her. "Give them a try. Go with your brothers and eat at the table."

He handed the banana bowl to Gabe to carry and turned back to his dinner plans. Sauce. How hard could it be? He dumped the small can of tomato paste into a saucepan and added some water. He tried mixing it together but the paste just swirled unhelpfully in the cold water. Maybe he needed to heat it up. He sprinkled in some salt and pepper and set it to simmer. He glanced at the timer only to realize, *fuck*, he hadn't set the timer.

The pasta pot unhelpfully hissed at him and boiled over. Dom slapped off the heat and dumped the pot into a colander. The strained pasta was disintegrating at the ends but was stuck together and still hard in the middle. How had he managed to both under AND over cook the spaghetti?

Still trying to salvage the meal, he carried the dripping pasta back to the stove and poured it into his makeshift sauce, mixing it until it kind of came together. The starch from the melting pasta actually helped the sauce thicken. Proud of his concoction, he used tongs to fill bowls for the kids and carried them to the table, where he thought they'd be sitting.

"Kids?" he asked as he followed the sound of the television into the living room. *Oh shit.*

Gabe just wiped his peanut butter hands on his pants and the couch, Sofia had lost half of her raisins on the floor, and Enzo was smearing his bananas on the coffee table.

"I told you to eat at the table! Look at this mess! Who's going to clean this up?" Dom asked, his voice rising in frustration.

Sofia's lip began to quiver. Enzo leapt past quivering, straight into piercing sobs. *Damn it.*

"I'll help, Dad." Gabe ran to the kitchen for a towel and began smearing the banana even further around on the glass-topped surface.

"It's okay, son. I'll take care of it. Let's all go wash hands. Dinner is ready."

By the time he'd waged war on germs and cleaned up the ensuing bathroom flooding, the noodles had gone cold. Sitting in their booster seats around the table, all three took their first bites with varying degrees of concern. Gabe picked out one noodle to inspect it, as if sizing it up for a fishing hook, before lowering the whole thing into his mouth. Sofia poked at hers with her fork and sniffed it skeptically. Enzo dove right in, shoving a handful of noodles into his mouth, and promptly choking on them before spitting them back out on the table.

"It can't be that bad." Dom cut Enzo's noodles into smaller pieces before handing him back his bowl, which the toddler dumped into his lap. His own hanger threatened to spill over, but Dom bit his tongue. He realized he'd handle cleanup better with a full stomach. Dom's stomach growled, and he twirled the pasta on his fork and took a big bite.

He wanted points for actually chewing and swallowing. Holy hell, what a disaster. The pasta was unfortunately as gross as it had looked, and the sauce was vile. This dish might have made sense with some pickles and vodka added, because it was definitely more Bloody Mary than Bolognese. He looked at his kids' faces as they tried to eat what he'd made for them and cringed.

"Okay, change of plans. You kids hop in the tub and play. I'm going to order pizza."

They cheered and raced for the tub, shedding clothes as they went. Dom made the call and read off his credit card number with only a small wince at the cost.

He'd told Jo he'd handle it, and handle it he did. Forty minutes, five towels, and two cheese pizzas later, all of his children were bathed and fed.

Did it happen in the right order? Who was to say what was right and wrong in the order of childcare operations? Was everyone full and happy? Yes. Did they make it into bed? Absolutely not.

Dom collapsed on the couch and all three of his little munchkins curled up with him. Gabe leaned into his right side, Sofia sat on his left thigh, and Enzo curled up on his chest. Thoroughly worn out, he leaned his head back against the couch, and they all fell fast asleep.

～

THAT WAS how Jo found them, a pile of limbs and tender curls, clinging to their Daddy. She'd left Frankie tucked into their bed in search of a water bottle. She was parched and figured she should hydrate before climbing into the hot shower to try and relieve some of the pain in her breasts. The sight of her people all curled up like puppies in a basket made her smile.

When her awareness zoomed out to take in the state of the room, she groaned. What a mess! Had Dom helped? Yes. That hour-long nap had made her nearly human again. But was the cost too high? Possibly. She'd likely spend a solid hour tomorrow cleaning up the trail of snacks.

Heading into the kitchen, Jo let out a gasp. Dear God, what had he done? A congealed mess of pasta was caked in one of her pans, the floor was an unholy mess, and the greasy pizza boxes sat stacked on top of the range. Nothing had been put away. And how many utensils had the man used?

Her husband was a very handy man, but this was not his forte. She appreciated the attempt, but she also wished he'd looked before he leapt into action.

Never again, she vowed. If Dom offered to help with dinner, she'd have to come up with a way to let him down gently. She snagged a piece of cold pizza and her bottle of water. This help came with too high a price tag.

They did all look peaceful and happy though. Maybe not too high a price...

Careful not to wake them, she tiptoed back to her bathroom and let the warm water in the shower work its magic on her swollen breasts. When she came back to bed, she used the blue bulb again to clear the baby's nose. Finally able to breathe, Frankie turned to her and began to nurse, relieving some of the awful pressure and lulling Jo into a doze.

Cleaning and scrubbing could wait till tomorrow. With everyone around her blessedly quiet, Jo closed her eyes and slept.

1 year ago

Jo was busy prepping Friday dinner when the doorbell rang. That would be Jake. She deliberately let Frankie get the door and was intrigued by her reaction. After watching her youngest stutter through a stilted welcome, Jo stepped in.

"For God's sake, let the man in!" Jo bustled up the hallway. "I swear to God, I raised her with manners. Come on in, Jake. It's good to see you again." Jo leaned up and bussed his cheeks before relieving him of the wine and flowers he'd brought.

"Thank you for having me. I hope it's not too much trouble."

"The more the merrier on a Friday night." Jo smiled and nodded her head toward the kitchen. "Come with me while I put these in water."

Jake followed her back and watched her carefully as she arranged the hydrangeas and tea roses he'd brought in her favorite vase. Satisfied it was balanced, she placed it on the island where she could enjoy it while she cooked.

"Thank you again for inviting me to dinner." Jake reached for the bottle of wine. "Can I open this for you?"

Jo buried her nose in the flowers and inhaled deeply. "Someone's been spilling my secrets."

"Pardon?"

"People only bring my favorite wine when they're trying to butter me up. Who told you and what do you want?"

"No one had to tell me. I remembered the bottle you chose at Christmas and figured it would be one you liked. And I might be angling to get invited back for whatever is making this kitchen smell amazing."

He winked and made Jo laugh and hand over the wine key. "Well, aren't you clever? Are you a useful sort in the kitchen, or should I dismiss you and your wine to go join the crew on the couch?" Jo asked.

"I can boil water, and I grill a mean cheese sandwich, but please don't make me go watch baseball."

"Okay, you can stay and get your first lesson in Italian cooking."

She set him to slicing eggplant and zucchini for sautéing, explaining details as she went and juggling the other dishes currently cooking.

"Try this and tell me what you think." Jo handed him a forkful of linguine in a light, creamy sauce speared to the utensil with a clove of roasted garlic and a sun-dried tomato. He moaned and she took that as a vote of approval.

"I think you are a treasure, Jo Valenti." He captured her hand that reached for his fork and pressed a kiss to her knuckles.

"What's all this?" Dom blustered as he entered the kitchen and traded his empty beer for a full one from the fridge.

"I'm trying to convince your wife to run away with me and cook linguine every day," Jake teased, but Dom didn't laugh. His face fell, and Jo huffed her irritation.

Did he really think she was going to have her head turned by a man half her age? If Alessi, her silver fox, hadn't managed it, Jake sure wouldn't. Besides, Jo had already determined that Dom was it for her.

"Oh Dom, don't be ridiculous. He's helping me put dinner together, which is more than I can say for any of the rest of you."

"You always shoo us out of the kitchen!" Dom protested as he snagged a stuffed pepperoncini from the tray of appetizers in the fridge.

"Because your idea of helping is snacking on the antipasti!"

"I fixed the leaking faucet last week," Dom grumbled.

"And after only two weeks of me nagging. I am truly grateful." She patted Dom's cheek. It had taken him much longer to get to some of their projects over the years. Two weeks was nothing to sneeze at. It felt good to tease her husband again though. She'd missed this easy banter. "Now go round up our children. Dinner's ready."

Jo sat back and enjoyed the conversation as it flowed around her table as easily as the dishes were passed. Having this bit of normalcy settled her. She hadn't missed another Friday dinner since that awful fundraiser had driven home how precious they were. She hadn't given up on her dreams for their retirement, but she realized that maintaining this tradition was also something she wanted.

They had always been the house that her children brought friends to. Now they were showing up with partners, and she was delighted. This was part of her life she definitely wanted to savor. Perhaps at a slightly lower decibel though…

Jo cleared her throat, trying to restore some semblance of manners around the table. "So, Jake, tell me about the new series," Jo prompted. Given the way Frankie and Dom both had their "innocent" faces on, she knew something was up. Maybe Jake would slip up and let her in on it.

"We are redoing a winery for an investor down south near Gilroy."

"Oh, really? How on earth did Dom get involved in that?" She sipped her wine to hide her smirk.

"The, ah, investor, liked the show and approached us about doing a renovation special," Jake hedged.

Dom jumped into the gap. "Remember that wine tasting tour you dragged me to with your group? I figured I could make it look better than that place."

Jo's smile slipped as she turned on her husband. "Don't go poking at my group. You know they are the only way I get out of this house anymore. I was just curious about the new show, since it is clearly interesting enough to make you break your word."

Her temper was rising, and she couldn't be held accountable for what she said if he provoked a fight.

"Now Jo, don't start..."

"Did you or did you not promise me that you would retire once the show was doing well?"

"I did, but..."

"Mom, I'm the one who pushed for the show." Frankie jumped into the fray to keep her father out of the line of fire. Jo had seen this tactic before. "Dad was going to pass, but I wanted a chance to prove to him that I can run the business. If I can pull this off, he's agreed to step back and let me run things day to day with Adrian. Isn't that right, Dad?"

Jo could tell when her youngest was trying to get something past them, and right now she had Dom over the barrel for something. What the hell was going on?

"Um, uh, that's right. I'm not really involved in the new show."

"Then when are you retiring?" Jo pressed, not buying any of it.

"After the kids' weddings. I want to be able to cover for them so they can take honeymoons, but then I'll be done. I'll walk away."

"I'll believe it when I see it," Jo huffed. She turned a steely glare on everyone around the table in turn. "You all heard him. When you get back from your honeymoons, he is done. I'm holding you to it this time." She jabbed a pointed finger at Dom, who hunched his shoulders as if she'd actually made contact.

The rest of dinner flowed smoothly. The laughter and life updates flowed around the table and reminded Jo why she loved this.

As her kids began to clear the table, Jo pulled Jake from the melee with a gentle touch to the arm. "It's a nice night," she said. "Come sit on the porch with me while everyone else cleans up. Bring your wine."

Following her out the back door, Jake sat down next to her on the stairs leading down to the back garden and sipped his Montepulciano.

"You must think I'm crazy." Jo stared down at her hands and fiddled with her wedding ring, her wine forgotten on the stairs. She struggled to find the right words, but she felt Jake deserved an explanation for her behavior.

"Why do you say that?" Jake turned to lean against the newel post so he could look her in the eye.

"Here you've gone and made my family famous. You've made us a household name and business is booming, and all I want is for Dom to walk away from it."

"That's not crazy. That sounds like you've put a lot of energy into this company and into building your family. It's time for some of that to come back to you now."

The olive branch from the young man who had every right to resent her felt like she finally had someone on her side. She really wanted him to understand.

"It's just… Well, after Gabe died, I realized that none of this is promised. We aren't guaranteed a tomorrow, and I want to enjoy whatever days I may have left, with the man I love, instead of watching him work himself into an early grave."

"Dom is a lucky man to have you pushing him. When I left acting, it was against the advice of every adult in my life. But just like you said, life is short, and I'd already missed out on most of my childhood. I couldn't lose the rest of my life as well. Doing it without backup was miserable."

Jo took a long sip of her wine. She knew she was putting him in a difficult position, but she was going to ask for his help anyway. She needed to know someone was looking after Dom since she wasn't on set or in the office.

"This vineyard project… How involved is Dom really?"

"He's very hands-off on the build. Honestly, it's practically an honorary role. He's done some short on-the-fly explanations of what's going on, but Frankie is running the build. He is helping keeping the Million-Dollar Starter Home builds rolling for Adrian, but that's a short-term fix while Adrian is stretched thin."

"Okay. I guess I can be patient a little while longer. He's not as young as he once was, but he refuses to acknowledge it. I trust you to keep him out of the fray."

"You have my word."

CHAPTER 16

35 YEARS ago

JO OPENED her eyes and slid her hand across the cool sheets on the other side of the bed. She rolled and starfish stretched. It was Saturday morning, and Dom had left at five a.m. for his double shift. She missed him when these double shifts cropped up on the weekends, but she had to admire his work ethic. He and his brother had set a goal, and they were chasing it hard. It wouldn't be long before these overtime checks allowed them to get Valenti Brothers off the ground.

She sat up and her head spun. She grinned and waited for it to pass. If her calendar and the little plastic stick she'd hidden in her underwear drawer weren't mistaken, they'd be checking another long-term goal off their list in about seven months. She had an appointment with her gynecologist next week to confirm it.

Rubbing a hand over her still flat belly, she imagined Dom's face when she told him he was going to be a daddy. He was going to freak!

They had taken a few years to just enjoy being married and to get her teaching career established. She didn't want to be juggling kids and work before they were really solid, and with him trying to save money for the business, the time just hadn't been right. But after her cousin Elizabeth's wedding, they'd been a little careless with the condoms and now they were going to start their family sooner than they'd planned.

She was imagining a sweet little face with her eyes and Dom's chin when a sharp cramp pinched low in her belly. Wincing, she gingerly got herself out of bed and into the bathroom, trying to keep her stomach from revolting against her vertical position as it had the past few mornings. That queasiness had prompted her to buy the test at the pharmacy in the first place.

Her heart climbed up into her throat as she sat down heavily on the toilet and found bloody splotches in her underwear. No. *No no no no no no....*

Hanging on to a thread of hope, she called her doctor and a cab.

∼

DOM SCRUBBED a hand through his sweat-soaked dirty hair and tossed his hard hat on the couch as he stepped out of his cement-crusted work boots. He'd busted his ass on the double shift at the construction site, and all he wanted was a shower, dinner, and a beer.

He and his brother Tony had taken on as many extra shifts as they could manage between them. They were so close to their savings goal for opening their own construction firm. In another few years, Valenti Brothers would be a reality.

Lost in his daydreams for the future, he made it all the way into the kitchen of their one-bedroom apartment before it hit him.

No dinner on the stove. No lights on in the living room. No Jojo.

The hairs on the back of his neck stood up. Something was wrong.

"Jo?" He called her name into the quiet apartment. "Babe, are you here?"

There weren't many places she could be. As he searched their home, panic gripped his throat and refused to let him breathe. Were his parents okay? Were hers? Had there been an accident? Where would she have gone in such a hurry and not told him?

He shuffled through the papers on the kitchen table, looking for a note, but all he saw was a pile of utility and doctor bills. Dropping them, he strode back toward their bedroom, still calling for her.

"Josephine! Where are you?"

A quiet whimper drew him into the bathroom.

Jo sat naked from the waist down in the empty tub, with her head resting on her curled-up knees, crying silently. Her jeans were in a pile next to the toilet.

"Jo! What's going on? Are you okay?"

Jo raised her teary eyes and stared at the tile wall. The vacant sadness there terrified him. He reached a hand toward her shoulder and she flinched.

"I lost it," Jo whispered before tears crumpled her face.

Dom's head was spinning. What could she have lost that they couldn't replace? What would cause this level of grief?

"Lost what?" He glanced into the tub and blanched. "Babe, I think we should get you to the hospital."

"I've already been there. I was going to surprise you with the news after my appointment next week, but I started spotting this morning. So I went to the emergency room, and they…. They couldn't find a heartbeat…"

In thirty seconds, Dom found out he'd been a father and was

no longer. His heart broke a little in his chest and his throat clenched around his words. *What? How? When?* The questions could wait.

Stripping off his filthy jeans and sweat-stained T-shirt, he climbed into the tub behind Jo and pulled her back into his arms. He couldn't carry a child for her, but he'd do his best to carry her burdens while she fought through this. She looked so fragile, and the helplessness he felt made him want to punch his fist through some drywall. Fear battled anger for control in his mind. It took all of his strength and focus to sit still and just hold her. If he lost that battle, he'd be scooping her up in his arms and taking her back to that goddamn doctor and demanding he fix it.

Thankfully his rational mind was winning. Just barely. "So what do we do?"

"There's nothing to do. They said it should pass in a few days."

Jo turned and buried her face in his shoulder before letting her sobs escape.

"I'm sorry! I'm so sorry, Dom."

"Babe, no. You didn't do anything wrong. There's nothing to apologize for."

"I lost our baby."

"No." He took her by the shoulders and pushed her away so he could look her square in the eyes. "You did nothing to cause this. It's okay. It's going to be okay. We will be okay."

"What if this is something I can't do? We've always talked about a big family."

"Then we find another way to have that. We can foster or adopt. We will find children who need a loving home and give them that. I love you, Jo. We'll figure it out together. All that matters is that we're in this together. I won't lose you."

The fact that she didn't respond with "I love you, and I'm not going anywhere without you" rattled his composure.

He held her tight in his arms as she poured out her grief. He

ROUGHED IN

kept his own tightly bottled up. He was so fucking scared and overwhelmed, but he tucked it down deep for her. She needed him to be strong. Her rock. Her husband in good times and bad, in sickness and in health. He'd promised in front of God and everyone. He just hadn't expected the test to kick him in the teeth.

But he held her close, helped her get cleaned up and into bed, made sure she drank some water before she finally fell asleep. He did all the things he could think of to take care of her and show her his love.

So it was after midnight by the time he sat in the kitchen with his beer, dinner long forgotten, and let his own tears fall.

∼

31 years ago

FOUR YEARS LATER, tears streamed down his cheeks again, but there was no beer in sight, just a cathartic release of emotions. Jo was asleep in the hospital bed behind him, after battling for hours. In the quiet now, Dom could let down his guard. He wiped his hands down his cheeks, erasing the telltale tracks before she could see. He didn't want her to worry.

Leaning back in the vinyl-covered chair, he tried to get some sleep too. He'd been through the wringer today, watching Jo fight to bring their son into the world.

As if thinking of him had been enough to wake him, Dom heard a thin, fussy cry from the bassinet. Crossing the room, he lifted his son and cuddled him. Would he ever get tired of saying that?

My son.
Gabriel.

Little angel.

He was so small that Dom could hold him entirely in his two hands. Such a tiny thing to cause so much trouble. Through three months of bed rest, week after week of morning sickness that transitioned to vicious, sleep-stealing heartburn, and a stubborn heel that found purchase against Jo's rib, making a full breath hard to find, Dom had felt so helpless. The years of trying and loss had been hard, and followed by a difficult pregnancy; the road to parenthood had been a bumpy one. To be holding his son now broke Dom's heart wide-open along every scarred fracture line. He was bursting with love.

He loved Jo with his whole heart, had for years. How was it possible to feel so much more love in his chest after just one day?

And with it the weight of responsibility settled over his shoulders like a fifty-pound rucksack. He was now completely responsible for another human. If anything happened to him, he knew Jo was a talented and resourceful adult. She could take care of herself if she ever had to. God willing, he wouldn't ever have to test his theory, but he didn't worry about it. This tiny little baby was totally helpless. He would need to be protected and loved and provided for. And Dom vowed that he would not let his son down on that front. He'd do whatever it took to give his son the life he deserved.

He settled in the chair again and tucked Gabe against his chest. The baby settled back down with his head against Dom's heart and his little legs pulled up against him. When Dom readjusted the hospital blanket to cover him, Gabe kicked his right leg out hard, landing a solid knock between Dom's ribs, startling a grunt out of him. An athlete already, Dom mused, before realizing that this was what Jo had been feeling from the inside out for months.

"You owe your mama an apology, little man."

Dom anchored his son against his chest, one hand splayed

from his butt to his back, and felt his heart knit back together in this new size and shape. Gabriel would need his mama soon to nurse, so Dom would soak up this snuggle time while he could.

Closing his eyes, he thanked God for bringing his family through this, healthy and whole. Dom vowed to do his best to protect and provide for them, since God had seen fit to give him these angels to hold in his heart.

CHAPTER 17

1 year ago

Jo held Sofia's hand and coached her through another contraction. As the tension in her daughter's grip began to ease, Adrian burst through the door of the hospital suite, his eyes frantic.

"Sofia?"

"Here, my love. I'm fine. It's fine. We're having a baby," Sofia said as he leaned over the bed to kiss her forehead.

"Thank God you weren't alone."

"Honey, I haven't been alone for nine months. But yes, having Mom with me was a blessing."

"And now that you're here, I'll just step out to the waiting room." Jo kissed the hand she'd been holding. "Call me if you need me. I love you, baby."

"I love you too, Mom. Thanks for everything."

Jo walked out to the waiting room and found Dom sitting by himself. "Hey there, handsome. Is this seat taken?"

Dom looked up and shook his head, and Jo sat down, her shoulder pressing against his. "How's she doing?"

"Our girl is strong. She's doing just fine. Better now that Adrian is there to calm her down."

"So, we're gonna be grandparents, huh?"

"We sure are. You ready for this?"

"I don't know. Are you?"

Jo eyed her husband, trying not to let sarcasm take the lead. "I've been trying to get ready for a while now. You might have noticed."

Damn, lost that battle.

"I've been trying too, in my own way."

"And what way is that? Working yourself into the ground?"

Dom turned to look her straight in the eye. Whatever he was about to say was not the snark she'd anticipated. "No, I've been seeing a therapist to help me get past why I've been working so hard the last few years."

Jo sat in stunned silence. Never in a million years would she have guessed that was what he'd been up to.

"A lot of decisions I've made over the past few years have come from a place of fear and needing to regain control wherever I could. I was so afraid of losing anything else after…"

After losing Gabe. Jo heard what he couldn't say. Dom shrugged and kept talking.

"Anyway, he suggested maybe it'd be good for you to see someone too. And maybe for us to see someone together."

Dom was waiting for her reaction, and she struggled to find the right words.

He leapt into her gap. "Or not, I mean, it was just an idea. If you don't want to, that's—"

She stopped him with a hand on his arm. "I do. I think it's a good idea, Dom. Let's do it. You know, this grandparent gig is just one of the things I'd hoped to share with you in our retirement. If you're working on a way to get there, I'm happy to do that with you."

"I've been working on getting us there for years. Everything I've ever done has been for the good of this family." Frustration leaked from his voice and through his eyes. "And you haven't seemed that happy."

"You might have been working for your family, but you sure didn't work with us. Most importantly, you stopped working with me, Dom. You cut me out."

"I didn't—"

"You did. You started making decisions like no one else's opinion mattered."

"I didn't mean to. I was trying to take the burden because you seemed so close to breaking."

The shift in perspective made Jo dizzy. After not talking for so long, this flood of revelations was overwhelming. "I guess we have a lot to talk about, then. Make the appointment, Dom. I'll show up."

In the aftermath, a quiet settled around them. She leaned her head on his broad shoulder and set down the burden of distance she'd been carrying. Her mind was rioting with his news and the events of the day, and she was grateful she still had his support. She'd missed this all these months. They'd always been physically close, and she'd missed snuggling into his warmth and strength.

"Our baby is having a baby," Jo murmured.

Dom put his hand on Jo's thigh, and she put hers on top of his. He turned it over and gripped hers tightly. It was a tacit acknowledgement that they were in this together. Joy and fear chased each other through her heart, but she wasn't alone. Not anymore.

Jo glanced up as movement at the door caught her attention. Frankie stood there, a huge smile on her face.

"And what are you grinning about, young lady?" Jo returned

the smile and sat up, breaking contact with Dom's shoulder, but not letting go of his hand.

"Just got off the phone with Jake. Plotting a little surprise for the new parents." She crossed to the chairs where they sat.

"That sounds interesting." Jo paused and stared at Frankie, before she turned back to Dom. She gave him the look all parents developed, the one that said *Go along with this* with just a glance. "Do me a favor, honey. Can you go see if the hospital has a coffee shop? I'd love a skinny latte. It's going to be a long night."

"Sure thing, Jojo."

Dom strode from the waiting room, and Jo patted the open seat next to her. She had information to extract from her youngest child who thought she was good at being sneaky. "Come sit with me, Francesca." Frankie cringed at the use of her full name, but obeyed. "Your father does better with waiting when he has a job to do."

"Then why do you want him to retire so badly? He'll be bored out of his mind without something to do."

"Oh, I have plans for what we'll do." Jo wiggled her eyebrows and laughed at Frankie's reaction.

"Ew! Ma, seriously. I don't want to hear about any sexy plans you might have for Dad. Just... Gah! My mind's eye is burning."

Jo chuckled. The period where she'd been numb with grief had bled into the time where they weren't speaking, which added up to way too long apart. She had absolutely missed her sexual relationship with Dom, and had been plotting retirement plans for every room in their empty nest. But her daughter didn't need the details on that. "There are other things I like to do with your father, like traveling."

"Sure, that's what you meant," Frankie teased.

"Speaking of plans, what's this you're cooking up with Jake?"

"I asked him to send the crew over to knock out the last of the list at the new house, so it'll be done by the time they're ready to go home."

"That's very sweet of him to help." Jo wiggled her eyebrows suggestively at Frankie, preparing to tease more information out of her daughter on this "thing" with Jake.

"Ma..."

"I just want to know what's going on in your life."

"There is nothing going on except me busting my ass to make this show a success."

"So much like your father." Jo sighed and ran her hand down Frankie's still-wet hair.

"And that's bad?" Frankie asked.

How could Jo explain that the very traits that made her so strong could be a weakness as well, without breaking down her daughter? "I know you idolize your father, and that you are trying so hard to keep your promise to Gabe. But I am your mother, and I have a few things to say. Brace yourself."

Frankie took a deep breath before turning in her chair to fully face her mother. "Hit me."

Jo smiled softly at her antics before she crossed her hands in her lap. "I married a man who is very headstrong, driven, ambitious. He poured his energy into his family business, and we've had a good life. Losing Gabe...it woke me up. I'd been going along, making everything work, to follow his plans, for years. I didn't realize how little voice I had in our marriage until I spoke up and tried to use it, only to be ignored. Over the last two years, I've seriously considered leaving."

Frankie's jaw dropped. After a beat, she asked, "Why did you stay?"

"Because even when he's driving me insane, he's my person. I love him. And I haven't given up hope that we can find a new normal. It's also terrifying to think of starting over alone after a lifetime together."

"Why are you telling me this?"

"Because I see the way Jake watches you when you're not looking. And I see the way a phone call makes you beam. Be careful, baby. Working with the person you love is complicated and hard. I don't want you to compromise your dreams like I did."

"Ma, you are way ahead of me. No one said anything about love or marriage. Hell, we've only shared one kiss. There's no chance of anything there."

"Just be careful. You are too much like your father to react well to someone trying to run your life."

"Like I'd ever let that happen. You don't have to worry, Ma." Frankie leaned over and pressed a kiss to her mother's cheek.

"Whatever you say, baby."

Oh, to be young and think she knew everything again! Growing old and realizing how little you actually understood was the worst. She knew she had to let Frankie make her own mistakes, and she sincerely hoped that Jake didn't turn out to be one. Hopefully, she could help them avoid some of the pitfalls she'd stumbled right into. She might not have a classroom, but she was still a teacher at heart.

Later, when Jake arrived and Frankie jumped up to greet him, Jo suppressed a smile and gave them a moment before she cleared her throat, breaking the tension she could practically see dancing between them.

Frankie sat down and Jake took the seat next to her.

"Is everything okay on set?" Jo asked while Frankie went oddly silent.

"Yes, everything is rolling right along, and we're hoping to finish up Adrian and Sofia's new place while they're here."

"Oh, isn't that a sweet idea!"

"Frankie thought of it."

"That's my girl."

Frankie still hadn't joined the conversation, and Jo could see she was distracted.

"I'm just going to duck in and see how we're doing. If Dom comes back with my coffee, send him in."

"Sure, Ma."

That was the last she saw of her daughter for eight hours. When she'd arrived in the birthing suite, Sofia had been in transition, her contractions coming one on top of the other. It had taken both Adrian and Jo holding Fi's hands to help her breathe through them. They had waited for full dilation, and after only two hours of active pushing, her grandson had joined them with a loud wail.

Laughter and tears welcomed him into the world, and while Sofia cuddled her son to her bare chest and the nursing staff happily bustled around the room putting things to rights, Adrian came up behind Jo and gave her a hug.

"We did it."

"We sure did. Good work, Daddy."

"Good work, Nana." He squeezed her one more time before perching on the edge of the bed, his eyes full of love for his wife and son.

Jo felt tears welling in her eyes and left the room to give the young family some time alone. She made her way back to the waiting room, caught up in memories of her own birth stories. She did not miss that Frankie was wrapped up in Jake, fast asleep. She'd blinked, and her babies were grown! It still had the power to shock her.

She leaned over and brushed the hair back from Frankie's cheek.

"He's here," she whispered, and then repeated at full volume to rouse her daughter.

"Who's here?" Frankie jerked her head up and looked around the waiting room, trying to get her bearings.

"The baby!"

"It's a boy?"

Jo nodded with tears in her eyes. "Enzo and Natalie are on their way. Mrs. Félice is going to take Daisy to school. You'll all get to go in together to meet him."

Dom walked back into the waiting room and wrapped Jo up in a big hug. She leaned into his embrace and let the tears fall. This family they'd made, this legacy still stood strong. Today was for joy.

"He's so beautiful. So perfect. And he cried so strongly," Dom said, his voice thick with tears.

Graciela, Adrian's mother, tentatively walked through the doors, leaning on her daughter Mahalia.

"Oh, Abuela Cici! He's here! Come and meet him!" Jo wrapped her daughter's mother-in-law in a big hug and hustled her back. Frankie rose to follow them, but her mother stopped her. "No, let us go alone. The rest of you wait for Enzo and Nat."

Watching Graciela fuss over her daughter and grandson warmed Jo's heart. Sofia had found a good partner in Adrian, and she was happy he'd become part of their family. A marriage would be even better, but that was coming. Jo tempered her impatience.

When Frankie and Enzo came in with their partners to meet their nephew, Jo teared up again. Her family circle felt complete for the first time in years. Did she wish Gabe was here? Absolutely, but the ache felt smaller in the face of this joy somehow.

"Does little man here have a name?" Frankie asked.

"He does." Sofia cleared the tears from her throat and addressed the whole room. "His name is Gabriel Luis Valenti Villanueva."

Jo and Graciela burst into tears at hearing their beloveds' names honored with new life.

"You named him for your *papá*?" Graciela reached a hand to her son.

Adrian squeezed it and nodded. "And Sofia's brother. They were both men we'd be proud for our son to take after," he said.

Jo gasped out a sob and proceeded to drench Dom's shirt with happy tears. By the time the nurse showed up to shoo them all out, there wasn't a dry eye in the house.

As she and Dom headed home to get some rest, Jo felt a lightness in her chest that had been missing for years. It took her a while to recognize it as peace.

CHAPTER 18

42 YEARS ago

JO SAT IN HER CLASSROOM, surrounded by piles of books and supplies, about thirty seconds from a meltdown. This was happening. Really happening. In three short days, she'd have thirty children in her classroom, staring expectantly at her, waiting to learn. And it would be her job to teach them.

Back-to-school panic dreams had begun two weeks ago. Despite the veteran teachers on her team assuring her that it was all normal, Jo couldn't quite shake the belief that the one about vomiting in class was more premonition than nightmare.

Today she'd finally been able to get into her classroom to begin putting it all together, and two hours in she was completely overwhelmed. She had a vision for a cozy, carpeted reading nook, desks organized in small groups, and bulletin boards that would rotate themes and content with the month and unit changes. She didn't lack the design or inspiration. The physical energy to do it all was seriously in question though. The thought of getting all this work done in three short days made her want to curl up in a ball and cry.

A quick knock on her doorframe startled a yelp out of her.

"Dom! What are you doing here?"

"I brought you a first day of school present. Can I bring it in?"

"Of course!" Jo scrambled up from the floor, happy for a distraction. "You didn't have to do anything."

"Today's a big day. I wanted it to be special." Dom grunted as he carried in a big wooden box. When he cleared the doorway and turned, she could see it was a bookcase.

He set it down carefully, and she ran a hand over the smooth walnut-stained finish. Mother Goose and fairy tales covered every inch of the elaborate trim. The left panel was hand-carved with Jack climbing a beanstalk up the side of the shelves, the giant's magical kingdom across the top panel, and Jack and Jill tumbling down the far side. The edge of each shelf featured different story elements woven together—roses, harps, keys, knives, waves, and more.

"Dom, it's beautiful! This must have taken you ages!"

"A few weeks. I've been whittling on my lunch breaks."

She pulled him into a hug and pressed a firm kiss to the lips she loved. This man of few words showed up for her in action every time. He already worked so hard for his own dreams. Here he was, making time and space in his day to support hers.

"It's just gorgeous. Thank you, honey. The kids are going to love it."

"If you tell me where you want it, I'll move it for you. It's a little heavy."

"Right over there in the corner, please. Wait, I'll unroll the carpet first."

"I can do that. You keep doing what you were doing."

With the calm efficiency of someone who worked with his hands for a living, Dom sliced open the plastic wrap and unrolled the rug in the corner before placing the beautiful bookcase on top of it, anchoring her reading area.

He turned and surveyed the piles of books she was sorting. "Looks like you've got a lot of heavy lifting to do. I don't have to be back at the job site until two. If you point me in the right direction, I can help."

Jo's heart swelled with love and gratitude. This man of hers… She sighed.

"You can put the science books in that cupboard there. Thank you, love."

∼

31 YEARS ago

JO LOOKED around the classroom that had been hers these last eleven years, and her eyes welled with emotions. Bittersweet joy, fondness, anxiety, gratitude, sorrow, grief, and more battered her from all sides so quickly that she couldn't pull them apart to manage them. Instead, they all hit her at once, and she was helpless to do anything but feel.

She'd put so much of her life into this room and the hundreds of children who'd passed through its door. Now that she was staring down a new phase of her life, the idea of leaving behind everything she'd known, the good and the bad, was overwhelming. True, she wanted to be a stay-at-home parent, but that didn't mean she had any idea how to actually do that. She knew teaching and was damn good at it.

The kids had thrown her a goodbye party that made her cry. And a few of her favorite parents had shown up after school with bottles of wine and advice, which made her openly weep. When her principal had popped in with cupcakes, Jo fully lost her shit.

Thankfully, Principal Pam had seen her through more than one crying jag and took it all in stride. Jo was grateful to have worked for such an amazing leader.

She would miss the community she'd built here, but she also knew that leaving right now was the best thing for her growing family. Still, knowing it was the right decision didn't make it any easier to pull off. She'd emptied her desk of personal items, packed a box with all of the letters, art, and handmade gifts that kids had given her over the years, and put everything else away for the next teacher who would come into this space.

Reflecting on the chaos of her first year, she hoped that the systems she'd organized would make things easier for the woman who would take her place. Another first-year teacher, Pam had said. Jo had left her an encouraging note in her desk drawer.

Boxes of books Jo had bought for the classroom over the years were stacked by the door. She would really miss those Scholastic book fairs. Now her beloved bookcase stood empty. She rubbed a hand over her barely-there belly, and imagined filling up the shelves with board books and stuffed animals instead.

When Dom came to pick her up, she was ready. She helped carry the boxes out to his pickup truck, and teared up again when he came out with the bookcase he'd so lovingly built for her. It was the end of an era, but Jo took joy from the idea that the fairy tales and nursery rhymes would grace her own children's nursery and hold all of their treasured tales.

With a final wave of fond farewell, Josephine Valenti stepped into the next phase of her life with no regrets, only happy memories.

~

1 year ago

. . .

JO PULLED into the driveway at the vineyard, a case of wine in her trunk and a smile on her face.

Frankie was sitting in her truck and hopped down to say hi with a hug. "Hi, Mom! What brings you out here?"

"My senior group went to a garden walk hosted by the local winemakers association down here. I thought I'd stop by on my way back and see how everything is going. Got a minute to show me around?"

"Of course I do. You won't believe what happened this morning..."

Jo followed Frankie into a house that still felt half done. Jo knew enough about construction to know that this was months from done, if the rest of the rooms looked like the ones she'd seen. She tamped down her annoyance at the slow progress. She still had that flicker of hope that Dom was going to stick to his promise this time. She wandered, wrapped up in her own thoughts, until Frankie's words penetrated her haze.

"I found out that Jake has been lying to me. For months!"

"About what?"

"The show and all the things that have been going wrong around here. He's been manipulating all of it to create tension for the show."

"It seems like that is pretty standard for reality shows, isn't it?" Jo pointed out.

Frankie pushed back. "It seems dishonest when you are doing things to trip up the person you're sleeping with, especially when the shit he pulled could have cost me a hundred grand."

"That is a valid point. Men." Jo sighed. "Always putting payment before people. If I had a nickel for every time someone else's kitchen remodel took precedence over my needs, I'd be a wealthy enough woman to pay off the debt he's driving you into."

Jo thought back over all the years of frustrations. She didn't want to bring her daughter into the mess between her and Dom, but she also didn't want her to make the same mistakes.

"Jake put his job first every time. He continually set me up to fail. It's a miracle I didn't veer off budget long before now."

"That's not a miracle. That's your own hard work. You've done wonders with this place on a shoestring. It's going to be beautiful." Jo took a deep breath and stopped to face Frankie. "You know I don't like to interfere in your love life, but I have to say this. Be very careful about falling for a man who will put his job before you. It's painful to always play second fiddle to his ambition."

"I thought I did love him, Ma. I thought what we had mattered. But now it all feels false. If he lied to me about this, what other lies did I fall for? How can I trust anything he says?"

"Broken trust is the hardest thing to repair, even for someone as skilled at fixing things as you. Do you still want him?"

"I don't know, Ma. I want the him that only I get to see when we're alone. I want the him he is away from here."

"Darling, you don't get to have just one part of him. You have to take him as a whole. The good, the bad, the ugly. Is dealing with his ugly worth it for a shot at his very best?"

Jo had learned this lesson too well. She loved so many things about Dom, but she couldn't separate that part of him from the things that drove her crazy.

With the help of her new therapist she was working her way around those things, slowly. All of her flailing for the last few years had only brought her back to the realization that home was where she wanted to be, with Dom by her side. She hadn't given up on the other things she'd wanted to try, but she'd discovered that she didn't want to do them alone. She could also acknowledge that the manic pressure to do all the things and the emotional brittleness she felt in the wake of Gabe's death were not a healthy response.

ROUGHED IN

They walked out of the back door. Jo turned and gasped as she took in the views of the rolling vineyards and the mountains that came right down to the edge of the property. The drought-dry brown grass and shrubs that covered them met with the green of the grapevines and created a beautiful contrast. It would show even better in the spring when everything was lush and green from the snow runoff.

She could see why the owner had built here. It was a lovely property, and if the wine association was anything to judge by, there was a great community of winemakers down here. Whoever had bought this place was in for such a fun adventure.

"This is beautiful, Frankie. I'd like to come back and see it once it's up and running. This land is like a little slice of heaven, and the work you've done is turning it into a masterpiece."

Frankie grinned. "I think that can be arranged."

They walked back around the exterior of the house toward Jo's car, and she scanned the parking lot, hoping to see Dom. Anticipation of seeing her husband was a new and welcome change.

"Ma, how will I know?"

Frankie's question pulled her attention back from her swirling thoughts. "Know what, darling?"

"How will I know if I can trust him again?" Frankie asked quietly.

"You'll have to see how he handles this blowup. Watch what he does and what he says. Try and figure out why he's making the choices he's making, and then decide if you can live with that." The words from her therapist flowed straight from her lips. Somehow it was easier to say them than to think about them, but she could see the truth in them. No one was perfect. If she was being honest with herself, this stop today wasn't a pleasure stroll. She wanted to talk to Dom about his reasons for a few things. She hadn't seen him yet, but he'd said he'd be here today…

"Thanks, Ma. I love you."

"And I love you, baby. I'm going to stroll over to craft services for a coffee before I hit the road, but I don't want to keep you. Will I see you at dinner Friday?"

"I'm planning on it."

"Good."

Jo walked off toward the food and beverage tables. Dom never could resist a free buffet. But instead of her husband, she found the man tying her daughter in knots.

"I think that's the first time I've seen you with coffee in your cup but not drinking it." She watched as he dragged himself forcefully from his thoughts.

"Hi, Jo."

"You really stepped in it this time, huh?" She smirked and grabbed a bottle of water.

"I see you ran into Frankie."

"Yes, I came by to see my daughter and check out how the build was going. She mentioned that you sabotaged things to make the show more interesting."

"Every challenge only makes the show better, which is good for both of us. But she won't even let me explain."

Jo crossed her arms, not willing to let him off the hook so easily. If her baby was questioning, he could stand a little pressure too. "So, she's pissed because you made her life harder on purpose, and you're upset that she won't let you mansplain to her why she's wrong? That's a real hot take."

Jake dropped his head and stared at his coffee again. "That's not what I meant."

"No, but it's what you said. Words matter, Jake, and actions matter more. You should have told her."

"This is just how reality TV works. My God, Jo, she's been on MDash for two seasons. How could she not know?"

"Because she isn't some Hollywood actor who grew up

playing the game. She put her dreams and her heart in your hands, Jake, and your lies betrayed her on both counts."

"I never lied to her. I never told her I wasn't doing it. She didn't ask."

Jo gave him the patented mom-look that had him dropping his head in shame. "Oh, so we're using four-year-old logic now. A lie by omission hurts just as much."

Jake flushed red and rubbed his neck. Jo was glad to see her words were getting through.

"I never meant to hurt her," he protested.

"And yet you purposely made her job harder, knowing what she stood to lose if she failed."

"But she hasn't failed. She's brilliant, smart, and funny, and a damn good leader on the site. This show is only going to showcase her strengths."

"Can you guarantee that? I heard about the multiple versions of the pilot. Can you promise me that only the good one will get used?" Jo propped her hands on her hips, and Jake shrugged his shoulders up toward his ears.

"It was never going to air, Jo. My execs were nervous about trusting so much responsibility and money on an untried woman who had shown them nothing but humor and hijinks on the other show. I had to cut together a backup version with Dom's voiceovers so they would move forward with the show. But I edited that version so closely. No offense to Dom, but it's nowhere near as good as Frankie's solo pilot. She shines onscreen, solving problems and getting things done."

"But at what cost? She has put the rest of her life on hold. She's made sacrifices on the build and called in favors to make it all work. Personally and professionally, she put herself on the line for this. You stole that time and energy from her." Jo felt each of Frankie's sacrifices to her bones. Jake had to realize that there was a cost to his way of doing things.

"She would have worked this hard on the project anyway."

"Exactly. You didn't have to manipulate her to get her effort."

"I didn't manipulate her. I tweaked the situation."

"Don't you try semantics with me, young man. I know bullshit when I smell it. Put yourself in her shoes. Imagine how it feels to know that a person you've worked with has been scheming behind your back the entire time, knowing it could ruin your career and your financial stability. Now imagine how much worse that is coming from someone you're in a relationship with. You should have told her before you slept with her."

Watching him blush and stutter was endearing. When was the last time he'd had his mother call him to task for something? She did like him, and if she could help him be a better man for her baby, she would.

He ran a hand over his mouth, his beard rasping in the sudden silence. "I, uh, I didn't mean to—"

Jo silenced him with a glare. "Don't finish that sentence. I hope you meant to, and I hope you treated her with respect. If you haven't, you need to fix that."

"How do I fix it if she won't talk to me?"

"Well, for starters you could apologize. And I don't mean this rambling defense of inexcusable behavior that you've just trotted out for me. I hope you've gotten that out of your system, so you don't spew that crap at her. The best apology is only three words long, but you have to mean them. I. Am. Sorry." Jo ticked off the words on her fingers. "Next, you need to back those words up with actions. She needs to see that she can trust you again. It won't happen overnight, but I happen to know my daughter is pretty special. She is worth the work and the wait."

Jake nodded and retreated into his thoughts. Jo pulled him from his musings with a firm grip on his shoulder. She stood in front of him now, and he won points for meeting her eyes in spite of his shame. She needed him to understand and not give up hope, so she laid it on the line.

"In spite of all this, I think you could be good for each other. Play it straight, Jake. Apologize for what you did wrong, acknowledge your fault, and tell her how you'll change. That's what you do when you love someone."

He nodded and dropped his head. Jo let him have his moment and scanned the work site for her husband again. This time she was rewarded with Dom striding across the parking lot.

"Ryland! We need to have a talk."

Jo could do Jake one more favor since it served her own purpose. "Dom, don't beat the boy up. He knows what he did is wrong, and he's going to fix it."

Dom pulled up short, confused. "But...but... Did you know about the...?"

"Double pilot? Yep." Jo linked her arm through Dom's elbow and turned him away. "Come walk with me through the vines, Dom. I need to talk to you."

Dom was still blustering, but he allowed her to lead him toward the gravel drive. She called back to Jake as they were about to turn the corner.

"Don't mess this up, Ryland. I like having you around."

CHAPTER 19

32 years ago

"Dom, we need to talk."

Oh shit, what had he done now? That tone of voice from Jo usually meant he was in for a *serious* conversation. "Sure, babe."

"Come sit down at the table."

He cautiously lowered himself into the chair across from her. She slid a plastic tube across the table at him.

"We're pregnant again."

Dom's heart leapt into his throat and blocked his words. He bounded from his seat and was around the table in a flash, pulling her into his arms for a twirling hug and then his lap as he took her chair.

She laughed and swatted at him playfully, but then her serious face came back. "I'm glad you're happy. So am I, but I'm also scared. I've been throwing up again in the mornings, just like last time."

Dom held her closer, as if he could keep all of the bad memories at bay using his hug as a shield. "Have you seen your doctor yet?"

"I go next week, but I'm already exhausted. I don't know how I can keep this up and teach, let alone split my time later."

He rubbed a hand up and down her back. "So don't go back to work."

"What do you mean, don't go back to work? Dom, I have to work. We have bills and babies are expensive."

"So is daycare, according to the guys at work. And with my parents gone, and yours retired down in Florida, that's what we'll have to rely on. I don't see Aunt Dulcie as a viable option."

"No, she'd probably put bourbon in the bottle."

"But how else am I supposed to get the baby to sleep?" Dom said in his best imitation of his aunt.

Jo laughed and pulled them back on track. "So, seriously, how would we make up the loss in income?"

"I'll take on extra shifts, maybe get a second job."

"Dom, you're already exhausted."

"So are you, and you're carrying our kid! My shoulders are strong. Let me carry us for a while. I know I'd rather have the peace of mind knowing our kids are being raised by you than a stranger."

"Oh, it's kids plural now?"

"I like to be optimistic. So let's talk logistics. You want to finish the school year or no?"

"There's only two months left, and I'd hate missing all of the fun stuff after making it through the hard parts. I want to finish this year with my kids."

"Okay, and then you'll give notice, spend the summer resting, and once the baby gets here—"

"If the baby gets here."

"*When* the baby gets here, you'll be a stay-at-home parent for a few years. And then we'll reassess the whole job thing. I can carry us at least that long."

"Are you sure?"

"Is that what you want?"

Jo nodded her head softly.

"Then that's what we'll make happen. We're a team in this, Jo, just like everything else. You are doing the amazing part right now, carrying a baby. I'm just the grunt labor keeping the lights on. Let me do this for you. Let me do this for us, for our family."

He put his hand on her belly, marveling at the idea that she was carrying their child. His wife was a miracle.

She placed her hand over his. "Let's do this, together."

Was he nervous? Of course. He'd be a fool not to be worried about another miscarriage, and Dom Valenti was no fool. Had he maybe bitten off more than he could chew with this financial plan? Likely, but that hadn't stopped him yet. He made the impossible possible every single day. Was he one hundred percent sure that whatever came next they'd face together and get through it even stronger? Absolutely. That's what Valentis did.

∾

1 YEAR *ago*

DOM STOMPED after Jo as she paused at the trunk of her car to grab a bottle of red wine and the emergency blanket, before continuing down the gravel path that wound down into the vineyard. Dom was still fuming over Jake's betrayal and didn't notice how far they'd walked until he realized he couldn't see the house anymore.

Spreading the blanket on the ground, she sat and patted the

ground next to her. He lowered himself slowly, carefully settling his bones next to hers.

"I can't believe what Jake pulled. How dare he?" Dom began.

"Interesting," Jo mused as she held out her hand.

Dom dug for his pocketknife, and popped open the corkscrew. He gestured for her to hand him the bottle and set about opening it. "What's interesting?"

"That you're so mad at Jake for being like you. Is it any wonder Frankie fell for him?"

She took the wine back from him for another swig, while Dom reeled from her words. "What the hell is that supposed to mean?"

"Explain to me how Jake making decisions for his business and not consulting his employees is any different from you unilaterally signing up our family for this show in the first place?"

"That was different."

Jo offered the bottle of wine and he took a pull.

"Not bad, right?" Jo asked, and he nodded his approval. "Now explain."

"Explain what, Jo?"

"Give me the explanation I couldn't listen to a year and a half ago. Tell me why what you did is so different from what Jake has done."

Dom stalled, balking at opening up that particular box of emotions. "Will it make a difference? You've made your anger pretty clear."

Jo was undeterred. "I've been seeing that therapist we discussed. She made the point that intention matters. I'd like to know what your intentions were."

"Jo, my intentions were the same they've been for the last forty years. I was just trying to take care of you and the kids."

"Bullshit. It wasn't the same, Dom. In the past, when you had some crazy idea, we talked about it and said yes together. Then suddenly you cut me out. Was it because you knew I'd say no this time? You didn't trust me to understand?"

Dom realized just how far he'd gone astray. It had never been a question of trust. He needed to trust her with this now if he was ever going to fix things between them.

"After... After Gabe died, you were so broken, so fragile, Jo. I've never been so afraid. You're my rock, and you were just... gone. I felt like I couldn't add to your burden."

"Dom, taking care of our family has never been a burden. I don't need protecting."

Dom held up a hand to forestall her argument. "At the time, it felt like I had to do something to find solid ground again. The opportunity came up, and I jumped."

"Hell of a jump." Jo took a long sip of the wine.

Dom stared into the space between them. "You have to know, Jo. I hear you and I'm trying. I know you want me to be done, but I can't walk away until I'm sure the kids are taken care of. This honestly seemed like a shortcut to stability."

"I can see that now. I still don't agree with how you went about it though."

"How about you?" Dom took the bottle back and sipped. She wasn't the only one who had questions.

"What about me?"

"You left. I lost you after the funeral, and you never came back. You've been going out all the time, doing things with anyone but me. I'm not an idiot. Why?"

Jo sat silent, trying to find the words.

"My whole world shifted that day."

Dom nodded but stayed quiet, giving her space.

"I couldn't just go back to the way things had been, because nothing felt the way it did before. I felt this urgency to do all the things I'd been putting off doing before it's too late. I had to fill every hour with something so that empty feeling didn't creep back in. And I got angry that you weren't on board. Do you know what I learned, in my manic 'doing'?"

"Tell me."

"I don't actually like doing a lot of those things without you. I want this retirement *with* you. But I was afraid if I stopped for even a second, I'd get swamped again. And if I went back to my old life, it would feel like giving up. On Gabe, on me, on us…" She trailed off, choking up.

Dom opened his arms, and she shifted into his embrace. He'd missed this. The warmth, the comfort, the balm to his soul when he held her in his arms. He fought tears of relief.

"I missed you," she whispered against his neck.

"I missed you too."

"Things aren't okay yet."

"No, we have some work to do, but we'll get there. I have faith in us, Jo."

~

42 YEARS *ago*

JO SAT on a bench on the quad, letting the sun warm her face, contentment making her sleepy. She would be graduating with her teaching degree in a few short weeks. She'd just wrapped up her last final, and she had a job offer in hand from a nearby school district. She wouldn't be moving away after all, and she couldn't wait to tell Dom. As usual, he was late.

They had a date to meet on the bench for a picnic, and though her stomach grumbled its annoyance, she smiled and sat back to wait.

Life was good. Jo would be the first person from her family to graduate from college. She'd worked damn hard to make that happen. She'd earned this moment to bask in the glow of her achievements.

It felt good to be a little lazy today. Maybe she'd convince Dom to drive over to Santa Cruz this weekend. A quick day on the beach where he'd told her he loved her sounded like the perfect way to celebrate the start of this next chapter.

Or maybe they could go apartment hunting. She knew her parents weren't super keen on the idea of her moving in with him before marriage, but it felt right. She wanted to start this next part of her life with him by her side. And it wasn't like they needed to live apart before they got married, if they got married. The virginity ship had sailed, and bon voyage! She was not going back to living under her parents' roof, that was for damn sure.

She'd suggest the house hunting when he showed up. If he showed up. She checked her watch. He was already fifteen minutes late. Had he forgotten their lunch date? No, he must've gotten hung up on a job site. He'd been putting in a bunch of overtime hours as the summer construction season ramped up.

Jo scanned the quad again, seeing friends and strangers scurrying along the paths around her, off to the next class or to study at the library. She was nearly done with all of that. A bit of melancholy pinched in her chest. She would miss this place and these people, this season of her life. But it was time.

She needed to spread her wings and learn to fly on her own now.

She couldn't wait to get into her own classroom and start making an impact in the lives of children. Her stomach growled again, interrupting her daydream. Maybe she'd just go grab a quick sandwich from the student union.

She turned to pick up her backpack from the ground and saw Dom walking slowly toward her, from the opposite direction than she'd been expecting him. Something was off.

Dom—big, outgoing, powerful Dom—was walking with those broad shoulders she loved hunched and his hands in his pockets. He hadn't looked up from the sidewalk and appeared to be talking to himself.

Jo's peaceful mood disintegrated. What was wrong?

CHAPTER 20

42 YEARS ago

"Just do it, you idiot. Get it over with."

Dom twitched his hand nervously in his pocket. He'd spent half an hour in his car just trying to get up the nerve to get out. He knew he was late and that she'd be waiting, but his feet felt like he'd walked through freshly poured concrete and forgotten to scrape.

Once he said what he needed to say, everything would change. He didn't want things to change. Weren't they happy? Hadn't the whole job thing worked out? Why the hell was he even thinking about messing with a good thing? And yet change was coming, and he'd never been one to back down from a challenge.

He steeled himself for the hardest conversation of his life.

He sat next to Jo on the bench, still struggling to find the words he needed to say.

"Hi, babe," she said. "You okay?" She pressed a hand to his forehead. "You don't look so good."

He didn't notice he was bouncing his knee until she shifted her hand to still it. He took that hand in his, marveling at how small and precious it looked in his work-roughened grip, and squeezed it three times, their secret code for "I love you." She squeezed back four times to say "I love you too."

"Why are you still dating me?" Dom blurted into the awkward silence between them.

"Um, because I love you? Did you miss the squeezes, silly?"

"But why?" He shifted away from her on the bench and angled his shoulders so that he could look directly at her. He needed to see her face when she answered. "Why do you love me? You could have any guy on this campus. You've got a bright future ahead of you with this teaching thing. You are so smart and confident, not to mention beautiful and kind and sweet and...I just can't figure it out. I'm just your average construction meathead."

"Yeah, but you're my meathead," she teased, but he shook his head. He couldn't let her joke him out of this. When she spoke again all traces of laughter were gone from her voice. "Let me get this straight. You can't figure out why I'm with you?"

He nodded, his heart in his throat, choking off his words.

"I think I fell for you that first night when I kicked your ass at pool. There you were, this big, strong guy, but instead of the bluster and outrage I'd been expecting, you laughed and came back for more. You surprised me. You weren't afraid to lose to me."

"You're wrong. I'm terrified of losing you." Dom dropped his head and muttered, still not understanding.

"That's not—"

Jo stopped and gripped his face in her hands, forcing him to look her in the eye.

"Babe, I'm right here. And I'm going to stay right here. Why? Because I have never felt so respected, so cared for, so loved as I have in the last year and a half. You've supported my dreams and made me part of yours. We make a hell of a team. Dom, you think I could have any guy on this campus? You're right, I could, but I don't want them, because they aren't you."

Dom leaned forward until their foreheads touched and he let out the breath he'd been holding. "I needed to hear you say that. I didn't realize how much, until I walked over here with this ring in my pocket."

He leaned back to pull the little black velvet box that had been taunting him for weeks out of his front jeans pocket and was rewarded with a gasp from Jo.

"Dom, is that…"

"My dad gave me one piece of advice about choosing who to marry. 'Aim high,' he said, and I listened. I will probably never understand why you fell in love with me or why you chose to stay. You deserve so much more than I can offer you right now. All I can promise is to never stop trying to give you more. More laughter, more security, more adventure, more love… Josephine Bertelli, I love you like crazy. Will you marry me?"

Dom thought his heart was going to beat right out of his chest while he waited for her answer. The blood pulsing in his ears made it almost impossible to hear her response. Almost.

"I'll think about it."

Dom barked out a laugh, and the vise in his chest loosened. The first time she'd said that had been after what he considered their first date. She'd said it to him again and again over the course of their relationship when she was going to say yes, but wanted to make him sweat a bit first.

She put a finger on her chin and mimed deep thought, fighting a grin, and he hauled her onto his lap and kissed that smile right off her face. When they came up for air, he was breathless and she was serious.

"Of course I'll marry you. I love you, Dom. I can't wait to see the life we'll build together."

Dom slid the small diamond ring on her finger. He'd wanted it to be bigger but his overtime hadn't covered as much as he'd hoped. "I love you too, Jo. I know it's not much, but someday—"

She cut him off with another kiss. "It's perfect, and I love it. Because I love you."

She kissed him again, and he returned it, heart full of the promise of the future and the love that flowed between them like wine. He'd meant what he said. He'd never stop working to earn her love, and maybe someday, if he was very lucky, she'd have everything she deserved in this life and more. He couldn't wait to get started.

∼

1 YEAR *ago*

THEN DOM COVERED Jo's lips with his own, and they stopped talking altogether. This reunion of their hearts and bodies was just as important as the one taking place between their minds. Jo lost herself in the simple pleasure of kissing her husband. After so many months apart, she felt home again.

Her blood heated beneath her skin and prickling nerves came shivering back to life as his hands roamed down her arms and around her back. His taste mingled with the wine and went straight to her head. She poured all of her longing into the kiss, feeling so much relief that this wall was being broken down between them.

His hands dipped lower to grip her hips and cup her ass, and she groaned, both from pleasure and frustration. She leaned back and broke the kiss. Dom's face fell, and she held up one finger before stripping off her blouse. Then she climbed back onto his lap, this time facing him, knees astride, so she could get as close as she wanted.

Dom said everything he needed to without words. His eyes spoke of his gratitude as they traced every dip and curve she'd revealed. His hands whispered reverent words of love as he ran them over every stretch mark and wrinkle and bump and line, blissfully remaking his acquaintance with her body. His insistent erection, pressing between her legs, shouted that even after all they'd been through, he still wanted her, badly.

Today it was enough. When he snapped the clasps undone and her bra fell forward, Jo shrugged it off and leaned into his mouth. Dom kissed and licked and sucked her deeply, just the way she liked. She clutched his head to her breast and rocked against him. With a growl she felt to her soul, Dom rolled her onto the blanket and made quick work of her jeans and boots. Just as eager, she tried to help him get his shirts off, but only succeeded in pinning his arms.

Laughter bubbled up in her throat and escaped before she could catch it. She hadn't expected this joy, and that melancholy thought caught in her chest. Tears threatened on the edge of her laughter, and Dom sat back on his haunches, giving her space.

She propped herself up on her elbows, and he slowly untangled himself from his button-down blue cotton shirt. He left his undershirt on though and paused. "Are you okay? Do you want to keep going or…"

"Or what?"

"Or we could go back to making out like teenagers… Or we could stop."

"You would stop right now?"

"Jo, I'll do whatever you need me to right now. I love you."

"And if I said I needed you to put your face between my thighs…"

"I'd say I'll buy you a new pair of underwear because these are about to get ripped off. But only if you're sure. Why the tears?"

Jo hadn't realized that they'd fallen down her cheeks, and she swiped them away. "Just sad for all the time we lost."

"Then let's make up for it."

"Let's." She didn't let him tear her underwear, because a good pair was hard to find, but she shimmied out of them with an alacrity that left no doubt of her willingness.

When he settled between her legs, his groan of satisfaction as he licked her and slid two fingers inside her, pumping and pulling in all the right places, reverberated through her entire body, setting off an orgasm that was sitting way too close to the surface.

"Again," she gasped.

And her wonderful husband complied, edging her closer and closer now that the low-hanging fruit was out of the way. Every muscle tightened in anticipation as he relentlessly drove her higher. She'd ache tomorrow and smile at the memory.

"You. I need you, Dom."

He shoved his jeans and underwear down to mid-thigh, too eager to bother getting them all the way off. The rough denim brushed her ass as he slid home, slow and deep, hooking her legs with his arms and holding her wide-open to him. Pinned down by his weight, his cock filling her deeply, Jo moaned with pleasure and closed her eyes.

"No, Jo, look at me. I need you."

She opened her eyes and saw the man she loved and missed staring down at her. He held her gaze, making her see him and acknowledge who was giving her this pleasure. She opened her heart and gave it right back to him, rocking her hips, clenching deep, trying to hold him as tightly as he held her.

Together they raced for that second peak, breath mingling, frantically chasing this love between them. When his breathing changed, Jo reached down and rubbed her clit hard, sending herself over the edge, and Dom followed right behind. She caught him as he collapsed against her chest, and relished his body pressed to hers.

Something elemental had clicked back into place between them. She knew they still had a lot of work to do together to forge a stronger union, but today had been a vital step back toward each other.

Dom rolled them to their sides and chuckled, still winded from their exertions. "Wasn't expecting that. I'm out of shape."

Jo reached down and squeezed his ass, pulling him tight to her. "I like your shape just fine, but if you're suggesting we get back in practice, I'm not arguing."

Dom took her hand in his and squeezed it three times before kissing her with a seriousness that jarred against the light post-coital banter.

"That's a deal, *partner*." His voice had gone soft and rough, like he'd swallowed a handful of paving gravel. "That's a deal."

She squeezed back four times.

~

5 YEARS *ago*

AFTER A LONG DAY of trying to hold his shit together at work, Dom walked into a dark house. A TV blared with some stupid theme music, but all the lights in the house were off. Flicking switches as he went, he passed through the living room and into the kitchen, finally spotting Jo, curled up on the couch in the family room, illuminated by the blue glow of the screen. A Rick Steves travel special flashed across the screen before switching to the local PBS station's fundraising drive.

"Hey, babe. How was your day?"

"Hmmm."

Dom was used to her grunted responses now. It had been three weeks since the military funeral, and Jo had yet to speak a full sentence to him. He scanned the kitchen for any signs that she'd eaten anything today.

He saw two coffee cups in the sink, one empty, one full. Elena must have come by. Sure enough, he opened the fridge and found a casserole inside sitting on a lonely shelf. Jo still hadn't left the house or gone grocery shopping. Dom added it to his to-do list for the next day. Written in Sharpie, the directions scribbled on the foil top told him everything he needed to know.

Macaroni and Cheese 350° for thirty minutes or until bubbly. Love, E

He put the dish in the oven and turned on the heat. Thank God for Elena. She'd been keeping food in their fridge for weeks.

"Babe, I'm going to go hop in the shower, okay?"

"Mhmmm."

Dom climbed the stairs and stripped out of his filthy work clothes. When he tossed them in the laundry bin, he noticed it was full. A quick shuffle showed him it was all his clothes. Jo hadn't changed out of her pajamas in a week.

Her behavior was starting to scare him. She'd never shut down like this before, and he had no idea how to get through to her. He'd tried talking, listening, cajoling… Tonight he was at his wit's end.

He showered and as the hot water washed over him he had an epiphany. He came back downstairs in a T-shirt and a pair of comfy sweatpants with a small card in his hand.

He set the table for two and prayed both plates would get used. He heated some frozen vegetables in the microwave and pulled the casserole out of the oven. Dom even went so far as to open her favorite wine in hopes it would spark some appetite.

"Jo, come eat."

"Uh-uh," she muttered and rolled back toward the TV.

Dom crossed to the couch and picked her up. "Josephine Valenti, you need to eat something. You can go back to your show once you've showered and gotten some food in your belly." He carried her to the table and sat her down in her chair in front of a small plate of food.

Jo reached for the wine and downed half the glass in one gulp. Dom rescued it from her grasp and handed her the fork instead. When she actually put a piece of pasta in her mouth, it felt like a solid win.

Dom scrambled for a conversation topic that would keep her engaged at the table. "So, work was crazy busy today. You know the Ohan-Mars project? With the really exotic hardwood flooring? All of the wood got delayed! It's on a shipping container somewhere in the Pacific, but it was supposed to be here two days ago. Getting it all figured out was a nightmare. We are swamped. Do you...do you think you might be ready to come back into the office soon? We miss you, Jo. And it might be good to have something to get out of bed for."

Another bite of macaroni, but no words. Just a baleful glare and a shake of her head.

"Jo, I'm not sure how to help you, but I can see that you need it. I've got the card for the counselor the chaplain recommended. I'm going to call her and see if she can come by."

Jo shrugged. He took it as tacit agreement, since it wasn't an outright denial. Honestly, even if she'd said no, he'd have called for himself. He was grieving, yes, but he'd also never been so scared in his life. He didn't know how to help Jo, and he was worried that ignoring it would only make it more dangerous.

Leaving Jo at the table, Dom pulled out his cell phone and called the number on the business card.

"Hello? This is Dom Valenti. I need your help."

~

Dom finally took a deep breath when Jo emerged from her cocoon on the couch over the following weeks. But much like the butterfly, her soft and warm exterior had transformed into a brittle shell. Talking with the grief counselor seemed to help, but her interactions with Dom were brief and direct. She had graduated to using actual words, but was miserly in how often she dispensed them.

Eventually, she came back to work, but nothing seemed to please her. The everyday challenges of running the business office that she had once handled with ease now left her angry and frustrated, her fuse perpetually short.

"What is this?" she barked, slapping an invoice down on Dom's desk.

"Um, it's an invoice?"

"I can see that. Why is it different from the invoice I just sent out yesterday to these clients?" Her voice rose in pitch and speed, alerting Dom to her state of mind.

"We discovered that their ductwork was bad and added it to the project this morning. That reflects the new cost."

"Well, great. That's just great. Now I have to call them and explain the difference." Jo tossed her hands in the air before snatching up the offending paper again.

"That would be very helpful."

"They're going to think I'm an idiot who can't do her job."

"No, they aren't."

But she wasn't hearing that.

"So scattered she can't even get a simple invoice right…" Jo muttered on her way back to her office.

Dom thought the issue was settled, but Jo came back less than an hour later with the same look on her face. "Listen, whatever it is, we can figure it out. I'm sure it's not that bad, Jo."

"I quit."

That declaration rocked him back on his heels. "What? Why? What's the matter?"

"I'm the matter. I can't do this anymore. I can't pretend I'm content writing checks and shuffling papers. This isn't how I want to spend whatever time is left to me. I'm done." She laid the company checkbook on his desk and walked out the door, directly past the truck they had driven to work in together that morning.

Stunned, Dom rocked back in his chair and Tony peeked his head around the doorframe.

"What was all that?" Tony asked.

"Jo just quit."

"Maybe she just needs a little break. Maybe she came back too soon."

"I was just trying to get her off the couch. I don't know what to do anymore. Everything I try to do seems wrong."

"Well, just keep the lights on until she gets through it. It'll all be okay in the end."

Sure, Tony. It'll all be okay. The sarcasm burned in Dom's throat unspoken. Nothing was okay. Nothing would ever be okay again.

But he could keep things afloat until Jo came back. He'd promised to love and cherish, through better or worse. He could be her shelter until she was strong enough to face the wind. He picked up the phone.

"Fi, I need a favor."

CHAPTER 21

⌘

1 year ago

WHEN NEWS of the fire reached Dom, he was in the kitchen. Jo was making his favorite stuffed pepperoncini peppers for Friday dinner. In an unsettling wave of déjà vu, he sat heavily on a chair while someone at the hospital told him Frankie had been brought in by paramedics to be observed for smoke inhalation. The vineyard was burning.

He must have gasped, because Jo was by his side in an instant, taking his phone from his trembling hand and turning on the speaker.

"Repeat everything you just said, please. What's going on?" she demanded.

The caller hadn't even gotten through her first sentence before Jo was tugging him out of his seat and pushing him toward the door. "Get in the car. I'm driving."

Dom followed her blindly as she shut off the oven, grabbed her purse and keys, and sprinted out the front door.

He didn't say anything on the tense drive to the hospital. The ride passed in a blur. He let Jo talk to the intake nurse in the ER to find out where his baby was. It was too much. Too soon. Not again. Not ever again, he'd vowed. And yet here they were.

Jo led him to a seat in the waiting area and sat down next to him, draping her arm around his shoulder and pulling him close. "It's okay, Dom. She's going to be okay."

He just shook his head mutely, unable to put his fear into words. He didn't want to jinx it.

"I'll be the strong one today, Dom. You can lean on me. I've got you."

And she did. She carried him, through seeing his baby in a hospital gown, ashen against the white sheets with tubes taped to her nose. Through hours of waiting until they were allowed to bring her home. Through all of the phone calls to emergency response and insurance companies and Jake and the crew. Jo held it together and got them through it.

In the shadow of her competence, Dom sat in silence with some unpleasant truths.

He'd underestimated her. He should have known better. In all their years together, through all of the tough times and challenges, Jo had never broken. Not once. Not even when Gabe had died. She'd gotten fragile, but she'd never snapped.

Had he used that fragility as an excuse to take charge? He had so desperately needed to feel in control of something, anything, in a world spinning off its axis. Had he cut her out so he didn't have to listen to anyone else? It was an ugly realization that while he'd been telling himself he'd done all of this for her, part of the reason was much more selfish. He'd jeopardized everything so that he could feel powerful in a world that had cut him off at the knees.

Knowing that Frankie was safe and sound and that firefighters had managed to save most of the vineyard structures was a blessing, but Dom's heart still sat heavy in his chest at the end of the day. He was more determined than ever to make it up to Jo.

~

24 YEARS ago

"YES, Mrs. Miller... Yes, I know that's frustrating. As I explained..."

Dom held the phone away from his ear as Mrs. Miller told him exactly what she thought about the fact that his crew hadn't been able to get her sod laid because it had been ninety-five degrees today. It would have died before it had a chance. But Mrs. Miller was apparently having people over tomorrow and now they'd have to stay inside.

"Yes, I'm sorry you feel that way. The weather should break by Monday, and we will lay the sod then. Construction has its ups and downs, but by the end of the project you will have a backyard you can be proud of. I promise." He tried his best to soothe her, but he really wanted to ask her why the fuck she thought it was a good idea to host a garden party before the garden was finished!

No sooner had he hung up than the phone began to ring again.

4:59 on a Friday afternoon. He shouldn't answer it. He should let it go to voicemail. He should pretend he'd already left and go to Gabe's baseball game with his wife and their little ones. But being the owner of his own business meant responsibility came first, and he picked up the phone.

But instead of being a new project inquiry, it was his new foreman, Chad, calling from the spec house.

"What do you mean, Glenn walked off the job?"

"Uh, he said he had an appointment?" Chad explained, stumbling over his words.

Dom pinched his nose. Glenn had appointments at his local dive bar every payday. This was the last straw, for both Glenn and Chad. Glenn was good at drywall, but he wasn't worth the inconsistency. And Chad, he'd been on the job a month and still hadn't learned that he was the boss.

"Chad, did you remind him that he should have told us about this 'appointment' at the beginning of the shift and not the end?"

"Uh, no. I didn't think to."

That was the problem. Chad couldn't think on his feet. He couldn't adapt to a changing situation and read the subtext. He couldn't handle more than one complex task at once. And Dom was trusting the fragile reputation of his company to this dude?

Dom couldn't afford to keep him if he couldn't get the job done. He wouldn't have even chosen to hire Chad, but Tony had broken his elbow and was out of commission for a while, and Dom had needed immediate backup. The call had gone out among the Italian aunties, and Chad had been the least shitty choice. Which was still a shitty choice.

He didn't care if it would piss off his aunt's friend's cousin. This guy might have office skills, but a leader of men he was not. Dom wouldn't fire him right away, but he was done giving chances. Glenn, however, was done. Not only was Glenn's bailing to go on a bender affecting Dom's professional reputation as a builder who got things done on time and under budget. No, now it was impacting his family life as well.

Dom sighed deeply again, because he knew he would have to pick up the slack *and* go through the torturous hiring process again. *Damn it.* If he hadn't been burned so badly, he'd hire an office manager too. They desperately needed someone to help with the invoices and deposits. But if this was what he got hiring crew recommended by people he knew, Dom was reluctant to trust the process to find him someone he'd trust to handle his income.

And none of that changed the fact that Dom would be working late, again.

That drywall needed to be mudded tonight so that the sanding could get done tomorrow, or they'd lose the whole weekend. Dom didn't mind paying overtime to get a job done right when they were battling issues beyond their control like shipping delays or broken tiles. But paying extra to cover the incompetence of someone he'd just paid? *Hell no.*

"I'm on my way."

"Wait, you don't have to come over here." Chad's voice wavered, and Dom's Spidey senses tingled. "Doesn't Gabe have a little league game?"

"Yeah, he does. And because this asshole can't keep his head out of the bottle, and you can't keep him on the job, I'm going to miss it."

"Dom—"

"I said I'm on my way." Dom slammed the receiver down on the cradle and swore.

He'd only stayed late in the office to try and wade through some paperwork since Tony was out. If he'd been ten minutes faster, he could have avoided that phone call completely. Part of him wished he didn't know about the problem because then at least he could have enjoyed his son's baseball game. But the job would have still been fucked whether he'd gotten the call or not, and that was bad for business.

Being the sole provider for their family on top of running his own business meant that shirking on the business was shirking on his family, and that he could not tolerate. Even if Gabe would be disappointed in the short term.

If he didn't get the invoices done, no money would come in. If no money came in, they couldn't meet payroll. If he couldn't pay his guys their salary, he couldn't pay his either. And Gabe had needed new baseball cleats, along with a pair of tap shoes for Sofia. The other two babies would be getting into the mix soon enough. He had a short window to make this work, or he'd have to give up on this dream and go back to working for someone else.

Some days he actively longed to go back to juggling a full-time construction and part-time landscaping gig like he had when Gabe was born. Had he been exhausted? Absolutely, but at the end of the day he'd been done. No constant worrying. No putting out fires. Nobody else's career depending on his. He had severely underestimated the challenges of running a business with his brother.

Still, he'd do what needed doing. He'd taken the call at five o'clock on a Friday, and he'd be the one to clean up the mess.

Shuffling all the invoices and receipts into a hasty pile, Dom cursed math and swore he'd get to it tomorrow morning. He pulled up the hours Glenn had worked this week and wrote out a business check to cover it. He'd figure out the taxes and stuff later, or more likely he wouldn't, but as of right now, Glenn was no longer employed by Valenti Brothers.

He left a message on the home machine letting Jo know what was going on, and he drove to the Pit, Glenn's preferred dive. Sure as shit, there he sat, ponied up to the bar, several empties littering the mahogany counter in front of him.

"Hey there, Glenn. Heard you had an appointment. You okay?"

"Yeah, Dom, I'm good. Here, let me buy you a round. What are you drinking?" Glenn waved over the bartender, completely oblivious to the rage simmering under Dom's skin. "Hey Gary, get my boss here whatever he'd like, on my tab."

"Your tab is maxed out until you come back with some cash,

Glenn." The long-suffering bartender rolled his eyes at Dom, who nodded back.

"Gary, was it? Let me ask you a question. What time did Glenn roll in here today?"

"About four fifteen."

Glenn's gregarious face fell, and he began to backpedal. "You see, the doctor was running late, and I couldn't see him today after all, but I was hurting, so I came in..."

Dom held up a hand to stop his rambling defense. "I don't care."

Glenn's face sagged with relief for a moment before Dom started talking again.

"You see, you don't work for me anymore. I can't trust you to do the job you said you'd do. Here's your last paycheck that covers the hours through today." He laid the check on the bar, and tipped his head to Gary. "You might want to let him cash that here, so he can pay his tab."

Gary picked up the check before Glenn could react. "That is an excellent idea. Can I get you a drink, sir? On the house?"

"No, thank you. I have to go finish mudding a family room. Goodbye, Glenn. Good luck."

Dom turned and left, ignoring the spluttering expletives behind him.

He had no room in his life for incompetence. He couldn't afford the time or the cost.

～

He glanced at his watch as he pulled into the job site's driveway. If he hustled, hopefully he could still catch the last few innings. But one glance at the front yard killed that pipe dream. It was a spec house they were building, so no one lived there yet and the front yard was still a dirt patch. But that didn't mean the crew could treat it like a dump site. Tools caked with plaster lay on the front walk, just waiting for someone to walk away with them. White swaths of plaster runoff colored the brown dirt where the crew had attempted to wash down, leaving an eyesore for the neighborhood. Collecting material as he went, Dom made a mental note to chat with the boys about washing up out back instead.

Inside, it looked like more than Glenn had walked off the job. If Chad had called to tell him that everyone had been abducted by aliens, Dom would have believed him. Workstations left with drills still plugged in and wood half cut. Buckets of mud that would harden overnight and need to be thrown out and replaced. Fast food bags left littered in the corners.

How had they managed to get so much plaster in the front yard and still have dirty buckets left behind? And when had they left? Right after lunch? This looked like about a half day of work. They hadn't made nearly enough progress. Every day they ran over cut into Dom's profits, and it was his investment money on the line. *What a mess!*

Dom felt some justification for making the right call, but it still sucked to be the one to clean it up. Saving his charm to sweet-talk Jo out of being angry, he leaned his shoulder into this problem and got to work. At least the joint compound was still wet so he could get busy right away. He ran tape over the seams and smeared the mud over the gaps, smoothing behind him as he went.

At this point in his career, he could do this kind of work on autopilot. Tape, scoop, smear, scrape, repeat. The soothing repetition helped calm him down, and as he found his flow, he let his mind wander to the future.

Someday, he wouldn't have to worry about money so much. He'd be able to hire the very best crew and treat them well because Valenti Brothers would be so well respected in the Bay

Area that they'd have their pick of jobs. They'd be making good money and be able to give their families the life they deserved. And of course, Gabe, Enzo, and Seth would be running the crews for them, so they wouldn't have to rely on friends of friends who didn't know what they were doing. Those boys were growing up in the business, and someday, he and Tony would hand it all to them, knowing they'd given their sons a solid foundation for their future.

Someday, he'd be able to retire and give Jo every dream she'd ever had. She'd been so good about delaying travel and fun because of money and time and babies, not to mention the fact that airplanes still freaked him out. But by the time they retired, he'd figure all that out and take her on a tour of the world. They'd make love in every continent. Well, maybe not Antarctica. That seemed a bit cold. Dom spun out his own daydreams while he methodically worked his way around every seam. Someday, he'd give that woman the world.

But someday was not today. So Dom did what he did best—drove his mind and shoulder at a problem until it was fixed. No one else had to worry. He'd just take care of it. Tony didn't need one more thing to worry about on top of his elbow and trying to keep his own projects running. Jo didn't need to worry about this. He didn't want her to know how close they cut it every week. She had enough to worry about juggling the kids and the house and everything else. No, he was the provider, the fixer. It was his job to keep the business growing and running smoothly. If his hard work could provide a good life for his family, then he couldn't begrudge the time it took to do a job right.

CHAPTER 22

1 year ago

Dom struggled to keep to the speed limit as he drove Jo down for the final reveal at the vineyard. Valenti Vineyards was officially finished, and after months of waiting he was finally going to give her what she wanted. He wanted to be done with the reveal already, and Jo was getting anxious with the blindfold on.

"If this is some kind of trust exercise your therapist suggested, can't we just tell him we've done it? The suspense is killing me," Jo groused, and Dom had to chuckle.

Jo had never been particularly patient. He should have known better than to make her wait nearly three years for him to join her in retirement. This surprise would hopefully go a long way to making up for that.

Driving past the gate that now proudly proclaimed the new ownership, Dom slowed as he pulled in the driveway. This. This was his real legacy. Sofia and Adrian, Enzo and Natalie, and Frankie stood shoulder to shoulder in front of the grand estate they'd helped him create. The recent fire had done more than open his eyes to Jo's strength. It had also made him realize that bricks and timber were nothing compared to the foundation of his family. He couldn't quite remember now why it had felt so important to keep building. He had everything he needed right here. His children, his grandchildren, and hopefully after this reveal, his wife firmly back by his side.

"Showtime," he muttered as he climbed out of the car and circled it to open the door for Jo.

"Dom, what is going on?" Jo asked, exasperation and laughter coloring her tone. "Where did you take me?"

Dom's hands were shaking as he led Jo to their marks on the driveway. Had he done enough? Would this work? It had to. There was no other option.

"My Jojo." Dom's voice cracked on her nickname. He held her hands in his as they stood face-to-face, as he had that day so many years before in front of their priest, that day he'd promised to love and honor and cherish her.

Please God, let her see that's what I'm trying to do.

"Josephine Valenti, do you remember back when we were young and newly in love? When we'd sit out at the beach bonfires and dream with a bottle of wine between us?"

Jo nodded her head, but her smile dropped a little.

He hated that he'd dimmed that memory for her, but he pushed on. "My dream was to own my own business. You stood by my side every step of the way while we made that dream a reality. You took care of the kids and kept the office running and got the bills paid and gave more years to my dream than I ever had the right to expect. And I thank you for that. Because of your sacrifices, we have a legacy to pass on to our kids."

Jo kept her lips pursed, and he hoped that was because she wanted to see what he said next, and not because she was biting back an argument. Dom pushed on, putting his heart on his sleeve for the world to see.

"I remember your dreams too. You were going to be a teacher, and when we retired we were going to travel and drink wine and watch the sunsets over a plot of land in the country. Do you remember?"

His voice was thick with tears now, but he had to get it out. Jo's shoulders shook as she nodded. He sucked in a deep breath and kept going.

"You've taught our children how to be wonderful adults. I know that's not exactly how you pictured your career, but you have to know the difference you made in all of our lives. I hope this second part shows our appreciation. I hope..." Dom cleared the emotion from his throat. "I hope it's everything you dreamed we could have."

He untied the blindfold, and Jo turned to get her bearings. Her eyes widened as she realized where they were. "Dom, what are you saying? What does this mean?"

She clutched his arm as he turned her more fully toward the house. He didn't even know if she'd seen the cameras yet.

"It means this was all for you. For us. I'm walking away from the building business. I'm leaving it in very good hands," he said as he looked over his shoulder to where his legacy stood, watching. He could say with confidence that they could absolutely handle anything life threw at them.

For the first time, Jo realized she had an audience, and self-consciously wiped her cheeks. "Oh, Dom. This is too much. Is this what you've been hiding the last few months?"

"This, and a few other things I'll tell you about later. Do you like it?"

Dom held his breath while he waited for her answer.

"I'm overwhelmed. It's beautiful, of course, but I never thought it would be mine."

It wasn't quite the resounding yes he'd hoped for, so he launched into the pitch he'd sold Jake months ago. Once they made nice for the cameras, which were already making him jump out of his skin, he could tell her the rest.

"Well, it's fifty acres in the country, and I thought we could give making our own wine a go. I know you want to retire and travel and do all those things we dreamed, and we will. But let's be honest. You'll go nuts with me underfoot, and I'll go nuts without a project to tackle. This solves all of those problems, but still gives us the freedom to do those things we dreamed about all those years ago. Will you let me show it to you?"

Jo looked up at him, and Dom took courage from the love he saw there. For the first time in too long, Jo looked at him with hope and happiness. All of this was worth it for that alone. He'd keep doing the work to fix his mistakes, but today? Today was a good day.

∽

15 years ago

"Wait right there. And keep your eyes closed!"

Dom stood still where she'd placed him, and dutifully kept his head down and his eyes closed, but he couldn't resist asking, "Is this really necessary? I see finished projects every day."

"Yes, but you've never seen one of mine. And yes it is necessary. I want you to see the property from a renter's perspective, so I'm going to take you on a walk-through. I just have to... There...the lockbox was a little tricky." She walked back to him and looped her hand through his elbow. "Okay, Dom, you can open your eyes now."

Dom was content to let her play this out her way, so he raised his head and opened his eyes at her command. His astonishment was not feigned.

"Jo, what? When? Is this the same building?" He spun his head around, confirming that he was indeed looking at the right address. Jo had banned him from the site for the last two weeks, so he knew she'd been up to something, but he hadn't expected this.

Gone were the crumbling bricks and mortar on the facade, handled by his crew of tuck pointers. But he'd seen that. He'd inspected the results himself. It was the landscaping and styling that made his jaw drop. Bright and cheerful petunias lined the front walkway and climbing roses and baby cypress trees framed the exterior spaces between the entrances of each unit. Mulch had been laid around the base of the larger beds, and the freshly washed windows glittered in the sunlight.

"I had a few ideas for landscaping, and I got Gabe and Enzo to give me a hand digging."

Dom spun his head to goggle at his wife. She laughed at him. "What? Did you think I could be part of a construction company for ten years and not know how to use a shovel?"

Dom shook his head at that nonsense. "No, I just...I would have done this for you. You didn't have to do all that digging and planting yourself."

"I just told you, the boys helped with the outside. And besides, if I'd let you help, I wouldn't have been able to keep this a surprise. And the look on your face right now is worth every blister."

She tugged his elbow and he followed her up the front walk, taking in the sprinkler heads she'd plumbed and the edges she'd laid. She'd certainly kept the boys busy.

"Come on! I want to show you the inside. We kept most of the units empty and move-in ready, but we staged this one for showings, and Sofia and Frankie helped me get it all arranged. By the way, Sofia has already claimed this as her unit when she's done with college." Jo laughed and rubbed her hands together. "Our evil plan is already working!"

"Excellent." Dom steepled his fingers and raised one eyebrow, which made her laugh even harder.

As she got herself back under control, Jo straightened the hem of her suit dress and took a deep breath. She looked back up at him, this time with her professional customer service mask firmly in place. "You're going to be the first person to hear my tour speech. Welcome home, Dom."

She opened the door to the second unit on the first floor, the same one she'd walked him through four months ago when she'd convinced him to take this risk, and swept a hand in front of her to usher him in. The meaning was not lost on him. He stopped just inside the doorway and took it all in.

In his mind's eye, he could see the disaster it had been, all tight rooms and shoddy wiring, decaying pipes and twenty years worth of ignored or tenant-attempted repairs. He'd had serious doubts about Jo's vision and his own construction abilities.

When he'd last seen this space after months of work, it had been long stretches of refinished hardwood floors flanked by primed drywall. A blank canvas with a solid frame behind it. But now... Now it was a proper home.

"You painted," he said, stating the obvious because other words escaped him.

"It's still neutral, but it gives the space some life. And I'm okay with our tenants painting, so I wanted to show that here. But I'm getting ahead of myself. Welcome home! This unit is a two-bedroom, two-bath, nine hundred and fifty square feet with a dedicated parking space included in the rent. We are close to public transportation and walkable to the local schools. To your left, you'll see the main living space with plenty of room for a lounging area and more. We've opted to put a small dining table in and made the first hallway bedroom into an office space/guest room. But there is also a dining option here in the kitchen at the bar-height counter, which keeps the use of space flexible if you need to move the office out here."

The light golden tan color she'd put on the walls made him feel like he was standing in a ray of sunshine, and the seating area invited him to come sit down and relax. He could picture sneaking over here on Sundays to watch the game in peace. Of course, Jo probably wouldn't appreciate that in the middle of her tour, but it meant that her plan to stage the apartment was a sound one. He was already picturing ways he could use the space, instead of worrying over how much she'd spent on rugs and couches.

Dom turned to the kitchen and nodded. He'd complained at the expense and time when she suggested opening up the kitchen walls and putting in a wraparound counter and bay of cabinets, but seeing how it made the space feel open and welcoming, he could admit she was right. Everything fit together perfectly. Renters were going to love this.

Seeing her personal touches on the counters, from her vase filled with hydrangeas to the cookbook lying open next to the stove, Dom felt like he was walking into Jo's Tuscan Kitchen. The terra-cotta tiles on the floor and the faux granite countertops transported him into Jo's vision. She really had an eye for this design business.

When they built a project for a client, he went with whatever options they chose. When he was starting a building from scratch, they picked whatever matched the price point. He'd never really given much thought to how the space would be decorated afterward. That wasn't his strength. But he could see how this added value to his work.

This room told a story, and welcomed him to be the main character.

Jo picked up the tour and sold him on the low-flow water

fixtures in the bathroom and the durability of the lovely faux stone tiles. She took him through the office space where he recognized the old desk from their garage under a new coat of distressed paint.

When they got to the main bedroom, Dom was bursting with pride. Jo had done such a good job turning this into a home. He shouldn't be surprised. After all, she expertly built and maintained their home over the last twenty-plus years. But seeing her skill overlaying his own work tapped a new level of appreciation for his wife. She was taking Valenti Brothers' reputation for good work and making it stronger.

She was amazing. Maybe they could consider more renovation and flip projects in addition to complete rebuilds and new construction. It was certainly easier to see how it would work with Jo in the mix. An avenue to keep an eye on, for sure.

"As you can see, there is enough room for a king-size bed, but we've put a queen in to show how furniture might fit in as well."

"You're *my* queen." Dom put his hands on Jo's waist and backed her up so that her legs bumped the edge of the bed. "The apartment is beautiful, but I keep getting distracted by my sexy realtor." He kissed her neck and made her giggle. The dimple that made him weak appeared on her cheek, and he groaned.

"Really?"

"Yes, you are too sexy for my own good."

"No, I meant you like what I did to the apartment?"

"Yes, babe. This was a good idea. You made the right call about the wall in the kitchen despite the cost, and your staging has made it feel like a home. I can almost picture us living here." With a hand on her shoulder, he toppled her back onto the bed. "There, that's better."

He lay down next to her and propped himself up on his elbow so he could look at her face. Brushing the hair back from her cheek, he leaned in for a kiss.

"Imagine—the kids are all grown. We're finally taking that vacation to Italy you've always wanted. It's just you and me under the Tuscan sun, lazing in bed, eating good food, making love…"

He punctuated his dreams with kisses, and Jo leaned into both the imagery and his embrace.

"Strolling through art galleries, exploring old ruins and building new memories together over sunsets and bottles of wine. I can't wait, Dom. We're going to conquer this fear of flying you have and take on the world."

"As long as you're by my side. We make a hell of a team, Jo."

She pulled him back in for another kiss, sealing the promise of this shared future.

He'd blocked out an hour for this tour with Jo, and he was determined to make every minute count. He slid his hands under her fancy suit, destroying her composure and taking a little tour of his own over all of his favorite places. Every curve, every dip, testament to the lives she'd created and shared with him. Every shiver and gasp a renewal of the vows they'd made to love and to cherish so long ago. Every beat of her heart beneath his fingertips a reminder of the passion that still pulsed between them.

With four kids in the house, a quiet hour was hard to come by. Dom wasn't going to waste a second. He was going to show Jo exactly how much he loved her and her brilliant ideas.

CHAPTER 23

1 YEAR ago

JO KEPT GASPING for breath every time Frankie and Dom escorted her into a new room. She saw the perfect blend of Sofia's style and Frankie's craftsmanship. As they moved from room to room —complete with camera setups and makeup retouches as she couldn't seem to stop crying—Jo tried and tried to picture her family in these rooms. The great room was stunning, but she couldn't quite picture a Christmas here. The back bedrooms would be great for guests, but not for her grandchildren. She wanted them to pile into the beds their parents had slept in. The bathrooms were stunning, but none of them had the soaker tub with the perfect built-in tile ledge for her wineglass, like the one Dom had designed for their private bathroom at home.

The kitchen was tempting. She could create some amazing meals in that professional kitchen, and the wine cellar cleverly concealed beneath the kitchen island was icing on the cake. But she couldn't picture sneaking in for a midnight snack or making cookies with Daisy.

The public areas, like the tasting room and the bar, made complete sense if they were going to make their own wine. However, Jo knew many things about drinking wine but absolutely zero things about how to make it herself. Her mind reeled with all of the details, but she hoped she was putting on a good show for the folks at home who'd been following this renovation.

It truly was a beautiful space, and she was proud of all that her children had created. But it wasn't hers. Her home was the house an hour north that contained all her memories and dreams, her laughter and tears. She didn't want to leave that all behind. She didn't want to start over, making this new place feel like home.

Outside, the terraced decks were both functional and beautifully designed. Enzo's signature style showed off the beauty of the surrounding landscape while giving the viewer a taste of comfort and class.

Looking out over the vines that had survived the fire, she could understand why Dom had wanted this. The outdoor areas for entertainment were just screaming for a party. The genius of Enzo's landscaping design ran right up to the charred remains of the barn, bringing home the reality of the fire that had come too close for comfort. Jo flashed back to her baby lying in a hospital bed and pulled her in for a tight hug, just to reassure herself that Frankie was indeed fine.

By the end of the day, Jo was exhausted. After a full morning of filming, followed by a late afternoon wrap party where she'd personally thanked everyone involved, she had earned the glass of wine in her hand and five quiet minutes on the deck.

Gathering her thoughts today was harder than usual. Every time she thought she had them pinned down, they skittered off in new directions. Three minutes into the five she'd allotted herself, Dom slipped out the back door and joined her at the railing. He wrapped an arm around her shoulder, and she wrapped hers around his waist. The sun sat low on the horizon, half concealed by the mountains along the edge of the property. The evening air began to chill and so did her happiness.

"Domenico Valenti, what have you gone and done this time?" she asked quietly.

Dom sighed into her hair as he brought his head down to hers. "You don't like it."

"That's not what I said and not what I meant. Don't you twist my words."

Jo heard his deep breath, felt it as his chest rose and fell beside her cheek.

"You're right. I'm sorry. When I started, I was trying to give you what you wanted."

"And did you at any point think to bring me into the conversation?"

"You, ah, weren't exactly speaking to me, so I relied on a dated blueprint and a flawed understanding of local codes."

"Local codes?"

"Yeah, you know, like how it goes in your books. Guy and girl meet, fall in love, he screws up, and does this grand gesture to make it up to her."

"How do you know what happens in my books?"

"How many years have we been married? You've read a lot of books. And when you get excited about them, I listen. I even read a couple."

"And took notes, apparently." The vineyard began to make a little more sense to Jo. It was a plot twist straight out of a Harlequin Presents. "Dom, what's this really all about?"

"That's a story I'm still figuring out myself, so it might take a while to tell. You need more wine?"

She shook her head, and he led her over to the beautiful Adirondack chairs Seth and Nick had made out of wine barrels. He lit the firepit and settled back into the chair, and Jo tamped down on the urge to climb into her place on his lap. If she did that, she'd never hear this story. So instead she settled for the chair next to his and wrapped herself in the decorative throw Sofia had no doubt artfully arranged just so. With the darkness falling quickly, the fire created a little cocoon of light around them, giving the illusion that they were completely alone.

"When Gabe died... I... I lost my way a bit. You seemed so fragile, and I wanted to protect you. I needed to prove I could protect someone I loved. So I tried to take things off your plate, so you didn't have so much to worry about."

"I never asked you to do that."

"No, no, you didn't. And watching you handle Frankie in the hospital, I realized I hadn't given you enough credit. But at the time, the idea that I was protecting you let me rationalize cutting you out."

Jo gasped. Hearing him admit out loud what she'd believed for so long physically hurt.

"Jo, when Gabe died, I was reeling. I...I excluded you and the kids from so many decisions, especially about the show, because I needed to feel like I could control something, anything. And I'm sorry."

"Dom, where is all this coming from? Why couldn't you have told me back then and saved us all this heartache?"

"Couldn't see it. I've only been putting it all together with James, that therapist I started seeing."

Pieces began to come together in Jo's mind. So many times when Dom had been stressed during their lives together flashed past her memory. In hindsight, she could see the subtle ways he'd coped by reasserting control over the situation through charm or stubborn determination. "And the vineyard?"

"Well, after the show fiasco, I knew I'd pushed you too far. And though at the time I didn't know why, I wanted to fix it. You kept saying you wanted me to retire, and every time I thought about it, my chest would get real tight and I couldn't breathe. I...

I couldn't see a future past Valenti Brothers. Who am I if I'm not Dom Valenti, head contractor?"

Why didn't he say anything? Would I have listened? Really heard him?

Jo owned her own likely failure. She hadn't been in a place for that kind of conversation either. She had just assumed he'd be on board for whatever retirement plans she suggested. She hadn't asked for his input either, nor had she noticed that he was clearly panicking at the idea.

But that was then. Mistakes were made. What mattered was that they were having the conversation now. "You're Dom Valenti, Nonno and husband."

"Anyhow, I thought back to those nights on the beach when we'd talk for hours. Since you weren't talking to me at all anymore, I had a lot of quiet time to remember what you'd said. And I heard you when you said you wanted to travel. I'm gonna try and get over my fear of flying. James is helping me with that too. More control stuff. But it's never going to be something I can do regularly, so I wanted to give you a slice of Tuscany here. You also said you wanted a place in the country."

"I did say that. Forty years ago. And it is a beautiful property, Dom, but it's not home. It's not for me, it's for you. All I wanted was to spend time with you in our home, making more memories with the time we have left. This looks like a gorgeously designed time suck."

"You may be right. I was grasping at straws, and by the time I realized this was a short one, we were too far into it to turn back." His quiet admission floored her. "So much of Frankie's dreams and finances were tied up in this because of the network contracts that I had to see it through. So I stayed and kept working, filling in for the kids as they needed me. You know I'd do anything for our kids. And spending all this time on a new project let me avoid the reality that I can't give you what you want."

"Why? Why can't you give me what I want?"

"Because I don't know who that is anymore! You say you want Dom the husband, father, grandfather… Who is that? I don't see him in the mirror anymore." Dom's voice broke, and he turned his head to stare out at the darkened vineyard.

She couldn't let him retreat after they'd come so far. Giving up on keeping her distance, Jo set down her wine and crawled into his lap. "Then let's find him together. I miss you, the Dom I married, and I don't want to lose you again to some crazy, intense career. If you're bored, let's talk about it. If you're scared, turn to me, not away. If something's not working, we'll fix it side by side."

"What if he's gone?" Dom whispered hoarsely.

"He's not. You may not see him in the mirror, but I do. I'll help you find him again, and figure out who he wants to be now."

Dom buried his head against her shoulder and she pulled him into her embrace. When his shoulders began to shake with quiet tears, she held him closer and ran a hand down his back.

"It is a beautiful property, Dom."

"Yeah, it is. I can list it with the agent again, once we're out of the contract period—"

She silenced him with a kiss. "Don't. Who knows? Maybe you will need a hobby. But if we keep it, we are going to hire professionals to run this and make the most of it. I'm not letting another business steal you away from me."

"Deal. What is this 'hobby' thing you speak of?"

Jo laughed, and leaned into his shoulder. "You'll figure it out… For the record, as grand gestures go, this is pretty grand. Wait till I tell Elena you bought me a vineyard…."

"She and Tony already know. They might be doing some industry recon in Italy…"

"Domenico Valenti, you told your brother about my present before me?" She smacked him on the shoulder, and he captured her hand in his.

"Hey, it took a combined effort to make this happen. Your kids knew about it before you did too. And everyone just wanted you to be happy. Because it's been very clear that you haven't been happy for a long time, Jo."

"No, I haven't, but for the first time in a long time I feel like I could be. Like we could be together. Let's find that happy, Dom, whatever it looks like. For both of us."

She squeezed his hand three times, and he replied with four and the words that had always seen them through.

"I love you, Jo, and I'm not going to lose you."

"I love you too, Dom. And I'm not going anywhere without you."

~

6 MONTHS *ago*

"THANK you so much for agreeing to meet with us today." Jo ushered their guest into the living room of the vineyard house. They'd kept a lot of the furniture Sofia had used to stage the house because it was absolutely perfect. Jo settled herself on the sofa next to Dom, who still wasn't sure about this woman she'd invited over.

"It's my pleasure. I certainly couldn't pass up an opportunity to see the inside of this gorgeous place for myself!"

"The kids did a great job with it," Jo demurred, and offered her a glass of the red wine she'd opened for the late afternoon meeting.

"I can't wait for the show to air. I'd love to talk more about how to use that publicity for the good of our community."

This woman's networking game was on point. No wonder she was the president of the local wine association.

"I'm going to put you in touch with my soon-to-be son-in-law, Jake Ryland, about that. When I met you at that garden show a few months ago, I knew you'd be just the right person to ask for help. Frankly, this all feels a little overwhelming."

Camelia James tucked her blonde hair behind her shoulder and leaned forward. "I'm happy to help in any way I can."

Jo smiled and took a sip of her own glass of red before admitting near-blasphemy in wine country: "I don't want to run a winery."

"Well, um. I can see how that could be a problem."

Jo laughed at the way the younger woman's face carefully blanked and tact infused her voice.

"My darling husband bought this property on a lovely whim, but we know nothing about winemaking. And I refuse to spend my retirement—sorry," she leaned into Dom and put a hand on his knee, "*our* retirement taking on a completely new industry."

"Understandable."

"But I do not want to sell this place. I can see the potential from the hospitality side, from the wine business side, and from the property rental side. It's a good investment, and like you said, we'd like to spread the attention and wealth into our new community. But we cannot do this on our own. We need advice on how to make it all happen and have it not completely consume our lives."

"So, a few questions. Do you or your children intend to cultivate the grapes yourselves?"

"No, at least not in the short term. We can help keep an eye on things, but backyard gardening is my current level of expertise."

Camelia pulled out her cell phone and began tapping in notes.

"Do you want to make a Valenti Vineyards label wine? Or would you just prefer to sell the grapes to the highest bidder to be incorporated into established wine brands?"

Jo looked at Dom and could see the thought in his head before he said anything.

"Yes, I think we'd like to have bottles of our own wine made." She took his hand in hers, and he squeezed his agreement.

"Do you plan to distribute them widely or just keep them for the estate?" Camelia asked.

"I hadn't thought about that. How many bottles of wine do you think we'll have?"

"Given the acreage, depending on yield, you could have anywhere from five thousand to twenty-five thousand cases. The last owners didn't take very good care of it, and still sold a hundred tons a year to my father. If you ever change your mind on bottling your own, I'm sure he'd be open to renewing a contract."

Jo's jaw dropped. *Holy cow!* She hadn't imagined that level of scale. "I...I'm not sure."

Camelia tapped more on her phone. "That's fine. This is enough to get us started. I'm texting you the contact numbers for Julio Marcano, a local lawyer who works with the winegrowers association, Garrett Carter, who is the best vineyard manager around, and my cousin Jocelyn Meyer who runs a women-owned custom crush facility just a few towns over." She tapped her phone again, and Jo's buzzed in her pocket.

"See? I knew she was the person to ask." Jo elbowed Dom playfully. "We can ask smart questions, make some smart decisions, and then let very smart people follow through on those decisions."

"I guess," Dom groused. "But I still want to learn more about the process."

"That's a given if you're going to be in the wine industry,"

Camelia reassured him. "But these folks will be able to coach you through that process while you're getting started. And each year, you'll have the opportunity to make new decisions and try new avenues. Nothing in this business is forever." A shadow passed over her face and Jo wondered, but didn't ask.

"Thank you for this. This is exactly what we needed. We didn't know what we didn't know."

"My pleasure. As property owners, you both are automatic members of our local wine association now, and we have monthly meetings both to continue education and foster these connections. We might not be as well known as Napa yet, but we're working on it. Having another rental property plus wedding venue in the area, tied to a popular TV show and family wine brand, would be wonderful."

Dom bumped Jo's shoulder this time. "See? Someone appreciates my genius marketing scheme."

"I'd appreciate your genius a whole lot more if it would talk to me first before making major financial decisions."

"Touché," Dom conceded.

Jo turned back to Camelia. "Let me give you a tour of the grounds and get your opinion on what type of venue would best serve the area."

"Lead the way!"

CHAPTER 24

42 YEARS ago

DOM STOOD in front of the altar in the church he'd struggled to stay awake in every Sunday his entire life. The church he and his brother had been baptized in. The church his parents had married in. A shiver ran down his spine. No chance of him snoozing today.

The adrenaline and nerves coursing through his veins had kept him wide-awake last night. His skin was still buzzing right now as he waited. What the hell was taking so long?

He tugged at the stiff collar of his tuxedo shirt. Why did they make these things so damn tight? He'd even gone to the Big n' Tall store. Two weeks ago the fit had been perfect. Today he couldn't breathe.

"Quit pulling at that collar." His mother slapped his hand, much as she had when he'd turned church flyers into church flyers. He'd only thrown the one... The memory of the priest's face made him smile. Thank goodness Father Pietro had retired and wouldn't be serving today. "You'll wrinkle it."

"I can't even swallow, Ma!"

"That's not your bow tie's fault." She straightened the offending piece of silk he'd tugged askew and kissed his cheek. As she rubbed her lipstick off his skin, he was transported back to his childhood, even though she now stood on tiptoes to reach him.

Everything had been easier then. His father had held the weight of the world on his strong shoulders. His mother had held their home together with the strength of her heart. His brother had been a pillar to lean on and his best friend.

Still was. Dom grinned at the man standing next to him. The only thing that made this bearable was that Tony looked as uncomfortable as Dom felt.

For so long, these three people had been his rock, his home, his family.

Today he would take the step to start his own family. The nerves were appropriate. Giving Jo the kind of stability and love his family had given him was no small task, but he was determined to succeed.

He still wasn't quite sure how he'd convinced Jo Bertelli to give him the time of day, let alone marry him. But he wasn't going to question it too hard. She said she loved him, and he was going to hold her to it.

In less than an hour, she'd be Jo Valenti, his to have and to hold. Together they would build what his parents had. A solid, stable home. A successful partnership. A loyal and loving family.

God, they would make some beautiful babies. He hoped they all looked just like Jo.

Couldn't they just skip all this pomp and tradition and get to the baby-making part of the evening?

His smile shifted to a grin as he imagined taking off the big white wedding gown Jo was putting on right now. Tonight was gonna be fun.

A door slammed at the back of the church, and he jolted. *Right. Message received.* No sexy thoughts in church. He dutifully cleared his mind and tugged at his collar again.

Tony knocked his elbow from his spot right behind him.

"Knock it off, or Mom's gonna come back up here, and we'll never get this thing started."

"What the he— heck is taking so long?" Dom barely held back the curse word. Patience had never been his strong suit, and today was testing his limits. He checked his watch again. "We should've started five minutes ago."

"Maybe Jo came to her senses..." Knowing his brother was teasing him didn't help.

Dom turned a glare on Tony, who laughed and raised his hands in surrender. Dom bit back his instinctive response. He'd really never hear the end of it from Ma if he tore his tux before Jo even saw him in it. Besides, he was pretty sure wrestling in church was frowned upon.

"Do you want to talk football or go over the business plan again?"

"What? No. Are you crazy? I'm about to get married."

"I know, idiot. Those are two topics that generally hold your attention for more than five minutes. Just trying to distract you from the wait."

"I don't want to be distracted. I want to be married."

Once he was married, the rest would fall into place. Jo would start working in her classroom. He had a job lined up with a construction crew. They'd started scrimping for a honeymoon. After that, he and Tony were going to save up their money and open their own business as soon as possible. And he'd get to come home to Jo every night. The future looked bright indeed.

But he couldn't do it without Jo. Where was she?

She calmed him. She listened to his rants and brought him back to reason. She opened her heart and loved him unreservedly. She was the key to everything. And today, of all days, she was late.

~

JO LOOKED in the mirror and adjusted the veil over her face while she waited. The anteroom in the church hall sweltered in the summer heat, and she actively tried not to sweat off her makeup while her mother ran back to the car for the something borrowed.

In just under an hour she'd be Mrs. Josephine Valenti for the rest of her life. She tried and failed to suppress the grin threatening to split her face in two.

"You're sure? Really, really sure?" Her mother stepped back into the room, repetitively smoothing a small strip of fabric.

"Mama, of course I'm sure. I love Dom. You love Dom. You and Daddy gave us your blessing."

"I know, I know. It's just you're so young."

"I'm older than you were when you married Daddy."

"I know. *I* was so young!"

Jo shook her head at her mother's nerves. She was ready to start this next phase of her life with Dom. Whether her mother was ready to let her go was clearly another story.

"You worked so hard for your degree. I'd hate to see you give all that up for a man."

"I'm not giving up anything, Mom. I'm still going to teach. I'm gaining a partner. Don't you know women can have it all?" Jo tried to tease her mother into a smile with her favorite feminist phrase, but it didn't work.

"Yes, but now I'm afraid you'll get more than you bargained for. That I haven't prepared you for the real world well enough."

"Mom, I know all about the birds and the bees."

"It's an early stork I'm worried about."

"We're taking care of that. We aren't planning to start our family for a few years. We've talked about this."

Her mother gave her an indulgent smile. "So confident."

"Just like you taught me to be."

Her mother handed her the scrap of cotton she'd been worrying. "This is for you. It's a handkerchief from your Nonna Maria. She embroidered your initials on it the day you were born and told me to save it for the day you married."

Jo ran her fingers over the beautiful blue silk stitches and creased fabric, remembering the woman with the deep wrinkles and warm smile who'd made it for her. She imagined adding a *DV* next to the *JB* and enclosing them in a heart made of tiny perfect stitches.

"Thank you, Mom. I love it." She tucked it into the bodice of her wedding gown, in case she needed it. But she didn't anticipate any tears. She was too excited.

"You're positive this is what you want?"

Jo laughed and patted her mother's hand on her shoulder. "Positive. Dom is the man for me."

"Then I guess I can let you go with a clear heart. I love you, Josephine." Her mother blinked rapidly and pressed her cheek to Jo's, kissing the air and taking care not to mess up her makeup. "Touch up the powder on your nose, and I'll tell your father we're ready."

～

STANDING IN THE CHURCH VESTIBULE, her hand tucked into the crook of her father's elbow, Jo watched her friend and soon-to-be sister-in-law Elena walk down the aisle ahead of her and savored her last few moments as Daddy's little girl.

"You ready?" he asked gruffly, the tears he held back thickening his throat.

"Why does everyone keep asking me that?"

"Because this is a big decision."

"Well, the moment to ask that question was months ago when he popped the question."

"If you'll recall, I asked you then too. You can change your mind."

"I'll give you the same answer I gave you then. I'm sure. He makes me happy, Daddy."

"That ever changes, I want to hear about it."

"Oh, Daddy." She squeezed his arm. "I love you too."

The music changed and swelled. *About damn time.*

"Here we go." She bounced in her white heels before she took small, steady steps down the aisle, deliberately clamping down on her urge to sprint and jump into Dom's arms.

The look on Dom's face made her efforts worthwhile. She wanted to savor his shock. His jaw was dropped and his cheeks flushed, until she made eye contact with him and grinned. Then his slack lips stretched into her favorite smile, the one he used right before he said *I love you.*

She put her whole heart into her smile as she strode slowly toward her future.

As her father passed her hand into her soon-to-be husband's, Dom asked the only question that really mattered. "Ready?"

"Absolutely."

He squeezed her hand tight three times, linking their fingers, and a tear spilled over from his shining eyes.

She squeezed back four and reached into her bodice for the handkerchief. Everyone in the pews laughed and Dom grinned.

And so she started her married life as she meant to continue, surrounded by laughter and smiles.

CHAPTER 25

1 YEAR ago

JO WOKE up melancholy the morning of the double wedding. The conversation she and Dom had the day before with the couples therapist weighed heavy on her heart.

"I just wish Gabe had gotten to have all of this too. I get so sad and angry that he didn't get to find love or have kids or even just see his siblings' big day," Dom had said through tears.

"That is a normal reaction. Even this many years past the grief event, major life milestones can retrigger the feelings of loss," their counselor had said as she passed a box of tissues.

"My normal response would be to take control of the situation so I can keep others from feeling this way too."

Jo had cleared her throat and given him *the look*.

"But I realize it is also a way to control my own anxiety. As I've been reminded, acting impulsively and taking control isn't the best way to handle my emotions. So do you have any suggestions?"

"Before I answer that, let me ask Jo, how are you feeling about the weddings?"

"I am sad too. I wish Gabe could have been here to see his brother and sisters falling in love. There is a piece of our family missing and on days like today, it stands out." Jo hugged her arms around herself as if it would help hold her together while she lanced this wound.

"I wish to God he hadn't gone. I wish I'd fought harder," Dom said.

"You didn't fight at all. 'He's a grown man, Jo. He's made up his mind.' You all but gave him our blessing."

"Only because I'd done my best to change his mind the day before and failed. I did fail you, Jo, and him when I didn't win that argument. And now he's dead. But I never wanted him to go."

"You talked to him? And you didn't tell me?" Jo stared incredulously at Dom. He hadn't thought to tell her?

Dom met and held her gaze, remorse thick between his brows. "I needed him to tell you himself. I hoped you'd be able to turn him where I couldn't."

"I…I wish I'd known. I've been angry at you over that for years."

"I know. I deserved it." Dom dropped his head into his hands, and Jo ran a hand gently through his hair.

"No, you didn't. We all did the best we could. Is this…is this why it's so important to you to win arguments now?"

Dom shrugged, but she could see realization sinking in as he sat up straighter and his shoulders dropped. The therapist stepped into the conversational gap as they both fell silent.

"Thank you both for sharing these difficult emotions. I want to affirm that these are very common and reasonable reactions, especially around major life events. If I might make a suggestion?"

Jo and Dom had nodded together, hands entwined.

"Find a way to honor him tomorrow, to bring his memory into the family day. Maybe it's lighting a candle. Maybe it's asking the photographer to take a special picture. Let's take a minute to think about what that could be. And if you end up in a spiral, remember to breathe and ground yourself in the moment."

After so many years of coexisting and raising their family, each focusing on their areas of expertise, communication had stagnated around the mundane. Having the therapist there to help facilitate the process made actually talking about important things with her husband much easier. When she dropped into a defensive attitude instead of hearing the intent, the therapist called her on it. When Dom blustered and brushed off her concerns, the therapist stopped him and made space for Jo to explain and be validated.

And having a professional to guide them through the pockets of grief that continued to arise was a blessing.

Jo rose and began to get ready for the big day, confident that they could handle anything that came their way.

∽

THREE HOURS LATER, in the women's dressing room, Jo wasn't as confident. Hair and makeup was taking way longer than anticipated, the photographer's assistant had gotten lost on the way to the vineyard, and Dom was beside himself with nerves.

Sofia tried to help him fix the bow tie he'd mangled. "Daddy, knock it off."

"I can't help it. Damn thing is trying to kill me," Dom grumbled.

Jo stepped up behind him and pulled him in for a quick squeeze. She could feel the tension he was holding in, trying to make everything perfect for Sofia and Enzo and their partners today, while also grieving Gabe. "No, it isn't. It's making you look handsome."

Turning him so she could hold eye contact and his hand, Jo hauled in a deep breath for him to mimic. She pulled out the therapist's advice and prompted him softly.

"Remember, breathe through it, babe. Focus on the now." Grabbing her bouquet, she held the flowers between them, unconsciously mimicking their own wedding day. "Smell the roses. The girls need you."

Out of the corner of her eye, she saw the photographer framing them with her camera. She focused her attention on Dom as he did as bid and nodded his agreement.

"You're right. I've got this. You ladies seem to have everything under control in here. I'm just going to step out for some fresh air and see how the boys are doing."

Jo looked around the room at the barely controlled chaos as she crossed to zip Sofia into her dress, but didn't argue. The fact that Dom was willing to cede control over a situation that made him anxious was a big step forward.

"Now that he's gone," Jo teased, "break out the bubbly!"

Laughter and cheers greeted her suggestion. Stemless flutes were passed around filled with frothy golden wine that matched Jo's dress. She raised hers for the first toast.

"To my daughters, all three of you." She smiled at Natalie, who was already a daughter of her heart, before turning to include Sofia and Frankie. "In the face of fire damage, the births of my blessed grandbabies, and a rigorous production schedule, you have managed to adapt and stay resilient to make this day happen. I pray that you take this level of communication and flexibility into every relationship. I didn't realize how much it mattered until I lost it. You three amazing women deserve every ounce of happiness you can wring from life, today and every day. I pray that the paths you've chosen bring that happiness straight to your door. To love!"

She clinked glasses with each young woman in turn, tears held at bay through sheer will not to ruin her mascara.

"Now let's go get you married!

~

FROM THE DECK behind the house, Jo surveyed the wedding arrangements like a queen reviewing her troops. The white chairs had been set up beneath the open-frame structure Frankie had built to recreate what would have been the wedding venue. The hanging lights gave the whole scene a magical feeling. And it was nearly sunset, which meant they were right on time.

Behind her stood Sofia, Natalie, Frankie, and little Daisy in whites and pinks, each carrying a bouquet or basket of flowers that fit them and the vineyard theme perfectly. Roses and dahlias in shades of cabernet, rosé, and champagne, highlighted with subtle greens and blues from the succulents, created the perfect vineyard garden as the women arranged themselves for the procession down the aisle.

Jo made a mental note to ask the florist for the exact varieties so she could plant them around the property.

Only one person was missing from the lineup.

"Dom? Dom!" She called down to where he stood by the chairs. "Dom, it's time! Get up here."

She leaned against the railing as her husband strode toward her across the expanse, feeling a little like Juliet awaiting her Romeo. But they were not children, and their love was not a tragedy. She felt so lucky that they'd been able to repair the marriage they'd worked so hard to build. As he bounded up the stairs, there was nothing she wanted more than to feel his arms wrap around her and his lips press against hers.

But Daisy got to him first, grabbing his hand and spinning him around.

"Come on, Nonno, we gotta go smile and throw flowers."

Jo put her desires on hold. Her granddaughter was right. It was time to get this show on the road.

The music that had been playing in the background stopped.

"That's our cue, everyone." Jo bustled toward Dom. She wiped away the tear running down his cheek. "You okay?"

He nodded, silently.

Screw timelines. She tucked herself into his arms and held him through the big emotions she could feel vibrating through him. He sucked in a shuddering breath, trying to get himself under control. She squeezed him three times, and he squeezed four but didn't let go. She was his foundation today and always. "It's okay, babe."

"It is. It really is. Thank you for everything."

"Don't get us started again. Sentimental watering pot," Jo teased, smiling at her husband wearing his emotions on his sleeve. She ran a hand down Dom's cheek and gave him the kiss she couldn't contain any longer.

"Ewwww, Moooooom! My eyes!" Frankie gagged and covered her eyes like she had when she was ten and was thoroughly embarrassed by parental displays of affection.

Jo wiped her lipstick from around Dom's mouth and grinned at her unruly daughter. "Go line up, smart-ass, and take Daisy with you." Jo led Dom over to the brides who each tucked a hand into his elbow for their walk down the aisle.

Once everyone was arranged, Jo ducked out to take her seat, and Pachelbel's "Canon in D" began to play.

She watched as the grooms caught the first glimpses of their women in their finery. That powerful punch of love writ large on their faces took her right back to her own wedding day, seeing that expression on Dom's face. She turned to see how her husband was faring as her big, strong man proudly walked both brides down the aisle with tears racing down his cheeks unchecked.

Jo felt her own tears rising as she reflected that she'd almost lost all of this. How different would the day have been if she'd left Dom? If she'd let the rigid shell she'd constructed to protect herself isolate her from all of the love in this family? They had both made mistakes, both let grief take something precious from them. But they had also come through it together, actively working to rebuild what had cracked.

As Dom settled into the seat next to her, she pulled her grandmother's handkerchief from her cleverly hidden pocket and offered it with a knowing smile. She had his back, now and forever.

The ceremony was lovely, exactly as Sofia and Natalie had planned. At one point, Laurel, Natalie and Enzo's infant daughter, had begun to fuss, and Jo had gone to help. Her hips bounced and swayed in the long-ingrained pattern that mothers never lost. Nuzzling her nose into soft baby curls, she shushed and kissed and cuddled until the baby settled. When Graciela brought baby Gabe over and Brandy joined them with Laurel's twin brother, Ash, she counted her blessings up to four.

They made it through the rest of the ceremony and into the reception before Jo's mascara finally lost the battle. After the introductions and the blessing by the priest, Jo and Dom joined Sofia, Enzo, and Frankie at the head table. Supported by their spouses and partners, they held slim tapers in their hands. Openly weeping, Jo and Dom held a long match together and lit a single white candle set at an empty chair. Special for the occasion, they had brought Gabe's chair from her table.

Each of their children then lit their candles and carried them back to their seats to light all of the candles along the head table.

Jake carried his taper and lit the centerpieces of each guest table as well.

As the candlelight pushed back the darkening evening, Jo's heart swelled with it. Gabe's influence on everyone in this room lingered in ways she doubted he'd realize, but the collective glow around the party warmed her heart. Every time she looked at the empty seat, Jo felt Gabe's presence like a warm hug and knew he was here and watching, loving every minute of this special day. He might be gone, but he was held close in so many hearts.

Jo was determined to embrace the joy and love within her reach. So when her husband spun her into a dance and sang about loving her forever, she laughed and held him close. And when he led her down a darkened path, she followed, confident that brighter days lay ahead.

CHAPTER 26

14 years ago

"God, what time is it?" Dom asked, waking up with a start from a terrible nightmare of squealing tires and busting glass. He looked around frantically, confirming that he was indeed still sitting up on the couch, with Jo tucked against his side, a movie playing on the TV, and not in the middle of a car crash.

Jo rubbed her eyes and checked her watch. "Eleven forty," she said through a yawn.

"Twenty minutes to curfew." Dom stated the obvious, still trying to pull his brain from the horrible images that lingered.

"Do you think there will ever be a time we don't wait up for them to come home?" Jo asked.

"Not while they still live with us. Although next time I get to pick the movie."

"What? Why? *Blues Brothers* is a classic."

"It's giving my imagination too much fodder for all the ways Gabe could be getting into trouble right now." Dom ran a hand over his face, still trying to fully wake up.

"Crap, I didn't even think of it like that. Please tell me our kid isn't on a mission from God."

"Well if he totals twenty cop cars tonight, I think we'll have our answer."

"As long as he doesn't total his."

Jo poured herself another glass of wine. It was Dom's night to be the designated driver in case their seventeen-year-old son needed to be picked up. It was a deal they'd made when Gabe had started driving. No questions asked, no grudges held in the morning, if he or his friends ended up in any situation where driving was not smart. Gabe would call and either Dom or Jo would go pick him up.

Gabe had not activated that agreement yet, but one of them always stayed sober just in case.

"Why doesn't anyone tell you that having a teenager is as bad for your sleep as having a toddler?" Jo grumbled.

"Because if we had known it was going to reach that level of horror again, it would have broken us. Hell, if it were more widely known, the human race might go extinct!"

"Someday, Dom, someday I'm going to sleep in till noon." Jo waved broadly with her wineglass like an empress commanding her servants. "And it will be glorious."

"God, that sounds great. Someday I won't have to be on a job site at six a.m." Dom joined her in spinning fantasies.

"Someday we'll eat out regularly, so I don't have to cook every single day."

"We'll try every restaurant in town, when we won't have to feed six people, four of whom are growth-spurting."

"They eat so much!" Jo moaned, traumatized.

"What else are we going to do someday, Jo? I like this game."

"Someday I'm going to figure out how to get you on an airplane and we're going to see every city in Italy and then move on to France and Spain…"

"Have you thought about a cruise?" Dom asked hopefully.

"I don't want to spend my entire vacation on a boat crossing the Atlantic!"

"But someday we can take vacations for as long as we want. Time is no object."

"Hmmm, I'll consider it."

"What else?"

"Someday I'd like to go back to teaching. I miss the classroom and doing something that matters."

"What you do matters to me very much, Jo. Without you, Tony and I would never have been able to keep the business afloat. Because of you managing the finances, our children have a roof over their heads, food in their bellies, and college on the horizon."

"I know, but it's different helping an entire classroom of kids learn to read."

"I just want to make sure you understand that I see what you do for this family, here at home and at Valenti Brothers, and it matters."

"What about you, big guy?"

"What about me?"

"What's your what else?"

"I'm going to make my wife a very happy woman?"

"Is that a question or a statement?"

"Both? I don't know, Jo. I mean, I've definitely thought about leaving the business to the boys and retiring, but I have no idea what I'll do with myself after that. Probably drive you nuts with my harebrained schemes. You know me—I don't do well without something to do."

"So your something to do is going to be driving me crazy?"

"Only in the ways that make you happy." He nuzzled her neck. "Promise."

"Hmm, that doesn't sound too bad." Jo leaned back. "Add that to my list of what else."

She ran a tender hand through Dom's hair and he leaned into her palm. She supported his heavy head, and he closed his eyes to better absorb the pleasure. She kissed him, gently at first, and then as their chemistry sparked to life, with more fervor and tongue. If this waiting up for teenagers could involve more necking like one, Dom wouldn't complain. He slid his hand over her hip to pull her closer before sliding it under her sweater.

A choking cough and throat-clearing from the doorway breached his consciousness. Dom hadn't heard the door open, but there stood Gabe, eyes on the ground, shifting awkwardly. Dom turned Jo's wrist toward him so he could read the time. *12:02.* He pressed a kiss to the back of her hand and decided to give their son a little grace.

"Hi, Mom. Hi, Dad. Night, Mom. Night, Dad. I, uh, I'll just be going to bed now…" Their eldest son shielded his eyes and nodded as he beat a hasty retreat to his bedroom, returning the favor.

Jo looked at Dom wide-eyed, and they burst into simultaneous laughter. The giddiness of nerves releasing and the ridiculous role reversal of the situation was too much to contain, and they collapsed into each other's arms, cackling like hyenas.

"Someday…"

"Someday," he confirmed with a final kiss. "Now let's go to bed."

∼

Yesterday

. . .

"What should we do today?" Dom asked, trailing his fingers over Jo's bare shoulder, her hair tickling his nose as she burrowed deeper into the hollow of his neck.

"Mmhmm."

He chuckled and kissed the top of her head. After a dinner that started at nine p.m. that involved four courses and a bottle of wine, they'd strolled back to their rental apartment in the dark. Under a full moon and the influence of said wine, Dom had serenaded her with his best Louis Prima impression, much to the chagrin of the neighborhood cats. Jo had laughed and he'd glowed with that accomplishment all the way up the stairs of their third-story walk-up.

That glow had heated to an open flame as Jo had stripped out of her pretty wrap dress the moment he closed the door. They'd barely made it to the bedroom before combusting. Drunk on wine and laughter and the look in her eyes, he'd shown his wife that he loved her every way he knew how.

He touched every curve, every soft place, every change in texture. He traced a blueprint of his beloved with his fingers, the darkness concealing and revealing her at once. This woman he'd lived with through a lifetime of joys and sorrows opened her heart and body to him once again, and he felt the blessing in that. They moved together, each knowing what the other craved and giving it in abundance until love and passion bound them in that sweet moment of release together.

As the energy ebbed, Dom had rolled, tucking Jo against his side and anchoring her there with a strong arm, so they could sleep.

Now, with the Italian midday sun illuminating the naked woman in his arms, he felt that wash of gratitude again.

"What time is it?" Jo grumbled.

"Nearly noon," he replied, leaning back, moving his shadow to block the offensively bright light that hit her face.

She groaned and tried to hide by tugging the duvet over her head, accidentally clipping his chin with her clenched fist.

"Ouch!" He flopped back and rubbed his jaw dramatically.

Jo peered over the edge of the covers, remorse in her eyes but a grin teasing her lips. "Sorry, babe."

"Sure you are. You look positively torn up about it."

The light grin deepened into a sultry smile. Jo rolled even closer, hooking her leg around one of his. "Now that you're flat on your back though, all sorts of ideas are coming to me."

"Food, woman! I need food!" He chuckled and scrambled to his feet.

She slapped his butt as he walked past. "Quitter!"

That spun Dom around on his heel. "I never quit on us before, and I'm not about to start now." He dove back into bed with his wife and proceeded to show her just how good it could be when they turned toward each other instead of away.

~

Two hours later, freshly showered and lingering over their lattes at the café on the ground floor of their building, Dom and Jo took stock of the day.

"We could go visit that winery Elena and Tony told us to try, or we could go explore the *castello* on the hill..." Dom trailed off as he connected to the café Wi-Fi and a slew of emails downloaded. The chiming of his phone drew Jo's attention.

"Is everything okay?" Jo asked.

"Just got a lot of emails from the kids. The first one is from Sofia. Baby Gabe picture updates."

"Oooooh, let me see!" Jo snatched the phone and beamed as she scrolled. "He's getting so big! That is the only hard thing about being gone for two whole months—not seeing all the babies."

"Yes, well, I'm not anxious to get on a plane again any time soon, so let's make this trip last as long as possible."

Jo raised her latte in a toast and handed the phone back. "Not complaining. Looks like the next one is from Adrian."

"Hmm, he's got a question about one of our suppliers."

"Then he should call the supplier. It's his company now. Well, it's all the kids', but you know what I mean. You don't have to step in and solve every problem."

"I know. And I'm not solving the problem, just giving him information so he can solve it. It's a ten-second reply that will save him a fifteen minute chatty phone call. I promise I'm not getting sucked back in."

"Ten seconds?"

"Well, maybe fifteen between these fat thumbs and autocorrect. Honestly, I think he just likes making me feel like I'm in the loop."

"Okay, then." Jo waited while Dom typed out a quick reply. "What's next?"

"Huh." Dom frowned at the phone.

"Huh? What does 'huh' mean?"

"The next one is from Jake and Frankie. They are still pitching ideas for their new network, and they asked if we'd like to do a show—"

"Oh, dear God, absolutely not."

Dom held up a hand to stop her before her rant caught steam. "They want us to film our travels and vineyard explorations as a tie-in with the vineyard back home and then follow our journey to becoming winemakers."

"Dom. You were so nervous on the other shows that Fi and Frankie had to step in to host."

"I know, but you'll be there. I can just be the doofus learning new things and stomping grapes. I'll be the Lucy to your Desi."

Jo put a hand over his on the table. "You're the Dom to my Jo, and that's enough for me. I'm not saying no, but I don't want to do this right now. Not this trip anyway. We can revisit the wine series later, but this vacation is just for us."

"Agreed. Just for us." He turned his hand over and laced his finger through hers. "I'll tell him no, but gently."

"Any more urgent emails?"

"Natalie sent a video of the twins hiccuping in sync, and a picture Daisy drew."

"Ha! That I need to see."

As the video wound down, Dom set his phone to airplane mode so they wouldn't be bothered. "So, my love, what shall we do today?"

"Vineyard or castle?"

"Those are the two most likely options."

"What do you want to do?"

"Nope, I'm not answering first. I was recently accused of making too many decisions without your input. Not today."

"Starting small?"

"Only way to start is to start at all."

"Then…winery would be my vote."

"Excellent. I wanted to try that out too. It's like you read my mind."

"After over forty years of marriage, it shouldn't be that hard to do."

"And yet, we struggled with it a bit these last five years. I won't take it for granted again."

"Neither will I, babe. This trip has been good practice for us to learn how to talk to each other again. Thank you for making this finally happen."

"Jo, I never meant to hurt you. I'm so sorry it took me so long to figure it out."

"Neither of us were in a good place. This feels right. Healing, almost. Slowing down the pace of our lives to just be together. I needed this."

Dom tossed enough euros to cover their coffees and a bit extra on the table and held out his hand to his wonderful wife. "So did I, love. So did I."

"You aren't the same man I married all those years ago. You're not even the same man I raised my children with. But it turns out I love the man you are today even more. I can't wait for our third marriage to start."

Dom quirked a mysterious smile and tugged her to her feet. "Come with me."

Hand in hand, they strolled across the piazza and into a future that held lightness and hope for the first time in years. The solid foundation they'd built together over their many years of marriage had held up against the seismic shock of grief and depression. That deserved to be celebrated.

"Where are we going, Dom?"

"There's a shop over here I wanted to stop at." He pulled her to a halt in front of the picture window of a local jeweler. "We're finally getting that honeymoon, might as well have another wedding to go with it. Josephine Bertelli, will you marry me again?"

"No. Josephine Bertelli won't. But Jo Valenti will think about it."

∽

AFTER PICKING a band of channel-set diamonds to complement the engagement ring she refused to replace, they made their way out to the winery to exchange their vows. The brilliant Italian sun was sinking behind the rolling hills, taking its warmth with it, as it painted the sky red and purple by the time they made it out onto the patio. Jo and Dom didn't mind the chill or the encroaching darkness. They were glowing from the inside.

"Jo, I have loved you through the good times and the bad, through all of our ups and downs. And I still love you more today than yesterday. The thing I promised you years ago on a winter beach still holds true. Whatever comes our way, we'll figure it out together. I'm not going to lose you."

"Dom, we stumbled, hard, because we forgot how to lean on each other for support. We thought we each had to handle our emotions alone. I don't ever want to go back to that. I love you and the life we've built so much, and from here on out I'm not going anywhere without you. Whatever life brings us, for however long we have, we'll face it together."

"This isn't how it ends."

"No, love, it's just another beginning."

With a kiss and cheers from the folks nearby on the terrace, Jo and Dom Valenti reclaimed their dreams.

Did you miss where it all started? Check out Christmas Spirits, Opened Up, Stripped Down, and Roughed In to fill out the Valenti Family saga. Here is an excerpt from Opened Up:

OPENED UP CHAPTER 1

If one more thing hits my desk today, I'm going to snap.

Sofia Valenti cradled her aching head in her hands and questioned the wisdom of working with family once again. Joining Valenti Brothers Construction had always been her dream. But since Gabe's death, that dream had become a nightmare.

She pushed aside the stack of time cards she needed to process for payroll to give the contracts her cousin Seth had dropped off a first read-through. Dropping her cheater glasses down from their perch atop her head, she squinted at the fine print. Seth and his best friend, Nick Gantry, were incorporating their custom woodworking business into the larger family firm, and the details of the deal fell, as usual, onto Sofia's desk. The thought of woodworking drew her mind to the purchase order for cabinets that had landed on her desk late in the day. Needing to get that done so it could be filled first thing, she pulled it from the stack and laid it on top of the thick folder of legalese. The contract could wait.

Perfect. The order form was only half filled out. She clicked her computer screen awake and opened the supplier's website, while she let a soothing stream of curse words flow through her mind. Now she'd waste precious minutes looking up part numbers that damn well should have been filled in. This was not how she envisioned using her double degrees in Business Administration and Interior Design. Her thoughts drifted to the naïve but tempting dream she'd shoved into the back of her mind the day after Gabe died: the pretty, airy design studio, a waitlist of clients eager for her services, her father's respect. All of these goals had taken a back seat when her mother had lost her eldest son and fallen apart. She carefully tucked the dream away and turned her mind back to the pain-in-the-ass order.

Someone had needed to step in and keep the place running while her parents had dealt with their grief. Bills and contractors needed to be paid, and she'd needed a temporary job while she got her design business up and running. That had been three years ago. Truth be told, the mind-numbing work had gotten her through the worst of her grief after Gabe died, but now she needed more.

Basic cabinet package, bulk drawer pulls, the same retractable faucet kit they put in every house. The list never varied much. Valenti Brothers stood for good work at affordable prices, and their orders reflected that ethos. Though it hurt her creative soul, at least the part numbers were easy to find bookmarked on the site. With a few clicks, the order was entered, approved, and in queue for payment. If she was going to be stuck doing the office work, at least she could do it well.

As her mother and father, Josephine and Domenico Valenti, argued over how to pull back from the company and retire, the bulk of the day-to-day responsibilities fell on Sofia's shoulders. It had been months since she'd played with a design. No one even knew that she was available for design consults, because Dad never told anyone. Frustration weighed heavily on her mind as she tucked the PO into the appropriate file and pulled the contract back in front of her.

ROUGHED IN

The legalese began to blur, and her glasses fogged over. She pushed the glasses back into her hair and blinked away the tears. God, she needed a break. A week at the beach would do. Hell, even a weekend over in Monterey would work. The soothing waves and brisk sea air would clear out the cobwebs in her mind. Since that wouldn't be happening any time soon, she hauled in a deep breath and reached into her emergency drawer. Her stash of snack-sized candy bars was flush, and she chose one with care. Almond Joy. She could certainly use a little joy today. She unwrapped the candy and popped the whole thing in her mouth.

She wouldn't mind a little action involving nuts either, but she'd have to get out of the office regularly for that to happen. What had seemed like a temporary drought of male interest was turning into full-on climate change. The Almond Joy disappeared before she had a chance to taste it, so she reached for a mini 100 Grand. This time she focused on the chocolaty, sugary goodness filling her mouth and soothing her scrambling mind.

A hundred grand would certainly be nice right about now. If she had some reserves, she could finally get out from under her father's thumb. When she'd started, having everything wrapped up with a neat little bow had seemed ideal. The plan was simple: work for the family business, live in a family property rent-free, pull a small salary to cover expenses but not drain their coffers, with the understanding that someday she'd have equity in the firm and would make commissions from her design work. Now that little bow was pulling tighter around her neck every day, and her father didn't understand that she was suffocating.

If she was ever going to make a name for herself, she needed capital to invest and time to design. Right now, her bank account was crying by the end of the month. As long as she was stuck at this desk, trudging through paperwork and indulging in pity parties, her account was going to keep weeping.

Enough. She slid the drawer closed and double-checked her

planner. Two more hours before she could knock off for the family meeting her dad and Zio Tony had called. At least she knew she wouldn't have to rely on her freezer for dinner. Family meetings always took place around her mother's table, laden with food. She put her head down to focus on her remaining tasks, despite the images of her mom's lasagna triggering her salivary glands and tempting her to open the drawer just one more time.

Giving up on the contract until her brain was fresh, she rearranged her desk for the eighteenth time and began the rote task of entering payroll. In all her years of being the older sister, she had learned that she needed to leave on time. Enzo and Frankie would inhale more than their fair share if she was late. After the day she'd had, that was *not* happening.

∽

Adrian Villanueva heard the muttered curses as he pushed open Sofia's office door. That didn't bode well for his request, but he didn't have a choice. The tile that had arrived at the Chu project wasn't right, and he needed Sofia to call the supplier and sort it out before the warehouse closed for the weekend. He couldn't fall behind on that job, or it'd set off a chain reaction of delays and angry customers as his other sites suffered. He protected the Valenti Brothers' reputation as if he'd earned it himself.

Taking his life in his hands, he strode up to the prickly office manager's desk with a grin on his face. It wasn't a hardship to smile at Sofia Valenti. For years, he'd had to remind himself that, no matter how touchable her soft blonde waves looked or how her blue eyes twinkled at his jokes, she was off-limits. When he'd started working for her father as a teenage dropout, she'd been a sixteen-year-old stunner, and she'd only improved with age. Despite the fact that she was now old enough to choose her own partners, she was still the boss's daughter. He wouldn't do anything to jeopardize his relationship with Dom Valenti, certainly not while he worked up the courage to ask for the keys to his future. But in this case, his smile was wasted. She hadn't even looked up. He tried a different tactic in his charm offensive.

"Hello, beautiful."

"Ugh." She rolled her eyes, her manic fingers still flying across her number pad. The stack of time cards rapidly moved from one pile to another, her rhythm unbroken.

"I need your help."

"Get in line." He knew the snark was meant to be sarcastic. That was the usual tone she took with him, but the furrow between her brows looked like it was carved in granite. He wanted to smooth it away with his thumb, but he had a firm no-touching rule. The last thing he needed was to lose his precious restraint around her, and giving in to his impulse would trigger exactly that.

Focus on the problem. Get in, get out.

"The tiles on the Chu project are wrong. I need you to straighten it out with the supplier."

She closed her eyes and let out an ear-piercing scream. It surprised him into stepping back.

"What was that for?"

"Long story." She finally looked up, her slate-blue eyes brimming with anger and frustration. *Damn.* Nothing in his arsenal was going to smooth over whatever else was making her scream. His best option now was to muscle through the details and get out of her way.

"Here's the original order form and the packing slip. It looks like they switched the final numbers. We need to catch them before they leave, or we lose three days on this project, and I'll have to pull crews from scheduled work at other houses to finish."

"You've got to be kidding me! I need to be out the door in half an hour. I'm not a miracle worker."

"Could have fooled me."

"Yeah, yeah. Flattery will get you nowhere. Give me that." She snatched the paperwork from his hand and grimaced.

"So, got a hot date?"

Her head snapped up, eyes wide with surprise and...offense?

"Excuse me?"

"You said you had to leave. It's Friday night…"

"Screw you. When's the last time you saw me leave this office before eight p.m.?" She gestured to her small room, walls covered in mismatched sample cabinets and drawer pulls for the clients to see, and desk layered in papers.

"Just trying to make conversation. So why do you have to leave, then? It's well before eight, as you say."

"Dad called a family meeting. He's got something he wants to talk to us about."

Jealousy clenched briefly, even as he clenched his own fist in response. It was always this way. Family first. He'd started working for Valenti Brothers in high school as a general laborer. After his father had been deported, he'd been forced to become the man of the house far sooner than intended, working any and all hours to keep his mother and sisters safe and sound.

Over the last twelve years, he'd worked his way up, learning, apprenticing, proving his worth. He now led his own construction team, with Dom and Frankie leading the other two since Tony had officially retired last month. He'd always expected to work alongside the old man until Gabe had finished college and was ready to step in. But Gabe had chosen a different path, one that led him to the army and Iraq. One that hadn't led him back home.

He could see the opportunities, his own potential to fill that role. He wanted it so bad he could taste it: the stability, the power over his destiny, the sense of finally belonging. But as long as business was decided over family dinners, he was stuck, always on the outside looking in. He needed to get his ass in gear and ask Dom the question he'd been choking on for months. As casually as he could, taking care to bury his frustrations deep, he asked, "Oh, yeah? Any idea what about?"

She raced a highlighter across the invoice and reached for her phone, already tackling his problem.

"None. And if you don't get out of here, I'll never finish so I can find out. Shoo! Hello? Yes, can I speak to Javier? Thank you."

She continued entering numbers while she calmly reamed Javier a new one and wrangled a guarantee that the tiles would be delivered to the site by Saturday at ten a.m., no extra charge. He had no idea how she juggled it all, but better her than him. He backed out the door, wondering why that prim tone of voice turned him inside out.

～

Phone call done, payroll half entered, contracts still waiting, Sofia lowered her swirling head to her desk. *What nerve that guy has!* Calling her beautiful, asking if she had a date... She knew she wasn't beautiful, not by a long shot, but she didn't need to be teased about it at work. Once upon a time she'd dreamed she was a lovely princess in a beautiful castle just waiting for Prince Charming. But little girls' dreams often fade in the face of cold, hard reality, and hers was no different. Now, she was an overweight, underappreciated servant approaching thirty, trapped in a mismatched dungeon, and no one was coming to save her.

She hated that in spite of Adrian's insulting endearments and rude questions, the man still had the power to awaken the yearnings she kept carefully suppressed. There was no use getting turned on if there was no one to enjoy it with, so she tried to avoid it at all costs. But there was something about him...

His dark, chocolate brown hair, his peanut-butter-colored eyes, the perfect combination of sweet and nutty... She reached back into her drawer and pulled out the big guns, a double pack of Reese's cups. She slowly chewed the sugary treat and pretended that it filled the aching hole in her chest.

She'd watched him during her shy teen years, afraid to approach the boy who was already a man. He'd intimidated the hell out of her with his confident, cocky air. When she'd come back to the company after a few years of experience in college, she'd been ready to pursue the strong tug of attraction, but every minor advance crumbled against the firm wall of physical distance and relentless teasing he kept between them. If he'd pushed her away when she'd been young and beautiful, she could only imagine he'd run screaming if she approached him now. She'd packed on weight in the months following the funeral, and her sedentary job and borderline depression were keeping it there. She'd let herself go, and now she could barely find herself in the reflection in the mirror. She didn't have a chance in hell with a guy like him, so she did her best to keep her inappropriate longings well contained. Humor and sarcasm were her defensive weapons of choice.

She had to laugh or she'd cry. Adrian was a trusted employee and a minor jerk, no matter how attractive she found him. She could handle him and this pesky response he provoked. He probably had no idea that his words had wounded. Most men didn't. It likely didn't occur to him that words like "beautiful" or "gorgeous" *could* hurt. He would never imagine that his casual conversation rang like a condemnation in her mind. He had no clue, and that was why he could never know that his broad shoulders and strong arms made inner Sofia weak in the knees.

He would never know because she'd die sitting behind this

desk, all alone. She was well and truly stuck. The futility of her situation weighed on her heart. It wasn't fair. This wasn't how her life was supposed to go. The anger she tried hard to keep hidden from the rest of the family flared hot in her chest, lashing out at the one person who couldn't defend himself.

Damn it, Gabe. Why did you have to go and change everything? I want the life we had planned. I wish you were here.

But wishing would not make it so.

She shut the chocolate drawer firmly on her feelings and grabbed her purse. Time to see what Dad was up to.

VALENTI FAMILY TIMELINE

CHRONOLOGICAL ORDER

1977
Jo & Dom meet over pool
Hang out at the beach
1978
Dom proposes
Jo & Dom get married
Missed Honeymoon
Jo starts teaching
Dom builds the bookcase
1985
Miscarriage
1988
Jo finds out she's pregnant
They decide she'll stay home
1989
Gabe is born
Jo leaves the classroom
1990
Sofia is born
1991

Dom buys the construction business
1992
Enzo is born
1993
Frankie is born
Buy their forever home and begin renovations
Dom tries to cook
Baby Enzo's Christmas Pizzelles
1995
Jo begins to work at Valenti Brothers
1996
Dom struggles to juggle everything
1997
The family builds the tree house
2005
Jo pitches apartment renovation
Apartment project reveal
2006
Jo works in real estate
Dom helps with chores
Empty nest planning
2011
Dom & Gabe build the deck
Gabe & Seth enlist in the Army
2015
Gabe's death
Jo's breakdown
2018
Announcement of Million Dollar Starter Home
Jo joins Late Bloomers
Meets Alessandro
Coffee with Sofia
Winchester Mystery House

Dom buys the vineyard
Jo misses Friday dinner
Jo babysits Daisy & talks to Natalie
Halloween
Decked Out Christmas
2019
Vineyard show negotiations
Million Dollar Starter Home wrap party
Friday Dinner with Jake
Baby Gabriel is born
Jo confronts Jake at vineyard and talks to Dom
Vineyard fire
Vineyard reveal for the show
Jo & Dom talk about what they actually want
Bring in an expert to run the winery
Sofia & Adrian and Enzo & Natalie's weddings
2020
Travel Epilogue (pre-Covid)

CHRISTMAS SPIRITS EXCERPT

~

Want to start the Exposed Dreams series from the beginning? Try Christmas Spirits, my cross-over novella featuring Seth Valenti and Brandy Henderson.
Here's a little peek!

~

"I asked for a supra, non-fat, sugar-free, no-whip, eggnog latte."

Brandy Henderson narrowly refrained from answering Ms. Prada-purse-and-yoga-pants in the same bitchy tone. It was three weeks until Christmas, and Brandy was whipping and foaming drinks at Sweet Tea and Joe's as fast as she could while dealing with the customers in line waiting to order. She had to dig deep to find the spirit of the season at six a.m.

"That's what I made you, ma'am." She was proud of her even tone and friendly smile as she pitched her voice over the hissing steam spitting out of the espresso machine, her hands busy assembling the next order on auto-pilot.

"There's no way this is sugar-free. Make it again."

"I assure you, ma'am, I used the sugar-free eggnog syrup right here." Brandy gestured to the bay of syrup pumps next to her station. "Piccolo peppermint latte, for Ted?" She spun the finished drink on to the counter pick-up window.

"And I'm telling you, you screwed it up. Make me another goddamn coffee!" The woman's voice pitched higher and more shrill than the screaming steamer as Brandy foamed more skim milk.

The customer is always right. Brandy silently chanted the mantra as she sent an apologetic glance to the restless customers in line. Many of them were regulars who wouldn't mind, but she hated to keep them waiting.

"Yes, ma'am." She reached across the counter for the offending coffee and bobbled it. Since the woman hadn't put the cap back on completely, scalded milk splashed over the back of Brandy's hand and onto the counter. *Sonofabitch! That hurt.*

"You idiot! You splashed that on my purse." The woman began furiously blotting the leather bag with a handful of napkins.

Brandy bit her tongue against the pain of the burn and the insistent pressure of the sarcastic response desperate to break free. She glanced up at the clock, praying for Clare to hurry up and get there already. She didn't mind covering for her perpetually late friend, but this morning she needed help and she needed it now. Throwing the perfectly good coffee in the wash sink, Brandy assessed the damage. She ran her hand briefly under the cold water, praying it wouldn't blister. The normally tawny skin on her hand was turning an angry red. Damn. She didn't have time for a serious burn.

"Hello? I don't have all day!"

Not trusting herself to speak, Brandy silently and efficiently made another supra, non-fat, sugar-free, no-whip, eggnog latte, exactly as she had the last one. She may have wanted to put this loud, inconsiderate, rude woman in her place, but Brandy couldn't afford to lose this job and the tips it brought in. Not this close to Christmas. Her family was depending on her this year, and she wasn't going to let them down.

"Here you go, ma'am. Have a nice day."

"Next time, get it right the first time."

The worst part of working the early morning shift at the coffee shop was trying to get people their caffeine before they'd had any caffeine. Not ideal. She turned to the next person in line. Miranda, brevis Americano, extra shot, room for cream. She was already filling the order before she ducked back to the register to ring it up. Back in her rhythm, she took orders, counted change, and crafted the overpriced coffee and tea creations that seemed to power Silicon Valley. It wasn't a great job, but it was a means to an end. God, she couldn't wait for the end.

Tinkling bells pulled her from her trance. She looked up to see Clare with her straight inky black hair peeking out from beneath a ridiculous jingling red elf hat hustling behind the counter. The college girl looked like a member of a K-Pop girl band who'd gotten a make-over from Santa.

"Where have you been?" Brandy whispered with another glance up at the clock. She sprayed whipped cream to cover her words. "You're forty minutes late." Her hands never stopped flying.

"Bad traffic on 101."

A likely story. Even more likely, her new boyfriend had woken up horny. Brandy would never begrudge her friend a morning quickie, but she could sure as hell be jealous. It had been months since she'd had time for a date, let alone a third and all that entailed.

"Cover the front for a minute. I need to put some burn cream on my hand." She ducked into the back and rummaged in her pack for her first aid kit. Old habits died hard. As a former army medic, she never left home without her pack. She ran her hand under cold water as she popped an ibuprofen. She briskly cleaned and dried the wound site, applied a lidocaine cream, and loosely wrapped gauze around it. With any luck, she'd avoid a blister.

"There you are. Why is Clare working the front all by herself during the morning rush? Get your butt in gear, Brandy."

Perfect. Anna. Late and making assumptions without asking questions, as usual. Once again, Brandy bit back the words she longed to set free. Arguing with her boss would get her nowhere fast. She stowed her kit, tucked her rambunctious curls back under her cap, and dove back into the morning fray. If anything, the army had taught her that she could do hard things if she just put her head down and tackled the job head on. She could do anything if it brought her closer to her goal.

When she'd left the army two years ago, she'd immediately applied to nursing school only to find out there was a long wait-list. But nothing was going to keep her from her dream. She'd taken all the pre-reqs she could. Now, it was a waiting game to see when they would let her in. In the meantime, she'd keep earning her checks, helping her mom keep a roof over her half-siblings' heads, taking care of her step-father, and doing anything else that needed doing.

The incessant jingling of silver bells pulled her from her thoughts as Clare bobbed her head along to the piped in Christmas music while she worked the register.

"For God's sake, Clare. What possessed you to get the one with bells?"

"'Every time a bell rings, an angel gets his wings.' It gives me hope."

"It's giving me a migraine." Brandy grinned at her friend as she began making the medio Mexican mocha just ordered.

"There are going to be a lot of new angels before Christmas if you keep that up."

"Christmas spirit brings in the tips, Brandy." Anna commented from behind the other register. She shook the tip jar meaningfully. "You'd do well to remember that. Just look how much Clare brought in this morning while you were dawdling in the back."

"Yes, ma'am." She bit her tongue against her own defense, knowing she'd regret the lack of Christmas presents for the kids, no matter how good it would feel to spew the truth burning in her throat.

∼

"Watch your step!"

Seth yanked his thoughts from ruminating on his disturbing dream just in time to avoid taking a two-by-four to the face. His hard hat wouldn't have protected him from a broken nose. His boss, Antonio Valenti, gripped his arm and pulled him back, as if he was still a young child.

"Pay attention, son. If I have to file a workman's comp claim on you, I'm gonna make you do the paperwork. Actually, maybe I should knock you out. It might be the only way I get you to actually sit down in the office and learn the ropes. When you're running things, you will need to have a finger on every pulse. It's not all demo days."

Why did every word of criticism make him feel ten years old? Maybe because the same man was delivering them then and now, a pitfall of working for Dad. Seth didn't belong on the construction site. He knew it. The crew knew it. The only one refusing to acknowledge it was Dad. For two years, he'd been putting Seth on crews, giving him busy work, trying to convince him that he had a place in Valenti Brothers Construction. His plan was backfiring. While Seth appreciated the paycheck and the chance to do a little demolition every now and then, he didn't love the repetition of construction. What he would love doing was anyone's guess, so for now he would break down walls and haul supplies for his dad. He could help out his family while he figured out the rest.

The addition of an outdoor kitchen space on the back of a mid-century modern ranch was a two week job that his dad could do in his sleep. Though he could lay bricks or mud drywall with the best of them, Seth had no passion for it and zero patience for dealing with sub-contractors.

When he'd left the army two years ago, he had one unrelenting goal. *Just get home.* Beyond that, he had no idea what he wanted to do with his life. The job helping his dad was the least he could do, literally. His heart just wasn't in it, but he wasn't ready to risk his heart on anything important yet, so here he was on another job site, taking orders from his dad. But there was only so much of that he could take, especially on a day when demons from his past were chasing him.

He turned and headed for the front of the house.

"Where are you going?"

"Coffee run. I'll be back in fifteen."

SOMEONE SPECIAL EXCERPT

∼

Want to go back to where it all began? Someone Special was my very first romance novel. Meet Nick Gantry and Dani Carmichael as they fight their demons to find true love. Free on all platforms.

∼

"This is better than cable!" remarked Mrs. Grady, from her habitual perch by the window. Dani looked up from the stove. Something good must be happening two stories below on their normally quiet street. Dani briefly turned her attention back to the bubbling pots on the stove. Confident that her three meals were coming along nicely, she tucked unruly curls behind her ear and turned from the kitchen to join her neighbor at the window.

Below, two very muscular men with shirts removed, in deference to the fierce sun and brutal heat weltering up from the pavement, were wrestling an ugly sofa in through the double front doors of the building. Their lean muscles and trim waists twisted and flexed with effort. Dani's face flushed with heat, a welcome change from her recent numbness.

"They can move my furniture anytime! Then again, I'm not sure my blood pressure could handle it!" Mrs. Grady cackled. Dani continued to observe the scene below. While the slick and straining bodies held her gaze, the implications flooded her thoughts.

"I bet they're moving in the new tenant across the hall from us." An empty ache spread through her chest as Dani was hit by the grief that she managed to keep just below the surface. "Well, across from me. It will be strange having someone else living there in my old place." Her throat tightened at the reminder that she was living alone in Helen's apartment now.

She returned to the kitchen, grasping for calm, trying to avoid sinking into her grief. She drained the pasta, mixed in the homemade marinara sauce along with some freshly grated Parmesan, and reduced the chicken soup to a simmer. At least managing to create three large meals at once required her attention. She spun too quickly and knocked a wooden spoon to the floor. With a huff of frustration, she threw the offending utensil into the sink.

"Are you OK, Sunny?"

"Yeah, sometimes it just hits me that she's gone. That she won't sit at your Wednesday night dinner again. That she won't ever tell another crazy story about her service or her travels. That no one will be there when I open the door. It's just hard." Dani's voice cracked and her shoulders drooped under the weight of her sadness.

"I know, sweetheart. I miss her too. She was my best friend." Dani let herself be bundled into a hug, even though it was a poor substitute for the hug she missed.

"Mine, too. Now that she's gone, I feel lost."

"That's normal, dear. After all, you practically gave up your life to take care of her these last six months."

"What did I give up? A lackluster career in accounting and a dead end social life down in Houston? You know as well as I do, I didn't belong there." Dani shook her head. "No. I gained so much more, moving up here to help out. I met all of you, and got to spend more time with Aunt Helen. And with how quickly her health failed...well, I wouldn't have wanted to be anywhere else."

The pancreatic cancer had snuck in under the radar, and when they found it, it was too late. It hit vicious and fast. She'd been home for Christmas when Aunt Helen broke the news. Now, it was June and she was alone again.

"I know she loved having you with her. You were the grandchild of her heart."

Her grandfather's sister, Aunt Helen, had never married. She had no children of her own, and had spoiled Dani and her sister like crazy as a result. Summer trips wherever Aunt Helen happened to be living that year, fantastic surprises from abroad, and boxes of massive navel oranges every New Year's were her trademarks. And her stories! Dani had vivid memories of curling up at the foot of her chair and listening to her tell stories of her time in the Navy in her irreverent and slightly salty way. Dani let the fond memories roll through her mind.

"Remember how pissed she was when Dad brought up the idea of a nursing home?"

"Oh my goodness! I thought she'd have a stroke then and there, and save us another trip back to the hospital. She was not a woman to tolerate limits on her independence."

That independent spirit was her trademark, and Dani hadn't been able to stomach the idea of Helen losing that. When she had refused chemo and radiation, and begun to look at hospice care, Dani had offered to move into the vacant apartment across the hall and help take care of her. The move set her family at ease, and Dani felt blessed that she could help her surrogate grandmother wring every last drop of joy from her remaining days. They had visited favorite haunts and dear friends until leaving the apartment had become too difficult. Hospice nurses had come to handle Aunt Helen's medical needs, and given Dani a few much-needed breaks. Just handling her personal care had become around the clock job near the end. So Dani had given up her month-to-month lease on the apartment across the hall and moved to Helen's couch. Given the moving crew downstairs, she assumed her old apartment wouldn't be empty anymore.

Aunt Helen was gone, and Dani was as lost as ever. Everything she owned was in boxes and shoved into corners. She was surrounded by the remnants of her aunt's life, and it was difficult to see how hers could share the space.

She'd always had trouble figuring out where she fit in. She'd been raised to believe she could be whatever she wanted. But what if she couldn't figure out what that was? She'd bumped along okay until now, but she hadn't really pursued anything with passion. After going to college in Houston, she'd accepted a job working as an accountant at a multi-national energy firm. It had been lucrative, but it hadn't been satisfying, and her asshole ex-boyfriend even less so. She'd been sprinting on the hamster wheel and going nowhere. She had zero desire to hop back on. Coming home hadn't been a hardship, but what now?

"Moving in was the best thing for both of us. She kept her freedom, and I gained my own. But now I have too much freedom. I have no job, no friends, and no idea what to do about any of it. And I've got all of her estate to handle...I keep losing hours at a time just holding an afghan she knit or rearranging the framed postcards from her travels." The tears she'd been fighting to hold back ran silently down her cheeks.

"It's a big job. Don't rush it. You've got a lot to deal with. Losing Helen was hard on us all. Just keep putting one foot in front of the other. Come to our dinners. Talk to your friends.

Bake her favorite desserts. Share stories of her that make you laugh instead of cry. It will get easier with time."

The timer ding pulled Dani from her maudlin thoughts, and she bent to remove the shepherd's pie from the oven. She set it aside to cool and quickly packed everything else into the fridge. At least her neighbors would benefit from her lack of a plan.

Dani turned back from the fridge, wiping the tears of frustration and grief from her cheeks. She had to shake things up and move on with her life. It's what Aunt Helen had wanted, and she knew she had to live up to her end of the bargain. When Helen had agreed to let her come help, it was always with the understanding that when she was gone, Dani would take up the reins to her life and do something spectacular. *Now if I could just figure out what that is...*

"Well, Mrs. Grady, you're all set. You've got the shepherd's pie for Monday night, the spaghetti and meatballs for Wednesday, and chicken soup for Thursday. Make sure you nuke a vegetable to go with. I stocked your freezer today, so you should have plenty to choose from. Also, let Joe know that I left the fennel out of the soup this time, just for him. Tell everyone I said hi." She gathered her things and moved toward the door.

"Are you sure you won't join us, Sunny? I worry about you eating alone so much."

The use of her aunt's favorite nickname for her sparked a brief smile, but Dani shook her head. "I just...can't yet. Maybe next week." To be honest, she couldn't stand to see the sadness in her heart reflected back in the eyes of her aunt's friends. It was bad enough to feel it herself. "I'm going to go bake some cookies to welcome our new neighbor to the building. I'll extend an invite to your dinner party on Wednesday, if you'd like."

"The more, the merrier, I always say. And if he turns out to be a bachelor, send him over on Tuesday!" Still chuckling, Mrs. Grady closed the door behind her, and Dani waited to hear the bolt snick in the lock. She'd fallen into the habit of checking up on her neighbors when Aunt Helen had gotten too weak to do it herself. Making meals, listening for locks, dropping off mail, it didn't take long and helped a lot. Sometimes it felt like those were the only things she accomplished in a day.

"I really need to change that," she muttered.

Dani walked down the hallway, skirting past a pile of boxes left outside the door across the hall from hers. One of the moving men came out of the apartment for another load, and sent her an appreciative glance and smile. Dani ducked her head with a blush and quickly headed inside. Why hadn't she said hi? Why on Earth had she blushed? She had to get out more, preferably with a male of the species. Shaking her head over her reaction and the dismal prospect of that happening any time soon, she pushed aside her worries in the kitchen, baking her famous dark chocolate chunk cookies for her mystery neighbor.

ACKNOWLEDGMENTS

ROUGHED IN

This book was a labor of love. It was a difficult birth, often stalling, and there were many times I wished for an epidural, or a c-section, or some damn Pitocin before I finished the darn thing. To everyone who helped deliver this book baby, she is beautiful and I owe you every thanks. I am sorry for anything I might have said while I was out of my mind.

To all of my writing buddies online and IRL, both Nano & OSRBC, thanks for the laughter and writing sprints. OSRBC, Wicked Wallflowers, and HBs, you continue to build amazing communities of readers, and I am blessed to be part of you. Legends, thanks for holding my hand through the hyperventilating. To everyone at Friends For Eva, cheers! Thanks for tuning in every Wednesday to wine down. I love you all, even when you taunt me with glitter posts.

To Jen and Julia, this book would have been a hot mess without your guidance and liberal application of virtual red ink. Bless you for putting up with my repeated phrases and overuse of commas. Lucy, thank you for the covers on this series. I adore them.

To the writers I read and admire, thank you for creating the worlds that inspire me. Sarah and Jen, Jenny and Sarah, Kerrigan, Ro, Jasmine, Cass, Sophie, Naima, Lenora, and Leni thank you for always being just a text away with commiseration, encouragement, and inappropriate jokes. Never change. Tricia thanks for your eagle eyes. Darcie, thank you for long ranty walks in the woods. Jen and Jen I love you both. Why am I friends with ALL OF THE JENNIFERS? Because they make the bestest friends.

Mom & Dad, thanks for riding to the rescue and watching my kids while I chase this dream. To my three girls, these books are for you. This is all for you. I hope someday you see yourselves in every capable, intelligent, loving woman on these pages. To my husband, who supports this dream with as much passion as I do, you are my real life hero.

And to you, my dearest reader, for following this series to the end. I'm so glad that you enjoyed my world enough to come back. Fingers crossed, I'll have a new series for you to dive into soon. Thank you for your support.

RECLAIMED DREAMS

The last two years have been incredibly challenging. I almost stopped writing. The stress of a global pandemic married with moving house, three children schooling and a husband working from home, and several deaths in our immediate family broke my creativity for awhile. This book began as a 12 chapter novella I was going to release once a month to my newsletter followers. Obviously, it has changed from that initial plan quite a bit, but knowing that loyal readers were waiting for this story was the only thing that saved me.

To all of my friends in Friends For Eva, OSRBC, and the Coven Chat on FB, thank you for the continuous laughter and encouragement. To Sharon, Shari, Fedora, Tricia, Jenna, Stacey and Katie, your early eyes on this manuscript made it infinitely better. Jen and Julia, your amazing insights and edits are magical. Lucy, your covers give this series LIFE!

To my #latenightwritersclub on TikTok, thank you for showing up so I had to show up. You got my butt back in the chair and I will be forever grateful. To my IRL writer friends, Jasmine, Ro, Kilby, Amy, Wendy, Jenny, Sarah and more who held me up with hugs and glasses of wine and goat jokes, I love you all.

My parents who not only believed in this dream but have traveled thousands of miles to help with childcare are amazing. My kids who understand that when Mommy is outside she is working and not to be bothered are angels no matter what else you may have heard. And my amazing husband who wrangles bedtime every night so I have energy for my work and still makes me swoon is my real life hero. I couldn't do what I do without you.

And to you, my dearest reader, for allowing me the space and grace to finish this book the way it needed to be done. Thank you for the emails, messages, and posts that tell me how much these books mean to you. You are the reason I keep writing.

ABOUT THE AUTHOR

Eva Moore writes sexy contemporary romances featuring compelling characters finding love in the modern world. Pulling up her Chicagoland roots, she has chased adventures around the globe, with stints in France and Singapore. Eva now lives in California (at the wine end, not the movie end) with her college sweetheart and three gorgeous kiddos. She loves hearing from the outside world while she's hiding in her she-shed or playing on TikTok. Please visit her at https://www.4evamoore.com. If you want to stay up-to-date on new releases and bookish giveaways, join her newsletter at https://www.subscribepage.com/authorevamoore

ALSO BY EVA MOORE

Girls' Night Out Series
Someone Special (1)
Second Chances (2)
Three Strikes (3)
Forever Nights (4)
Christmas Spirits (5, novella)

Exposed Dreams Series
Opened Up (1)
Dirty Demo (1.5, novella available on Prolific Works FREE)
Stripped Down (2)
Decked Out (in Worst Holiday Ever Anthology) (2.5, novella)
Roughed In (3)
Reclaimed Dreams

Worst Series
Worst Holiday Ever
Worst Valentine's Day Ever

CPSIA information can be obtained
at www.ICGtesting.com
Printed in the USA
LVHW011315050122
707840LV00004B/59

9 781950 345052